FROSTBITE

A *Vampire Academy* GRAPHIC NOVEL

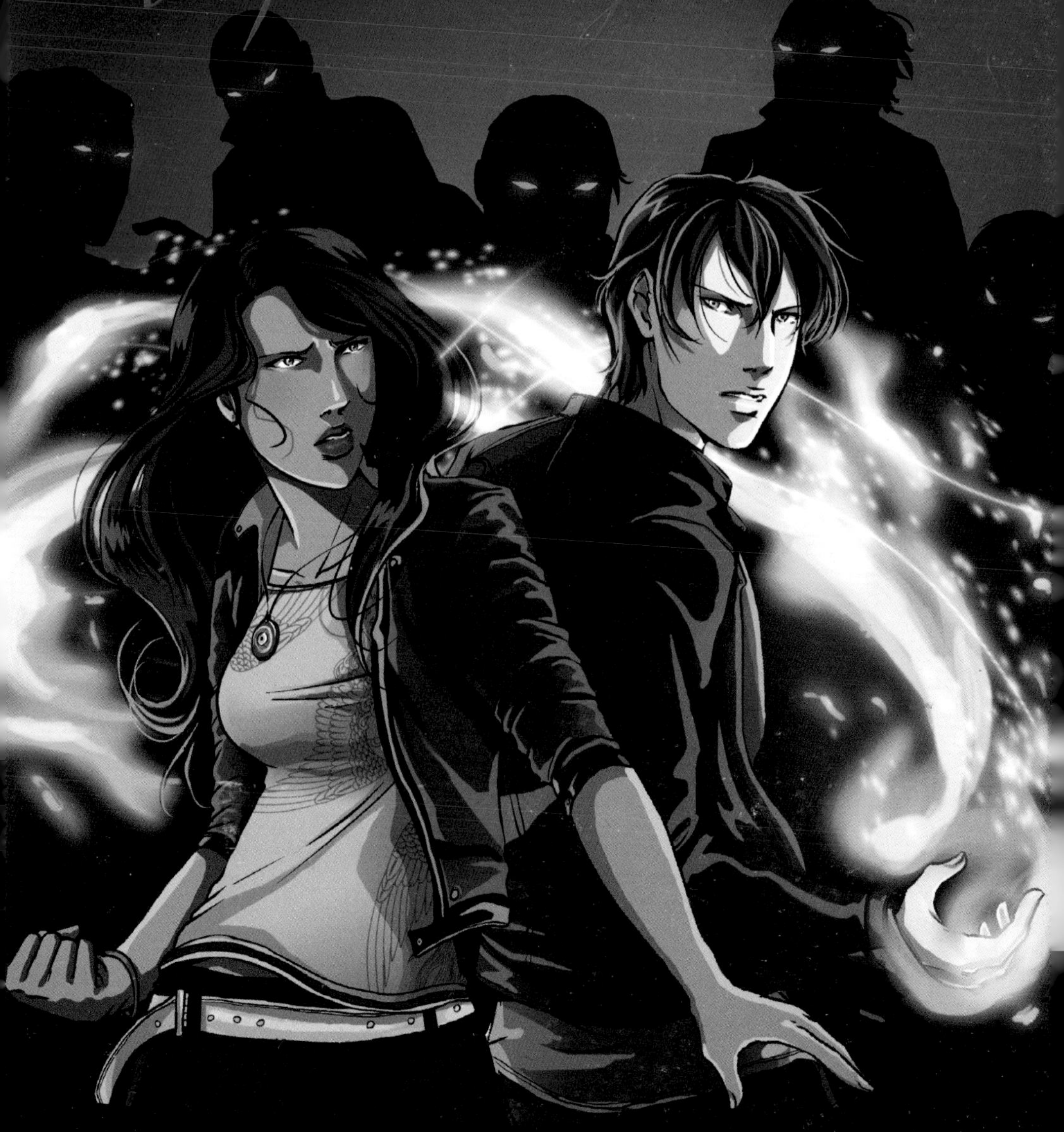

BASED ON THE #1 INTERNATIONAL BESTSELLING SERIES BY

RICHELLE MEAD

ADAPTED BY LEIGH DRAGOON • ILLUSTRATED BY EMMA VIECELI

COLORED BY VICKI PANGESTU, FORTRANICA, J-CON, FANDY, BUDI, RICHIE, & VINO OF CARAVAN STUDIO

COVER DESIGN AND LETTERING BY CHING N. CHAN

RAZORBILL

Published by the Penguin Group
Penguin Young Readers Group
345 Hudson Street, New York, New York 10014, USA.
Penguin Group (USA) Inc., 375 Hudson Street, New York, New York 10014, USA
Penguin Group (Canada), 90 Eglinton Avenue East, Suite 700,
Toronto, Ontario M4P 2Y3, Canada
(a division of Pearson Penguin Canada Inc.)
Penguin Books Ltd., 80 Strand, London WC2R 0RL, England
Penguin Group Ireland, 25 St. Stephen's Green, Dublin 2, Ireland
(a division of Penguin Books Ltd.)
Penguin Group (Australia), 250 Camberwell Road, Camberwell, Victoria 3124, Australia
(a division of Pearson Australia Group Pty. Ltd.)
Penguin Books India Pvt. Ltd., 11 Community Centre,
Panchsheel Park, New Delhi—110 017, India
Penguin Group (NZ), 67 Apollo Drive, Rosedale, Auckland 0632, New Zealand
(a division of Pearson New Zealand Ltd.)
Penguin Books (South Africa) (Pty.) Ltd., 24 Sturdee Avenue,
Rosebank, Johannesburg 2196, South Africa

Penguin Books Ltd., Registered Offices: 80 Strand, London WC2R 0RL, England

10 9 8 7 6 5 4 3 2

Library of Congress Cataloging-in-Publication Data is available

Printed in Canada.

PROLOGUE

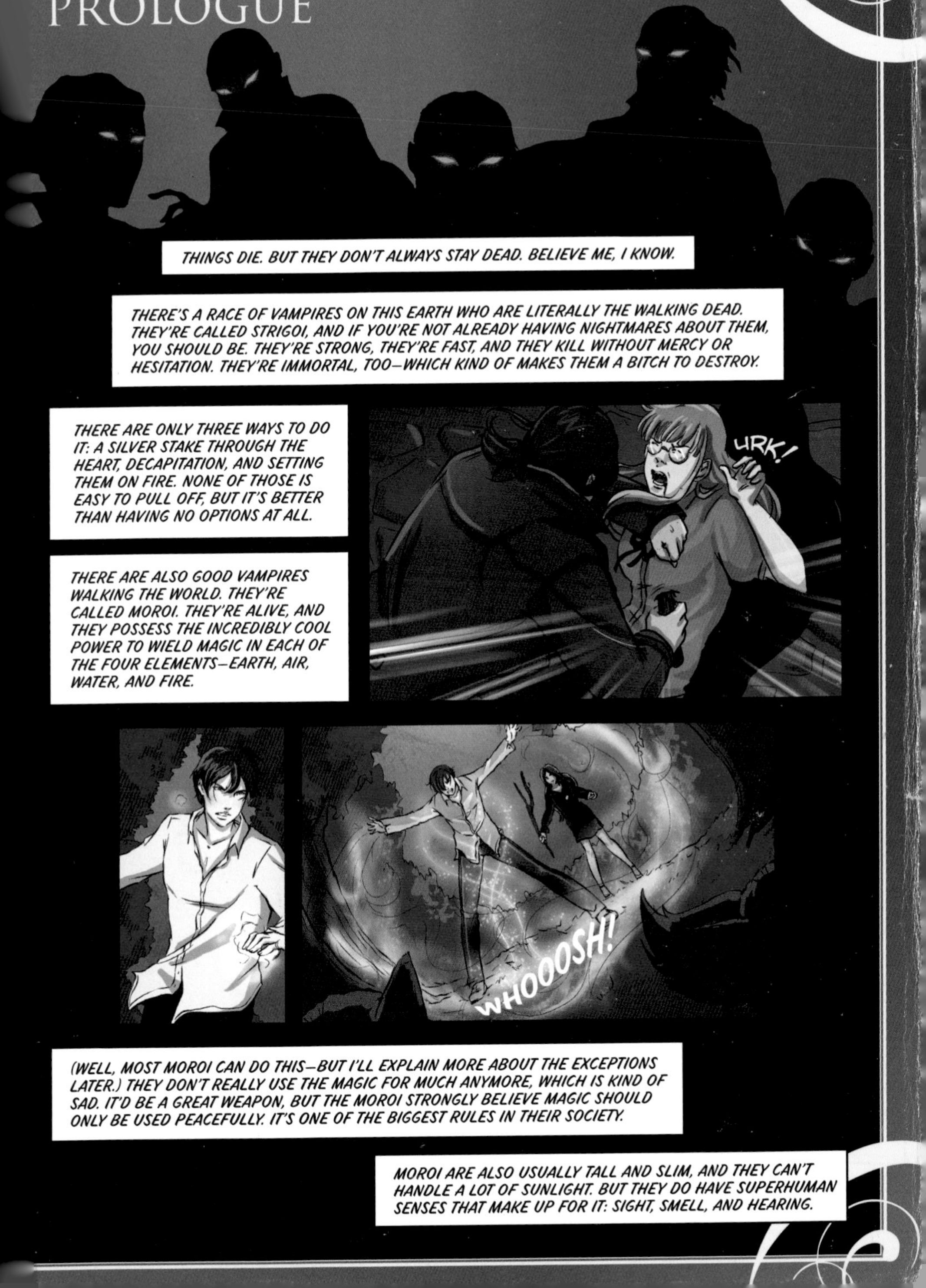
THINGS DIE. BUT THEY DON'T ALWAYS STAY DEAD. BELIEVE ME, I KNOW.
THERE'S A RACE OF VAMPIRES ON THIS EARTH WHO ARE LITERALLY THE WALKING DEAD. THEY'RE CALLED STRIGOI, AND IF YOU'RE NOT ALREADY HAVING NIGHTMARES ABOUT THEM, YOU SHOULD BE. THEY'RE STRONG, THEY'RE FAST, AND THEY KILL WITHOUT MERCY OR HESITATION. THEY'RE IMMORTAL, TOO—WHICH KIND OF MAKES THEM A BITCH TO DESTROY.
THERE ARE ONLY THREE WAYS TO DO IT: A SILVER STAKE THROUGH THE HEART, DECAPITATION, AND SETTING THEM ON FIRE. NONE OF THOSE IS EASY TO PULL OFF, BUT IT'S BETTER THAN HAVING NO OPTIONS AT ALL.
URK!
THERE ARE ALSO GOOD VAMPIRES WALKING THE WORLD. THEY'RE CALLED MOROI. THEY'RE ALIVE, AND THEY POSSESS THE INCREDIBLY COOL POWER TO WIELD MAGIC IN EACH OF THE FOUR ELEMENTS—EARTH, AIR, WATER, AND FIRE.
WHOOOOSH!
(WELL, MOST MOROI CAN DO THIS—BUT I'LL EXPLAIN MORE ABOUT THE EXCEPTIONS LATER.) THEY DON'T REALLY USE THE MAGIC FOR MUCH ANYMORE, WHICH IS KIND OF SAD. IT'D BE A GREAT WEAPON, BUT THE MOROI STRONGLY BELIEVE MAGIC SHOULD ONLY BE USED PEACEFULLY. IT'S ONE OF THE BIGGEST RULES IN THEIR SOCIETY.
MOROI ARE ALSO USUALLY TALL AND SLIM, AND THEY CAN'T HANDLE A LOT OF SUNLIGHT. BUT THEY DO HAVE SUPERHUMAN SENSES THAT MAKE UP FOR IT: SIGHT, SMELL, AND HEARING.

BOTH KINDS OF VAMPIRES NEED BLOOD. THAT'S WHAT MAKES THEM VAMPIRES, I GUESS. MOROI DON'T KILL TO TAKE IT, HOWEVER. INSTEAD, THEY KEEP HUMANS AROUND WHO WILLINGLY DONATE SMALL AMOUNTS.

THEY VOLUNTEER BECAUSE VAMPIRE BITES CONTAIN ENDORPHINS THAT FEEL REALLY, REALLY GOOD AND CAN BECOME ADDICTIVE.

MMMMM...

I KNOW THIS FROM PERSONAL EXPERIENCE. THESE HUMANS ARE CALLED FEEDERS AND ARE ESSENTIALLY VAMPIRE-BITE JUNKIES.

STILL, KEEPING FEEDERS AROUND IS BETTER THAN THE WAY THE STRIGOI DO THINGS, BECAUSE, AS YOU MIGHT EXPECT, THEY KILL FOR THEIR BLOOD. I THINK THEY LIKE IT. IF A MOROI KILLS A VICTIM WHILE DRINKING, HE OR SHE WILL TURN INTO A STRIGOI. SOME MOROI DO THIS BY CHOICE, GIVING UP THEIR MAGIC AND THEIR MORALS FOR IMMORTALITY.

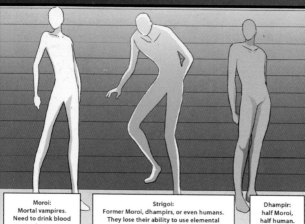

Moroi:
Mortal vampires.
Need to drink blood
to survive, can use
elemental magic.
Alive. Born.

Strigoi:
Former Moroi, dhampirs, or even humans.
They lose their ability to use elemental
magic when they turn. Moroi blood makes
them immortal and grants them extra
power and speed. Undead. Immortal.
Made as opposed to born.

Dhampir:
half Moroi,
half human.

STRIGOI CAN ALSO BE CREATED BY FORCE. IF A STRIGOI DRINKS BLOOD FROM A VICTIM AND THEN MAKES THAT PERSON DRINK STRIGOI BLOOD IN RETURN, WELL . . . YOU GET A NEW STRIGOI. THIS CAN HAPPEN TO ANYONE: MOROI, HUMAN, OR . . . DHAMPIR.

DHAMPIR

THAT'S WHAT I AM. DHAMPIRS ARE HALF-HUMAN, HALF-MOROI. I LIKE TO THINK WE GOT THE BEST TRAITS OF BOTH RACES. I'M STRONG AND STURDY, LIKE HUMANS ARE. I CAN ALSO GO OUT IN THE SUN AS MUCH AS I WANT. BUT, LIKE THE MOROI, I HAVE REALLY GOOD SENSES AND FAST REFLEXES. THE RESULT IS THAT DHAMPIRS MAKE THE ULTIMATE BODYGUARDS—WHICH IS WHAT MOST OF US ARE.

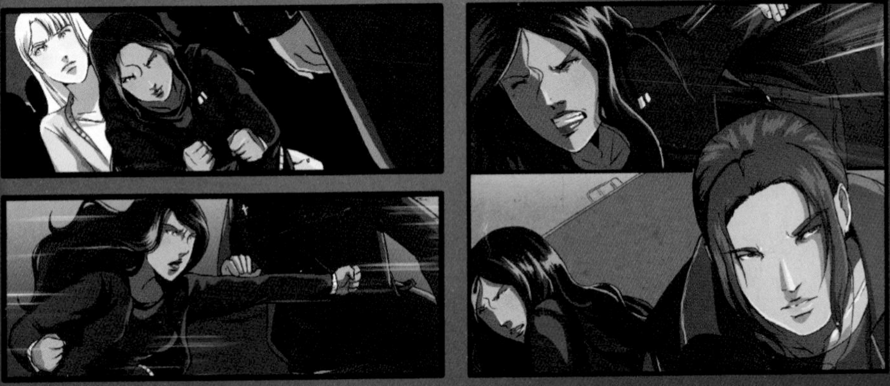

WE'RE CALLED GUARDIANS.

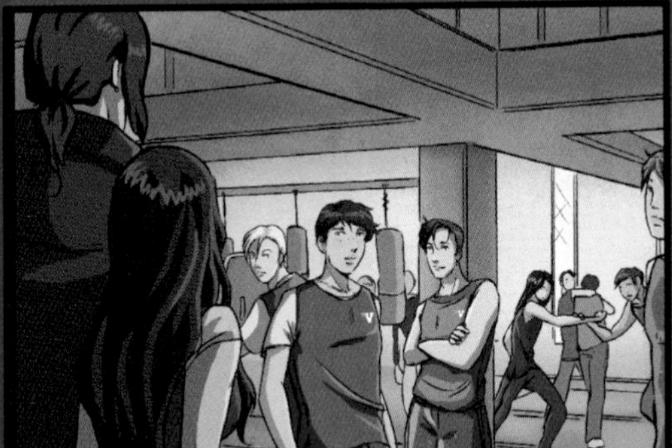

I'VE SPENT MY ENTIRE LIFE TRAINING TO PROTECT MOROI FROM STRIGOI. I HAVE A WHOLE SET OF SPECIAL CLASSES AND PRACTICES I TAKE AT ST. VLADIMIR'S ACADEMY, A PRIVATE SCHOOL FOR MOROI AND DHAMPIRS. I KNOW HOW TO USE ALL SORTS OF WEAPONS AND CAN LAND SOME PRETTY MEAN KICKS.

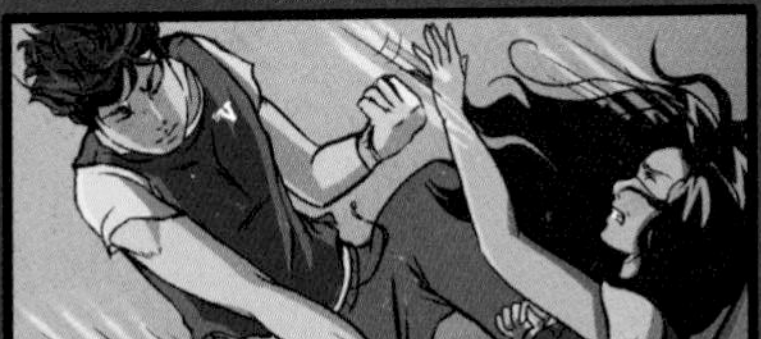
WUMP

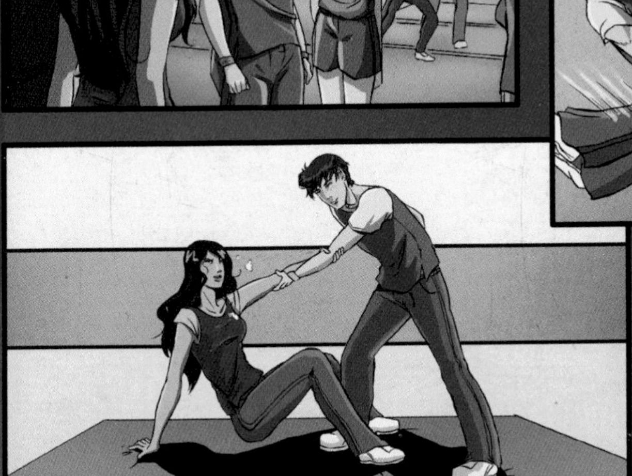

I'VE BEATEN UP GUYS TWICE MY SIZE—BOTH IN AND OUT OF CLASS. AND REALLY, GUYS ARE PRETTY MUCH THE ONLY ONES I BEAT UP, SINCE THERE ARE VERY FEW GIRLS IN ANY OF MY CLASSES.

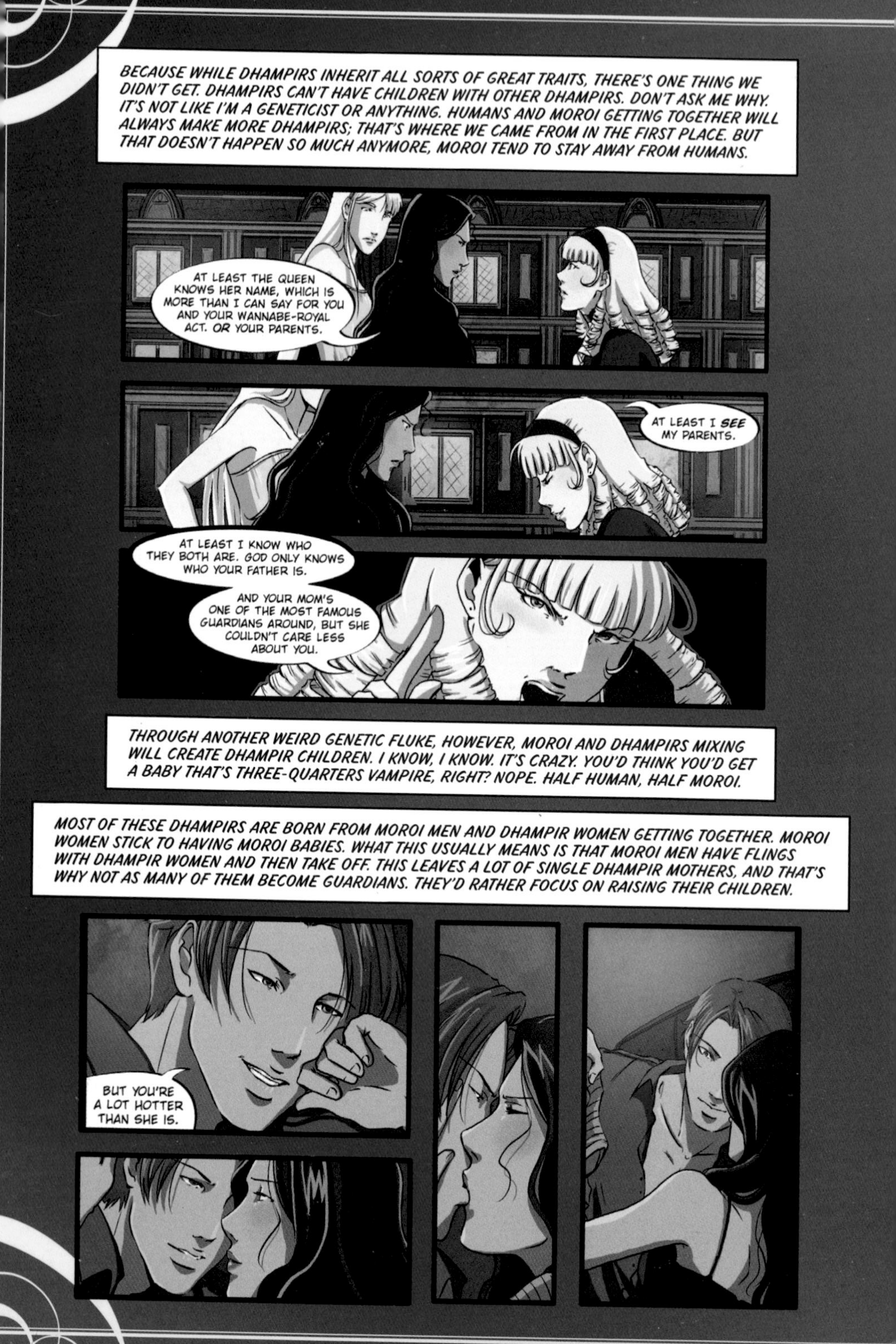
BECAUSE WHILE DHAMPIRS INHERIT ALL SORTS OF GREAT TRAITS, THERE'S ONE THING WE DIDN'T GET. DHAMPIRS CAN'T HAVE CHILDREN WITH OTHER DHAMPIRS. DON'T ASK ME WHY. IT'S NOT LIKE I'M A GENETICIST OR ANYTHING. HUMANS AND MOROI GETTING TOGETHER WILL ALWAYS MAKE MORE DHAMPIRS; THAT'S WHERE WE CAME FROM IN THE FIRST PLACE. BUT THAT DOESN'T HAPPEN SO MUCH ANYMORE, MOROI TEND TO STAY AWAY FROM HUMANS.
AT LEAST THE QUEEN KNOWS HER NAME, WHICH IS MORE THAN I CAN SAY FOR YOU AND YOUR WANNABE-ROYAL ACT. OR YOUR PARENTS.
AT LEAST I SEE MY PARENTS.
AT LEAST I KNOW WHO THEY BOTH ARE. GOD ONLY KNOWS WHO YOUR FATHER IS.
AND YOUR MOM'S ONE OF THE MOST FAMOUS GUARDIANS AROUND, BUT SHE COULDN'T CARE LESS ABOUT YOU.
THROUGH ANOTHER WEIRD GENETIC FLUKE, HOWEVER, MOROI AND DHAMPIRS MIXING WILL CREATE DHAMPIR CHILDREN. I KNOW, I KNOW. IT'S CRAZY. YOU'D THINK YOU'D GET A BABY THAT'S THREE-QUARTERS VAMPIRE, RIGHT? NOPE. HALF HUMAN, HALF MOROI.
MOST OF THESE DHAMPIRS ARE BORN FROM MOROI MEN AND DHAMPIR WOMEN GETTING TOGETHER. MOROI WOMEN STICK TO HAVING MOROI BABIES. WHAT THIS USUALLY MEANS IS THAT MOROI MEN HAVE FLINGS WITH DHAMPIR WOMEN AND THEN TAKE OFF. THIS LEAVES A LOT OF SINGLE DHAMPIR MOTHERS, AND THAT'S WHY NOT AS MANY OF THEM BECOME GUARDIANS. THEY'D RATHER FOCUS ON RAISING THEIR CHILDREN.
BUT YOU'RE A LOT HOTTER THAN SHE IS.

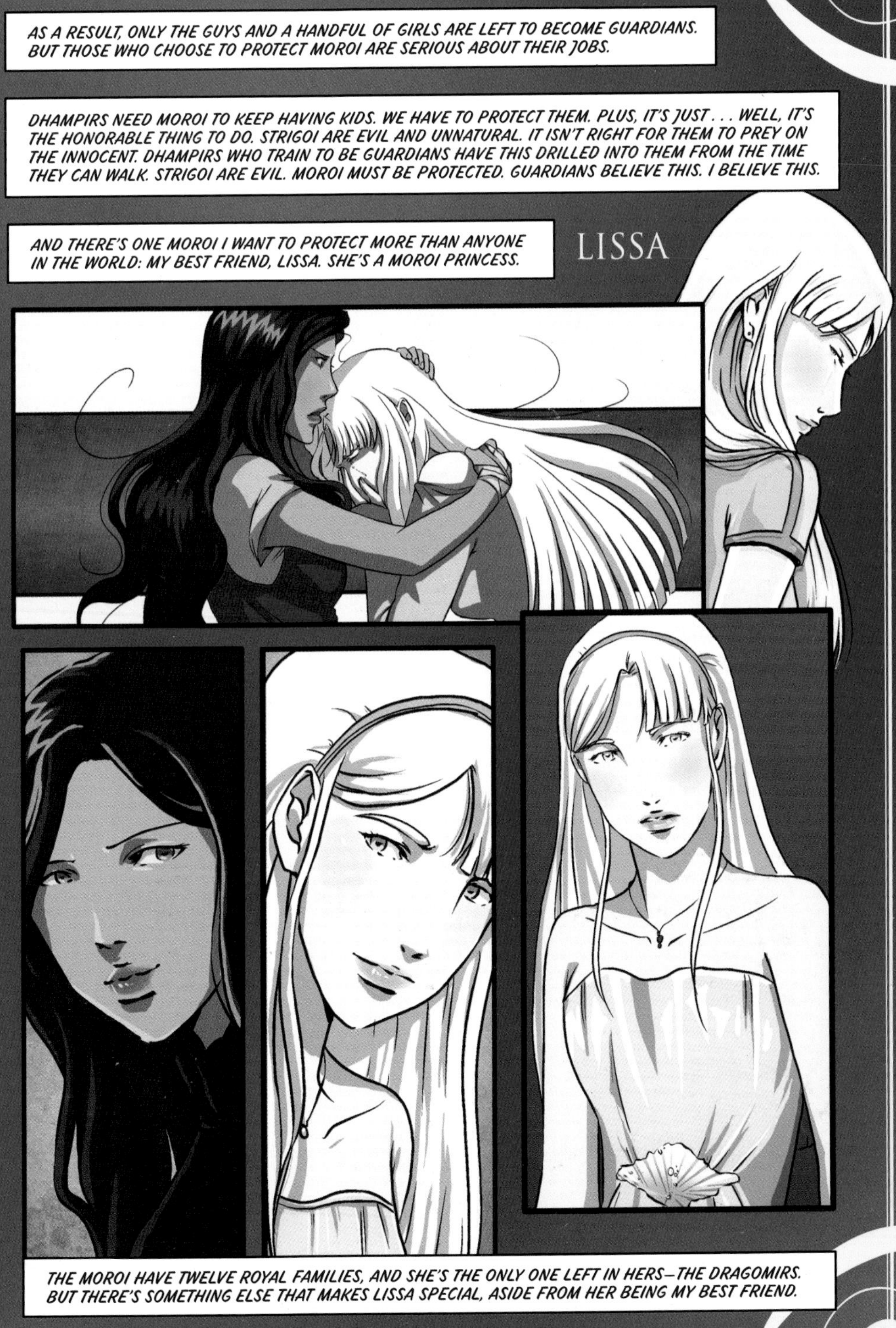
AS A RESULT, ONLY THE GUYS AND A HANDFUL OF GIRLS ARE LEFT TO BECOME GUARDIANS. BUT THOSE WHO CHOOSE TO PROTECT MOROI ARE SERIOUS ABOUT THEIR JOBS.
DHAMPIRS NEED MOROI TO KEEP HAVING KIDS. WE HAVE TO PROTECT THEM. PLUS, IT'S JUST . . . WELL, IT'S THE HONORABLE THING TO DO. STRIGOI ARE EVIL AND UNNATURAL. IT ISN'T RIGHT FOR THEM TO PREY ON THE INNOCENT. DHAMPIRS WHO TRAIN TO BE GUARDIANS HAVE THIS DRILLED INTO THEM FROM THE TIME THEY CAN WALK. STRIGOI ARE EVIL. MOROI MUST BE PROTECTED. GUARDIANS BELIEVE THIS. I BELIEVE THIS.
AND THERE'S ONE MOROI I WANT TO PROTECT MORE THAN ANYONE IN THE WORLD: MY BEST FRIEND, LISSA. SHE'S A MOROI PRINCESS.
LISSA
THE MOROI HAVE TWELVE ROYAL FAMILIES, AND SHE'S THE ONLY ONE LEFT IN HERS—THE DRAGOMIRS. BUT THERE'S SOMETHING ELSE THAT MAKES LISSA SPECIAL, ASIDE FROM HER BEING MY BEST FRIEND.

REMEMBER WHEN I SAID EVERY MOROI WIELDS ONE OF THE FOUR ELEMENTS? WELL, IT TURNS OUT LISSA WIELDS ONE NO ONE EVEN KNEW EXISTED UNTIL RECENTLY: SPIRIT. FOR YEARS, WE THOUGHT SHE JUST WASN'T GOING TO DEVELOP HER MAGICAL ABILITIES. THEN STRANGE THINGS STARTED HAPPENING AROUND HER. FOR EXAMPLE, ALL VAMPIRES HAVE AN ABILITY CALLED COMPULSION THAT LETS THEM FORCE THEIR WILL ON OTHERS.

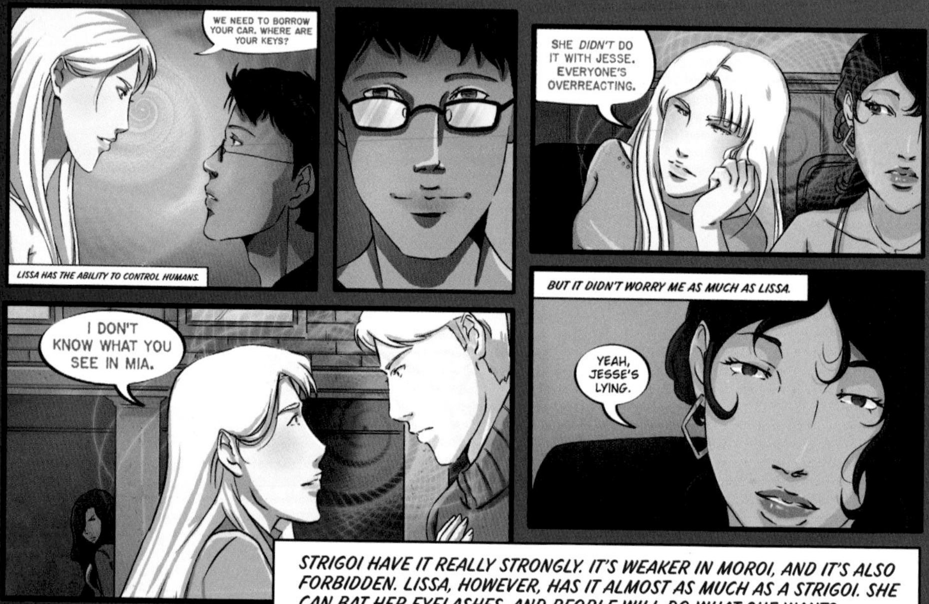
WE NEED TO BORROW YOUR CAR. WHERE ARE YOUR KEYS?
LISSA HAS THE ABILITY TO CONTROL HUMANS.
SHE *DIDN'T* DO IT WITH JESSE. EVERYONE'S OVERREACTING.
I DON'T KNOW WHAT YOU SEE IN MIA.
BUT IT DIDN'T WORRY ME AS MUCH AS LISSA.
YEAH, JESSE'S LYING.

STRIGOI HAVE IT REALLY STRONGLY. IT'S WEAKER IN MOROI, AND IT'S ALSO FORBIDDEN. LISSA, HOWEVER, HAS IT ALMOST AS MUCH AS A STRIGOI. SHE CAN BAT HER EYELASHES, AND PEOPLE WILL DO WHAT SHE WANTS.

BUT THAT'S NOT EVEN THE COOLEST THING SHE CAN DO.

I SAID EARLIER THAT DEAD THINGS DON'T ALWAYS STAY DEAD. WELL, I'M ONE OF THEM. DON'T WORRY—I'M NOT LIKE THE STRIGOI. BUT I DID DIE ONCE. (I DON'T RECOMMEND IT.) IT HAPPENED WHEN THE CAR I WAS RIDING IN SLID OFF THE ROAD.

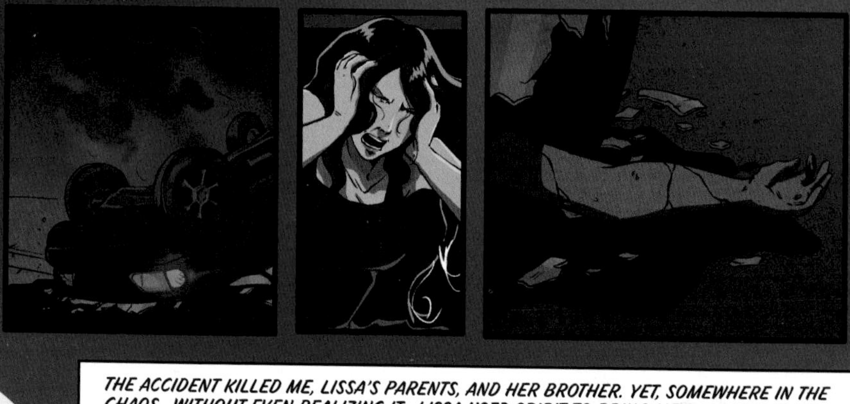

THE ACCIDENT KILLED ME, LISSA'S PARENTS, AND HER BROTHER. YET, SOMEWHERE IN THE CHAOS—WITHOUT EVEN REALIZING IT—LISSA USED SPIRIT TO BRING ME BACK. WE DIDN'T KNOW ABOUT THIS FOR A LONG TIME. IN FACT, WE DIDN'T EVEN KNOW SPIRIT EXISTED AT ALL.

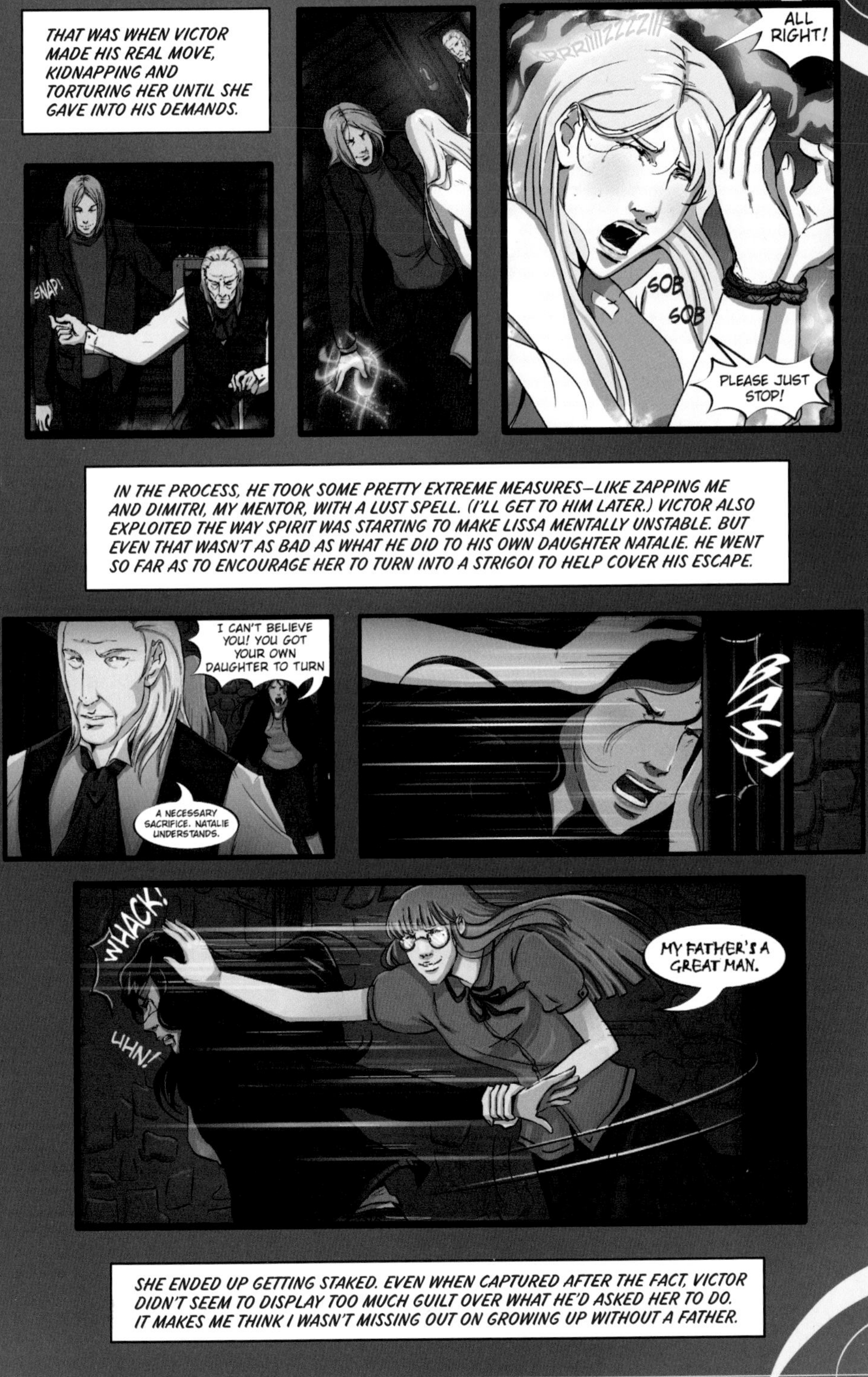
THAT WAS WHEN VICTOR MADE HIS REAL MOVE, KIDNAPPING AND TORTURING HER UNTIL SHE GAVE INTO HIS DEMANDS.
SNAP!
ALL RIGHT!
SOB
SOB
PLEASE JUST STOP!
IN THE PROCESS, HE TOOK SOME PRETTY EXTREME MEASURES—LIKE ZAPPING ME AND DIMITRI, MY MENTOR, WITH A LUST SPELL. (I'LL GET TO HIM LATER.) VICTOR ALSO EXPLOITED THE WAY SPIRIT WAS STARTING TO MAKE LISSA MENTALLY UNSTABLE. BUT EVEN THAT WASN'T AS BAD AS WHAT HE DID TO HIS OWN DAUGHTER NATALIE. HE WENT SO FAR AS TO ENCOURAGE HER TO TURN INTO A STRIGOI TO HELP COVER HIS ESCAPE.
I CAN'T BELIEVE YOU! YOU GOT YOUR OWN DAUGHTER TO TURN
A NECESSARY SACRIFICE. NATALIE UNDERSTANDS.
BASH
WHACK!
UHN!
MY FATHER'S A GREAT MAN.
SHE ENDED UP GETTING STAKED. EVEN WHEN CAPTURED AFTER THE FACT, VICTOR DIDN'T SEEM TO DISPLAY TOO MUCH GUILT OVER WHAT HE'D ASKED HER TO DO. IT MAKES ME THINK I WASN'T MISSING OUT ON GROWING UP WITHOUT A FATHER.

STILL, I NOW HAVE TO PROTECT LISSA FROM STRIGOI AND MOROI. ONLY A FEW OFFICIALS KNOW ABOUT WHAT SHE CAN DO, BUT I'M SURE THERE ARE OTHER VICTORS OUT THERE WHO WOULD WANT TO USE HER.

FORTUNATELY, I HAVE AN EXTRA WEAPON TO HELP ME GUARD HER. SOMEWHERE DURING MY HEALING IN THE CAR ACCIDENT, SPIRIT FORGED A PSYCHIC BOND BETWEEN HER AND ME. I CAN SEE AND FEEL WHAT SHE EXPERIENCES. (IT ONLY WORKS ONE WAY, THOUGH. SHE CAN'T "FEEL" ME.)

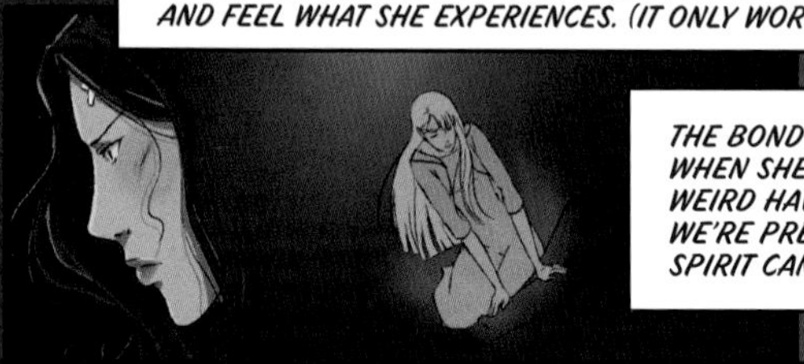

THE BOND HELPS ME KEEP AN EYE ON HER AND KNOW WHEN SHE'S IN TROUBLE, ALTHOUGH SOMETIMES IT'S WEIRD HAVING ANOTHER PERSON INSIDE YOUR HEAD. WE'RE PRETTY SURE THERE ARE LOTS OF OTHER THINGS SPIRIT CAN DO, BUT WE DON'T KNOW WHAT THEY ARE YET.

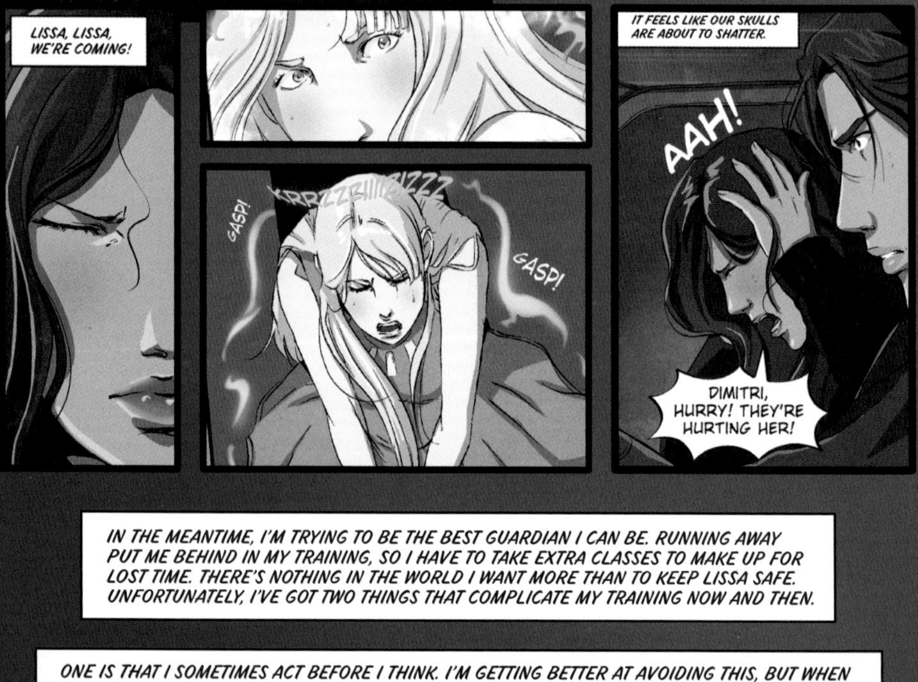
LISSA, LISSA, WE'RE COMING!
GASP!
GASP!
IT FEELS LIKE OUR SKULLS ARE ABOUT TO SHATTER.
AAH!
DIMITRI, HURRY! THEY'RE HURTING HER!

IN THE MEANTIME, I'M TRYING TO BE THE BEST GUARDIAN I CAN BE. RUNNING AWAY PUT ME BEHIND IN MY TRAINING, SO I HAVE TO TAKE EXTRA CLASSES TO MAKE UP FOR LOST TIME. THERE'S NOTHING IN THE WORLD I WANT MORE THAN TO KEEP LISSA SAFE. UNFORTUNATELY, I'VE GOT TWO THINGS THAT COMPLICATE MY TRAINING NOW AND THEN.

ONE IS THAT I SOMETIMES ACT BEFORE I THINK. I'M GETTING BETTER AT AVOIDING THIS, BUT WHEN SOMETHING SETS ME OFF, I TEND TO PUNCH FIRST AND THEN FIND OUT WHO I ACTUALLY HIT LATER. WHEN IT COMES TO THOSE I CARE ABOUT BEING IN DANGER . . . WELL, RULES SEEM OPTIONAL.

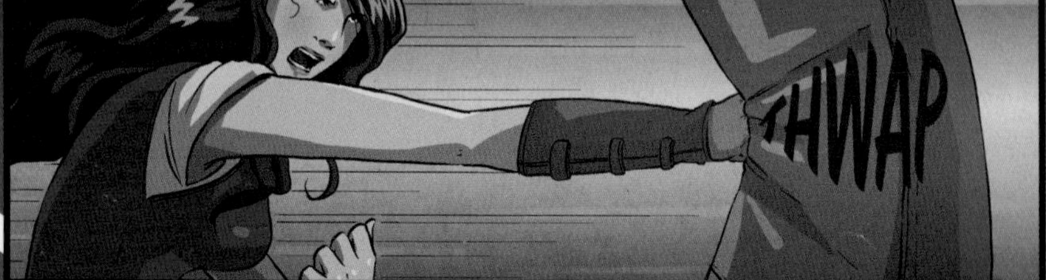
THWAP

DIMITRI

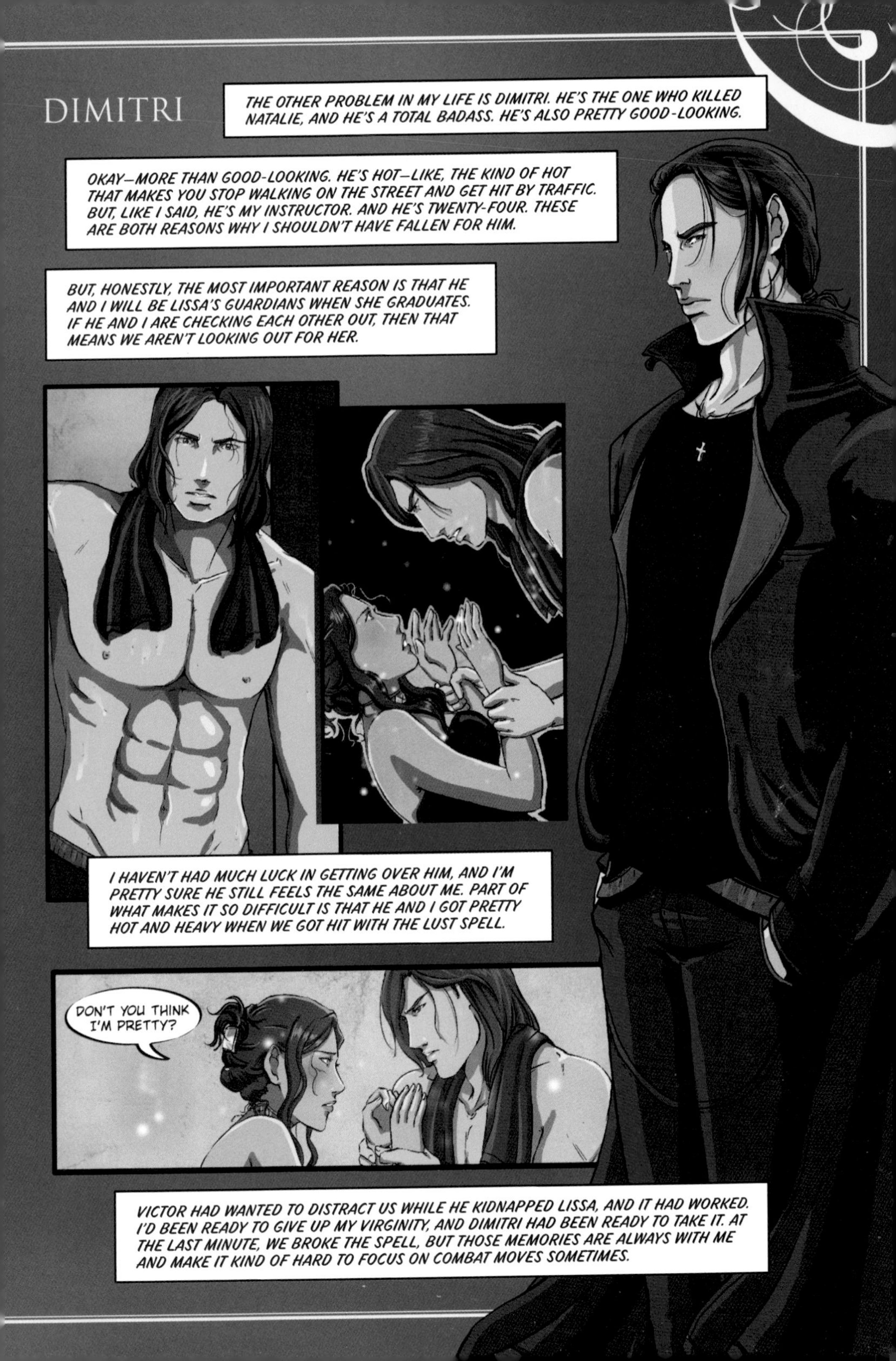
THE OTHER PROBLEM IN MY LIFE IS DIMITRI. HE'S THE ONE WHO KILLED NATALIE, AND HE'S A TOTAL BADASS. HE'S ALSO PRETTY GOOD-LOOKING.
OKAY—MORE THAN GOOD-LOOKING. HE'S HOT—LIKE, THE KIND OF HOT THAT MAKES YOU STOP WALKING ON THE STREET AND GET HIT BY TRAFFIC. BUT, LIKE I SAID, HE'S MY INSTRUCTOR. AND HE'S TWENTY-FOUR. THESE ARE BOTH REASONS WHY I SHOULDN'T HAVE FALLEN FOR HIM.
BUT, HONESTLY, THE MOST IMPORTANT REASON IS THAT HE AND I WILL BE LISSA'S GUARDIANS WHEN SHE GRADUATES. IF HE AND I ARE CHECKING EACH OTHER OUT, THEN THAT MEANS WE AREN'T LOOKING OUT FOR HER.
I HAVEN'T HAD MUCH LUCK IN GETTING OVER HIM, AND I'M PRETTY SURE HE STILL FEELS THE SAME ABOUT ME. PART OF WHAT MAKES IT SO DIFFICULT IS THAT HE AND I GOT PRETTY HOT AND HEAVY WHEN WE GOT HIT WITH THE LUST SPELL.
DON'T YOU THINK I'M PRETTY?
VICTOR HAD WANTED TO DISTRACT US WHILE HE KIDNAPPED LISSA, AND IT HAD WORKED. I'D BEEN READY TO GIVE UP MY VIRGINITY, AND DIMITRI HAD BEEN READY TO TAKE IT. AT THE LAST MINUTE, WE BROKE THE SPELL, BUT THOSE MEMORIES ARE ALWAYS WITH ME AND MAKE IT KIND OF HARD TO FOCUS ON COMBAT MOVES SOMETIMES.

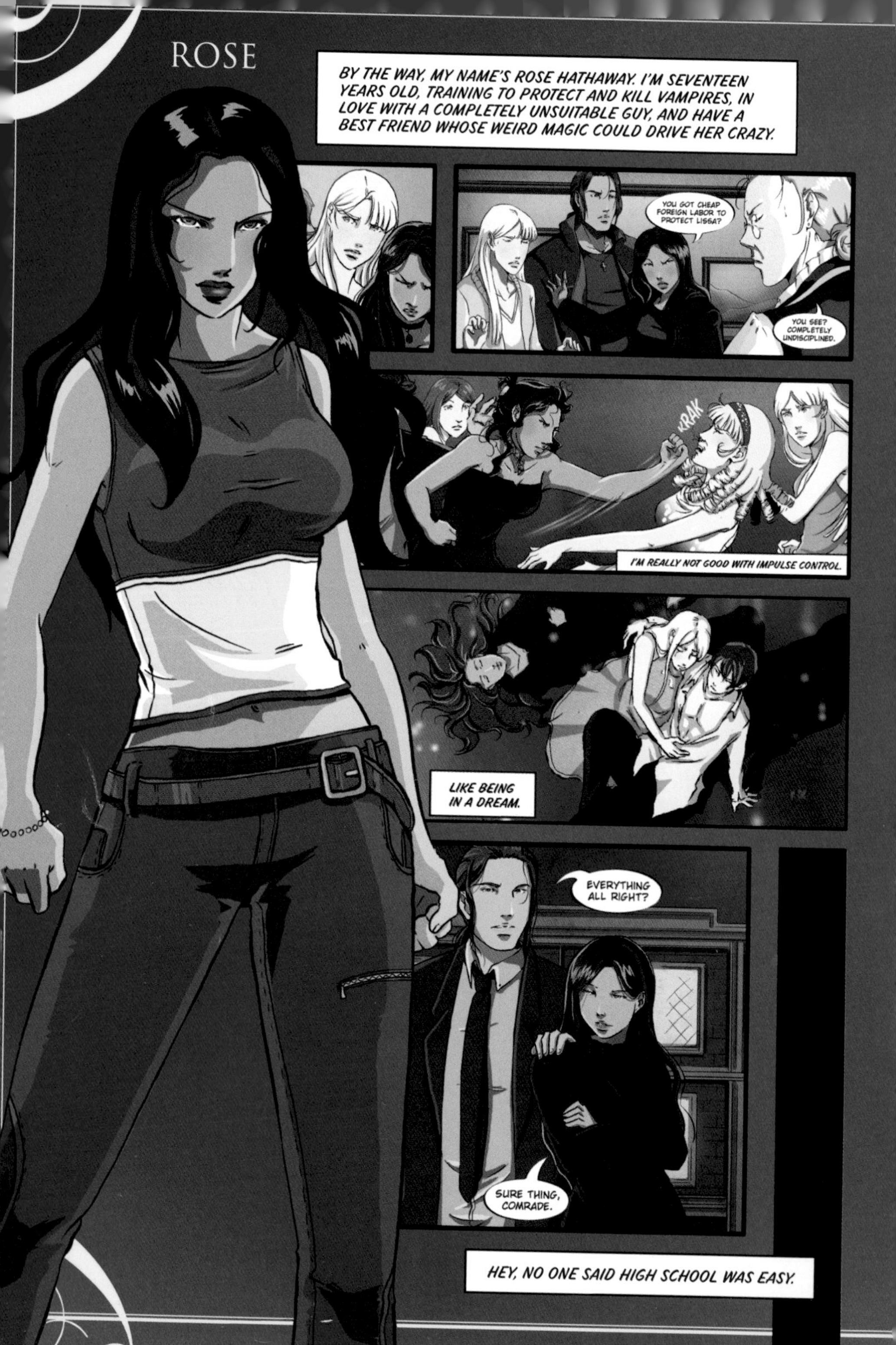
ROSE
BY THE WAY, MY NAME'S ROSE HATHAWAY. I'M SEVENTEEN YEARS OLD, TRAINING TO PROTECT AND KILL VAMPIRES, IN LOVE WITH A COMPLETELY UNSUITABLE GUY, AND HAVE A BEST FRIEND WHOSE WEIRD MAGIC COULD DRIVE HER CRAZY.
YOU GOT CHEAP FOREIGN LABOR TO PROTECT LISSA?
YOU SEE? COMPLETELY UNDISCIPLINED.
KRAK
I'M REALLY NOT GOOD WITH IMPULSE CONTROL.
LIKE BEING IN A DREAM.
EVERYTHING ALL RIGHT?
SURE THING, COMRADE.
HEY, NO ONE SAID HIGH SCHOOL WAS EASY.

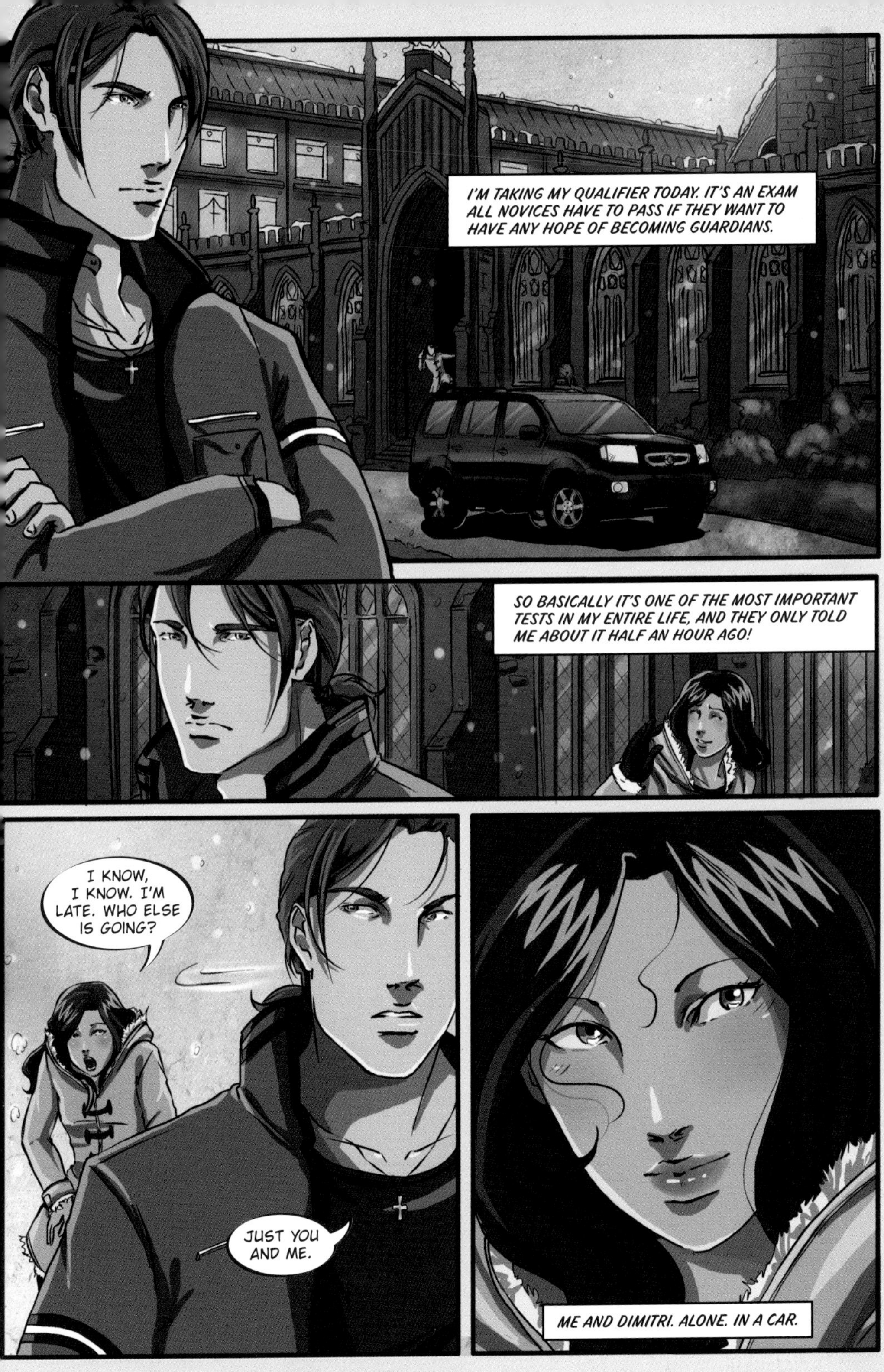
I'M TAKING MY QUALIFIER TODAY. IT'S AN EXAM ALL NOVICES HAVE TO PASS IF THEY WANT TO HAVE ANY HOPE OF BECOMING GUARDIANS.
SO BASICALLY IT'S ONE OF THE MOST IMPORTANT TESTS IN MY ENTIRE LIFE, AND THEY ONLY TOLD ME ABOUT IT HALF AN HOUR AGO!
I KNOW, I KNOW. I'M LATE. WHO ELSE IS GOING?
JUST YOU AND ME.
ME AND DIMITRI. ALONE. IN A CAR.

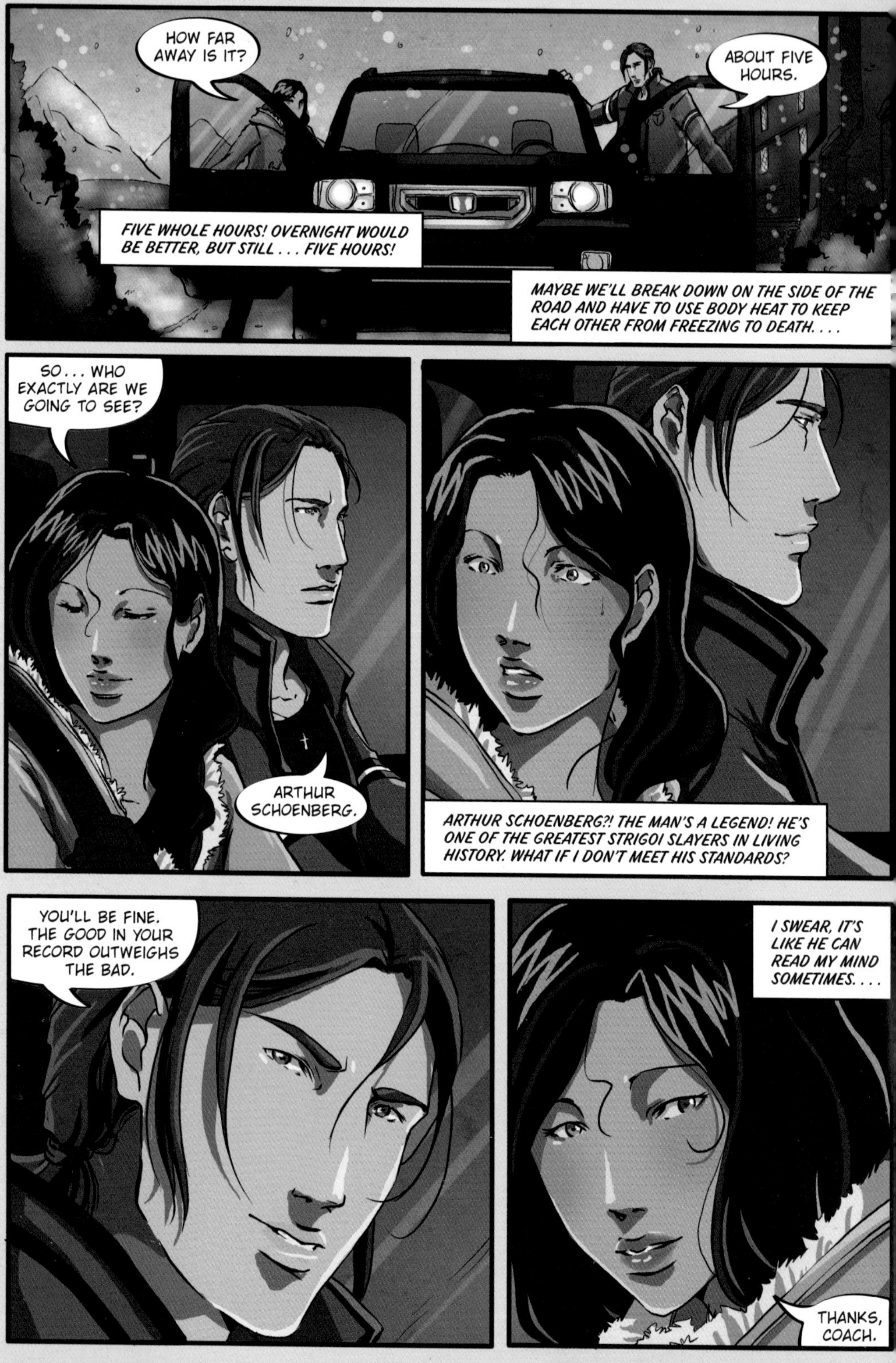
HOW FAR AWAY IS IT?
ABOUT FIVE HOURS.
FIVE WHOLE HOURS! OVERNIGHT WOULD BE BETTER, BUT STILL . . . FIVE HOURS!
MAYBE WE'LL BREAK DOWN ON THE SIDE OF THE ROAD AND HAVE TO USE BODY HEAT TO KEEP EACH OTHER FROM FREEZING TO DEATH. . . .
SO . . . WHO EXACTLY ARE WE GOING TO SEE?
ARTHUR SCHOENBERG.
ARTHUR SCHOENBERG?! THE MAN'S A LEGEND! HE'S ONE OF THE GREATEST STRIGOI SLAYERS IN LIVING HISTORY. WHAT IF I DON'T MEET HIS STANDARDS?
YOU'LL BE FINE. THE GOOD IN YOUR RECORD OUTWEIGHS THE BAD.
I SWEAR, IT'S LIKE HE CAN READ MY MIND SOMETIMES. . . .
THANKS, COACH.

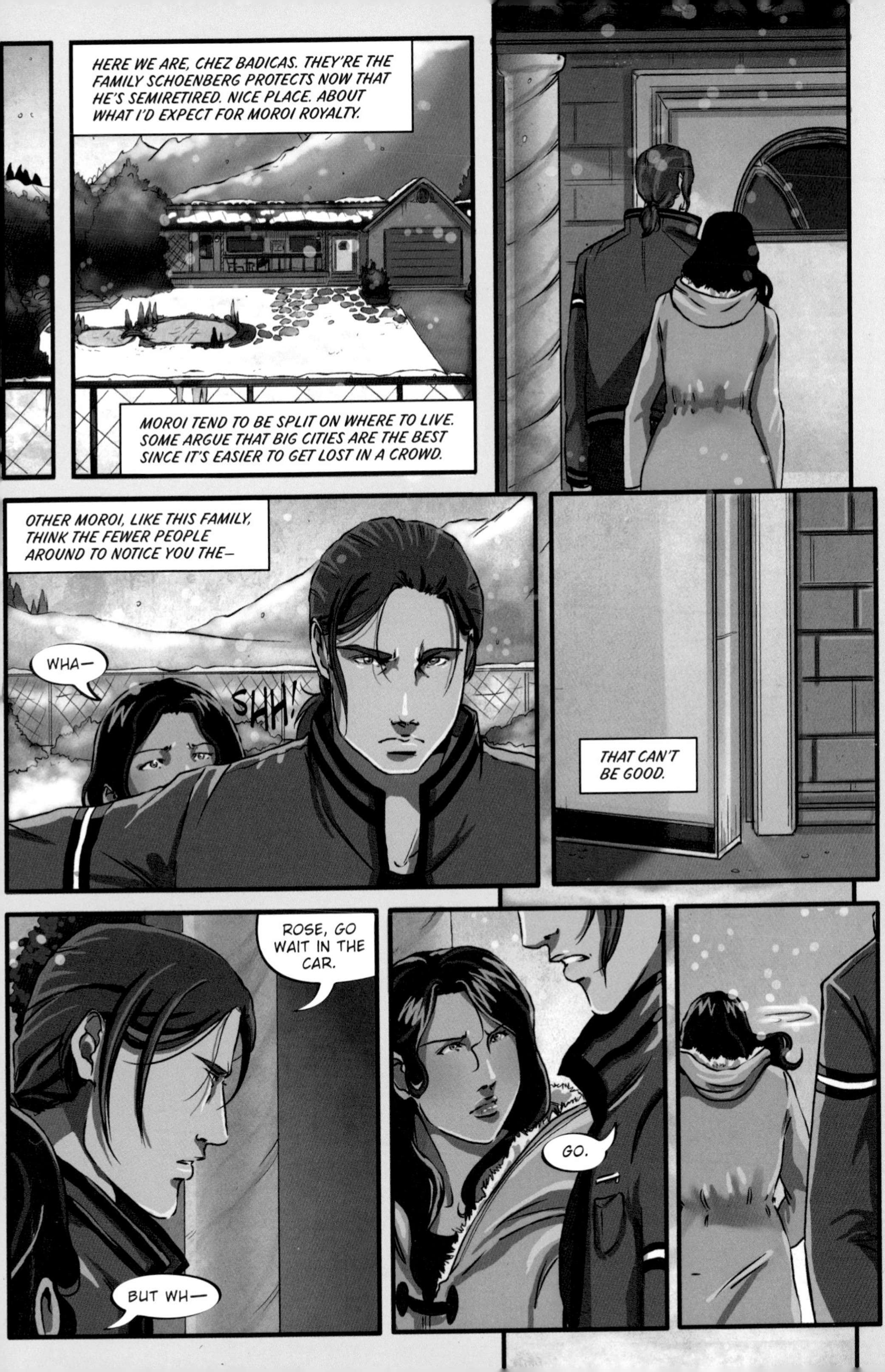
HERE WE ARE, CHEZ BADICAS. THEY'RE THE FAMILY SCHOENBERG PROTECTS NOW THAT HE'S SEMIRETIRED. NICE PLACE. ABOUT WHAT I'D EXPECT FOR MOROI ROYALTY.
MOROI TEND TO BE SPLIT ON WHERE TO LIVE. SOME ARGUE THAT BIG CITIES ARE THE BEST SINCE IT'S EASIER TO GET LOST IN A CROWD.
OTHER MOROI, LIKE THIS FAMILY, THINK THE FEWER PEOPLE AROUND TO NOTICE YOU THE—
WHA—
SHH!
THAT CAN'T BE GOOD.
ROSE, GO WAIT IN THE CAR.
BUT WH—
GO.

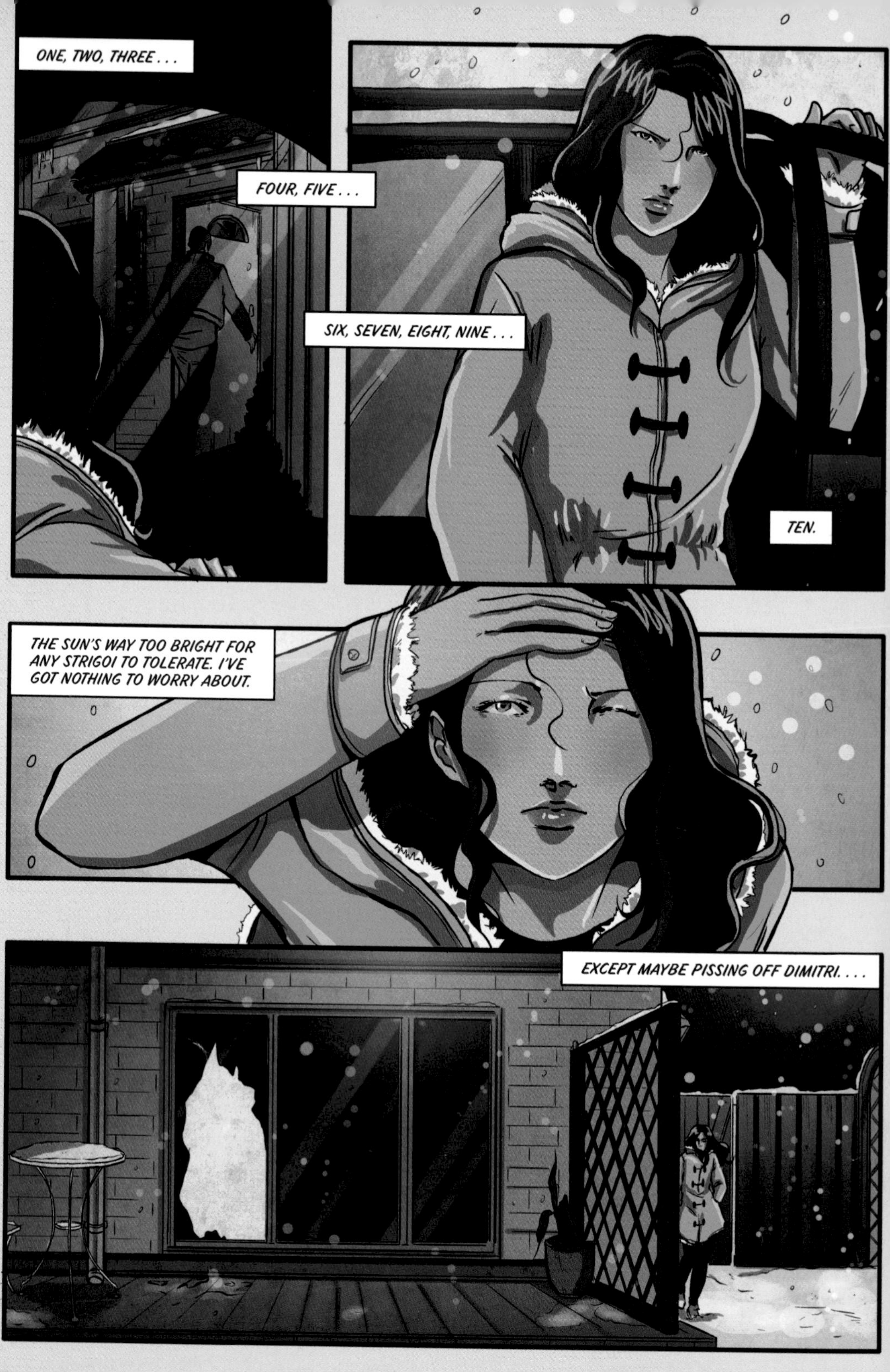
ONE, TWO, THREE . . .
FOUR, FIVE . . .
SIX, SEVEN, EIGHT, NINE . . .
TEN.
THE SUN'S WAY TOO BRIGHT FOR ANY STRIGOI TO TOLERATE. I'VE GOT NOTHING TO WORRY ABOUT.
EXCEPT MAYBE PISSING OFF DIMITRI. . . .

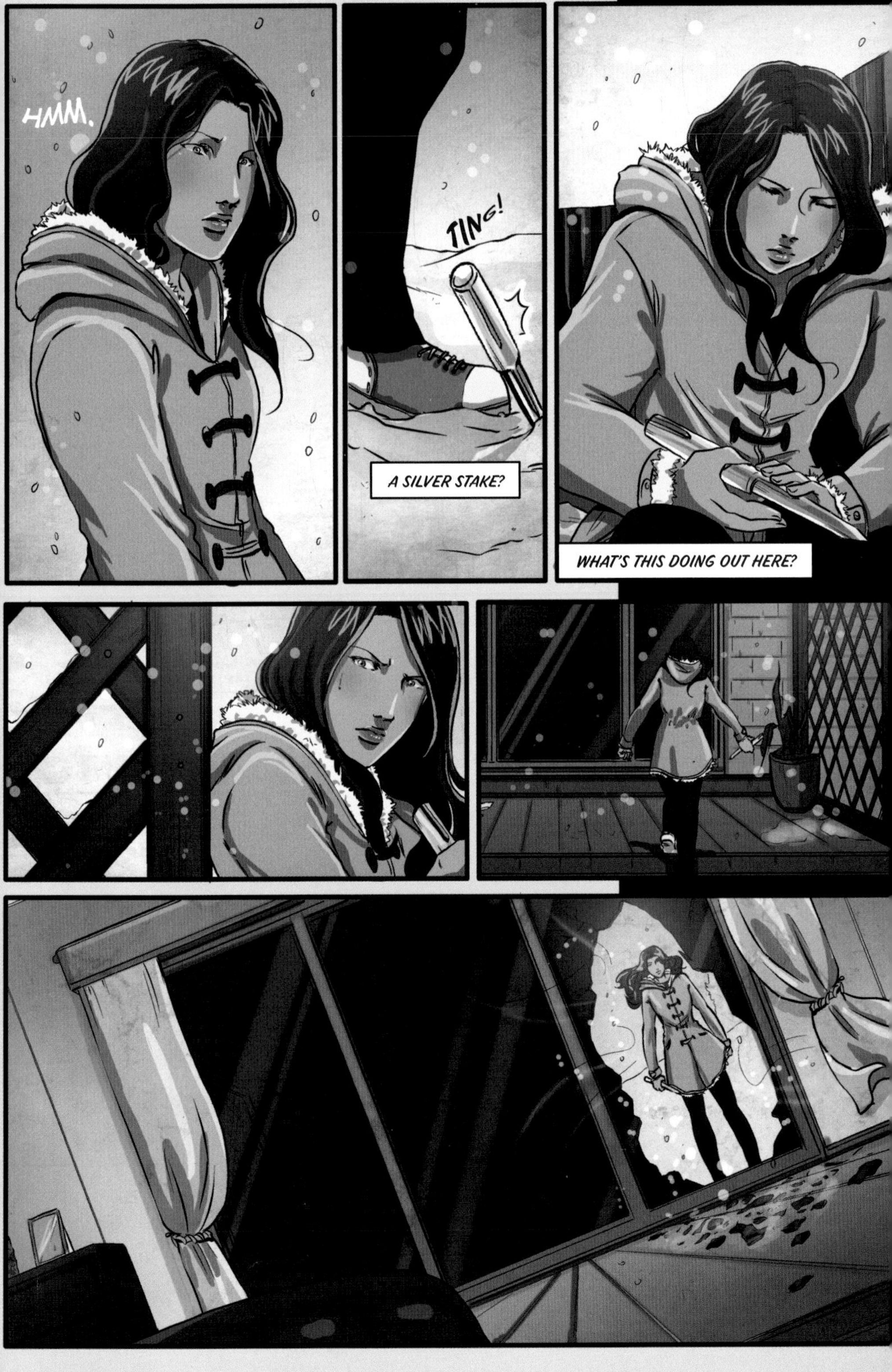
HMM.
TING!
A SILVER STAKE?
WHAT'S THIS DOING OUT HERE?

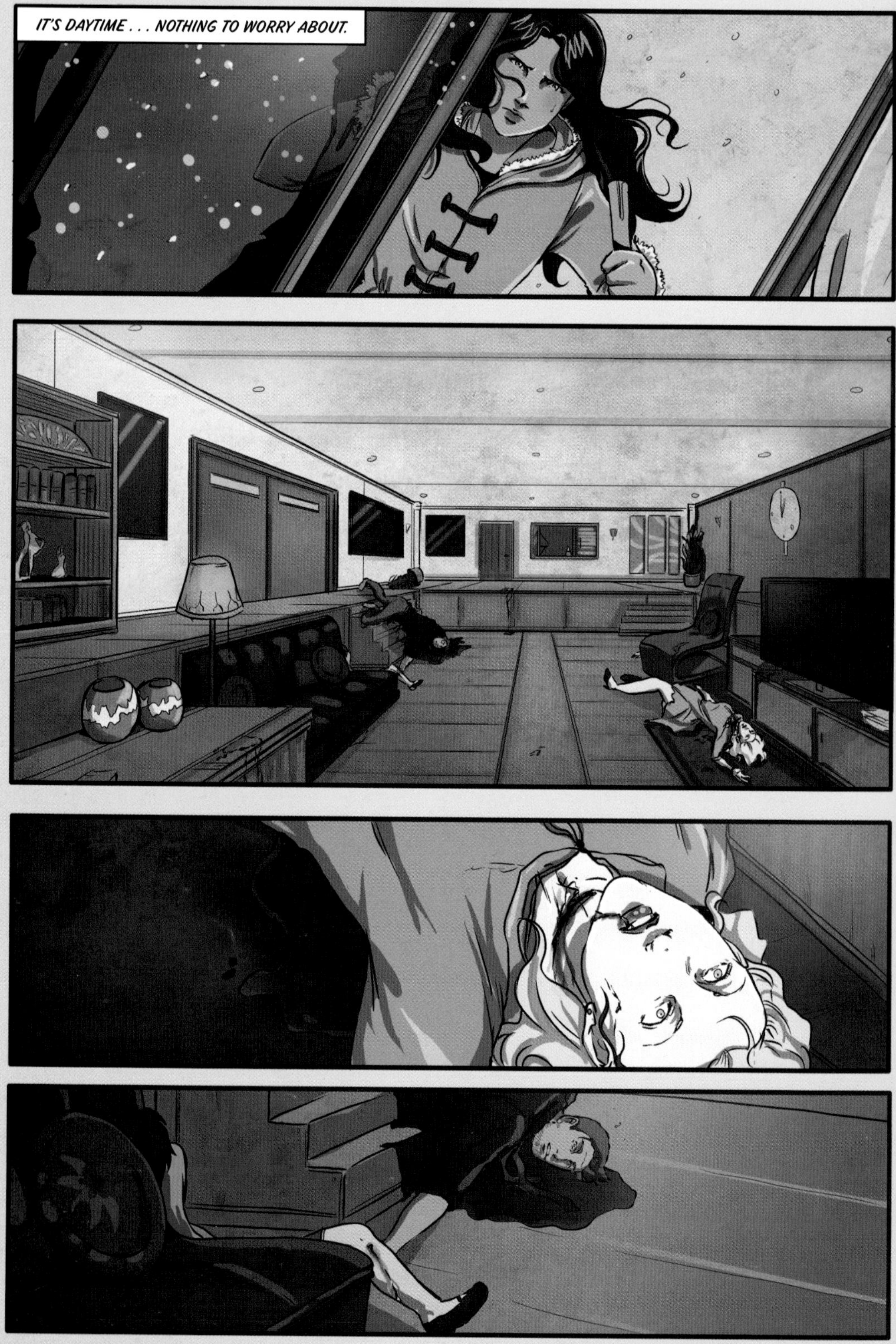
IT'S DAYTIME . . . NOTHING TO WORRY ABOUT.

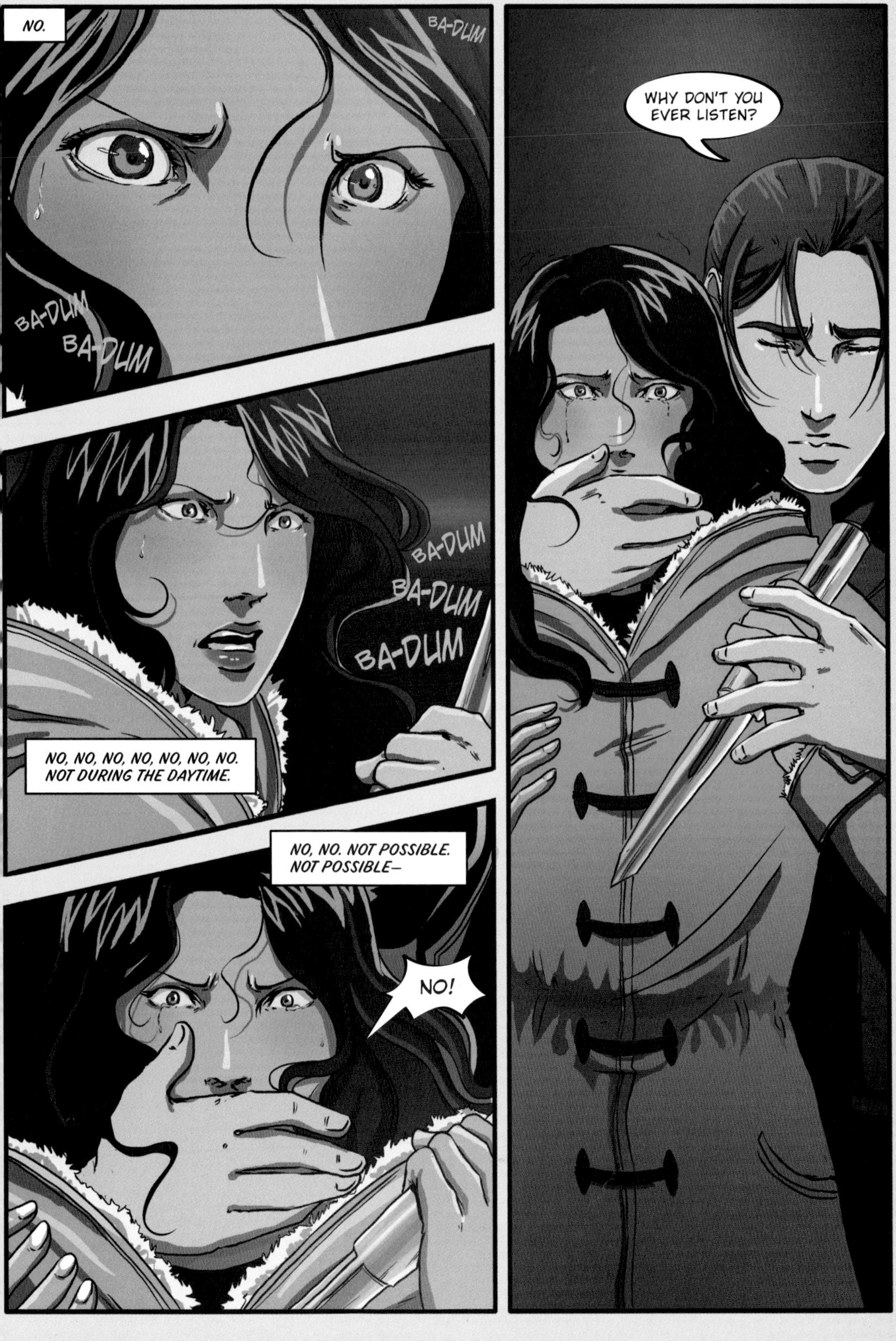
NO.
BA-DUM
BA-DUM
BA-DUM
BA-DUM
BA-DUM
BA-DUM
NO, NO, NO, NO, NO, NO, NO.
NOT DURING THE DAYTIME.
NO, NO. NOT POSSIBLE.
NOT POSSIBLE—
NO!
WHY DON'T YOU
EVER LISTEN?

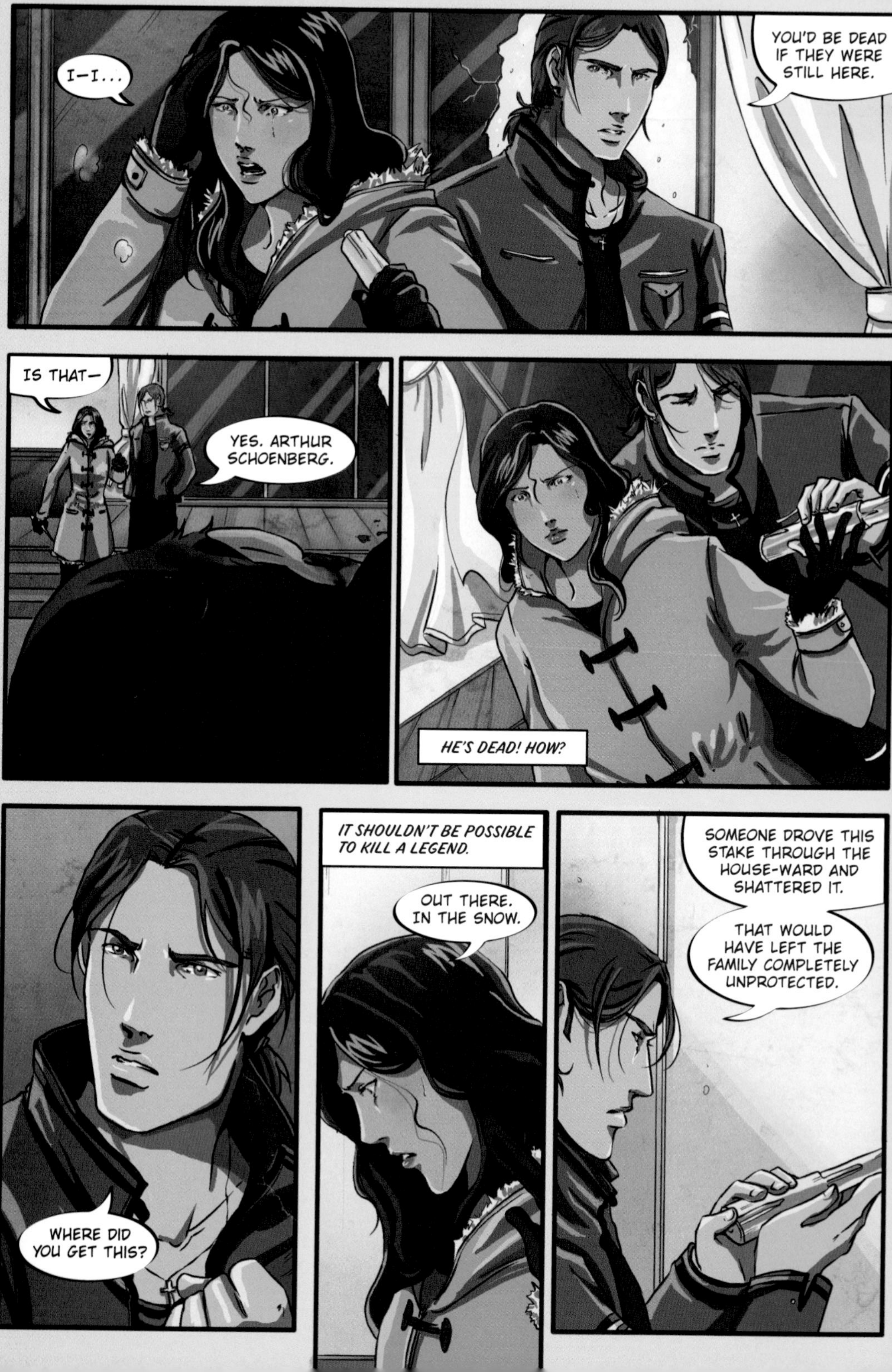
I—I...
YOU'D BE DEAD IF THEY WERE STILL HERE.
IS THAT—
YES. ARTHUR SCHOENBERG.
HE'S DEAD! HOW?
IT SHOULDN'T BE POSSIBLE TO KILL A LEGEND.
WHERE DID YOU GET THIS?
OUT THERE. IN THE SNOW.
SOMEONE DROVE THIS STAKE THROUGH THE HOUSE-WARD AND SHATTERED IT.
THAT WOULD HAVE LEFT THE FAMILY COMPLETELY UNPROTECTED.

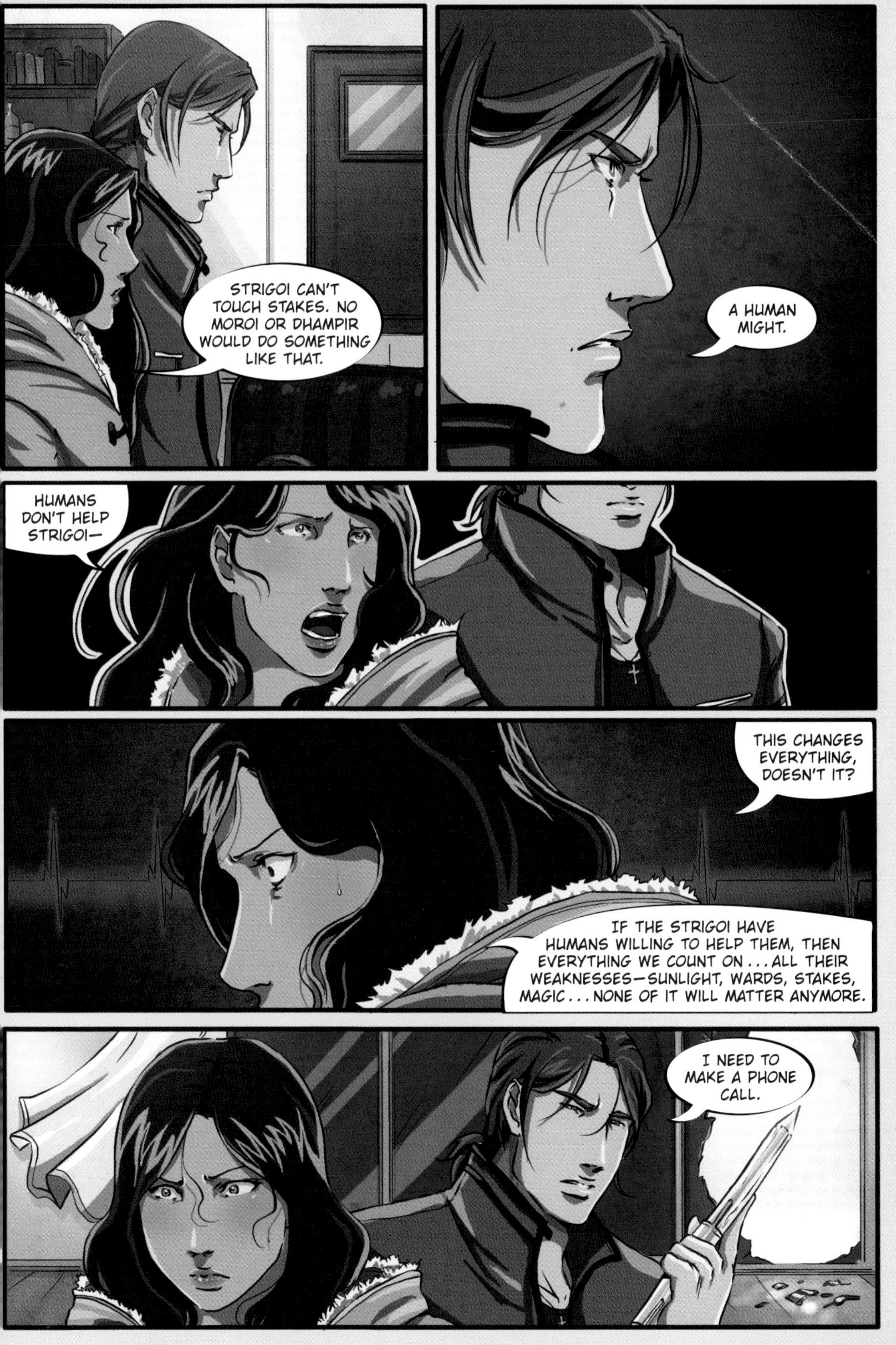
STRIGOI CAN'T TOUCH STAKES. NO MOROI OR DHAMPIR WOULD DO SOMETHING LIKE THAT.
A HUMAN MIGHT.
HUMANS DON'T HELP STRIGOI—
THIS CHANGES EVERYTHING, DOESN'T IT?
IF THE STRIGOI HAVE HUMANS WILLING TO HELP THEM, THEN EVERYTHING WE COUNT ON . . . ALL THEIR WEAKNESSES—SUNLIGHT, WARDS, STAKES, MAGIC . . . NONE OF IT WILL MATTER ANYMORE.
I NEED TO MAKE A PHONE CALL.

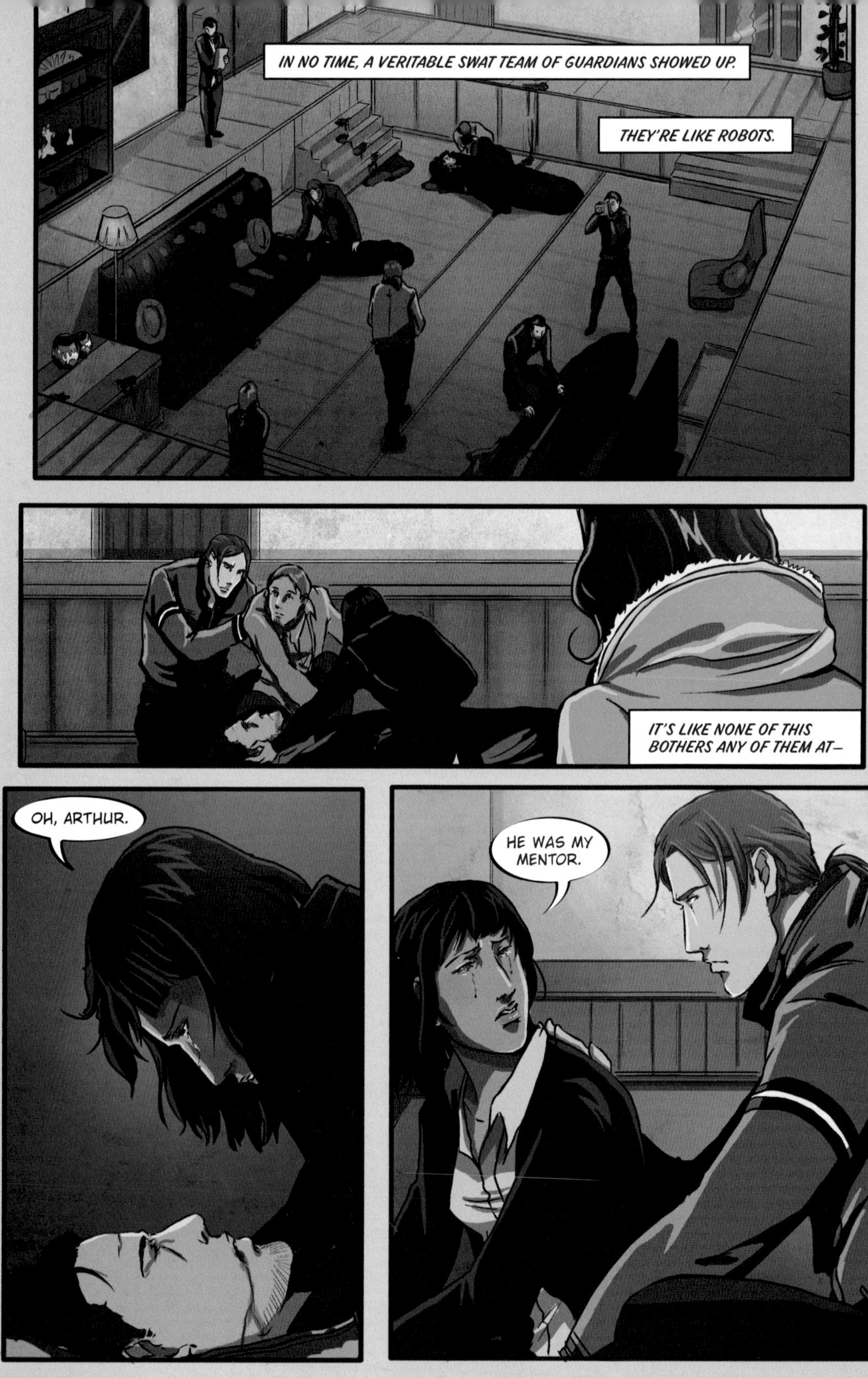
IN NO TIME, A VERITABLE SWAT TEAM OF GUARDIANS SHOWED UP.
THEY'RE LIKE ROBOTS.
IT'S LIKE NONE OF THIS BOTHERS ANY OF THEM AT—
OH, ARTHUR.
HE WAS MY MENTOR.

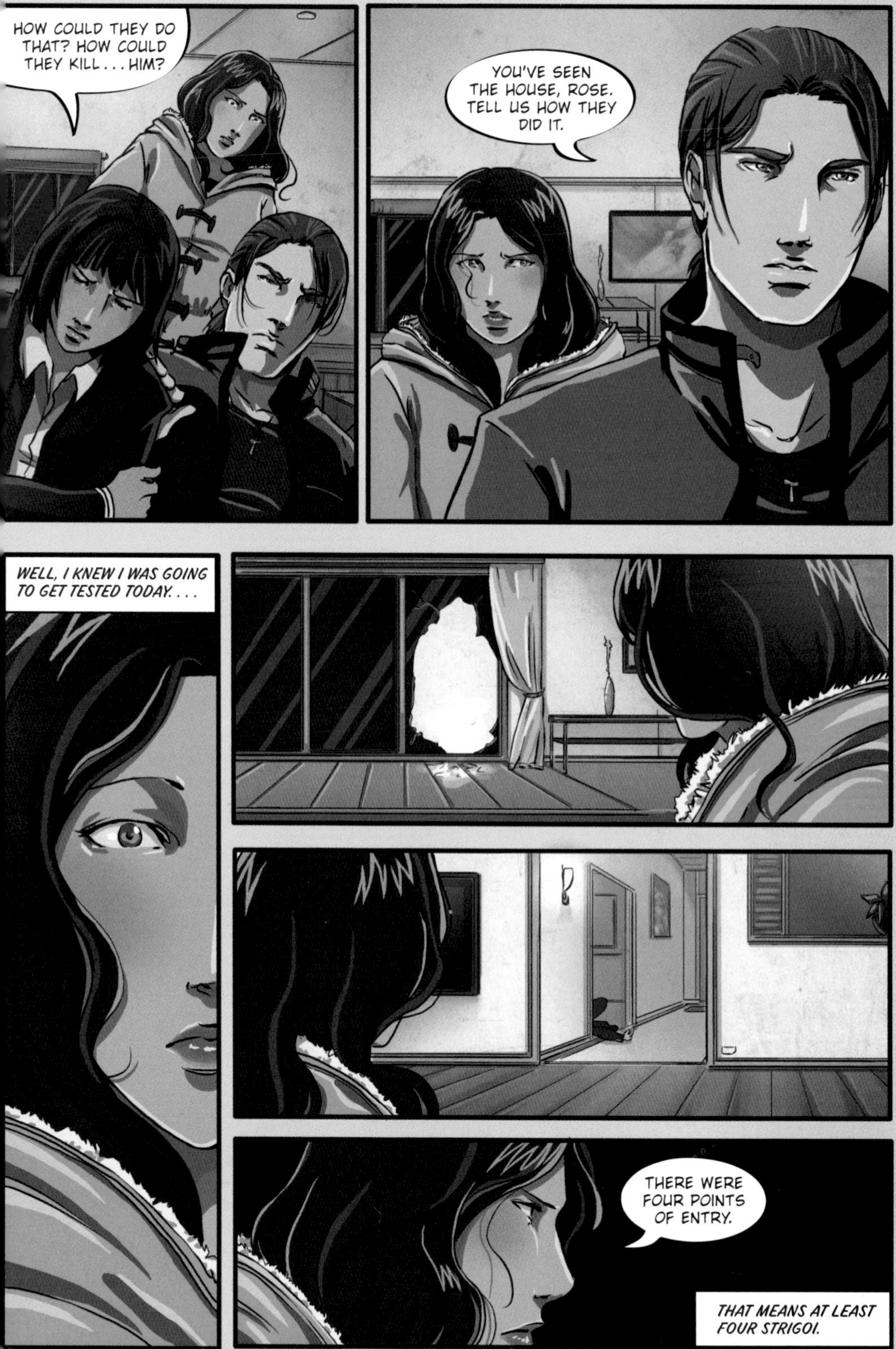
HOW COULD THEY DO THAT? HOW COULD THEY KILL . . . HIM?
YOU'VE SEEN THE HOUSE, ROSE. TELL US HOW THEY DID IT.
WELL, I KNEW I WAS GOING TO GET TESTED TODAY. . . .
THERE WERE FOUR POINTS OF ENTRY.
THAT MEANS AT LEAST FOUR STRIGOI.

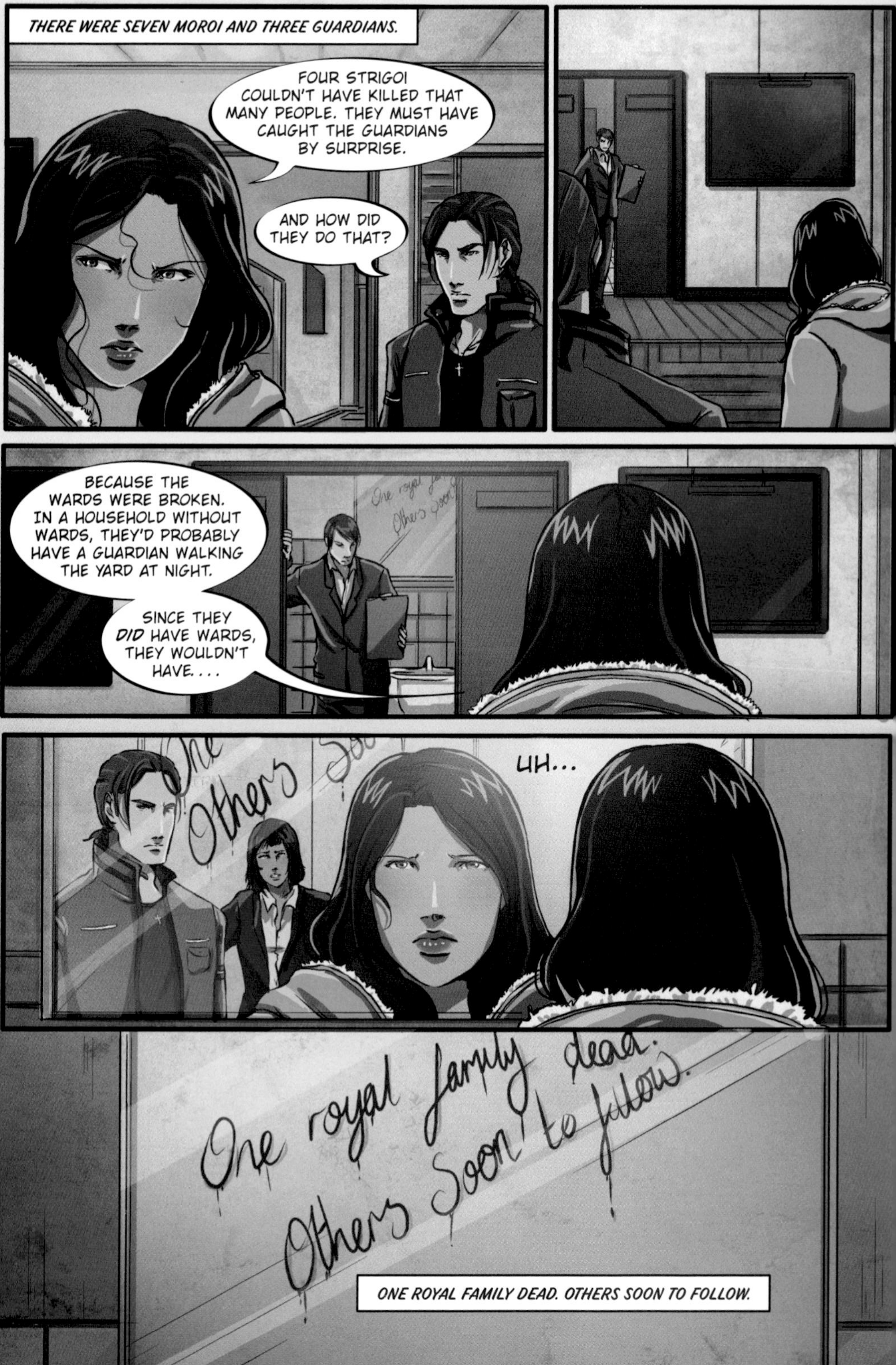
THERE WERE SEVEN MOROI AND THREE GUARDIANS.
FOUR STRIGOI COULDN'T HAVE KILLED THAT MANY PEOPLE. THEY MUST HAVE CAUGHT THE GUARDIANS BY SURPRISE.
AND HOW DID THEY DO THAT?
BECAUSE THE WARDS WERE BROKEN. IN A HOUSEHOLD WITHOUT WARDS, THEY'D PROBABLY HAVE A GUARDIAN WALKING THE YARD AT NIGHT.
SINCE THEY *DID* HAVE WARDS, THEY WOULDN'T HAVE. . . .
UH...
One royal family dead. Others Soon to follow.
ONE ROYAL FAMILY DEAD. OTHERS SOON TO FOLLOW.

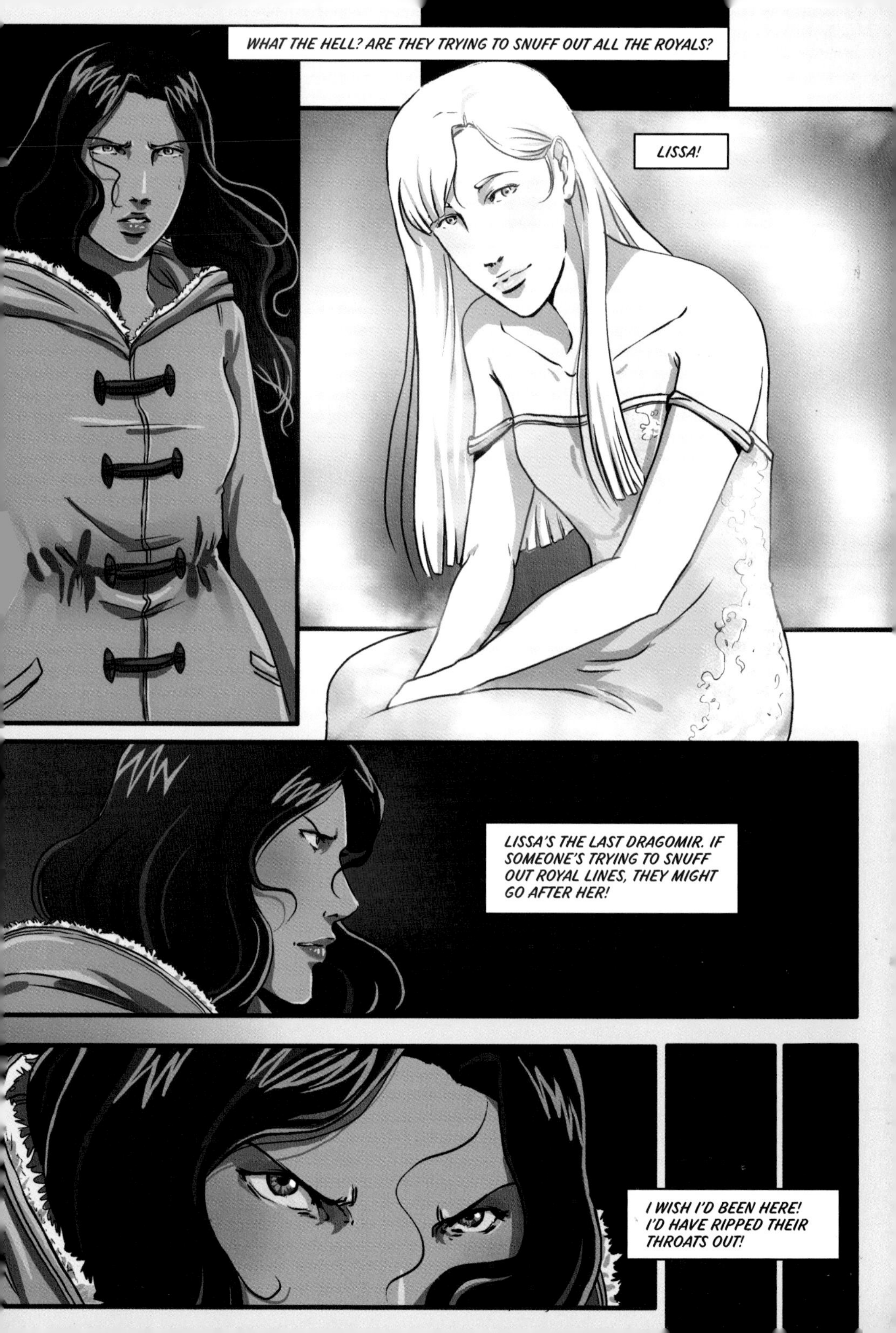
WHAT THE HELL? ARE THEY TRYING TO SNUFF OUT ALL THE ROYALS?
LISSA!
LISSA'S THE LAST DRAGOMIR. IF SOMEONE'S TRYING TO SNUFF OUT ROYAL LINES, THEY MIGHT GO AFTER HER!
I WISH I'D BEEN HERE! I'D HAVE RIPPED THEIR THROATS OUT!

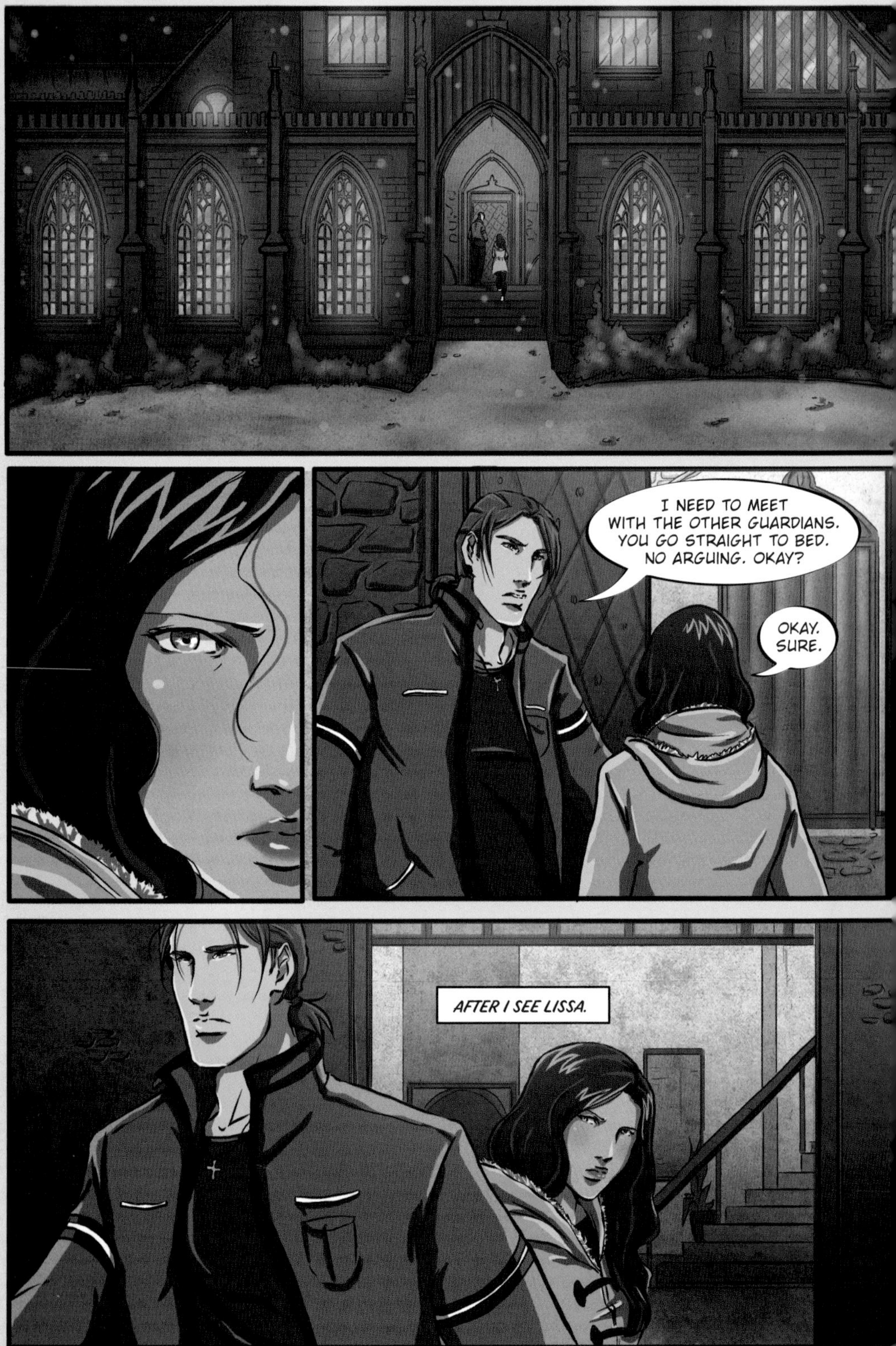
I NEED TO MEET WITH THE OTHER GUARDIANS. YOU GO STRAIGHT TO BED. NO ARGUING. OKAY?
OKAY. SURE.
AFTER I SEE LISSA.

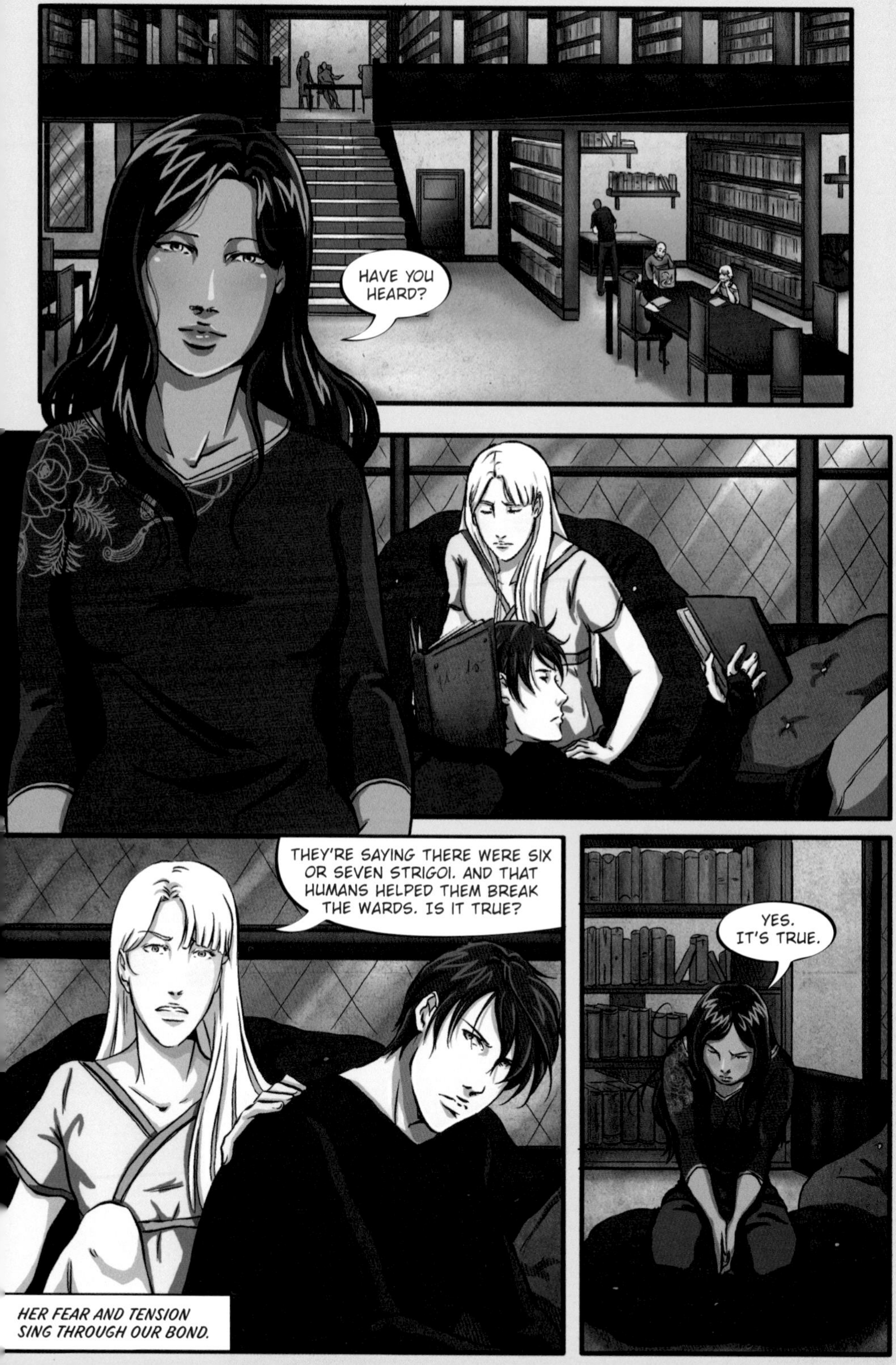
HAVE YOU HEARD?
THEY'RE SAYING THERE WERE SIX OR SEVEN STRIGOI. AND THAT HUMANS HELPED THEM BREAK THE WARDS. IS IT TRUE?
YES. IT'S TRUE.
HER FEAR AND TENSION SING THROUGH OUR BOND.

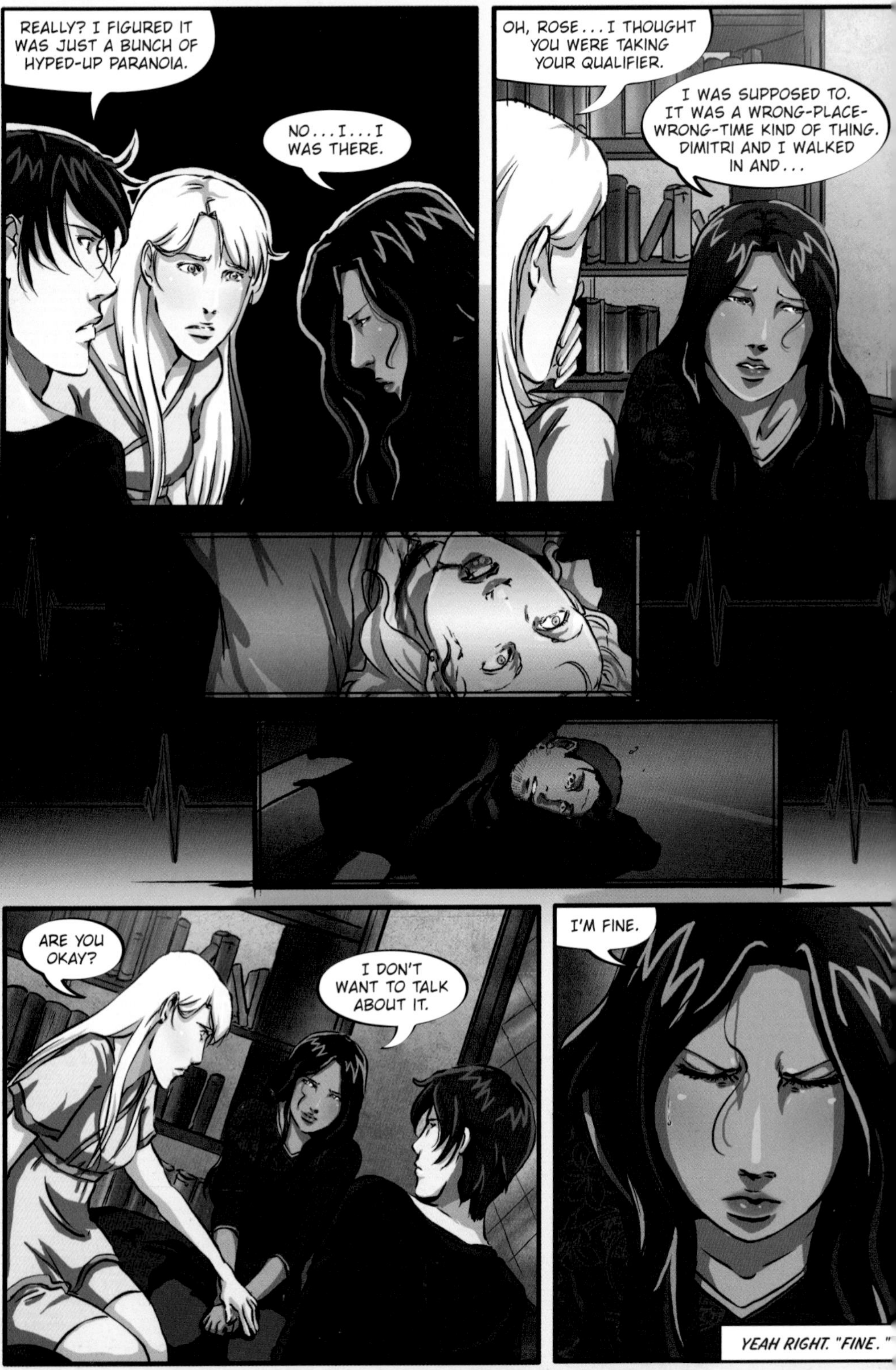
REALLY? I FIGURED IT WAS JUST A BUNCH OF HYPED-UP PARANOIA.
NO . . . I . . . I WAS THERE.
OH, ROSE . . . I THOUGHT YOU WERE TAKING YOUR QUALIFIER.
I WAS SUPPOSED TO. IT WAS A WRONG-PLACE-WRONG-TIME KIND OF THING. DIMITRI AND I WALKED IN AND . . .
ARE YOU OKAY?
I DON'T WANT TO TALK ABOUT IT.
I'M FINE.
YEAH RIGHT. "FINE."

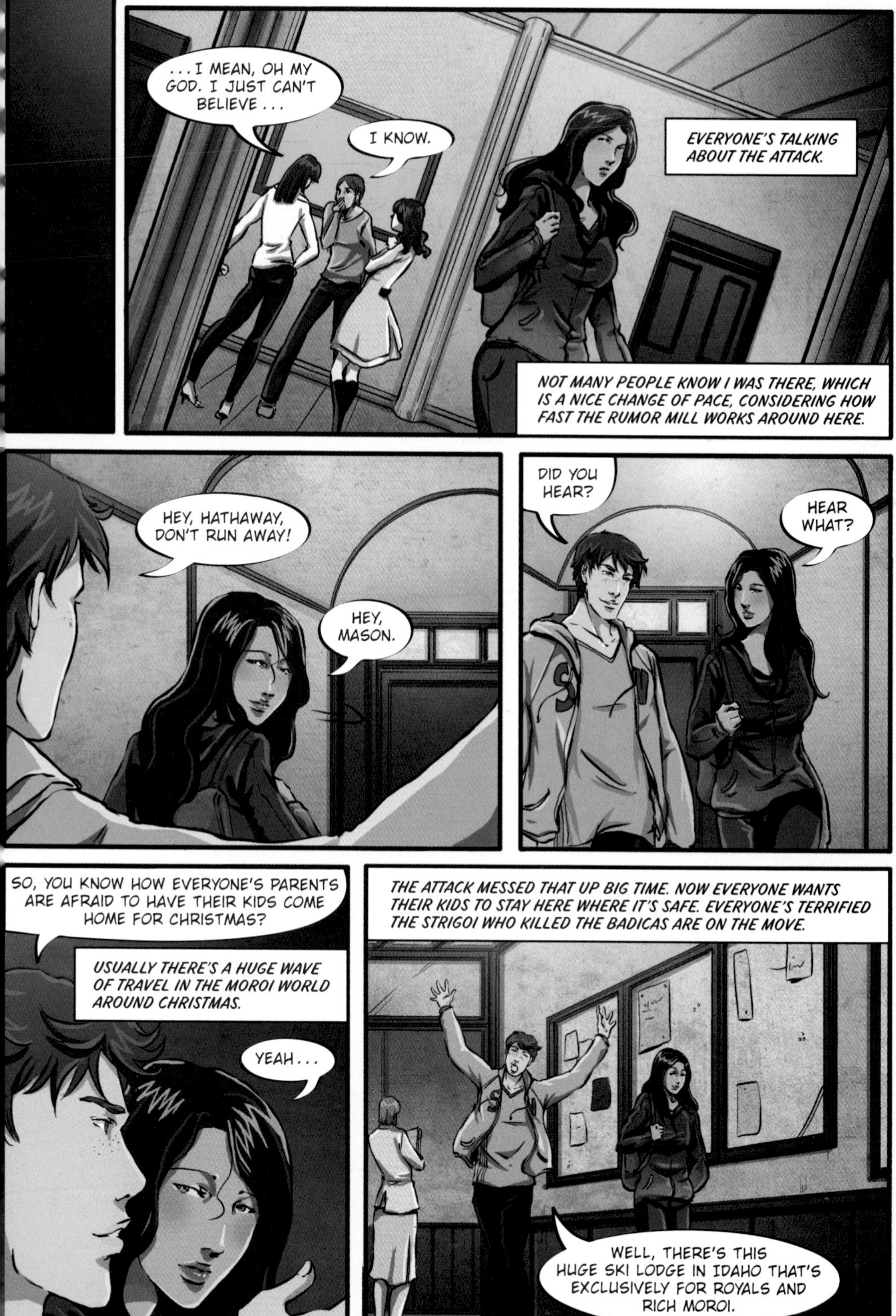
. . . I MEAN, OH MY GOD. I JUST CAN'T BELIEVE . . .
I KNOW.
EVERYONE'S TALKING ABOUT THE ATTACK.
NOT MANY PEOPLE KNOW I WAS THERE, WHICH IS A NICE CHANGE OF PACE, CONSIDERING HOW FAST THE RUMOR MILL WORKS AROUND HERE.
HEY, HATHAWAY, DON'T RUN AWAY!
HEY, MASON.
DID YOU HEAR?
HEAR WHAT?
SO, YOU KNOW HOW EVERYONE'S PARENTS ARE AFRAID TO HAVE THEIR KIDS COME HOME FOR CHRISTMAS?
USUALLY THERE'S A HUGE WAVE OF TRAVEL IN THE MOROI WORLD AROUND CHRISTMAS.
YEAH . . .
THE ATTACK MESSED THAT UP BIG TIME. NOW EVERYONE WANTS THEIR KIDS TO STAY HERE WHERE IT'S SAFE. EVERYONE'S TERRIFIED THE STRIGOI WHO KILLED THE BADICAS ARE ON THE MOVE.
WELL, THERE'S THIS HUGE SKI LODGE IN IDAHO THAT'S EXCLUSIVELY FOR ROYALS AND RICH MOROI.

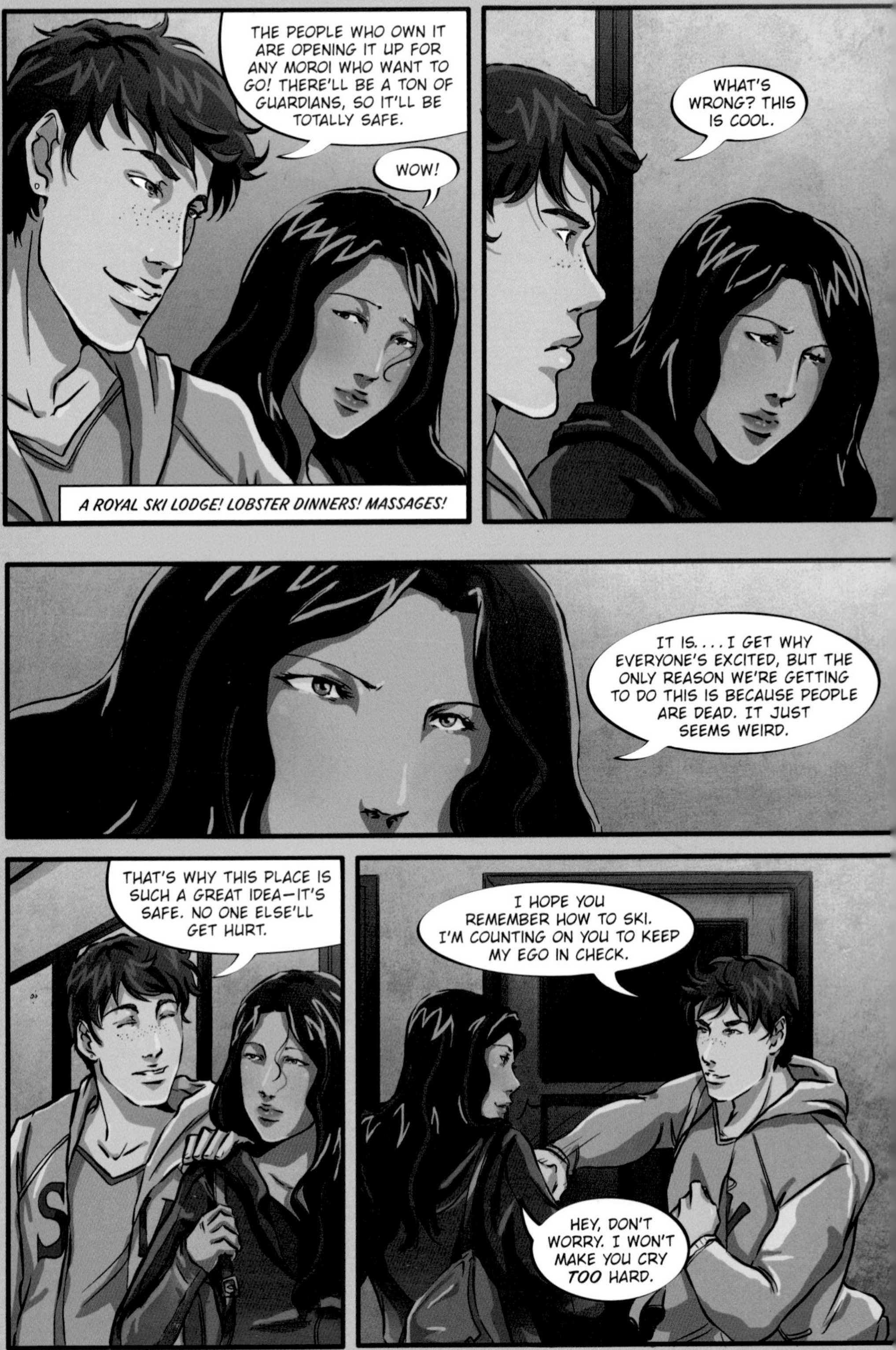
THE PEOPLE WHO OWN IT ARE OPENING IT UP FOR ANY MOROI WHO WANT TO GO! THERE'LL BE A TON OF GUARDIANS, SO IT'LL BE TOTALLY SAFE.
WOW!
A ROYAL SKI LODGE! LOBSTER DINNERS! MASSAGES!
WHAT'S WRONG? THIS IS COOL.
IT IS. . . . I GET WHY EVERYONE'S EXCITED, BUT THE ONLY REASON WE'RE GETTING TO DO THIS IS BECAUSE PEOPLE ARE DEAD. IT JUST SEEMS WEIRD.
THAT'S WHY THIS PLACE IS SUCH A GREAT IDEA—IT'S SAFE. NO ONE ELSE'LL GET HURT.
I HOPE YOU REMEMBER HOW TO SKI. I'M COUNTING ON YOU TO KEEP MY EGO IN CHECK.
HEY, DON'T WORRY. I WON'T MAKE YOU CRY *TOO* HARD.

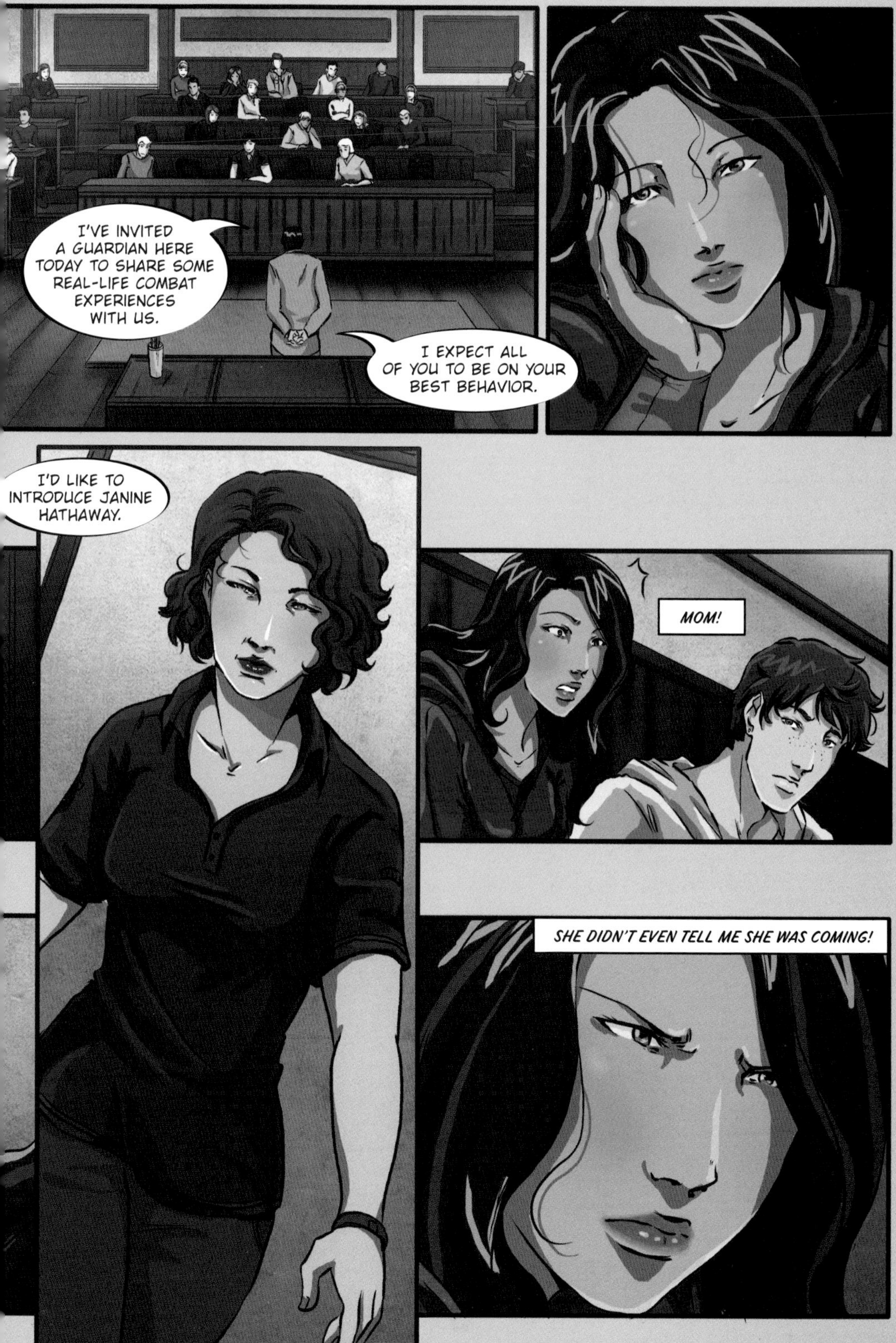
I'VE INVITED A GUARDIAN HERE TODAY TO SHARE SOME REAL-LIFE COMBAT EXPERIENCES WITH US.
I EXPECT ALL OF YOU TO BE ON YOUR BEST BEHAVIOR.
I'D LIKE TO INTRODUCE JANINE HATHAWAY.
MOM!
SHE DIDN'T EVEN TELL ME SHE WAS COMING!

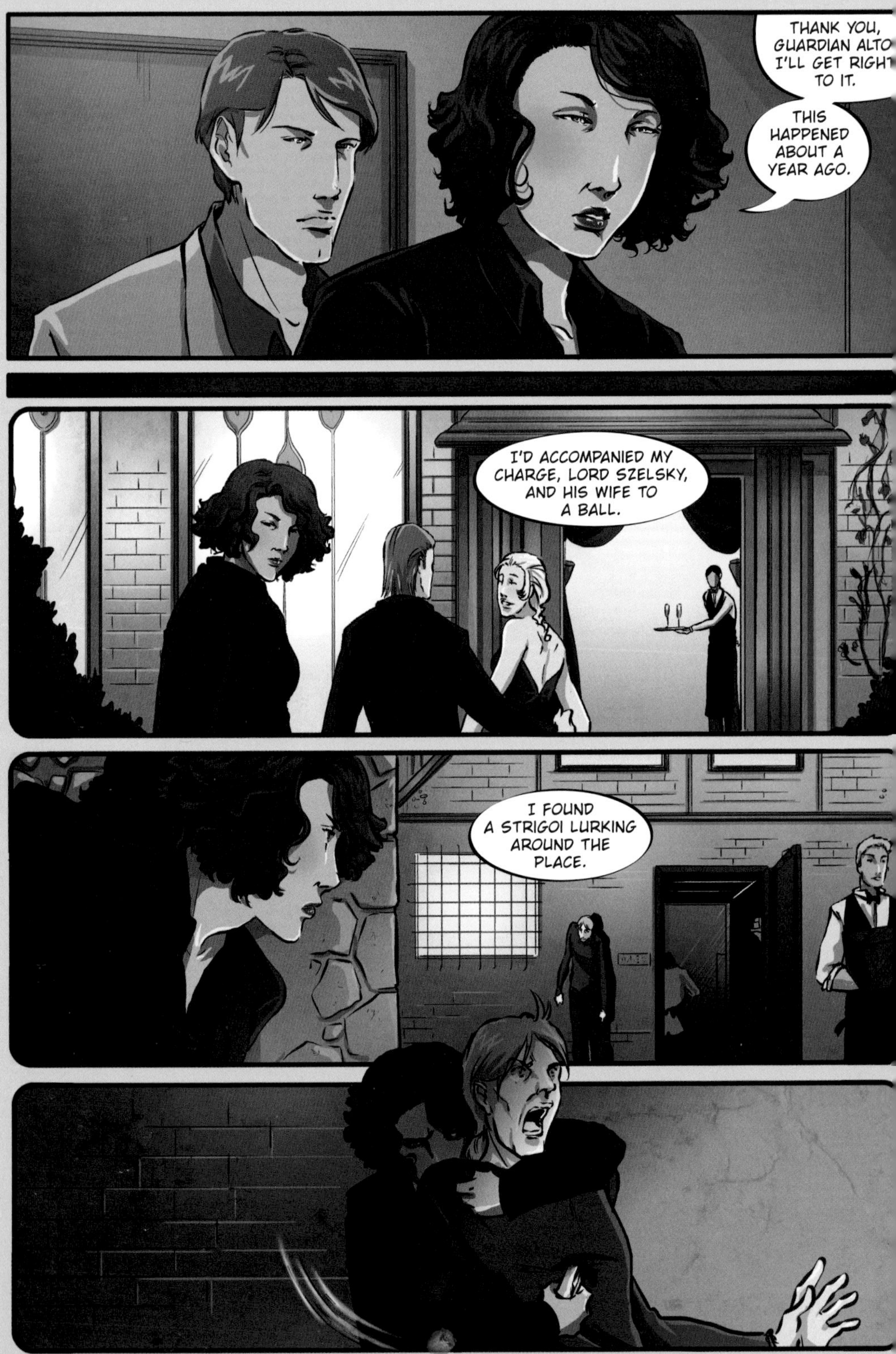
THANK YOU, GUARDIAN ALTO. I'LL GET RIGHT TO IT.
THIS HAPPENED ABOUT A YEAR AGO.
I'D ACCOMPANIED MY CHARGE, LORD SZELSKY, AND HIS WIFE TO A BALL.
I FOUND A STRIGOI LURKING AROUND THE PLACE.

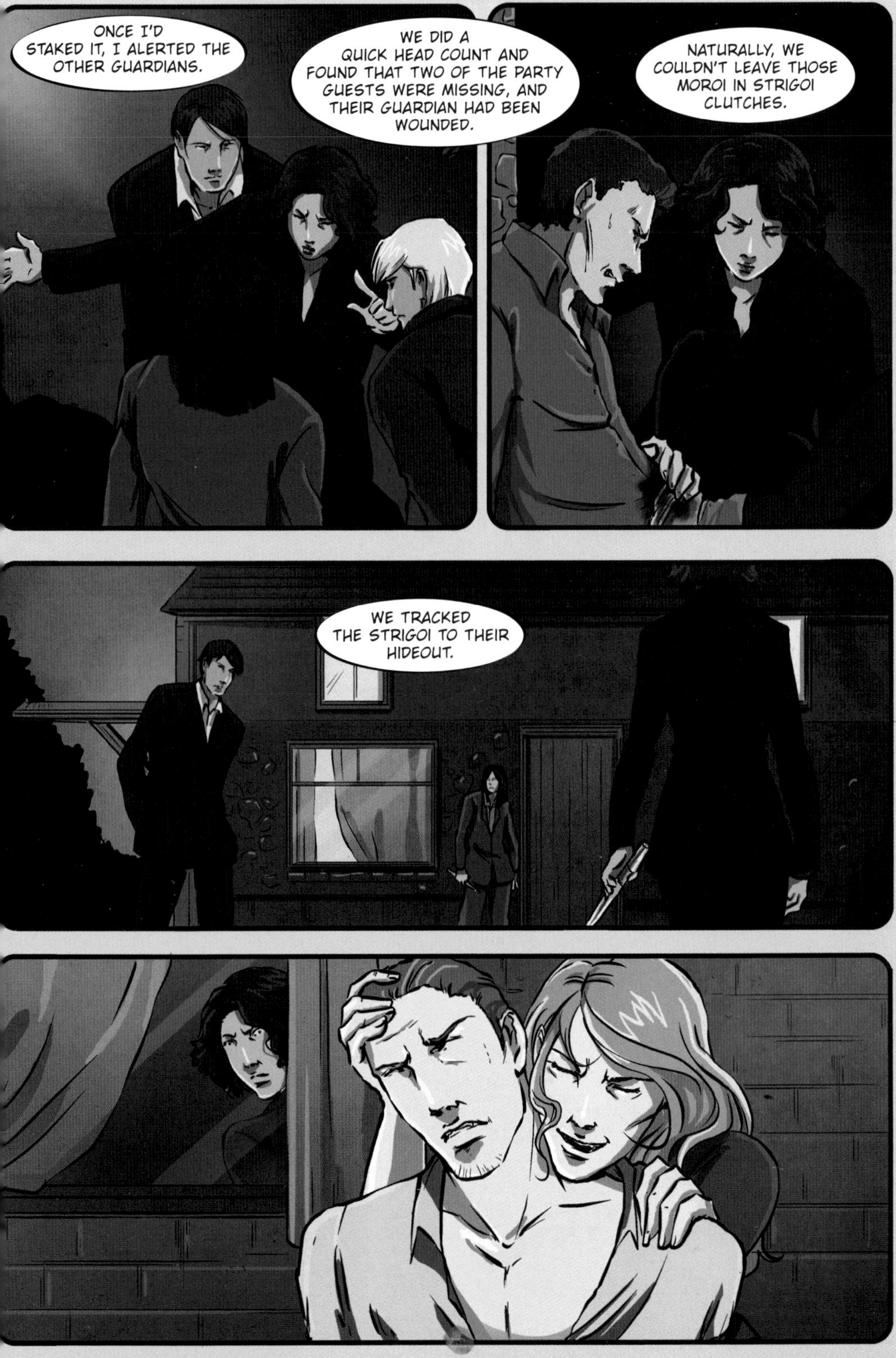
ONCE I'D STAKED IT, I ALERTED THE OTHER GUARDIANS.
WE DID A QUICK HEAD COUNT AND FOUND THAT TWO OF THE PARTY GUESTS WERE MISSING, AND THEIR GUARDIAN HAD BEEN WOUNDED.
NATURALLY, WE COULDN'T LEAVE THOSE MOROI IN STRIGOI CLUTCHES.
WE TRACKED THE STRIGOI TO THEIR HIDEOUT.

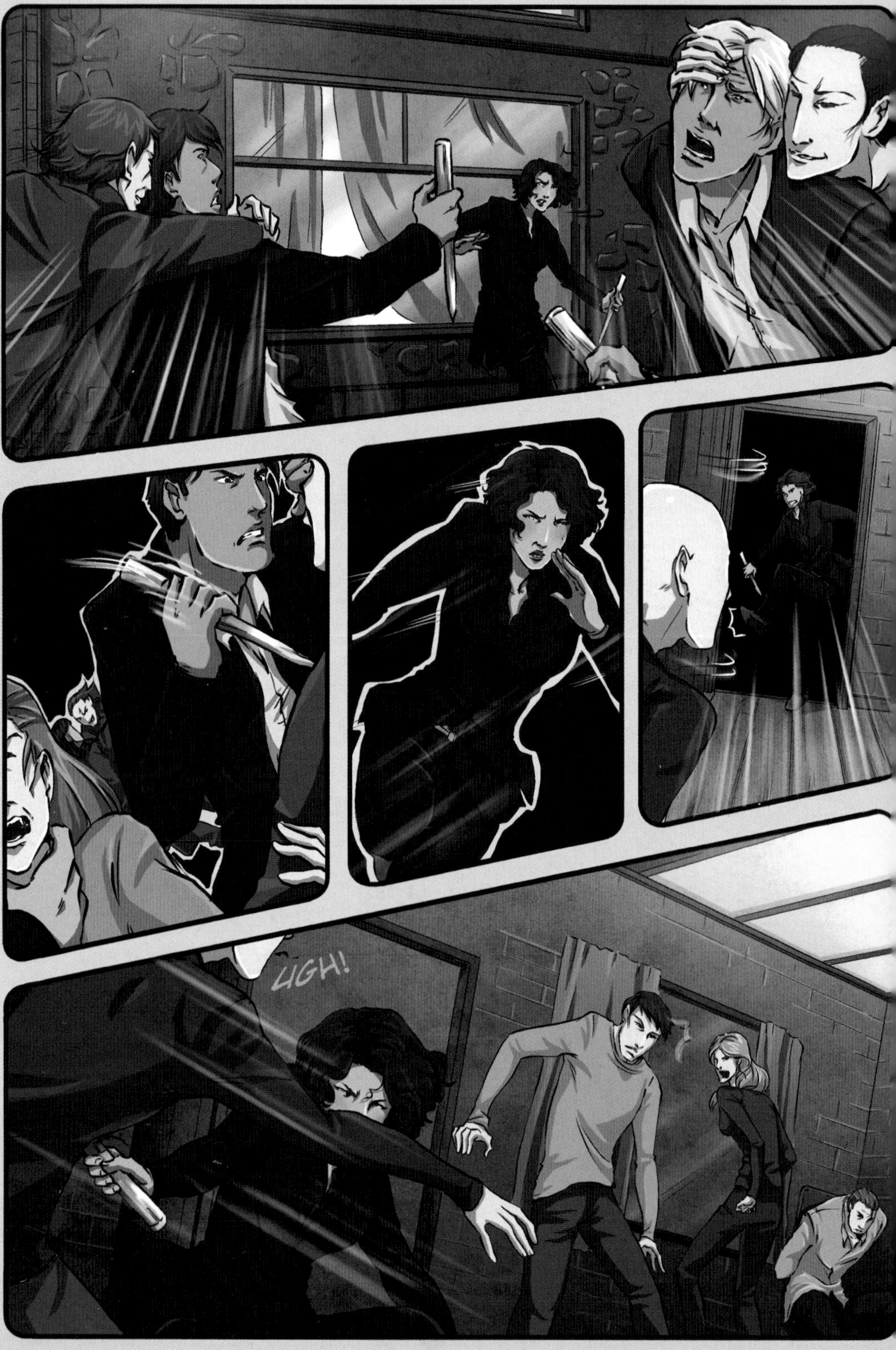
UGH!

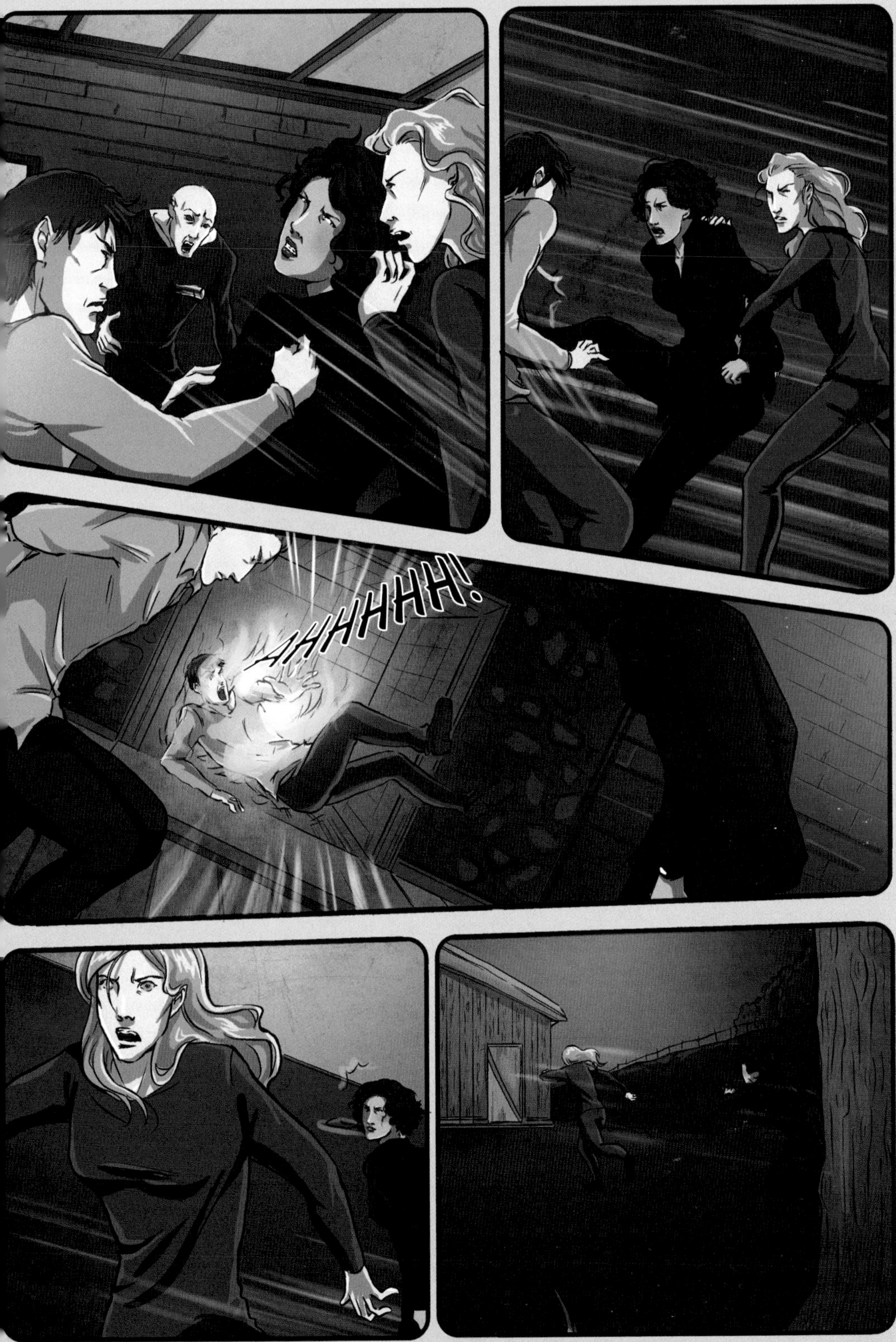
AHHHHHH!

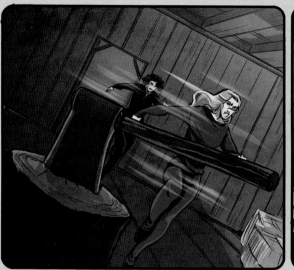

I WENT BACK TO THE HOUSE WITH A CAN OF GASOLINE I FOUND IN THE SHED.

THE ONE I'D THROWN IN THE FIREPLACE WAS STILL KICKING, BUT I DOUSED HIM WITH THE GAS AND HE BURNED UP PRETTY QUICKLY.

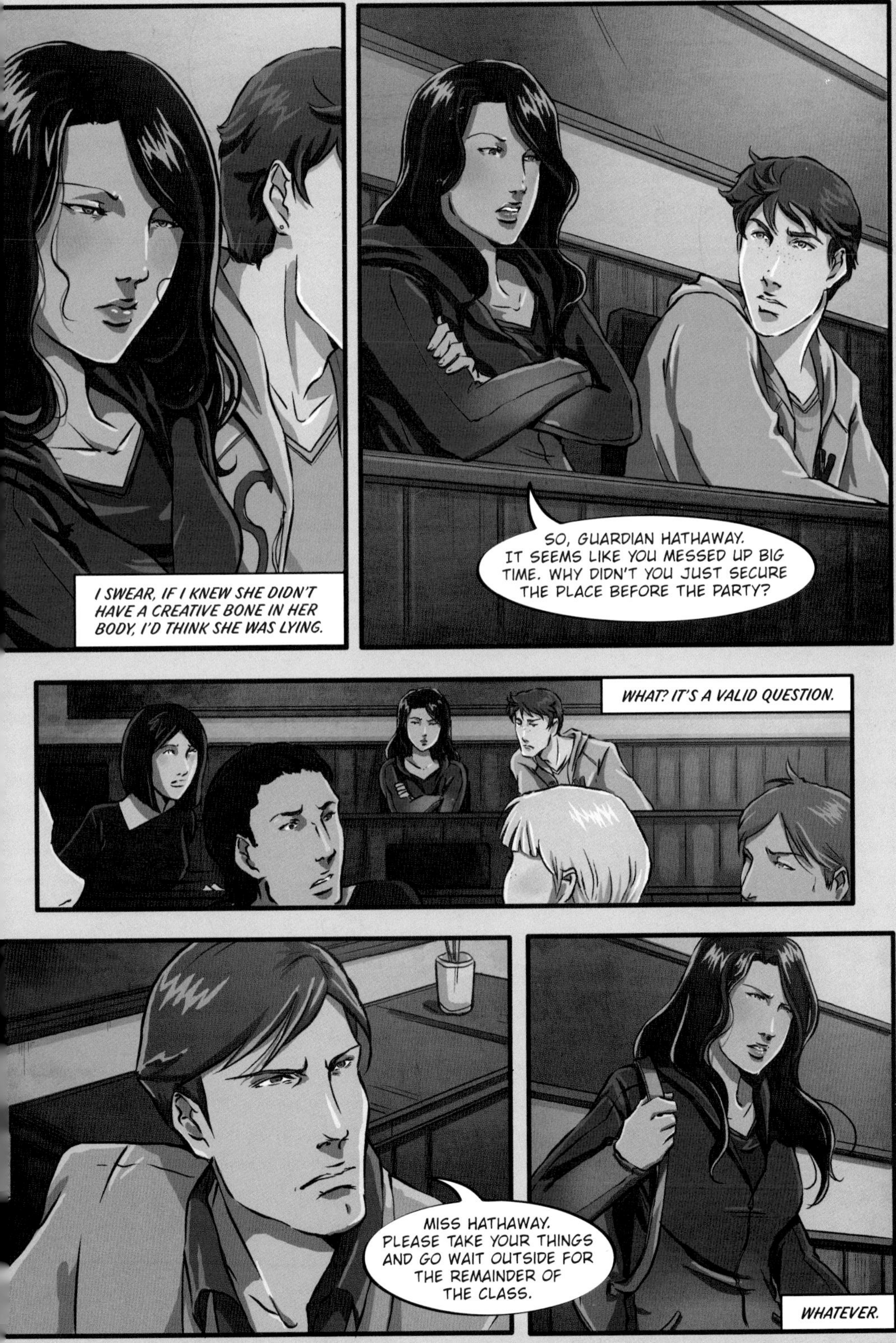

I SWEAR, IF I KNEW SHE DIDN'T HAVE A CREATIVE BONE IN HER BODY, I'D THINK SHE WAS LYING.
SO, GUARDIAN HATHAWAY. IT SEEMS LIKE YOU MESSED UP BIG TIME. WHY DIDN'T YOU JUST SECURE THE PLACE BEFORE THE PARTY?
WHAT? IT'S A VALID QUESTION.
MISS HATHAWAY. PLEASE TAKE YOUR THINGS AND GO WAIT OUTSIDE FOR THE REMAINDER OF THE CLASS.
WHATEVER.

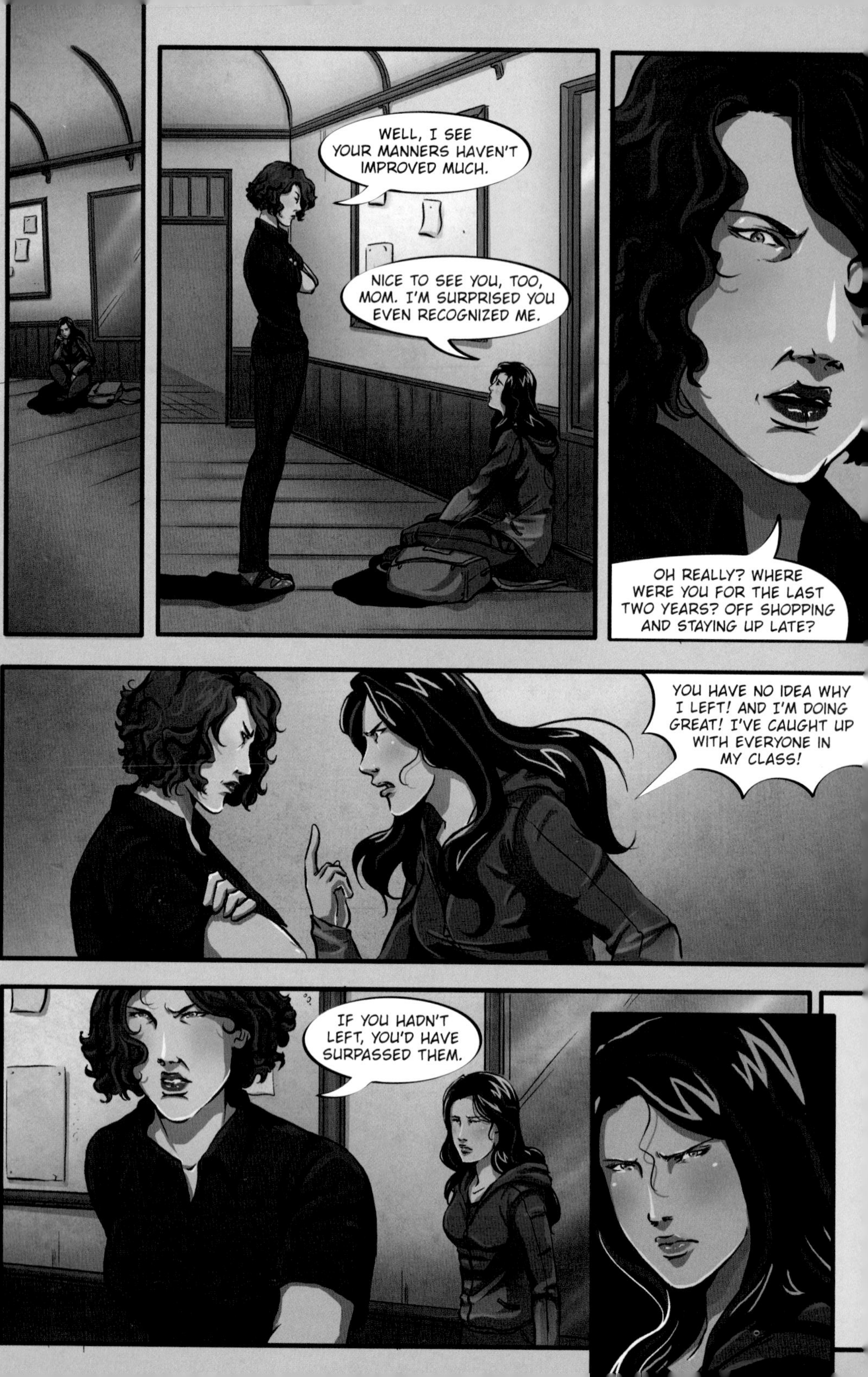
WELL, I SEE YOUR MANNERS HAVEN'T IMPROVED MUCH.
NICE TO SEE YOU, TOO, MOM. I'M SURPRISED YOU EVEN RECOGNIZED ME.
OH REALLY? WHERE WERE YOU FOR THE LAST TWO YEARS? OFF SHOPPING AND STAYING UP LATE?
YOU HAVE NO IDEA WHY I LEFT! AND I'M DOING GREAT! I'VE CAUGHT UP WITH EVERYONE IN MY CLASS!
IF YOU HADN'T LEFT, YOU'D HAVE SURPASSED THEM.

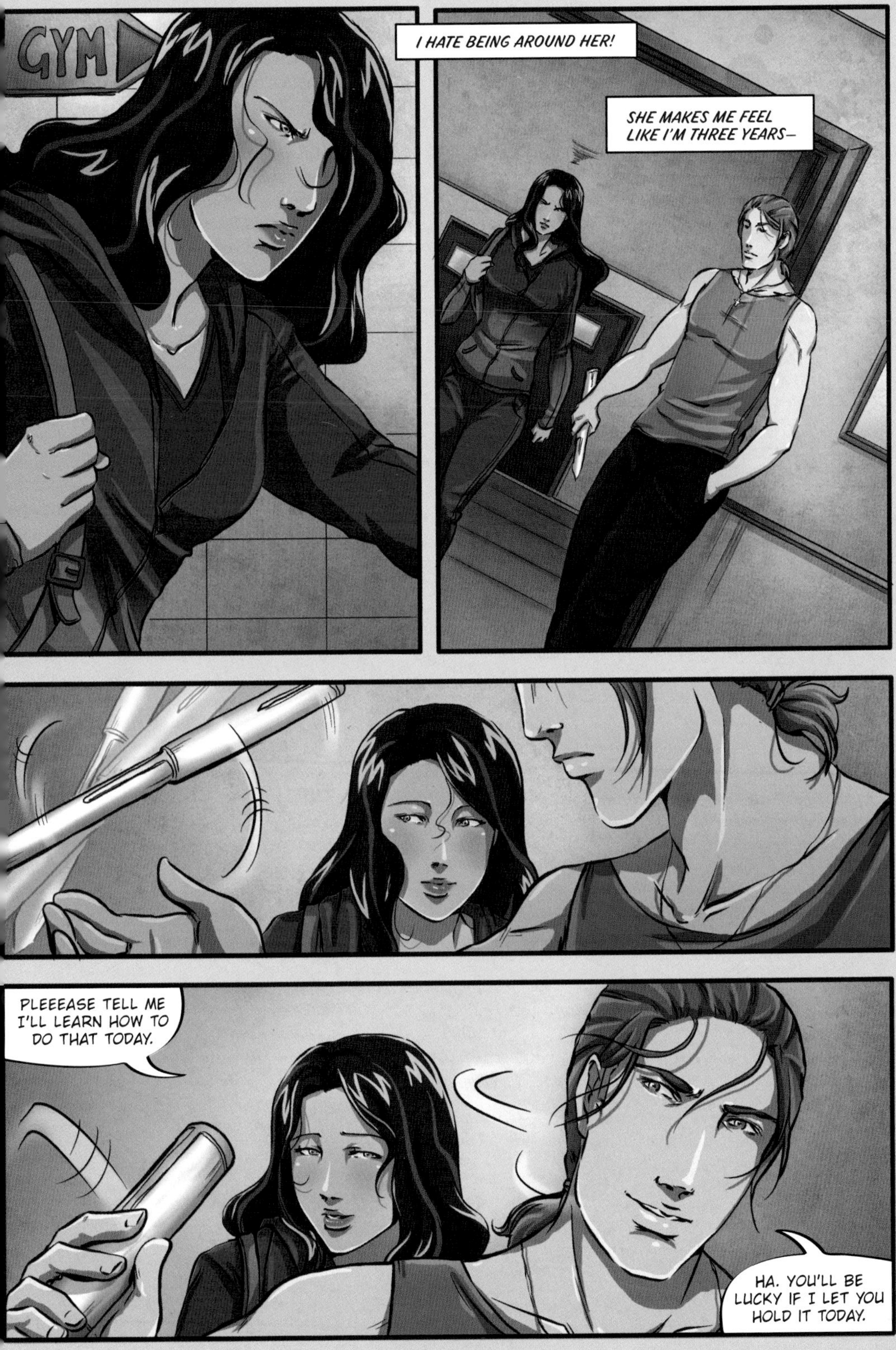
GYM
I HATE BEING AROUND HER!
SHE MAKES ME FEEL LIKE I'M THREE YEARS—
PLEEEASE TELL ME I'LL LEARN HOW TO DO THAT TODAY.
HA. YOU'LL BE LUCKY IF I LET YOU HOLD IT TODAY.

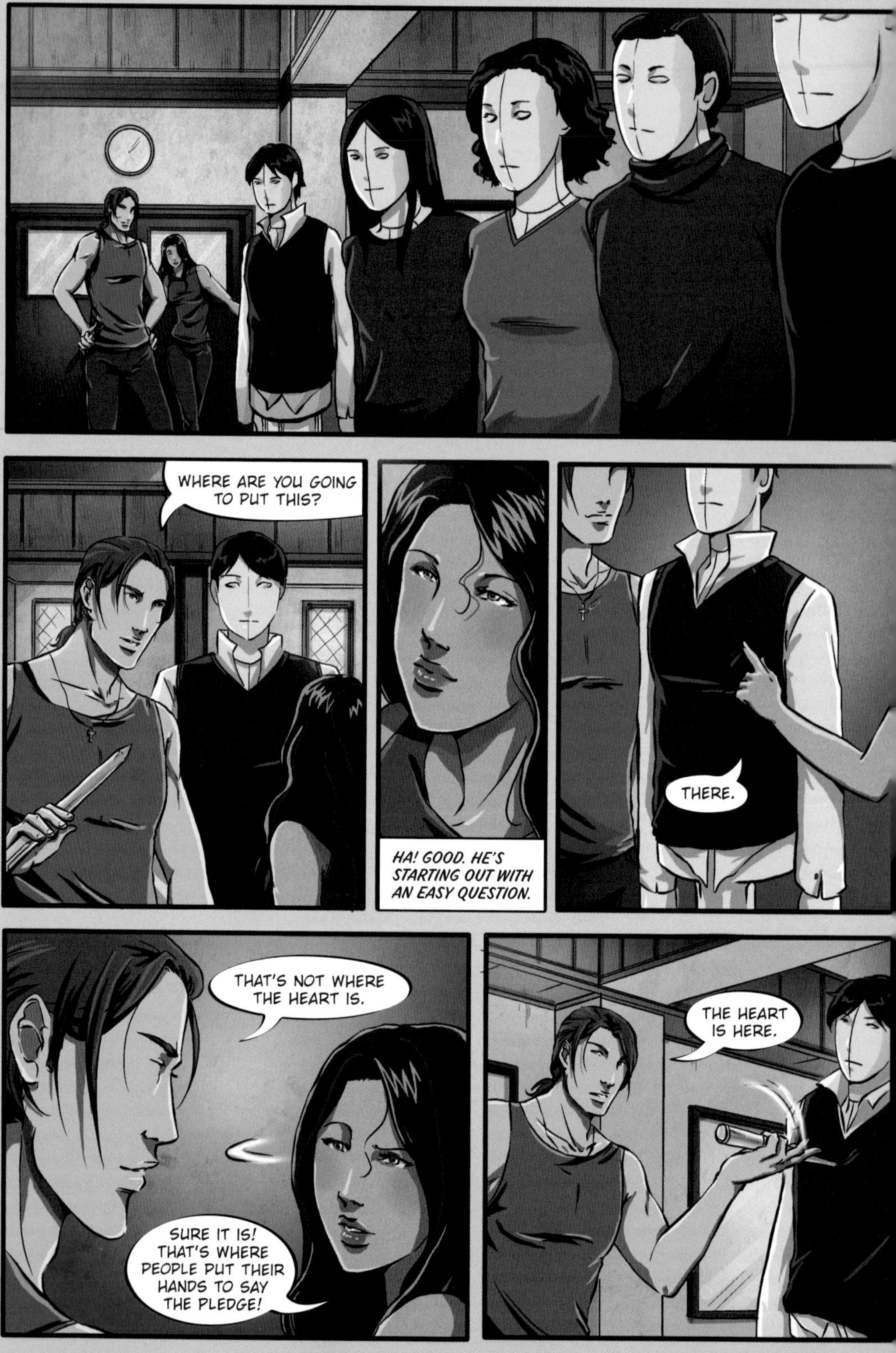
WHERE ARE YOU GOING TO PUT THIS?
HA! GOOD. HE'S STARTING OUT WITH AN EASY QUESTION.
THERE.
THAT'S NOT WHERE THE HEART IS.
SURE IT IS! THAT'S WHERE PEOPLE PUT THEIR HANDS TO SAY THE PLEDGE!
THE HEART IS HERE.

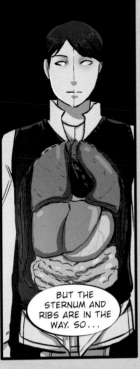

BUT THE STERNUM AND RIBS ARE IN THE WAY. SO . . .

HERE.

CHOK

TYPICAL. HE MAKES EVERYTHING LOOK SO DAMN EASY.

YOU'RE GIVING IT TO ME?

I'M SURPRISED YOU HAVEN'T RUN OFF WITH IT YET.

WHAT SHOULD I DO FIRST?

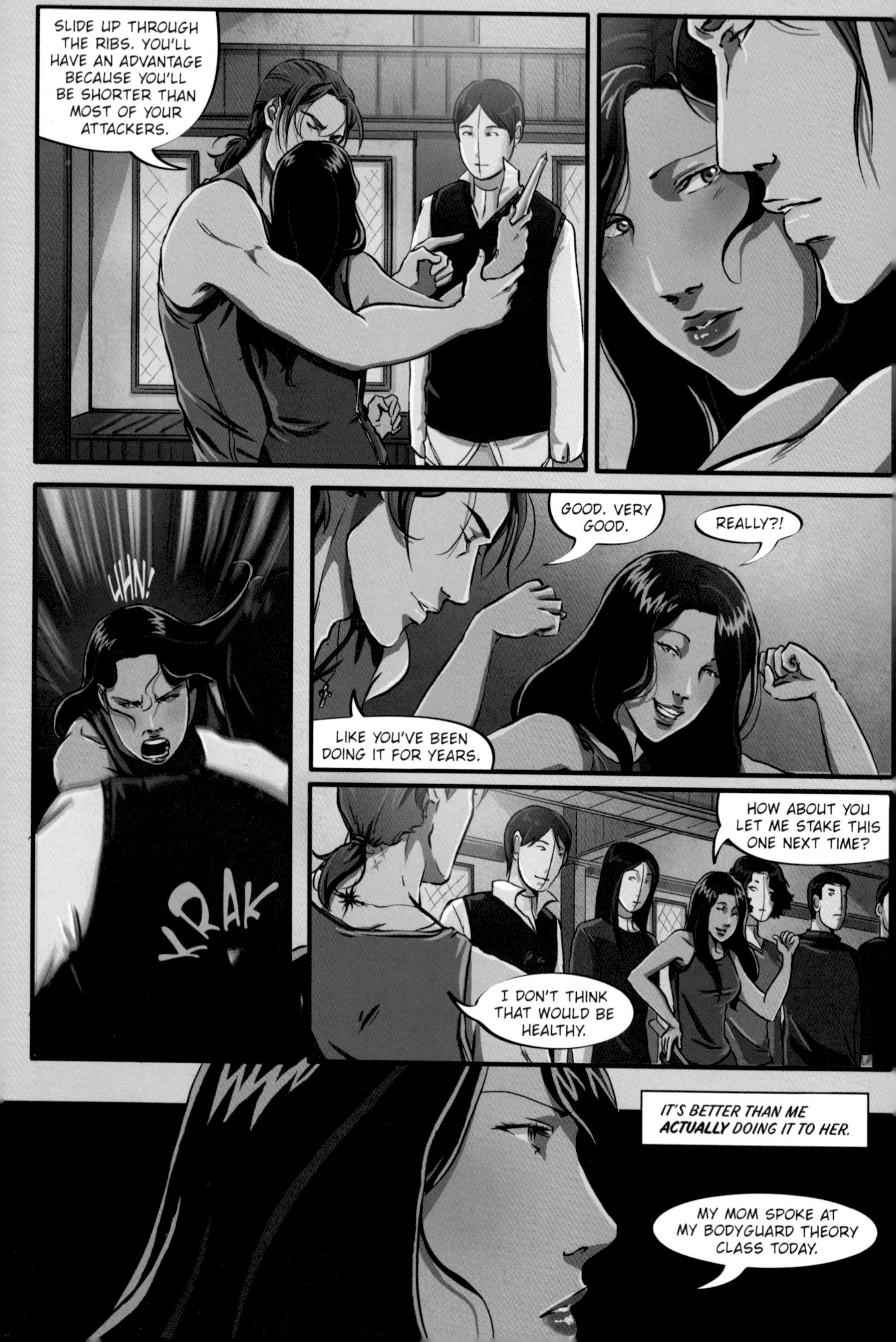
SLIDE UP THROUGH THE RIBS. YOU'LL HAVE AN ADVANTAGE BECAUSE YOU'LL BE SHORTER THAN MOST OF YOUR ATTACKERS.
UHN!
KRAK
GOOD. VERY GOOD.
REALLY?!
LIKE YOU'VE BEEN DOING IT FOR YEARS.
HOW ABOUT YOU LET ME STAKE THIS ONE NEXT TIME?
I DON'T THINK THAT WOULD BE HEALTHY.
IT'S BETTER THAN ME ACTUALLY DOING IT TO HER.
MY MOM SPOKE AT MY BODYGUARD THEORY CLASS TODAY.

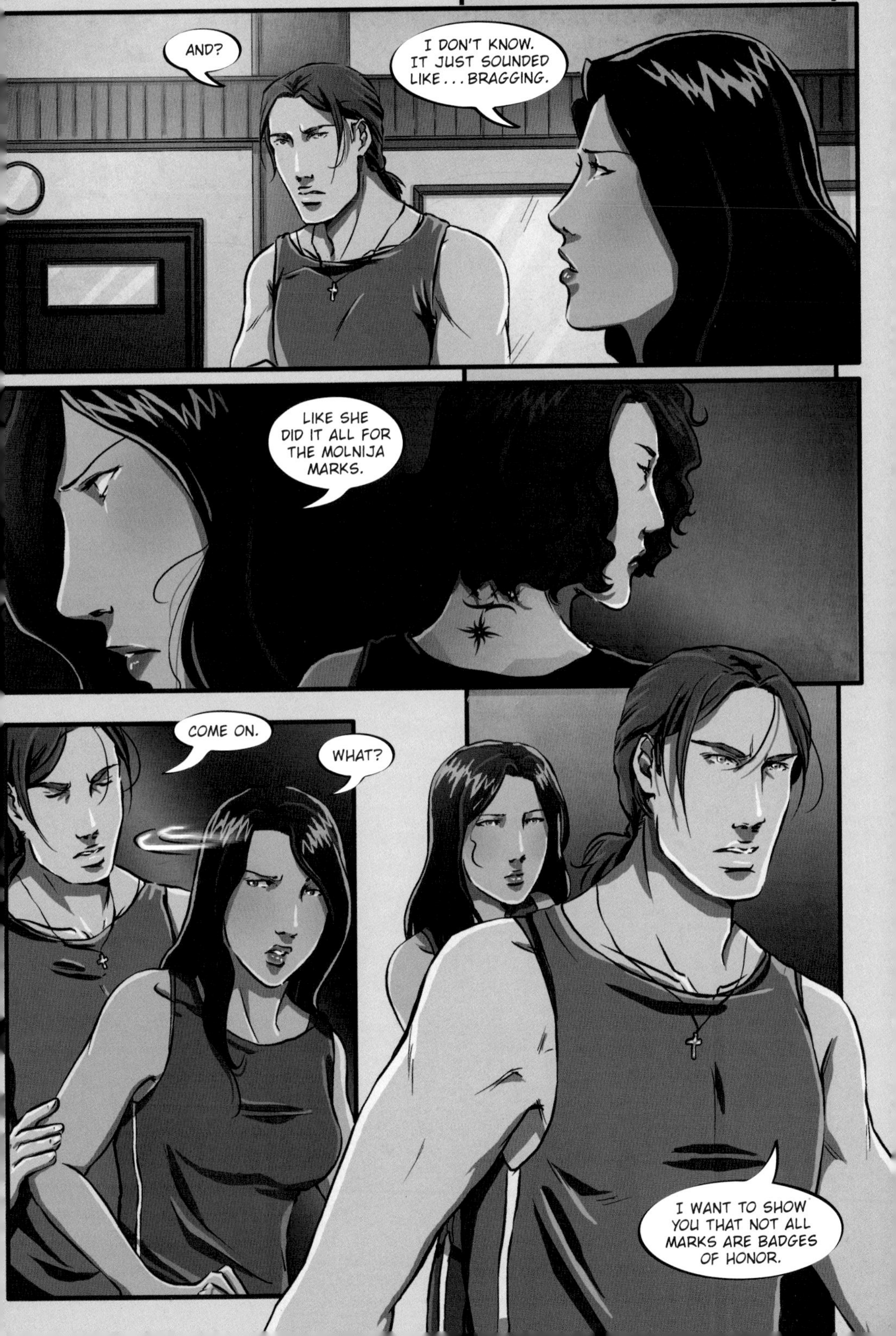
AND?
I DON'T KNOW. IT JUST SOUNDED LIKE . . . BRAGGING.
LIKE SHE DID IT ALL FOR THE MOLNIJA MARKS.
COME ON.
WHAT?
I WANT TO SHOW YOU THAT NOT ALL MARKS ARE BADGES OF HONOR.

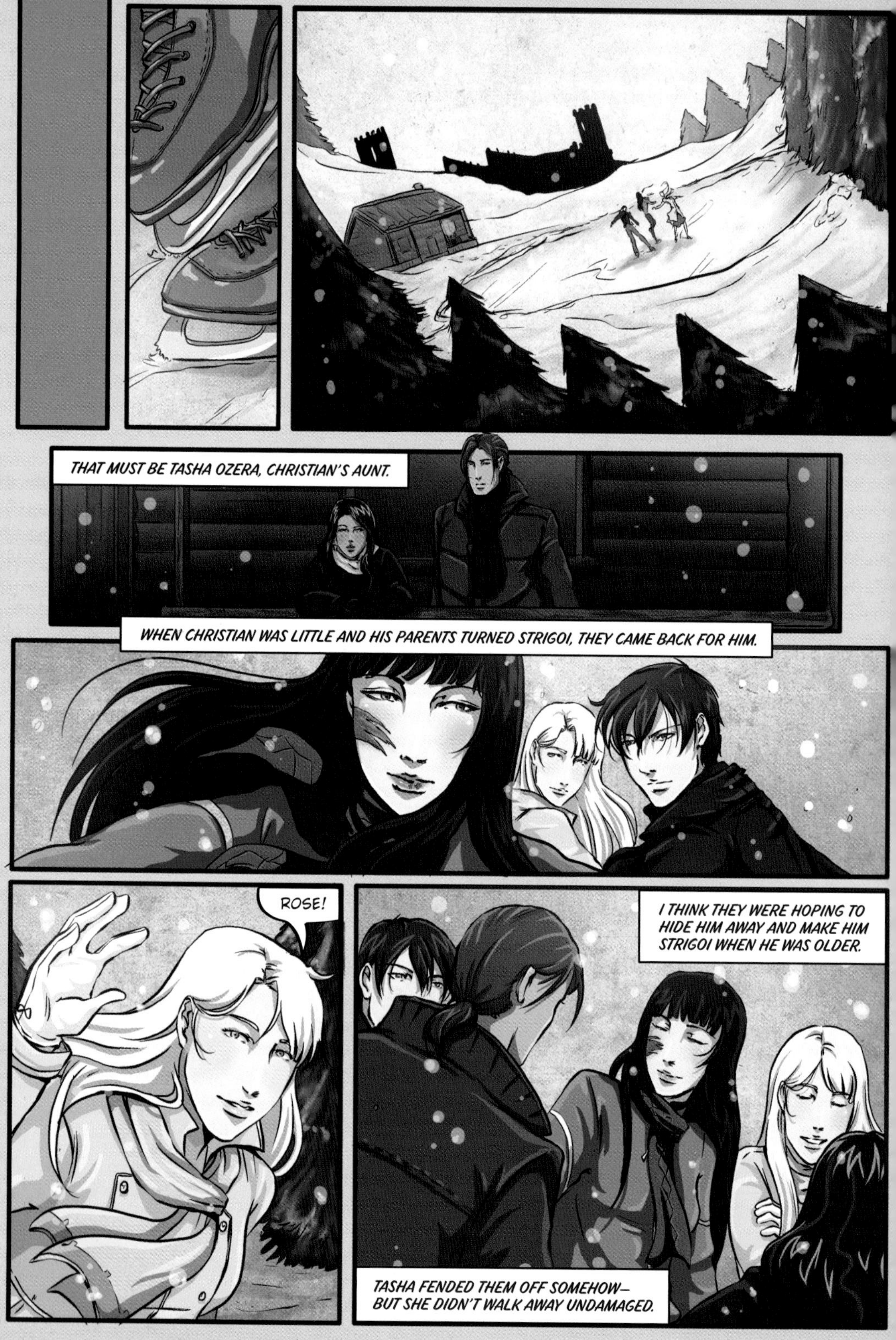
THAT MUST BE TASHA OZERA, CHRISTIAN'S AUNT.
WHEN CHRISTIAN WAS LITTLE AND HIS PARENTS TURNED STRIGOI, THEY CAME BACK FOR HIM.
ROSE!
I THINK THEY WERE HOPING TO HIDE HIM AWAY AND MAKE HIM STRIGOI WHEN HE WAS OLDER.
TASHA FENDED THEM OFF SOMEHOW— BUT SHE DIDN'T WALK AWAY UNDAMAGED.

SO, TASHA, ARE YOU COMING ON THE SKI TRIP?

YES. I HAVEN'T BEEN ABLE TO GO SKIING IN AGES. I'VE SAVED ALL MY VACATION TIME.

VACATION? DO YOU HAVE...A JOB?

SADLY, YES. I TEACH MARTIAL ARTS CLASSES.

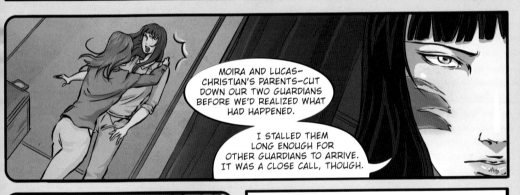

MOIRA AND LUCAS— CHRISTIAN'S PARENTS—CUT DOWN OUR TWO GUARDIANS BEFORE WE'D REALIZED WHAT HAD HAPPENED.

I STALLED THEM LONG ENOUGH FOR OTHER GUARDIANS TO ARRIVE. IT WAS A CLOSE CALL, THOUGH.

I DECIDED I DIDN'T WANT TO DIE THAT WAY. NOT WITHOUT PUTTING UP A REAL FIGHT. SO I LEARNED ALL SORTS OF SELF-DEFENSE.

ALL SORTS OF SELF-DEFENSE, HUH? MAYBE CHRISTIAN'S NOT THE ONLY ONE IN HIS FAMILY WHO DOESN'T HAVE A PROBLEM USING MAGIC OFFENSIVELY.

NOW I TAKE CARE OF MYSELF. I DON'T HAVE A GUARDIAN.

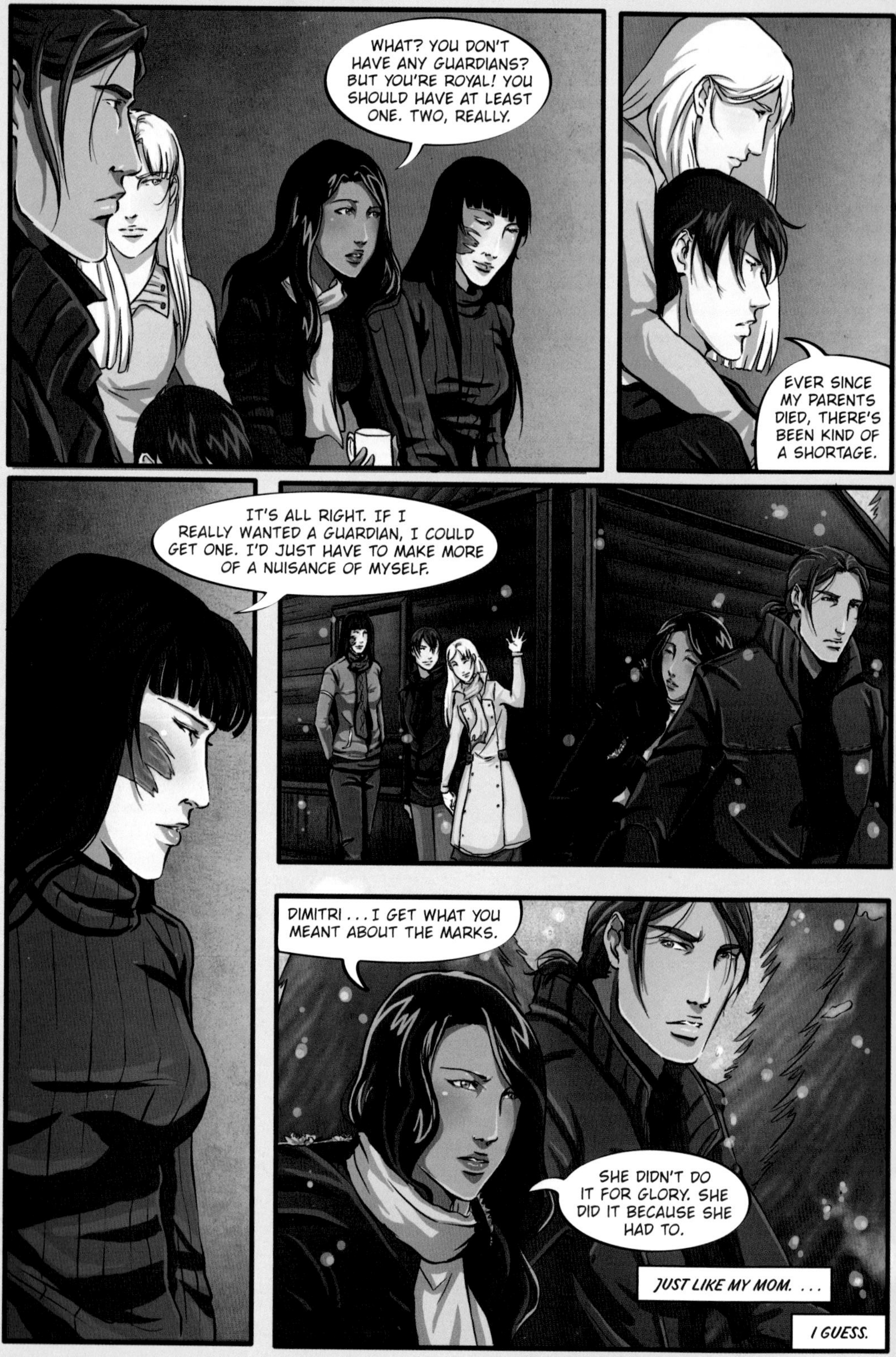
WHAT? YOU DON'T HAVE ANY GUARDIANS? BUT YOU'RE ROYAL! YOU SHOULD HAVE AT LEAST ONE. TWO, REALLY.
EVER SINCE MY PARENTS DIED, THERE'S BEEN KIND OF A SHORTAGE.
IT'S ALL RIGHT. IF I REALLY WANTED A GUARDIAN, I COULD GET ONE. I'D JUST HAVE TO MAKE MORE OF A NUISANCE OF MYSELF.
DIMITRI . . . I GET WHAT YOU MEANT ABOUT THE MARKS.
SHE DIDN'T DO IT FOR GLORY. SHE DID IT BECAUSE SHE HAD TO.
JUST LIKE MY MOM. . . .
I GUESS.

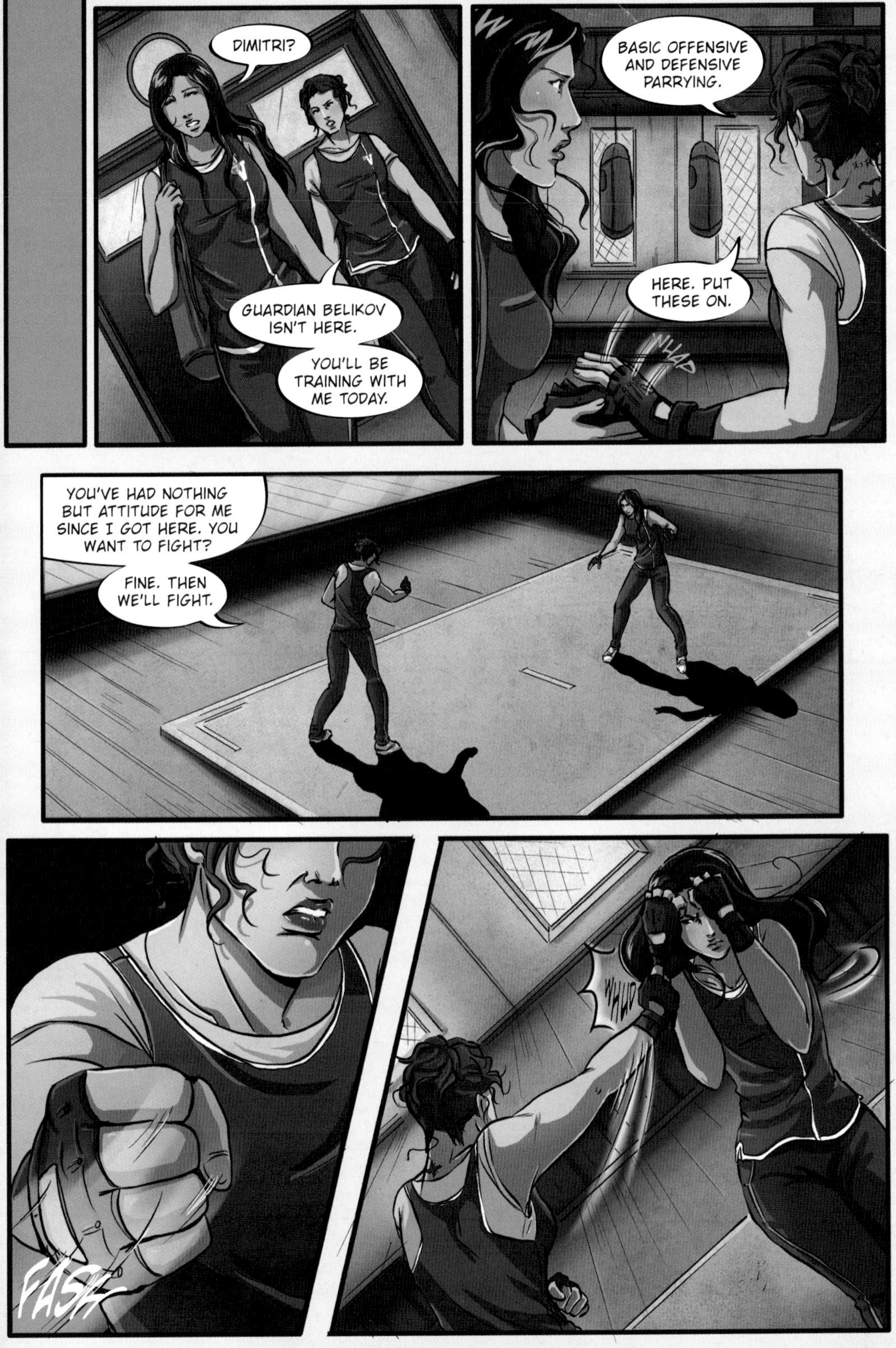
DIMITRI?
GUARDIAN BELIKOV ISN'T HERE.
YOU'LL BE TRAINING WITH ME TODAY.
BASIC OFFENSIVE AND DEFENSIVE PARRYING.
HERE. PUT THESE ON.
WHAP
YOU'VE HAD NOTHING BUT ATTITUDE FOR ME SINCE I GOT HERE. YOU WANT TO FIGHT?
FINE. THEN WE'LL FIGHT.
FASH
WHUD

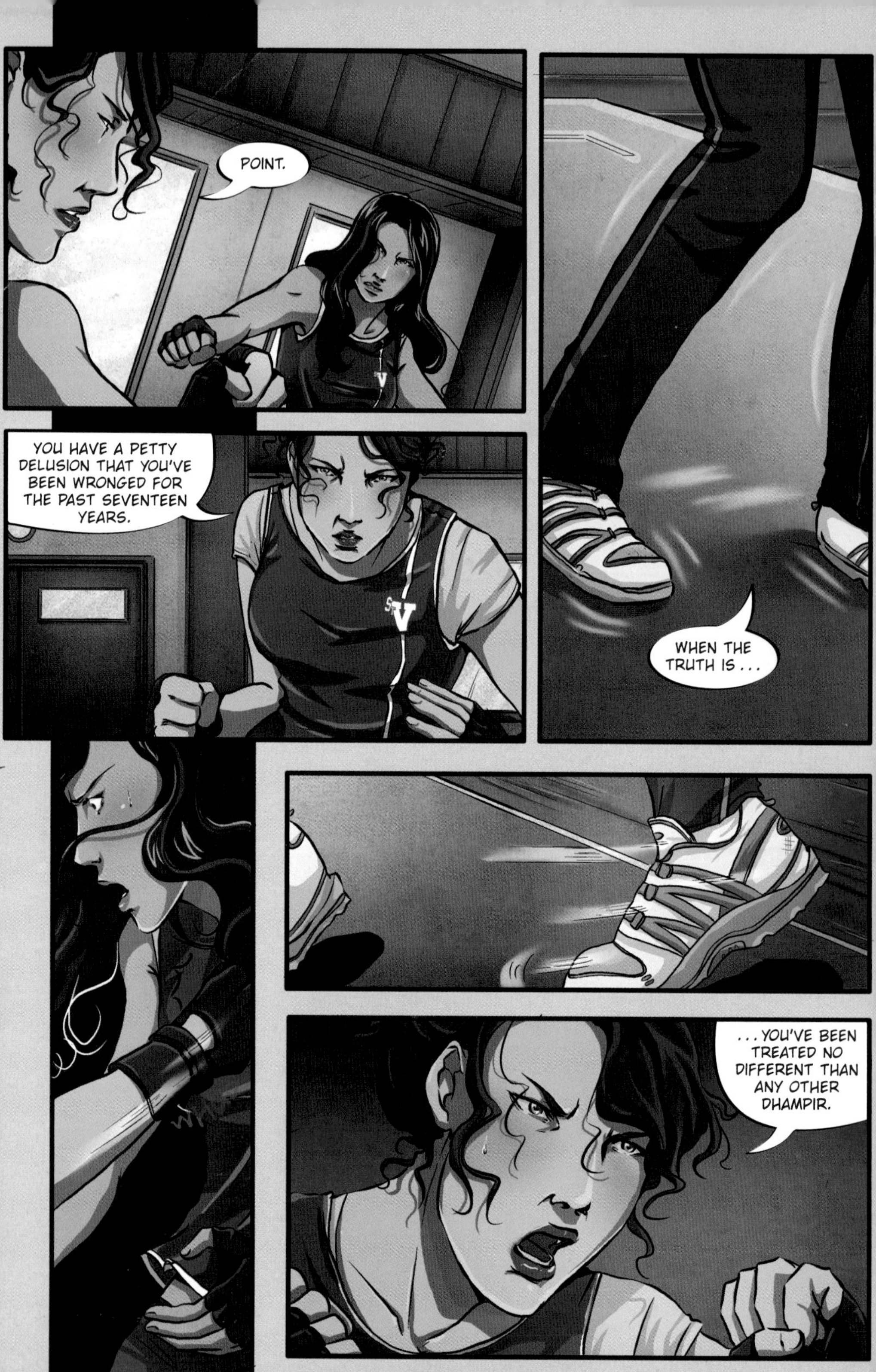
POINT.
YOU HAVE A PETTY DELUSION THAT YOU'VE BEEN WRONGED FOR THE PAST SEVENTEEN YEARS.
WHEN THE TRUTH IS . . .
. . . YOU'VE BEEN TREATED NO DIFFERENT THAN ANY OTHER DHAMPIR.

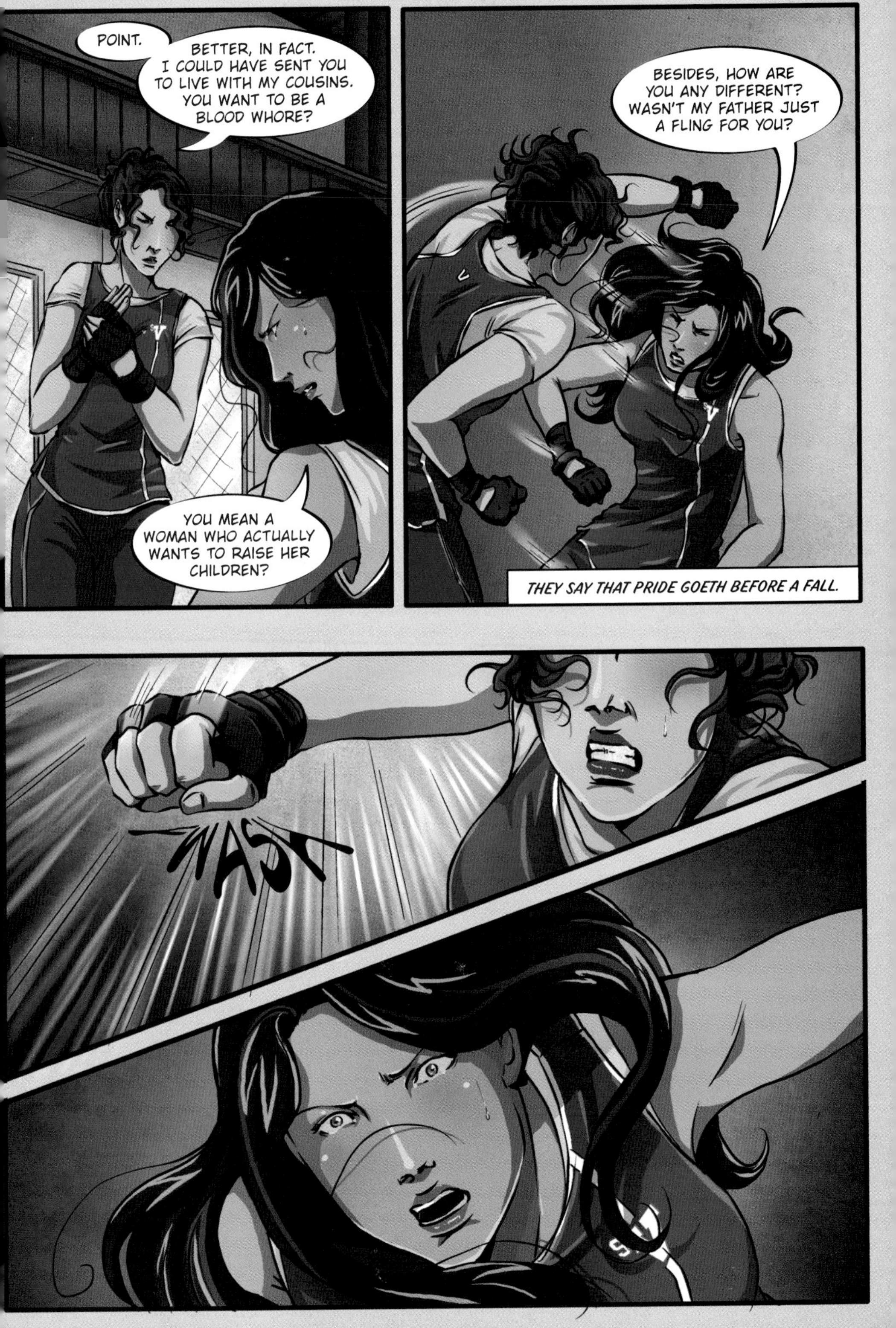
POINT.
BETTER, IN FACT. I COULD HAVE SENT YOU TO LIVE WITH MY COUSINS. YOU WANT TO BE A BLOOD WHORE?
YOU MEAN A WOMAN WHO ACTUALLY WANTS TO RAISE HER CHILDREN?
BESIDES, HOW ARE YOU ANY DIFFERENT? WASN'T MY FATHER JUST A FLING FOR YOU?
THEY SAY THAT PRIDE GOETH BEFORE A FALL.
WASH

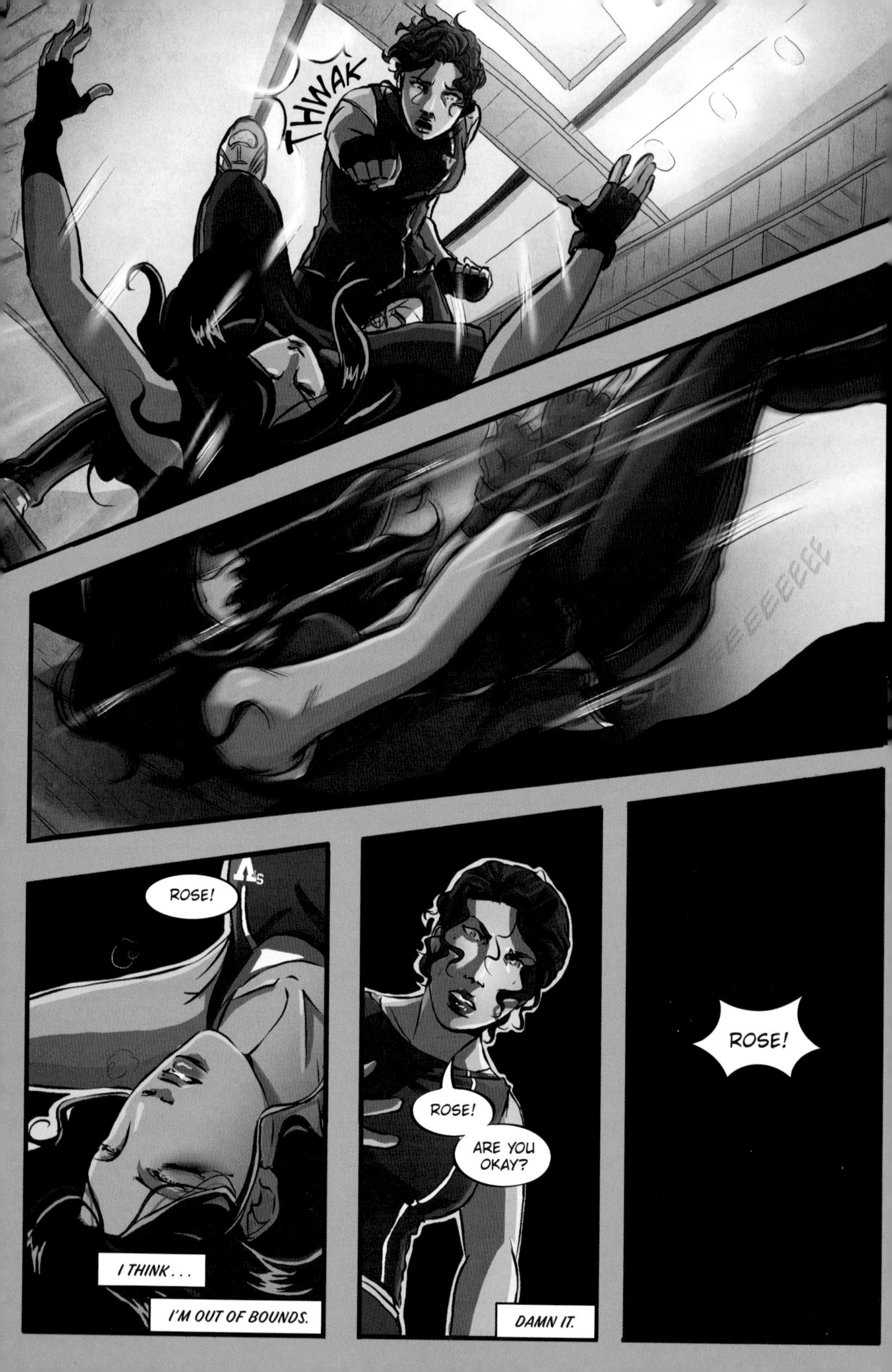
THWAK
ROSE!
I THINK . . .
I'M OUT OF BOUNDS.
ROSE!
ARE YOU OKAY?
DAMN IT.
ROSE!

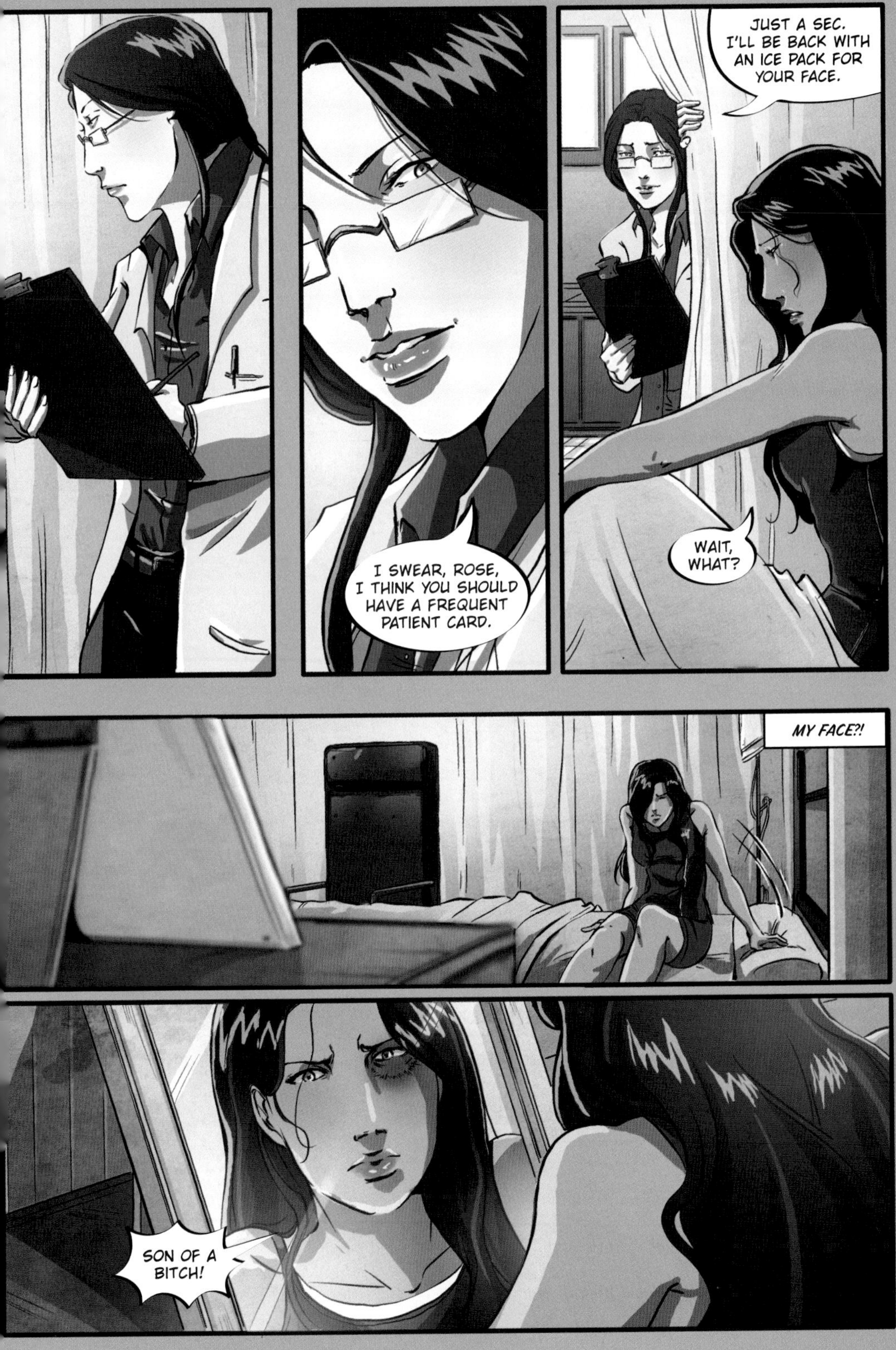
I SWEAR, ROSE, I THINK YOU SHOULD HAVE A FREQUENT PATIENT CARD.
JUST A SEC. I'LL BE BACK WITH AN ICE PACK FOR YOUR FACE.
WAIT, WHAT?
MY FACE?!
SON OF A BITCH!

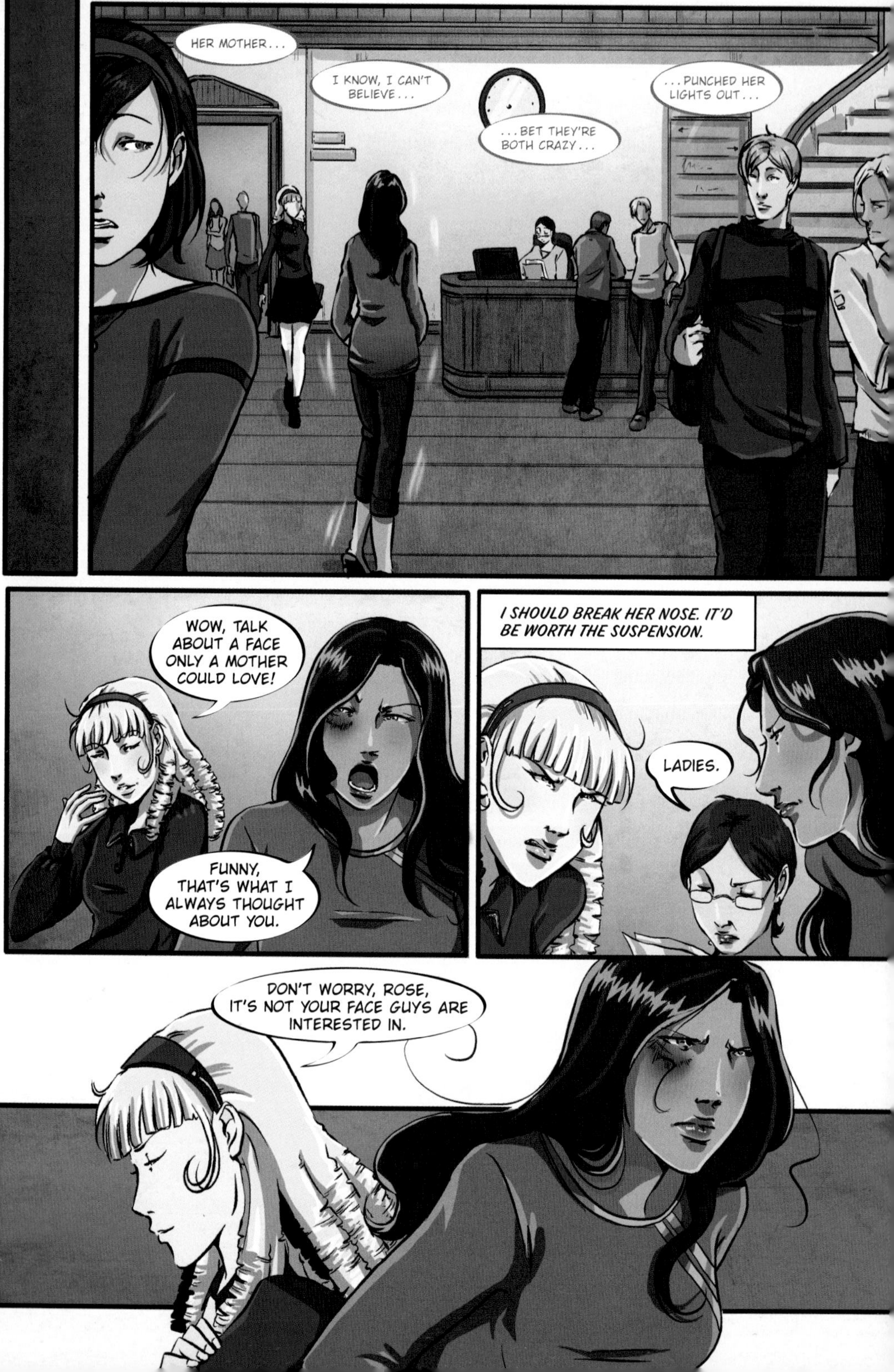
HER MOTHER...
I KNOW, I CAN'T BELIEVE...
...BET THEY'RE BOTH CRAZY...
...PUNCHED HER LIGHTS OUT...
WOW, TALK ABOUT A FACE ONLY A MOTHER COULD LOVE!
FUNNY, THAT'S WHAT I ALWAYS THOUGHT ABOUT YOU.
I SHOULD BREAK HER NOSE. IT'D BE WORTH THE SUSPENSION.
LADIES.
DON'T WORRY, ROSE, IT'S NOT YOUR FACE GUYS ARE INTERESTED IN.

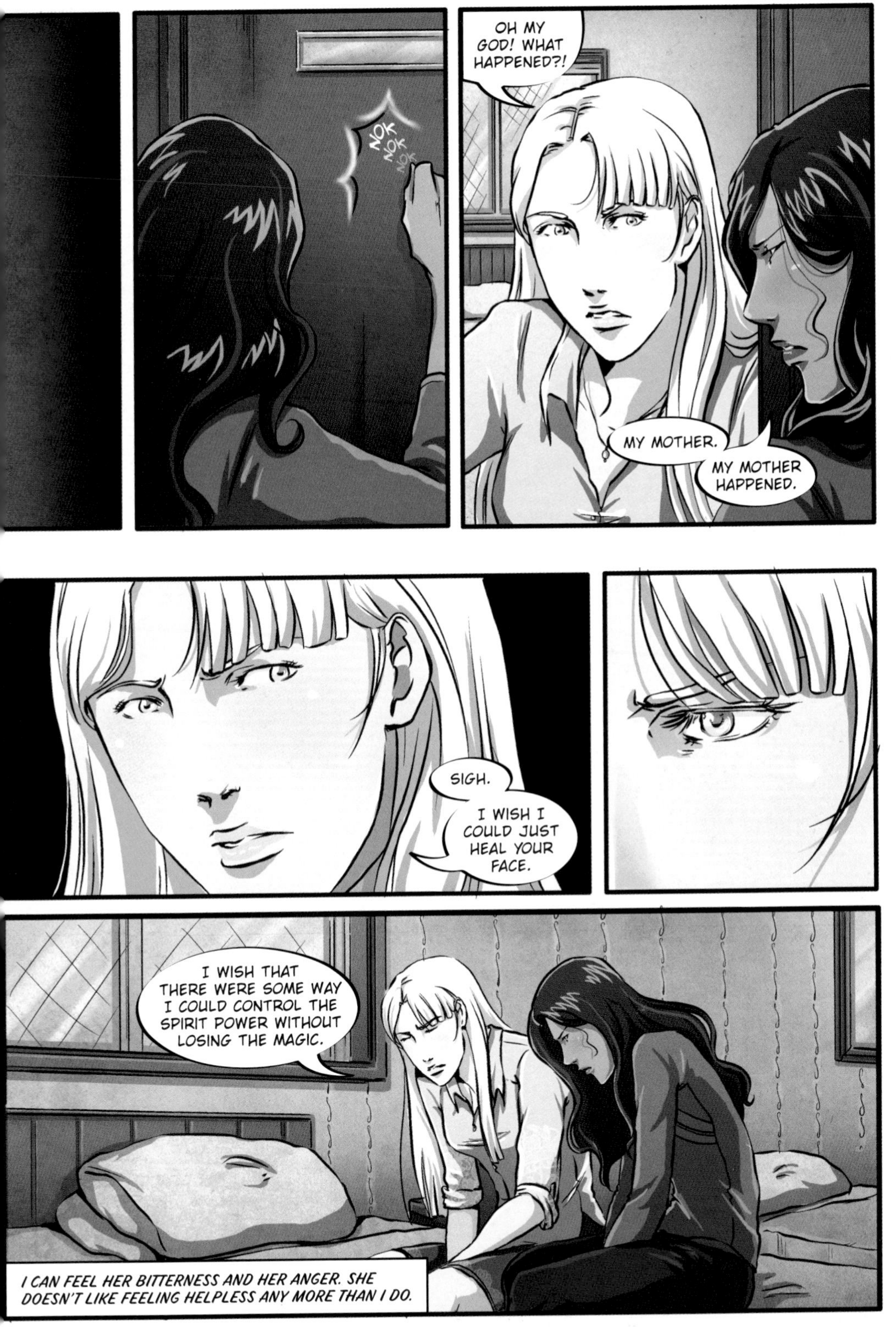
NOK
NOK
NOK
OH MY GOD! WHAT HAPPENED?!
MY MOTHER.
MY MOTHER HAPPENED.
SIGH.
I WISH I COULD JUST HEAL YOUR FACE.
I WISH THAT THERE WERE SOME WAY I COULD CONTROL THE SPIRIT POWER WITHOUT LOSING THE MAGIC.
I CAN FEEL HER BITTERNESS AND HER ANGER. SHE DOESN'T LIKE FEELING HELPLESS ANY MORE THAN I DO.

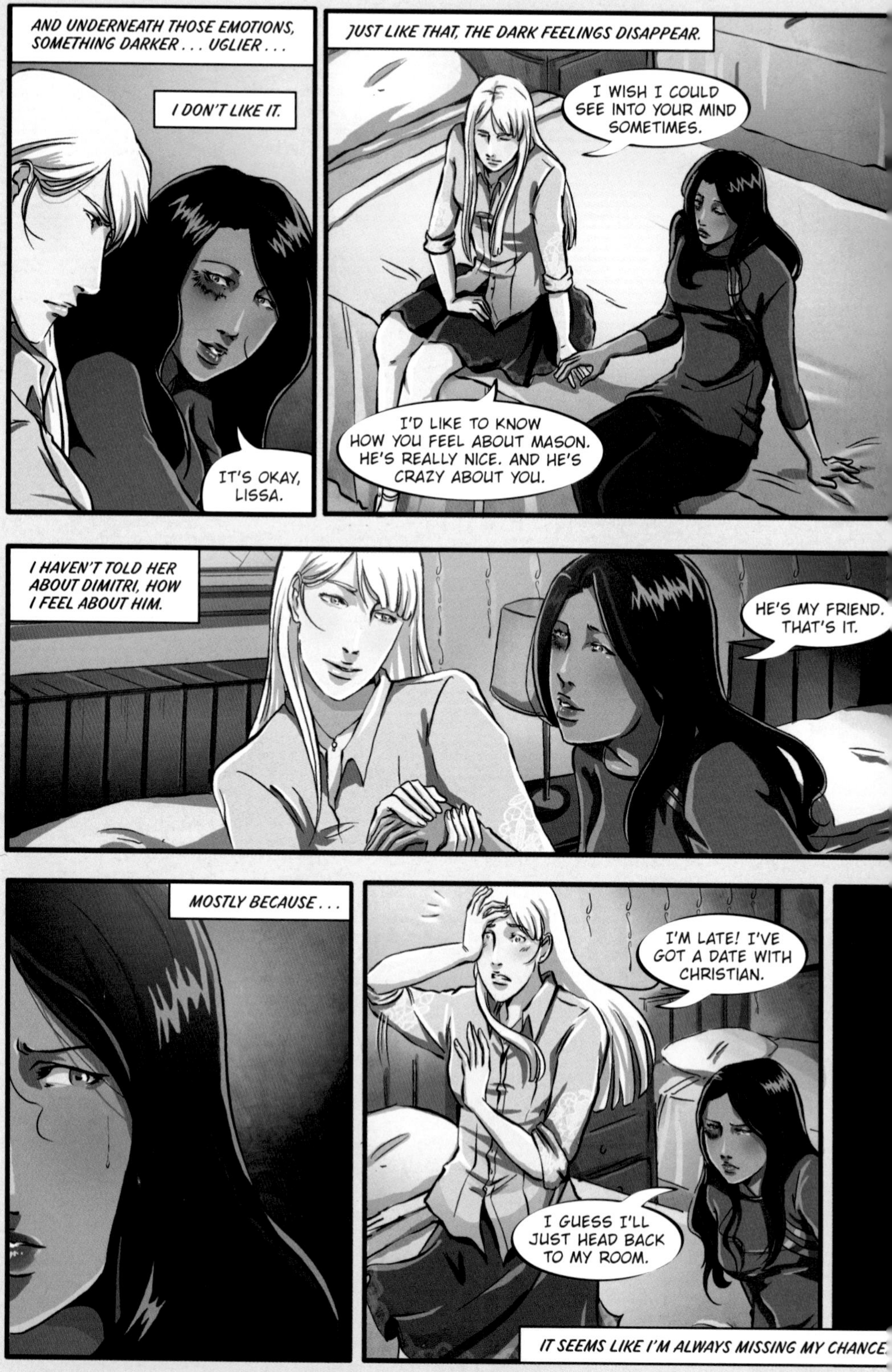
AND UNDERNEATH THOSE EMOTIONS, SOMETHING DARKER . . . UGLIER . . .
I DON'T LIKE IT.
IT'S OKAY, LISSA.
JUST LIKE THAT, THE DARK FEELINGS DISAPPEAR.
I WISH I COULD SEE INTO YOUR MIND SOMETIMES.
I'D LIKE TO KNOW HOW YOU FEEL ABOUT MASON. HE'S REALLY NICE. AND HE'S CRAZY ABOUT YOU.
I HAVEN'T TOLD HER ABOUT DIMITRI, HOW I FEEL ABOUT HIM.
HE'S MY FRIEND. THAT'S IT.
MOSTLY BECAUSE . . .
I'M LATE! I'VE GOT A DATE WITH CHRISTIAN.
I GUESS I'LL JUST HEAD BACK TO MY ROOM.
IT SEEMS LIKE I'M ALWAYS MISSING MY CHANCE.

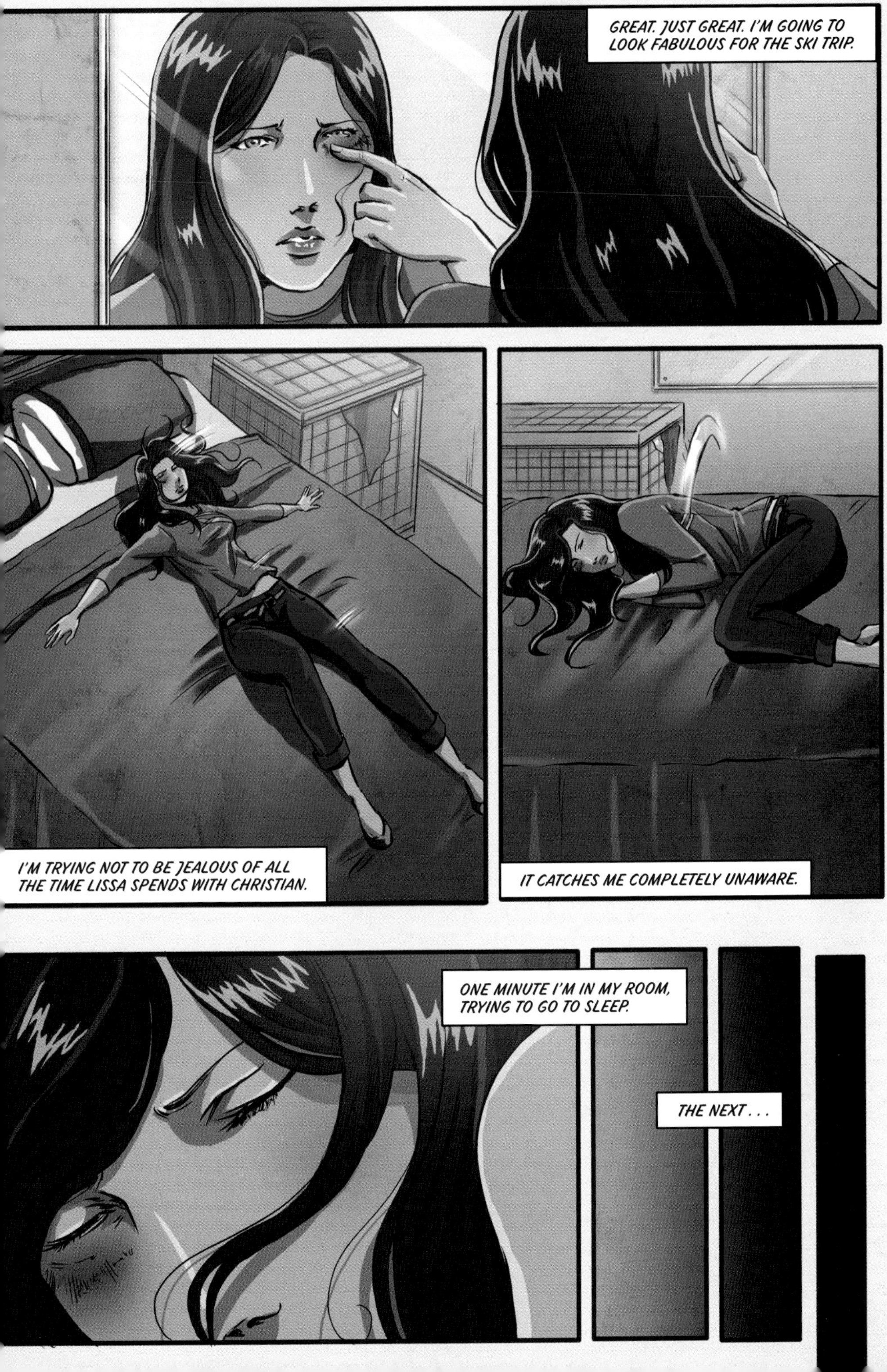
GREAT. JUST GREAT. I'M GOING TO LOOK FABULOUS FOR THE SKI TRIP.
I'M TRYING NOT TO BE JEALOUS OF ALL THE TIME LISSA SPENDS WITH CHRISTIAN.
IT CATCHES ME COMPLETELY UNAWARE.
ONE MINUTE I'M IN MY ROOM, TRYING TO GO TO SLEEP.
THE NEXT . . .

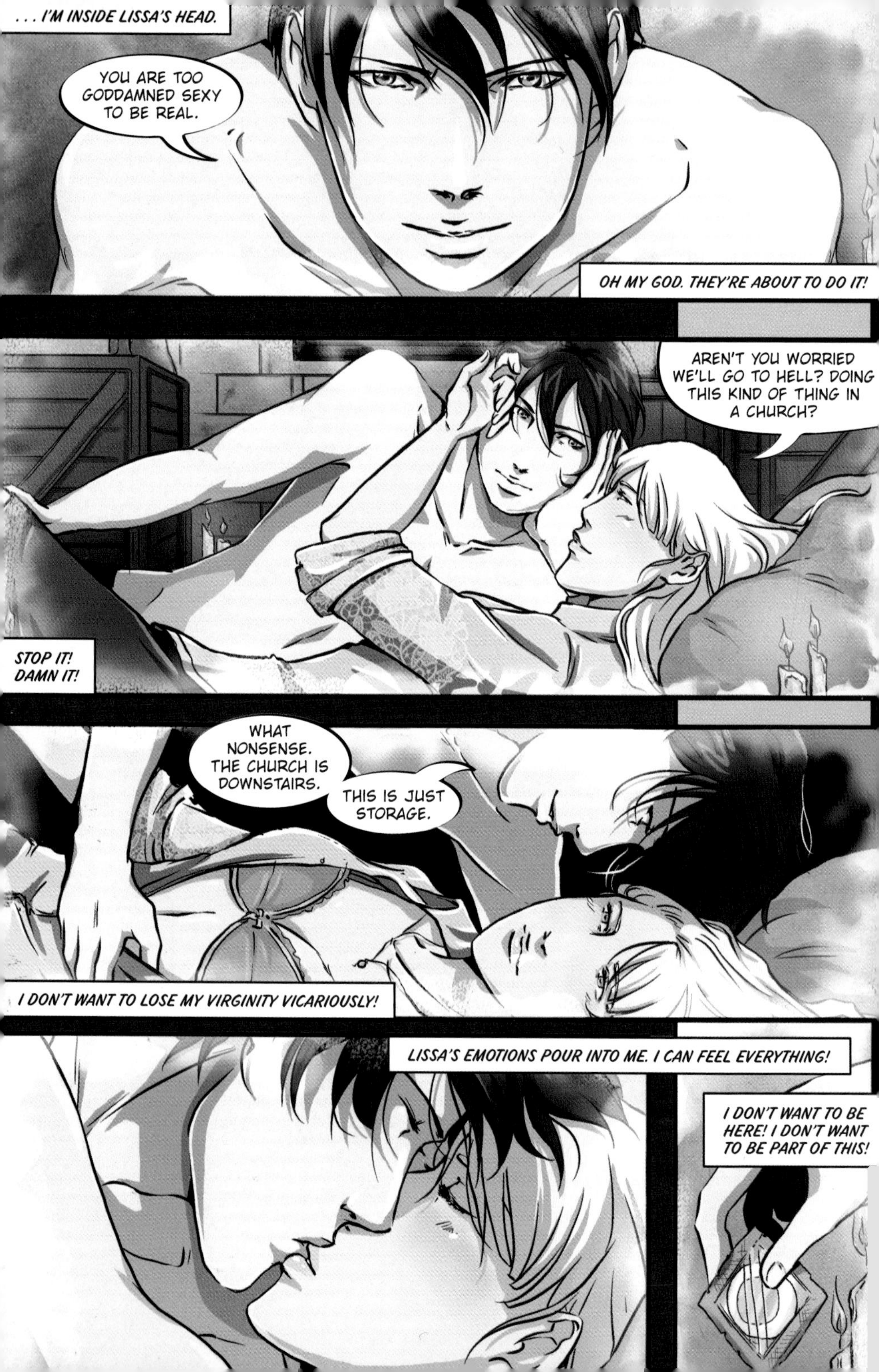

. . . I'M INSIDE LISSA'S HEAD.
YOU ARE TOO GODDAMNED SEXY TO BE REAL.
OH MY GOD. THEY'RE ABOUT TO DO IT!
AREN'T YOU WORRIED WE'LL GO TO HELL? DOING THIS KIND OF THING IN A CHURCH?
STOP IT! DAMN IT!
WHAT NONSENSE. THE CHURCH IS DOWNSTAIRS.
THIS IS JUST STORAGE.
I DON'T WANT TO LOSE MY VIRGINITY VICARIOUSLY!
LISSA'S EMOTIONS POUR INTO ME. I CAN FEEL EVERYTHING!
I DON'T WANT TO BE HERE! I DON'T WANT TO BE PART OF THIS!

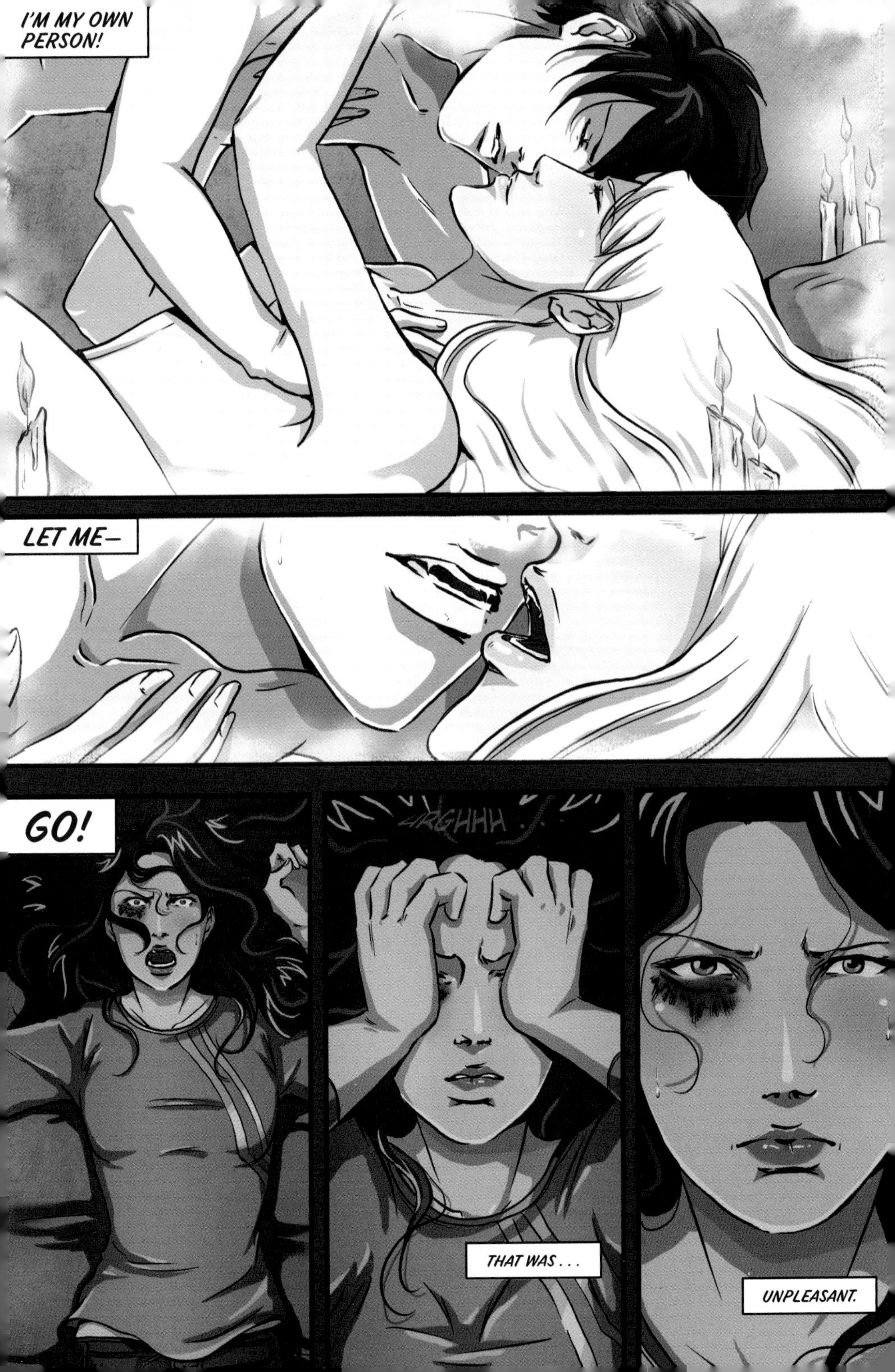
I'M MY OWN PERSON!
LET ME—
GO!
ARGHHH
THAT WAS . . .
UNPLEASANT.

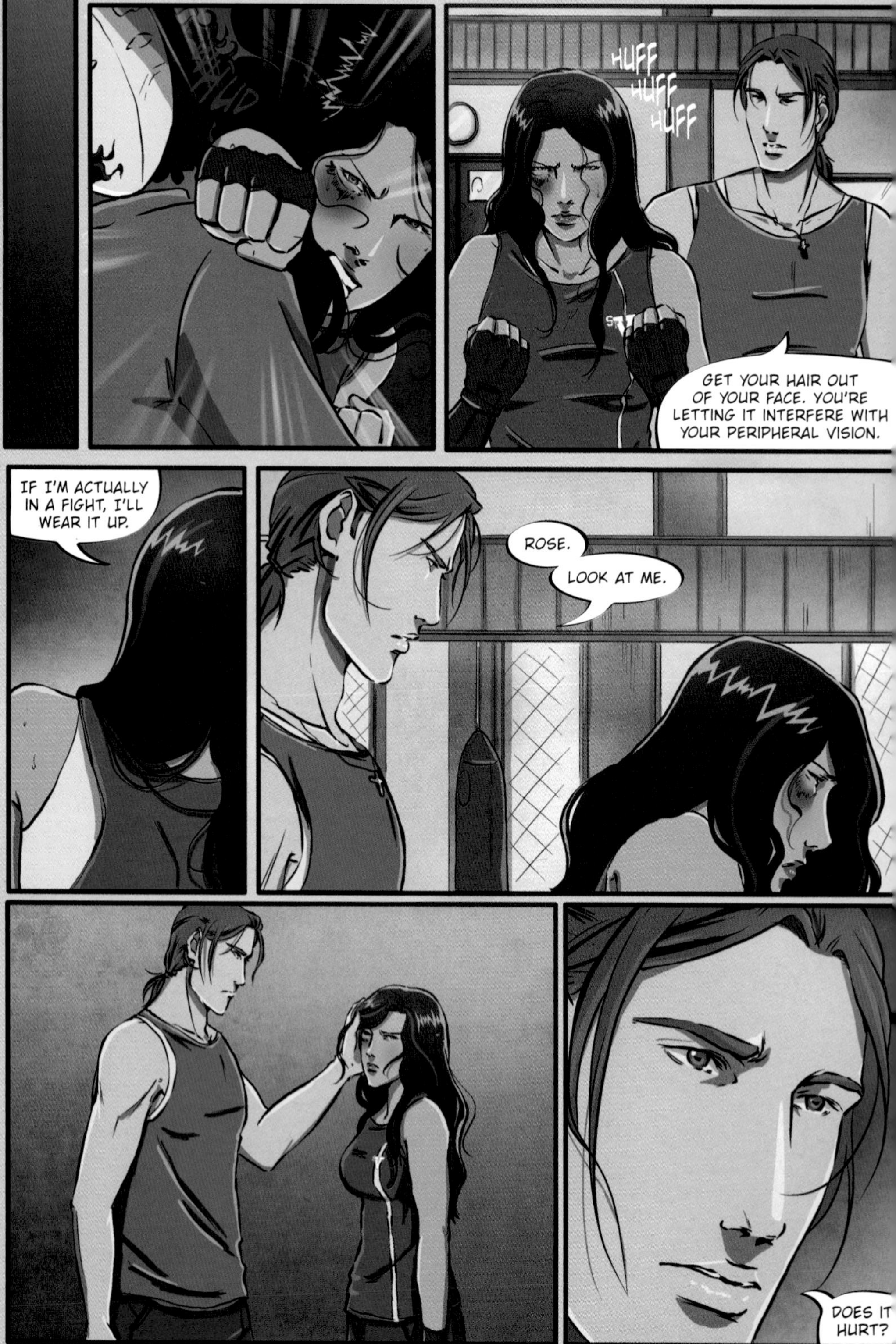
HUFF
HUFF
HUFF
GET YOUR HAIR OUT OF YOUR FACE. YOU'RE LETTING IT INTERFERE WITH YOUR PERIPHERAL VISION.
IF I'M ACTUALLY IN A FIGHT, I'LL WEAR IT UP.
ROSE.
LOOK AT ME.
DOES IT HURT?

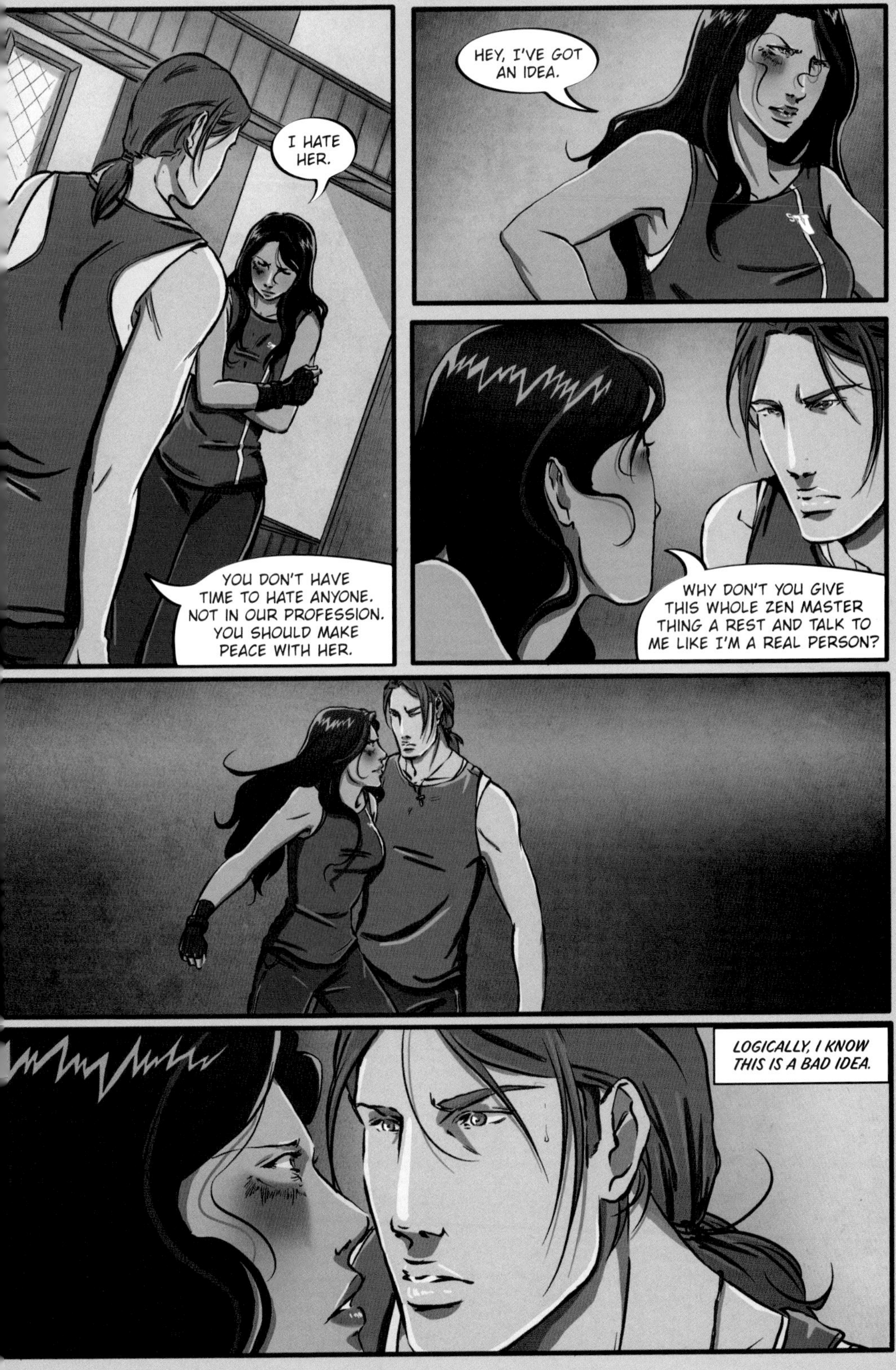
I HATE HER.
YOU DON'T HAVE TIME TO HATE ANYONE. NOT IN OUR PROFESSION. YOU SHOULD MAKE PEACE WITH HER.
HEY, I'VE GOT AN IDEA.
WHY DON'T YOU GIVE THIS WHOLE ZEN MASTER THING A REST AND TALK TO ME LIKE I'M A REAL PERSON?
LOGICALLY, I KNOW THIS IS A BAD IDEA.

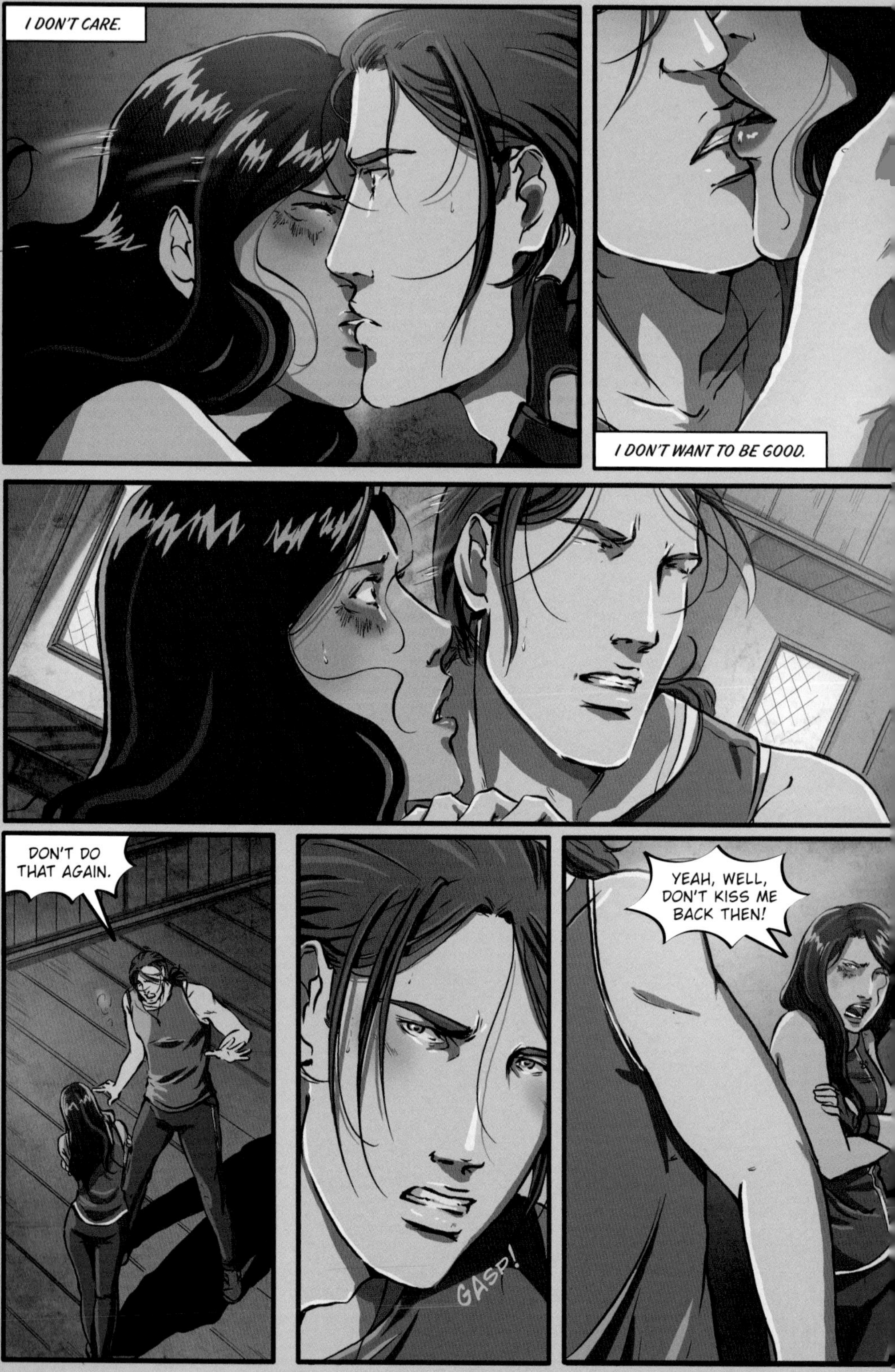
I DON'T CARE.
I DON'T WANT TO BE GOOD.
DON'T DO THAT AGAIN.
GASP!
YEAH, WELL, DON'T KISS ME BACK THEN!

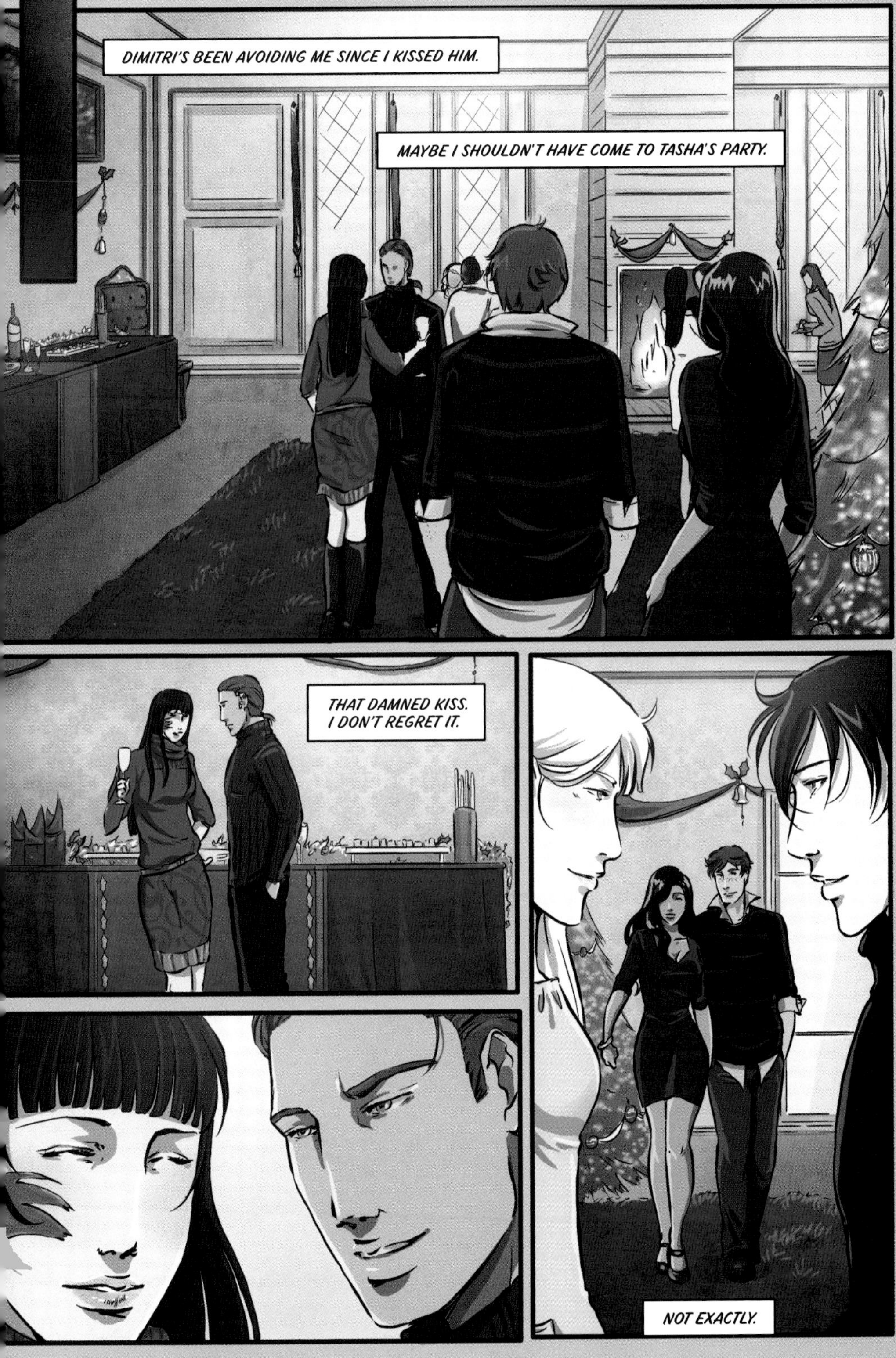
DIMITRI'S BEEN AVOIDING ME SINCE I KISSED HIM.
MAYBE I SHOULDN'T HAVE COME TO TASHA'S PARTY.
THAT DAMNED KISS. I DON'T REGRET IT.
NOT EXACTLY.

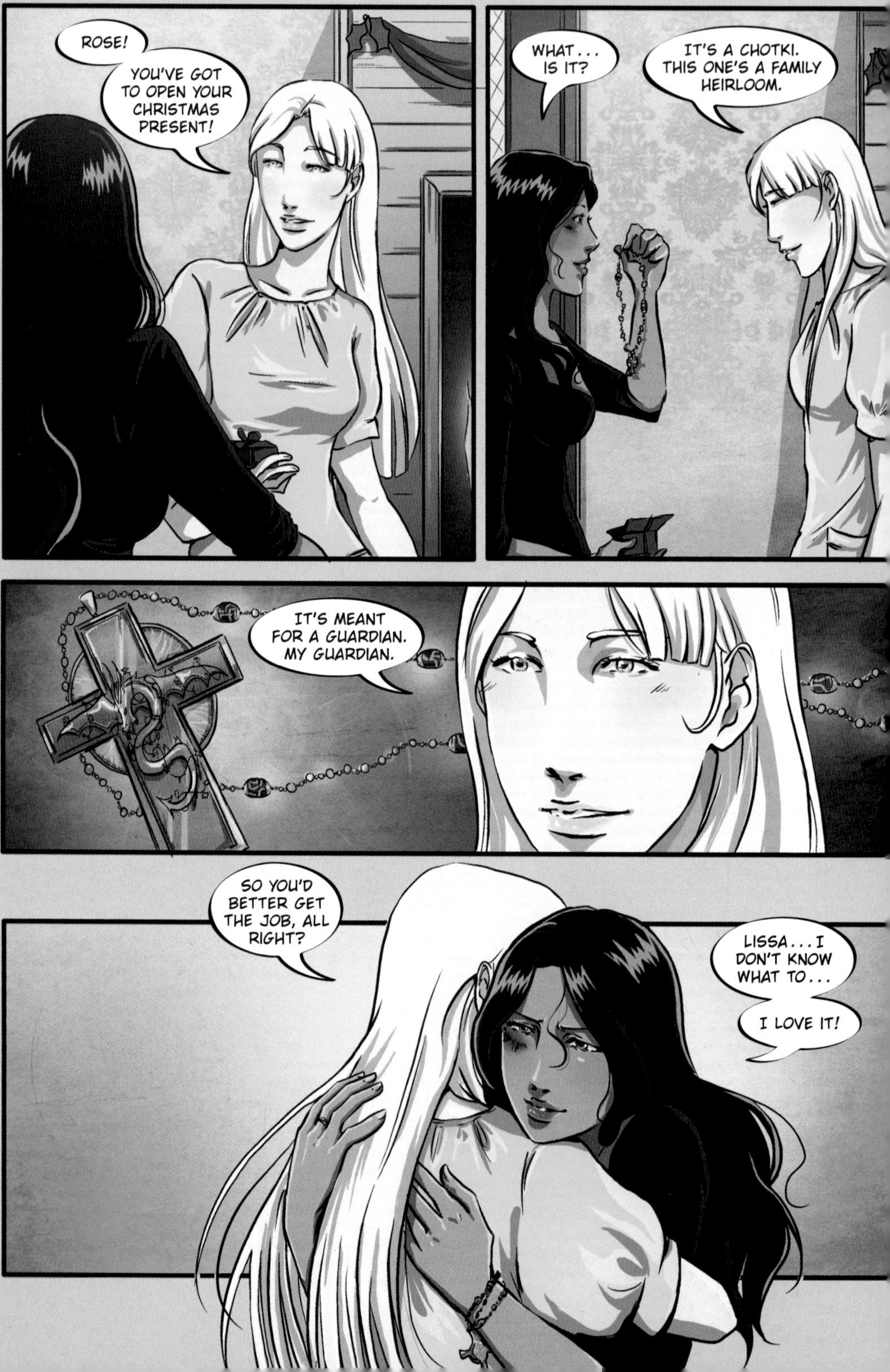
ROSE!
YOU'VE GOT TO OPEN YOUR CHRISTMAS PRESENT!
WHAT... IS IT?
IT'S A CHOTKI. THIS ONE'S A FAMILY HEIRLOOM.
IT'S MEANT FOR A GUARDIAN. MY GUARDIAN.
SO YOU'D BETTER GET THE JOB, ALL RIGHT?
LISSA... I DON'T KNOW WHAT TO...
I LOVE IT!

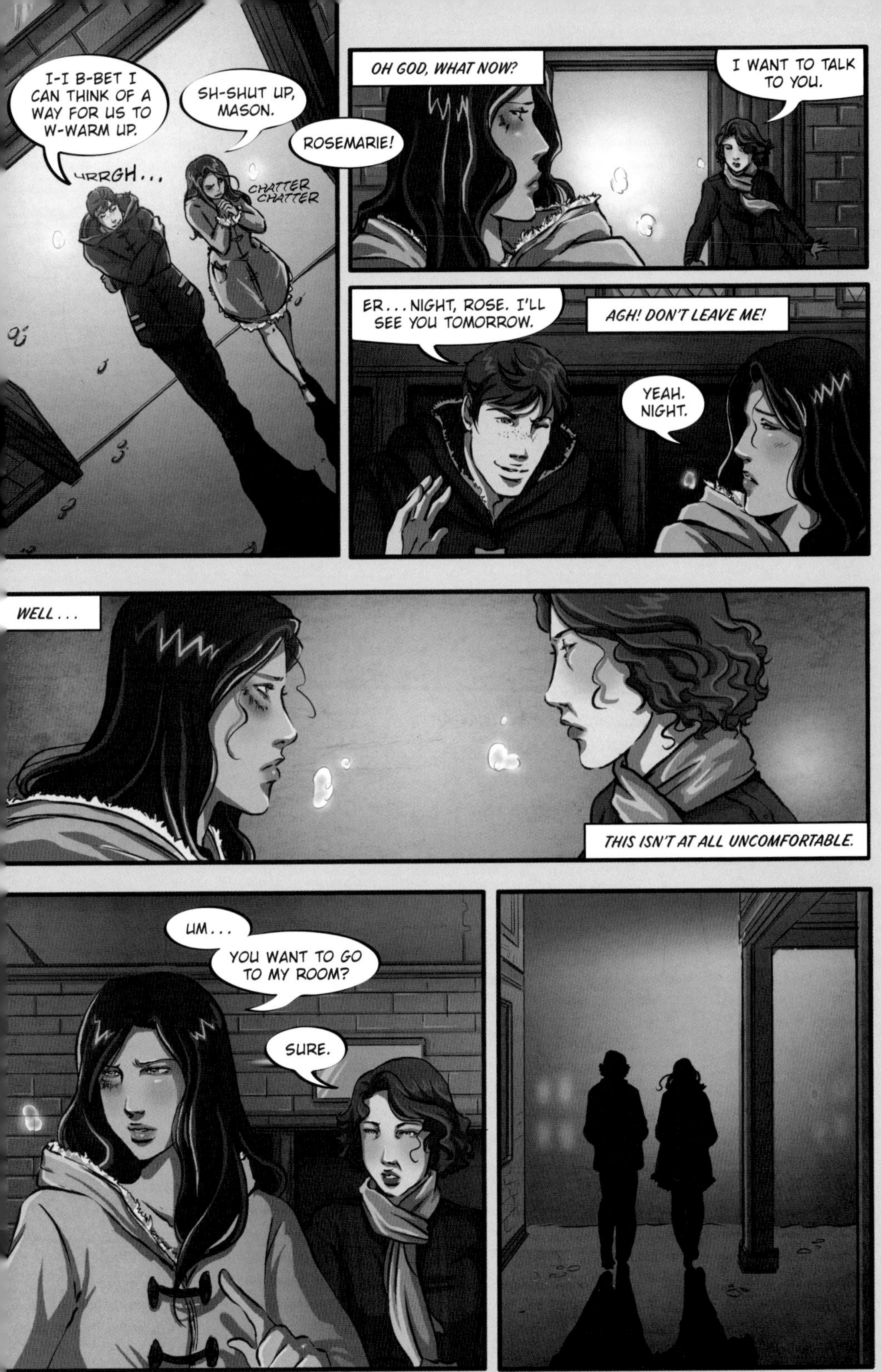
I-I B-BET I CAN THINK OF A WAY FOR US TO W-WARM UP.
SH-SHUT UP, MASON.
UHRRGH...
CHATTER CHATTER
ROSEMARIE!
OH GOD, WHAT NOW?
I WANT TO TALK TO YOU.
ER... NIGHT, ROSE. I'LL SEE YOU TOMORROW.
AGH! DON'T LEAVE ME!
YEAH. NIGHT.
WELL...
THIS ISN'T AT ALL UNCOMFORTABLE.
UM...
YOU WANT TO GO TO MY ROOM?
SURE.

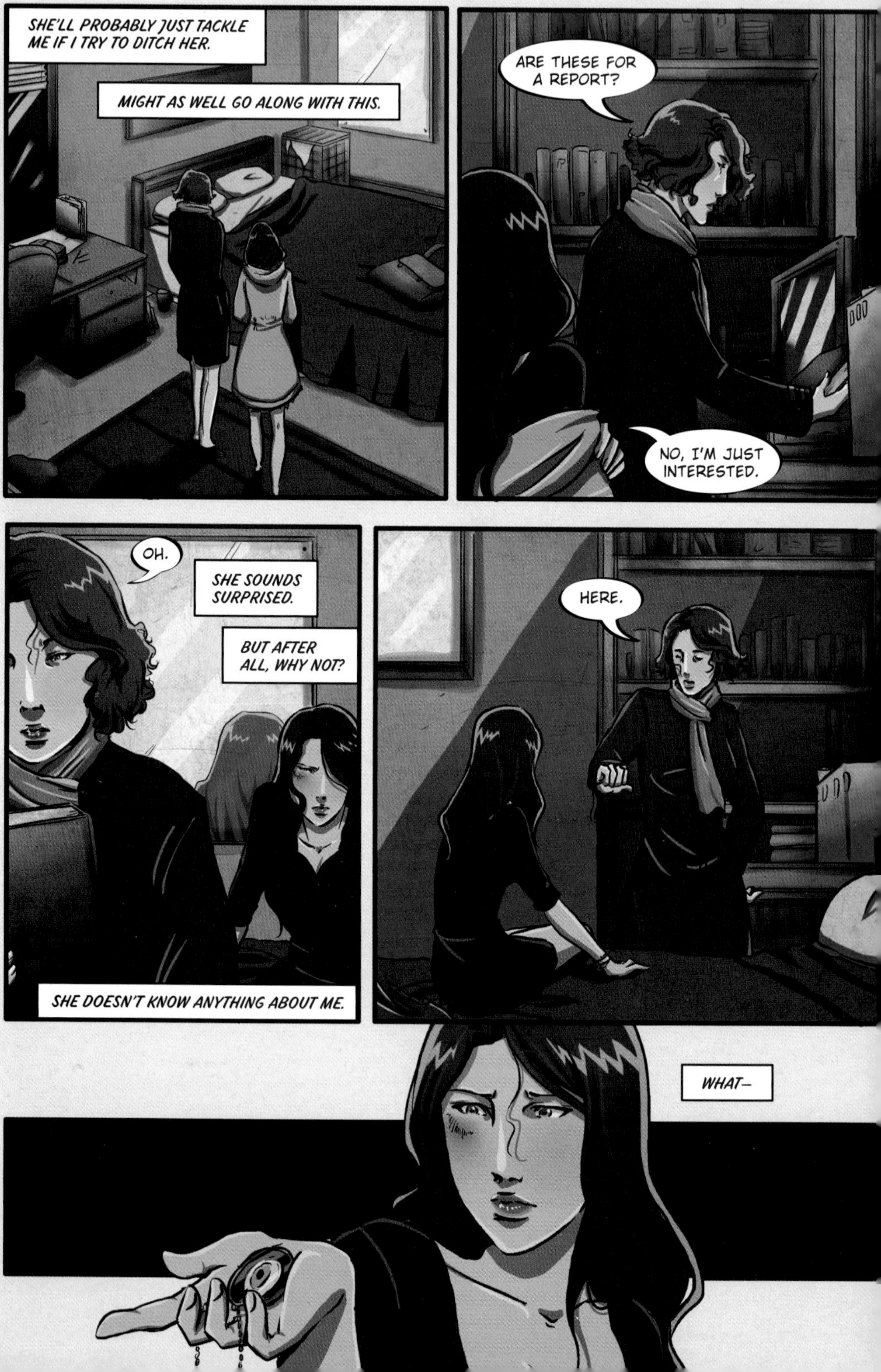
SHE'LL PROBABLY JUST TACKLE ME IF I TRY TO DITCH HER.
MIGHT AS WELL GO ALONG WITH THIS.
ARE THESE FOR A REPORT?
NO, I'M JUST INTERESTED.
OH.
SHE SOUNDS SURPRISED.
BUT AFTER ALL, WHY NOT?
SHE DOESN'T KNOW ANYTHING ABOUT ME.
HERE.
WHAT—

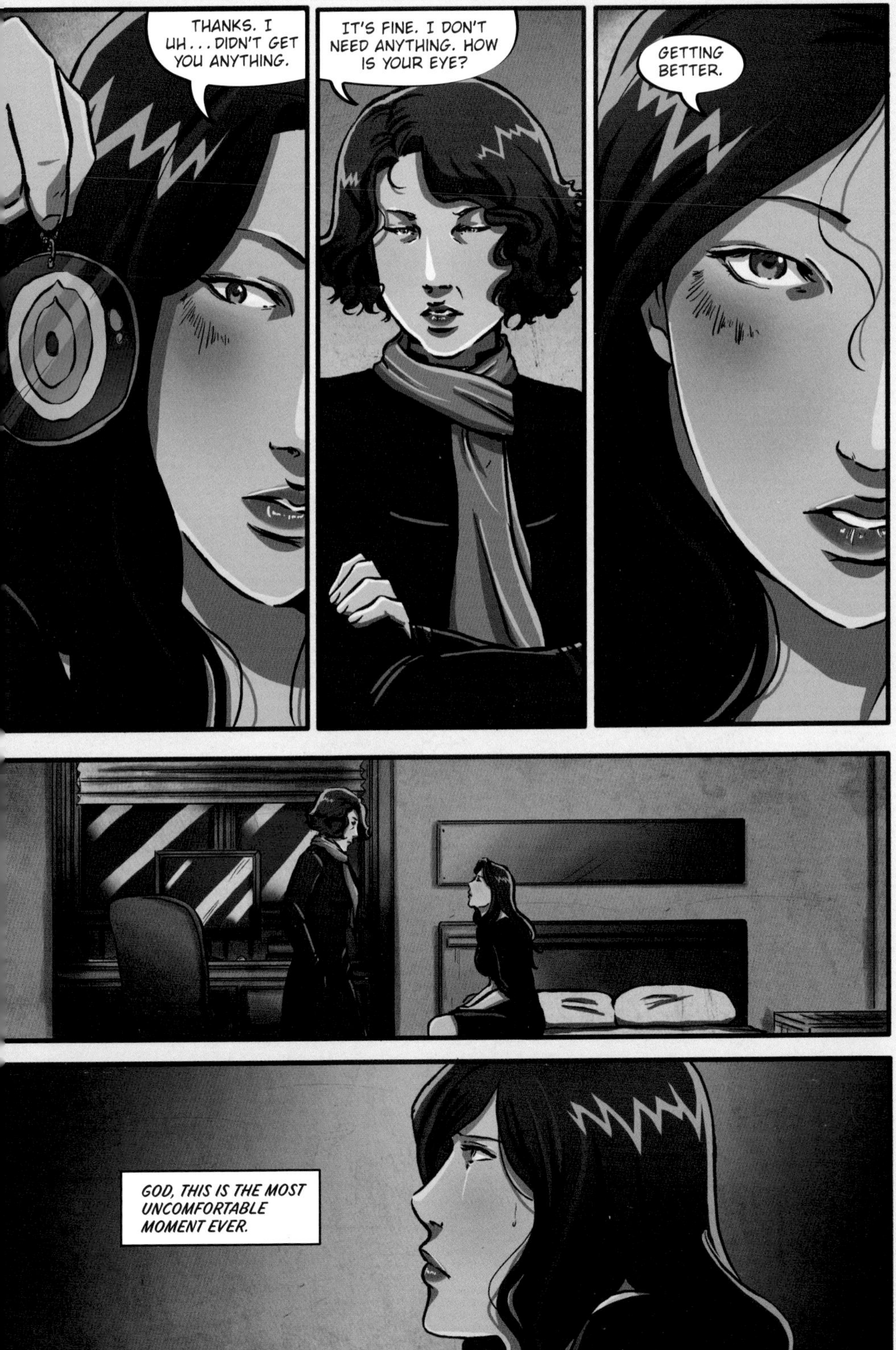
THANKS. I UH . . . DIDN'T GET YOU ANYTHING.
IT'S FINE. I DON'T NEED ANYTHING. HOW IS YOUR EYE?
GETTING BETTER.
GOD, THIS IS THE MOST UNCOMFORTABLE MOMENT EVER.

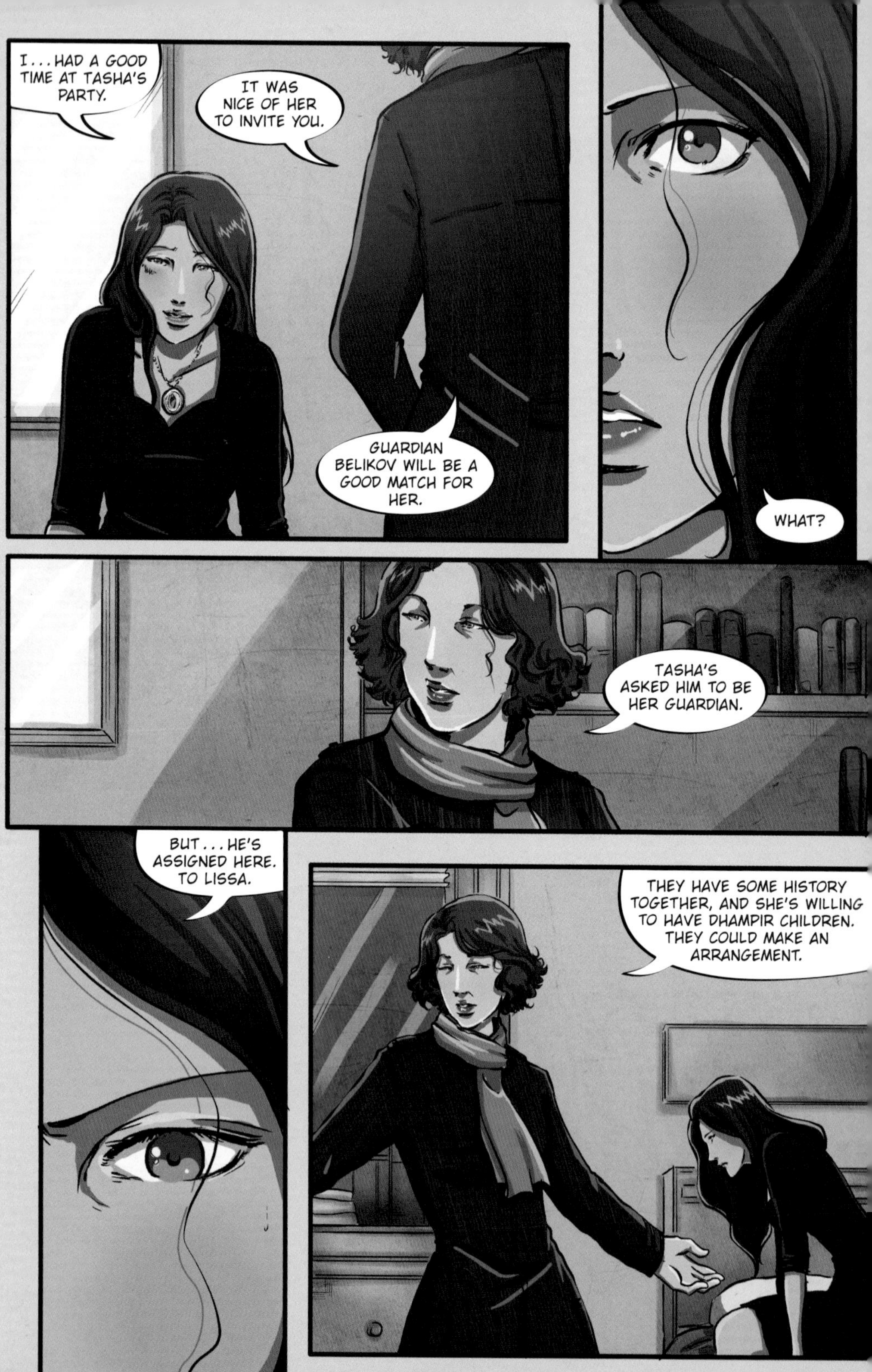
I . . . HAD A GOOD TIME AT TASHA'S PARTY.
IT WAS NICE OF HER TO INVITE YOU.
GUARDIAN BELIKOV WILL BE A GOOD MATCH FOR HER.
WHAT?
TASHA'S ASKED HIM TO BE HER GUARDIAN.
BUT . . . HE'S ASSIGNED HERE. TO LISSA.
THEY HAVE SOME HISTORY TOGETHER, AND SHE'S WILLING TO HAVE DHAMPIR CHILDREN. THEY COULD MAKE AN ARRANGEMENT.

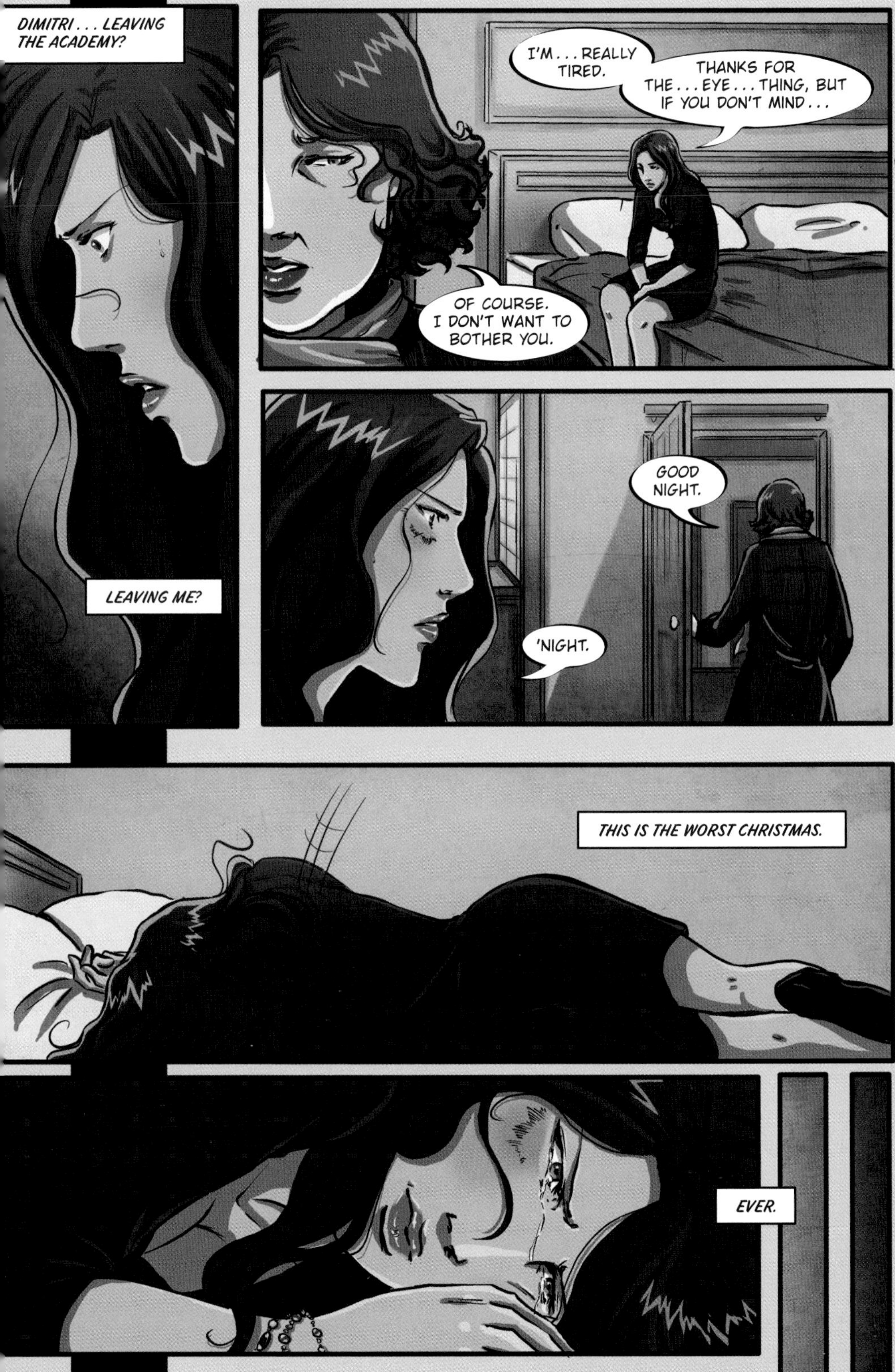
DIMITRI . . . LEAVING THE ACADEMY?
LEAVING ME?
I'M . . . REALLY TIRED.
THANKS FOR THE . . . EYE . . . THING, BUT IF YOU DON'T MIND . . .
OF COURSE. I DON'T WANT TO BOTHER YOU.
GOOD NIGHT.
'NIGHT.
THIS IS THE WORST CHRISTMAS.
EVER.

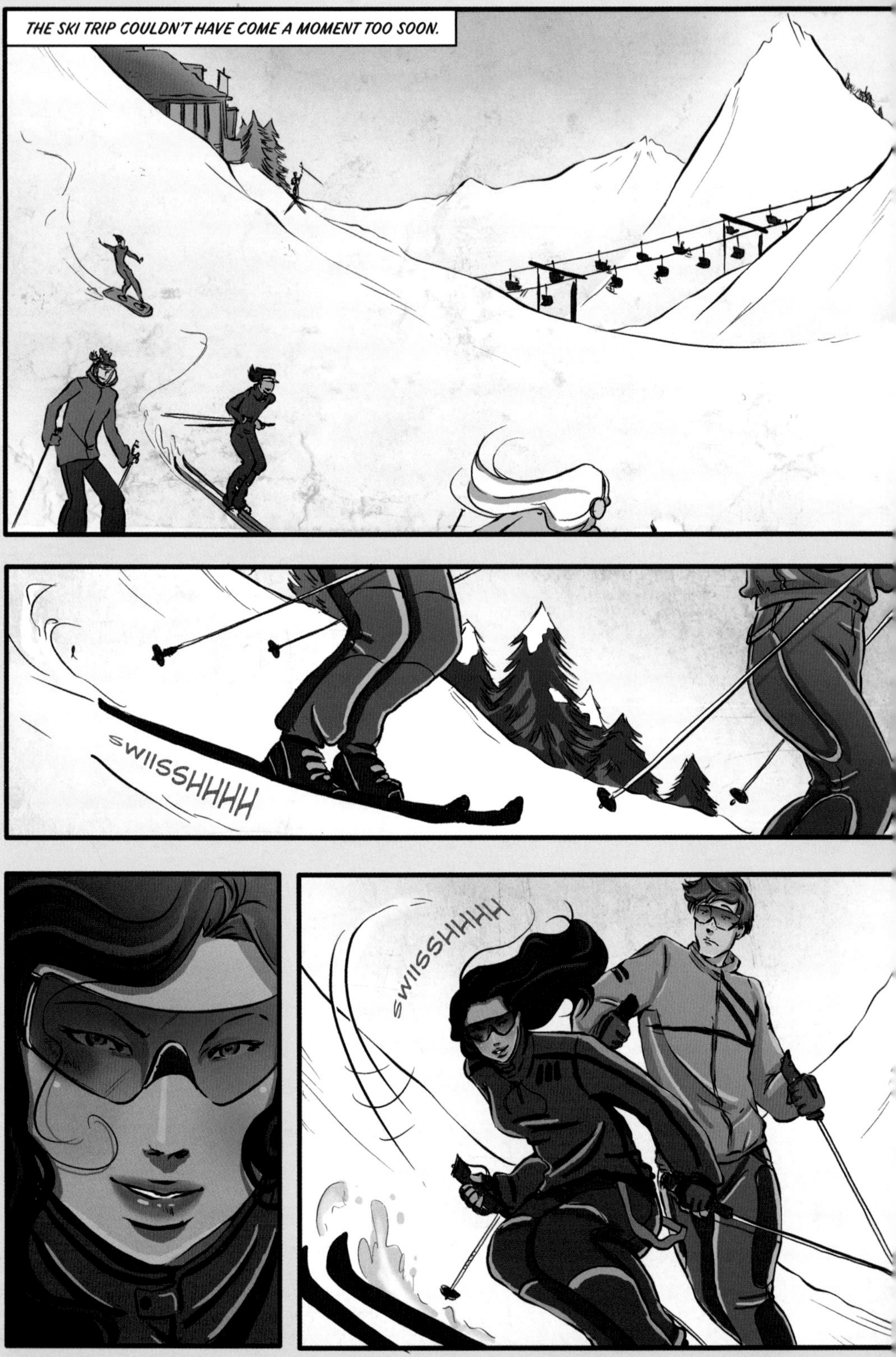
THE SKI TRIP COULDN'T HAVE COME A MOMENT TOO SOON.
SWIISSHHHH
SWIISSHHHH

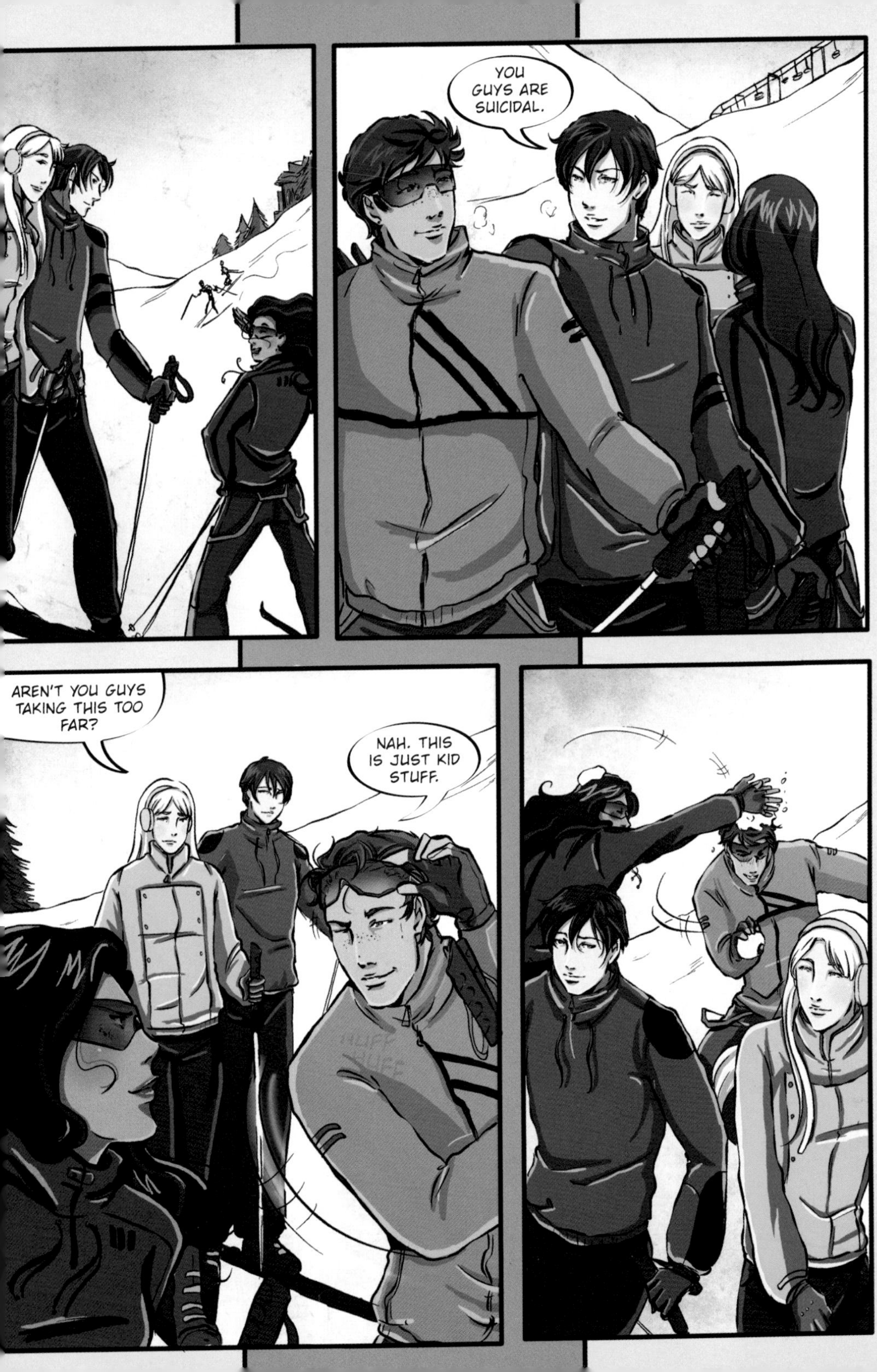
YOU GUYS ARE SUICIDAL.
AREN'T YOU GUYS TAKING THIS TOO FAR?
NAH. THIS IS JUST KID STUFF.
HUFF HUFF

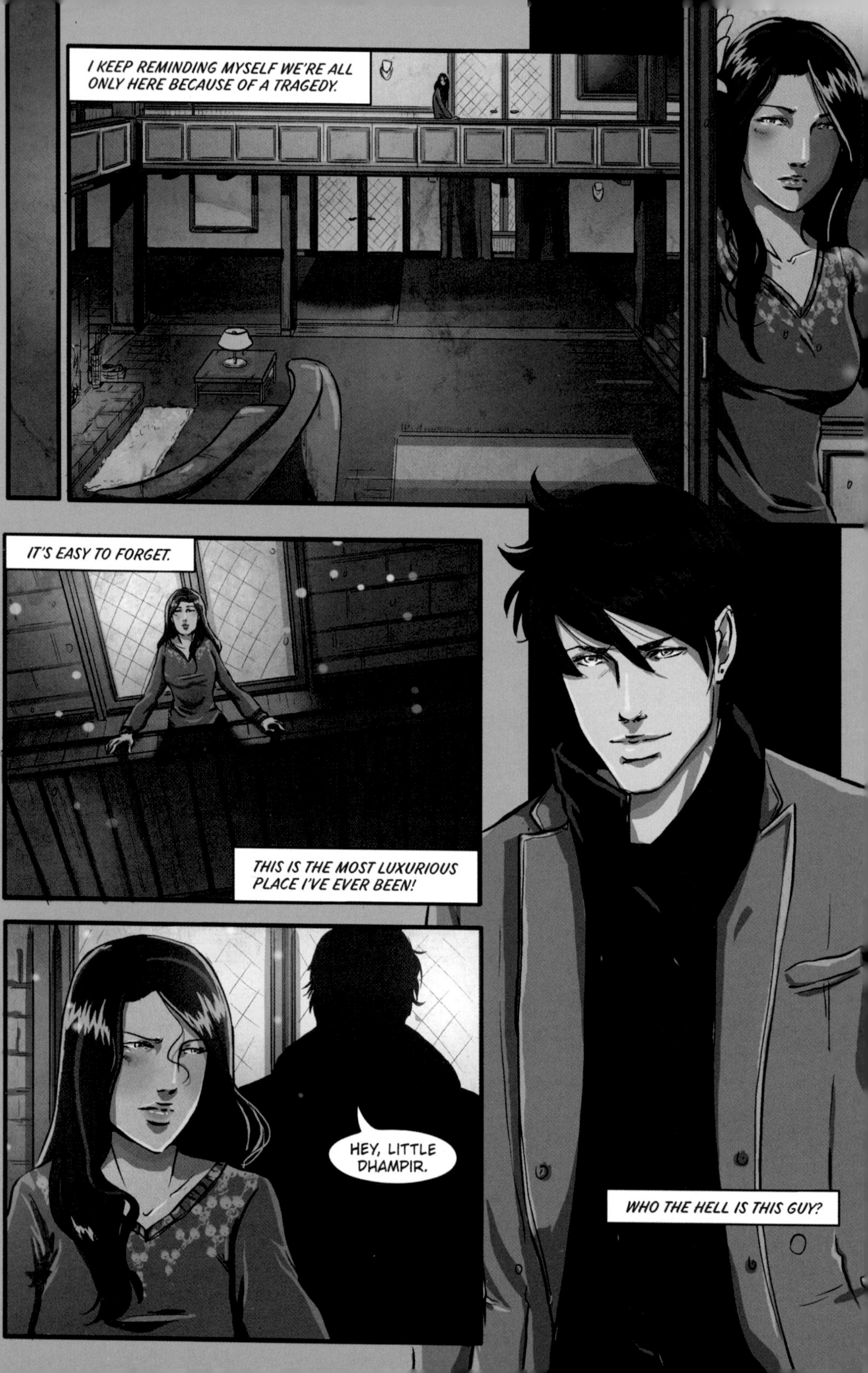
I KEEP REMINDING MYSELF WE'RE ALL ONLY HERE BECAUSE OF A TRAGEDY.
IT'S EASY TO FORGET.
THIS IS THE MOST LUXURIOUS PLACE I'VE EVER BEEN!
HEY, LITTLE DHAMPIR.
WHO THE HELL IS THIS GUY?

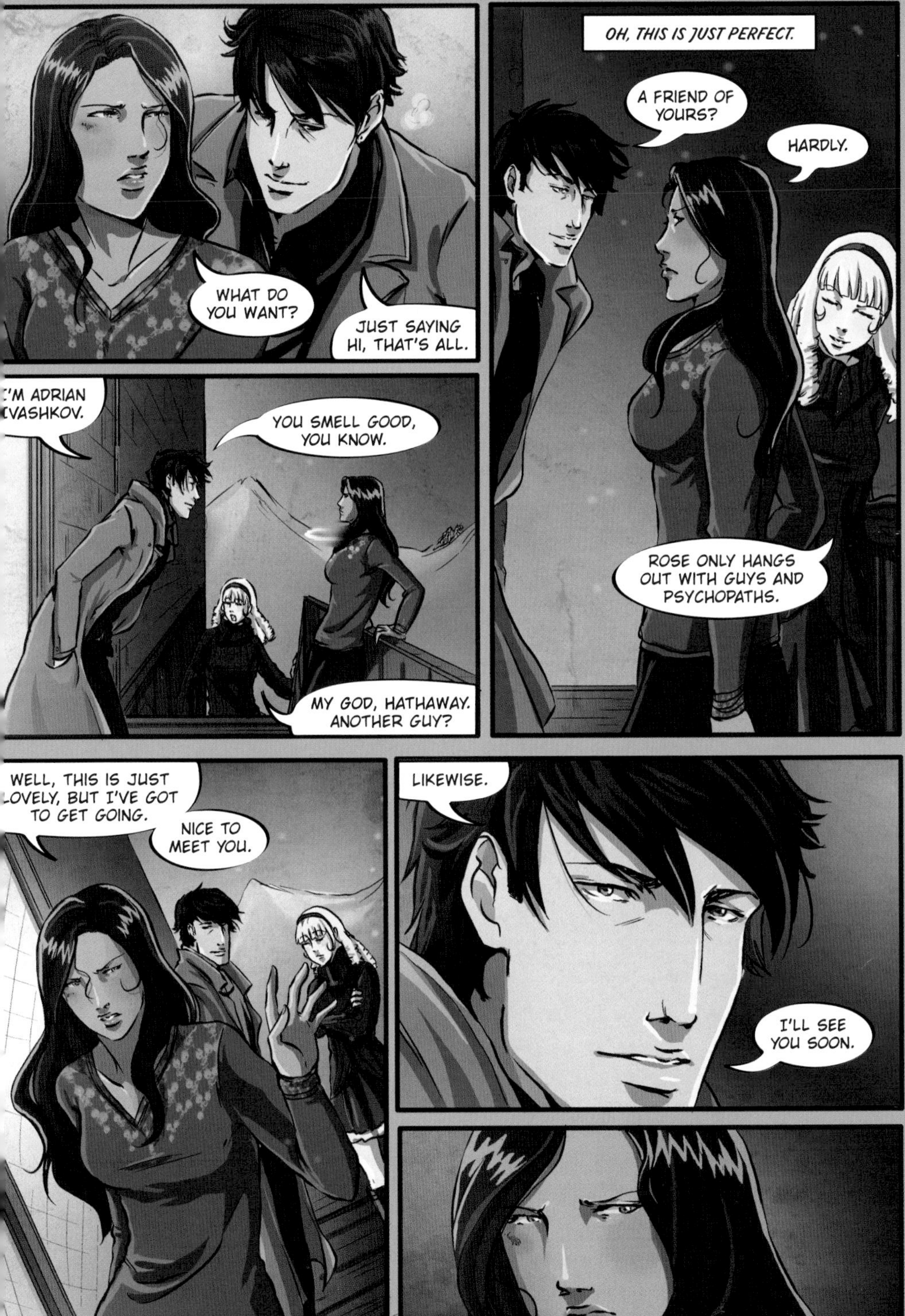
WHAT DO YOU WANT?
JUST SAYING HI, THAT'S ALL.
OH, THIS IS JUST PERFECT.
A FRIEND OF YOURS?
HARDLY.
ROSE ONLY HANGS OUT WITH GUYS AND PSYCHOPATHS.
I'M ADRIAN IVASHKOV.
YOU SMELL GOOD, YOU KNOW.
MY GOD, HATHAWAY. ANOTHER GUY?
WELL, THIS IS JUST LOVELY, BUT I'VE GOT TO GET GOING.
NICE TO MEET YOU.
LIKEWISE.
I'LL SEE YOU SOON.
ARGH. NOT IF I CAN HELP IT.

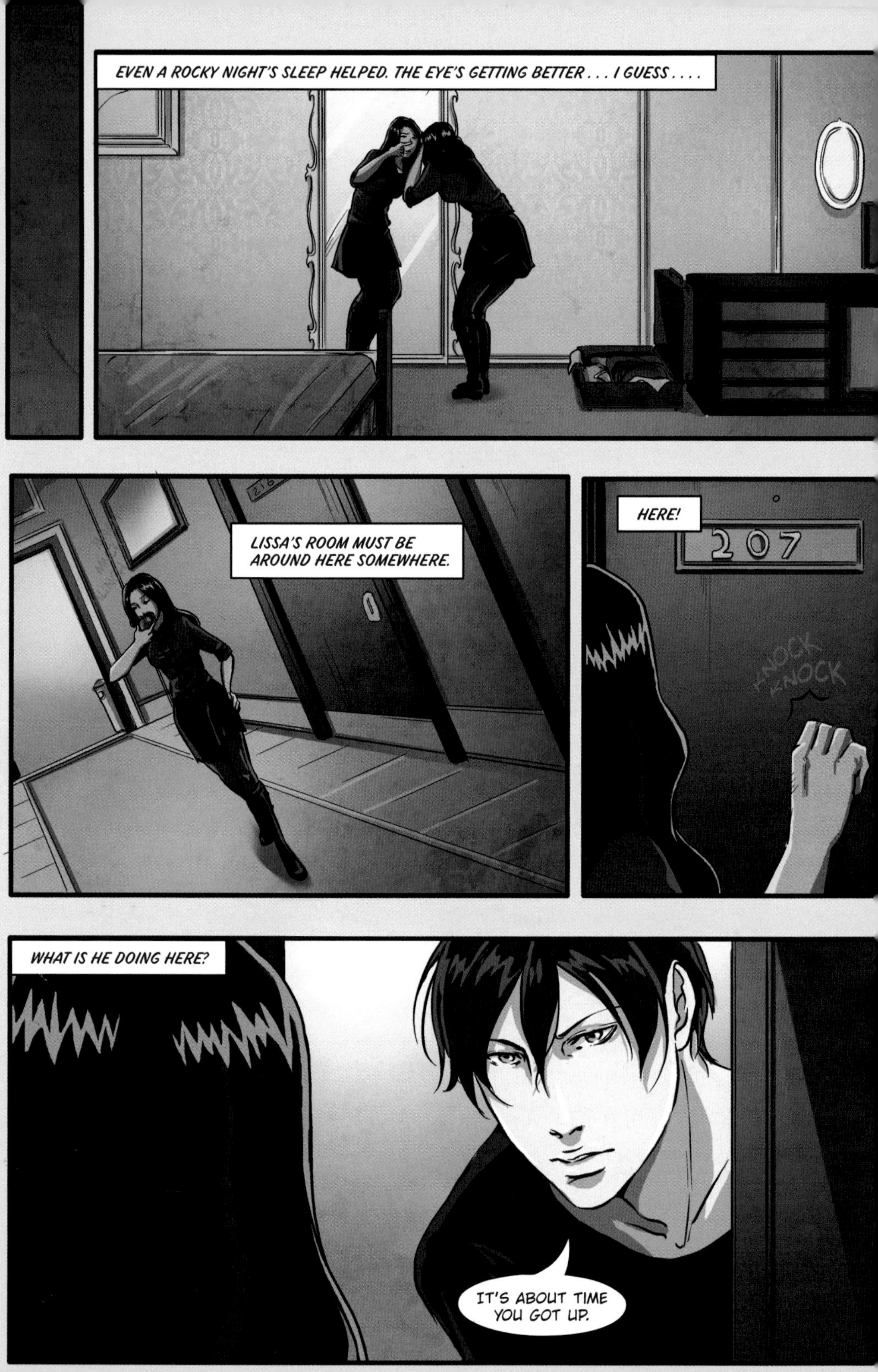
EVEN A ROCKY NIGHT'S SLEEP HELPED. THE EYE'S GETTING BETTER . . . I GUESS . . . .
LISSA'S ROOM MUST BE AROUND HERE SOMEWHERE.
HERE!
207
KNOCK KNOCK
WHAT IS HE DOING HERE?
IT'S ABOUT TIME YOU GOT UP.

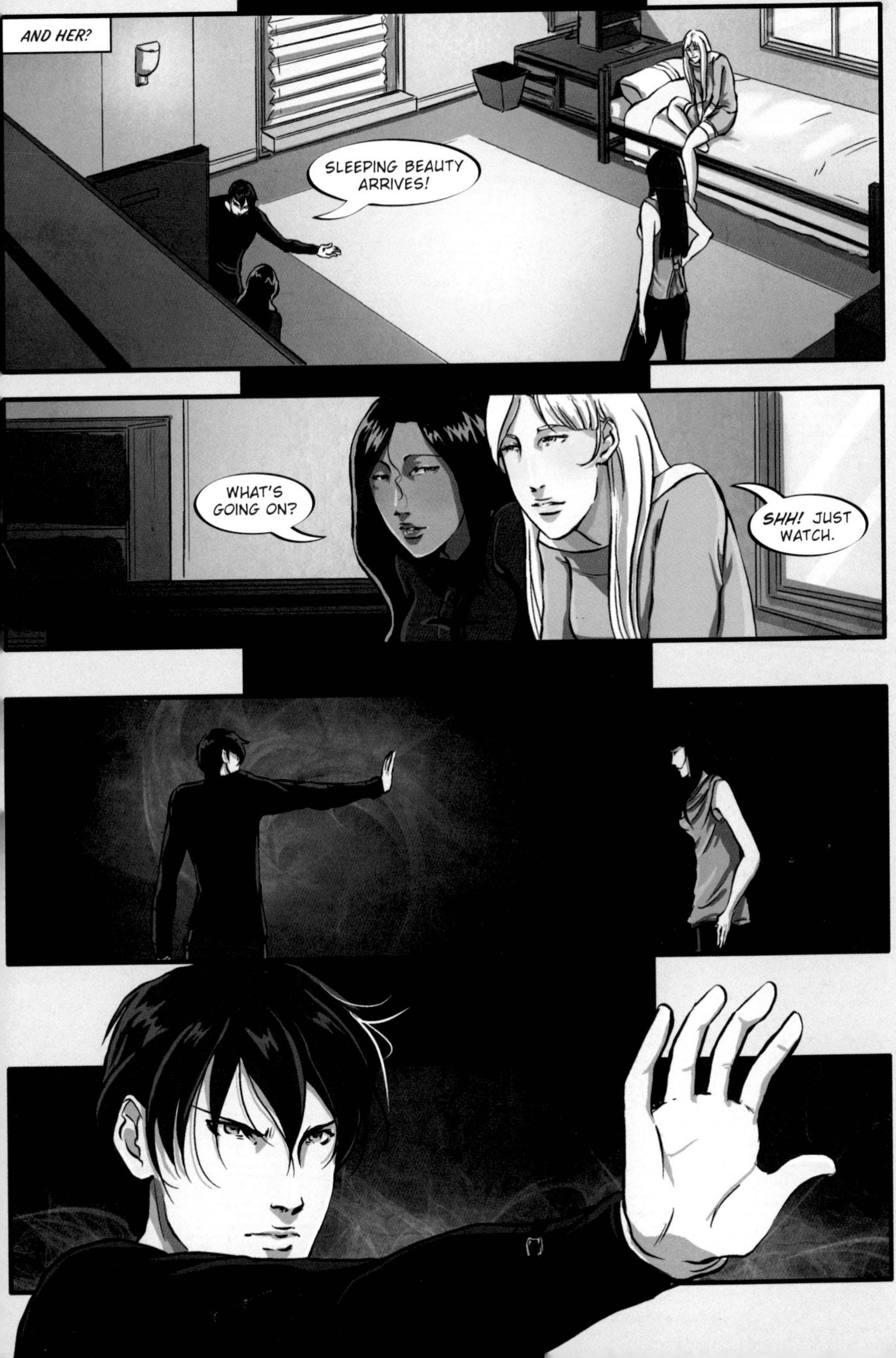
AND HER?
SLEEPING BEAUTY ARRIVES!
WHAT'S GOING ON?
SHH! JUST WATCH.

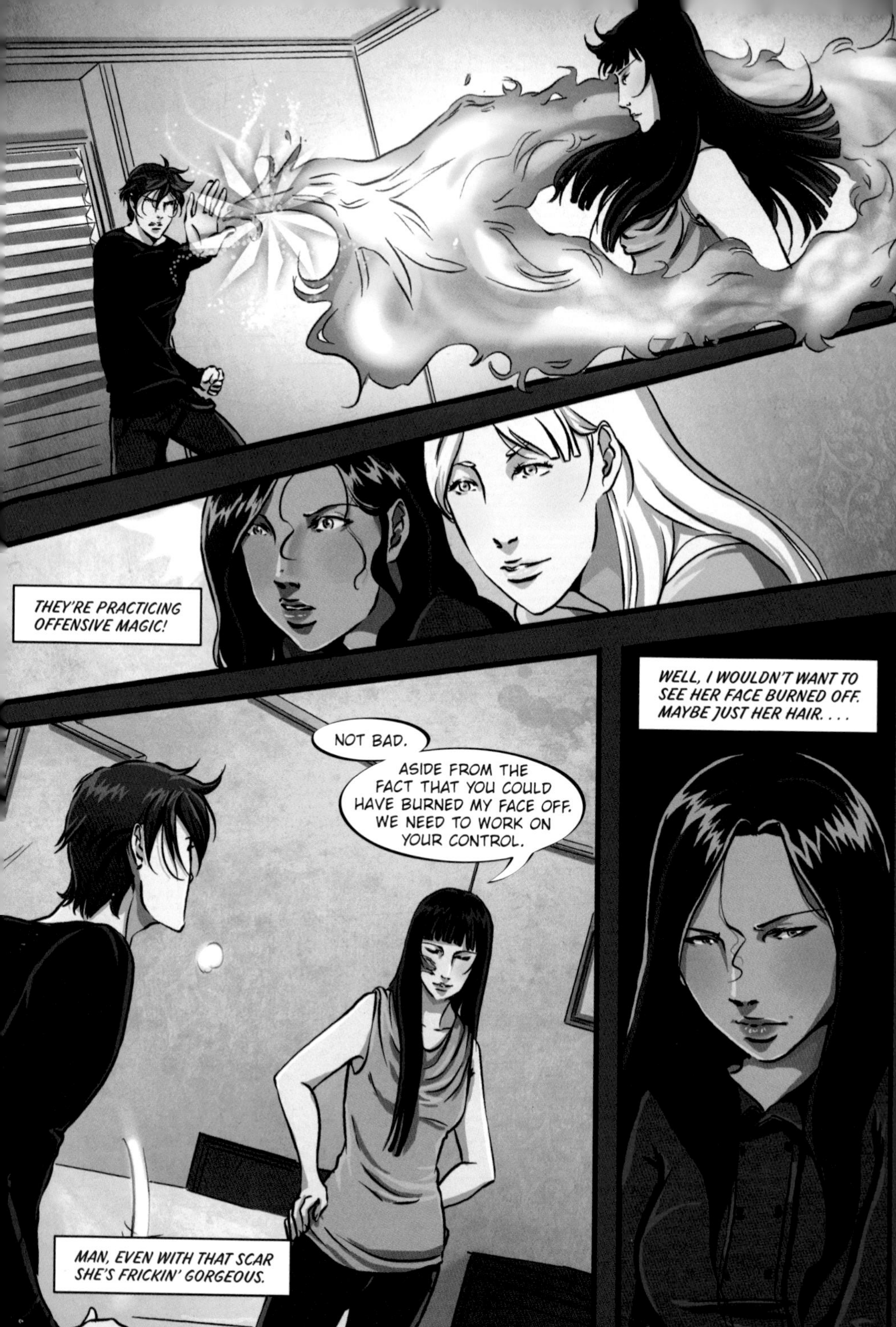
THEY'RE PRACTICING OFFENSIVE MAGIC!
NOT BAD.
ASIDE FROM THE FACT THAT YOU COULD HAVE BURNED MY FACE OFF. WE NEED TO WORK ON YOUR CONTROL.
MAN, EVEN WITH THAT SCAR SHE'S FRICKIN' GORGEOUS.
WELL, I WOULDN'T WANT TO SEE HER FACE BURNED OFF. MAYBE JUST HER HAIR. . . .

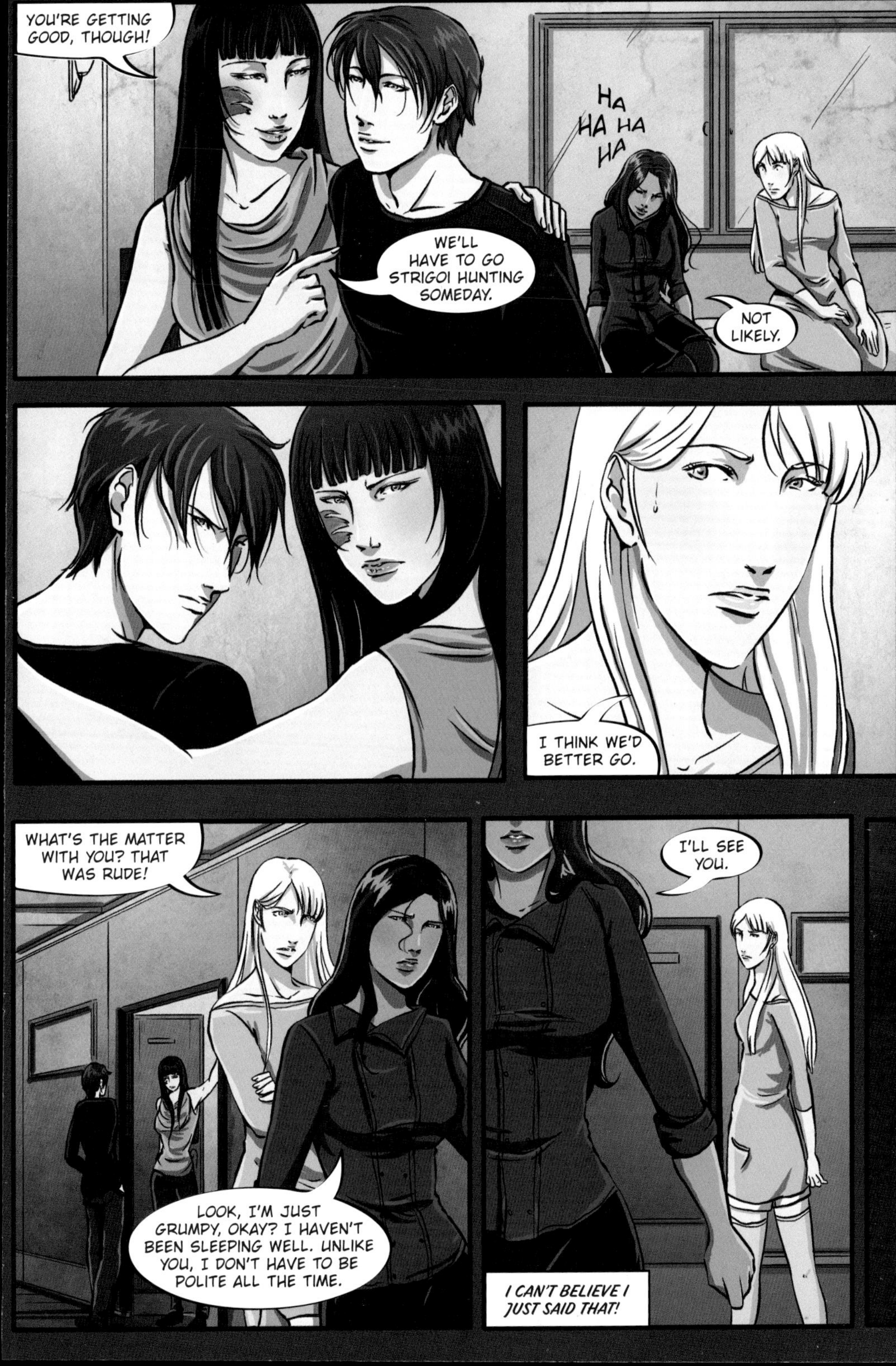
YOU'RE GETTING GOOD, THOUGH!
HA HA HA HA
WE'LL HAVE TO GO STRIGOI HUNTING SOMEDAY.
NOT LIKELY.
I THINK WE'D BETTER GO.
WHAT'S THE MATTER WITH YOU? THAT WAS RUDE!
LOOK, I'M JUST GRUMPY, OKAY? I HAVEN'T BEEN SLEEPING WELL. UNLIKE YOU, I DON'T HAVE TO BE POLITE ALL THE TIME.
I'LL SEE YOU.
I CAN'T BELIEVE I JUST SAID THAT!

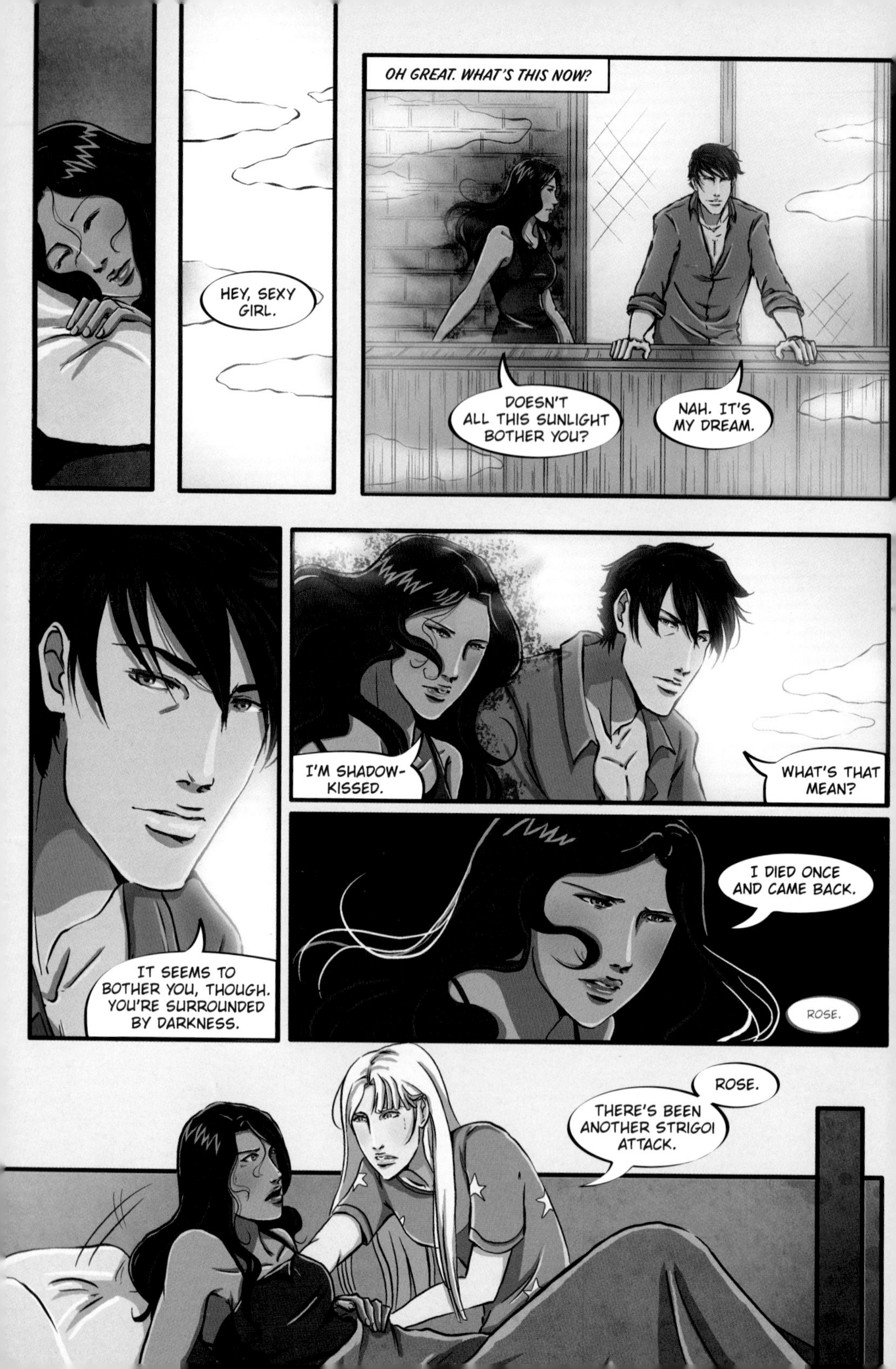
HEY, SEXY GIRL.
OH GREAT. WHAT'S THIS NOW?
DOESN'T ALL THIS SUNLIGHT BOTHER YOU?
NAH. IT'S MY DREAM.
I'M SHADOW-KISSED.
WHAT'S THAT MEAN?
IT SEEMS TO BOTHER YOU, THOUGH. YOU'RE SURROUNDED BY DARKNESS.
I DIED ONCE AND CAME BACK.
ROSE.
ROSE.
THERE'S BEEN ANOTHER STRIGOI ATTACK.

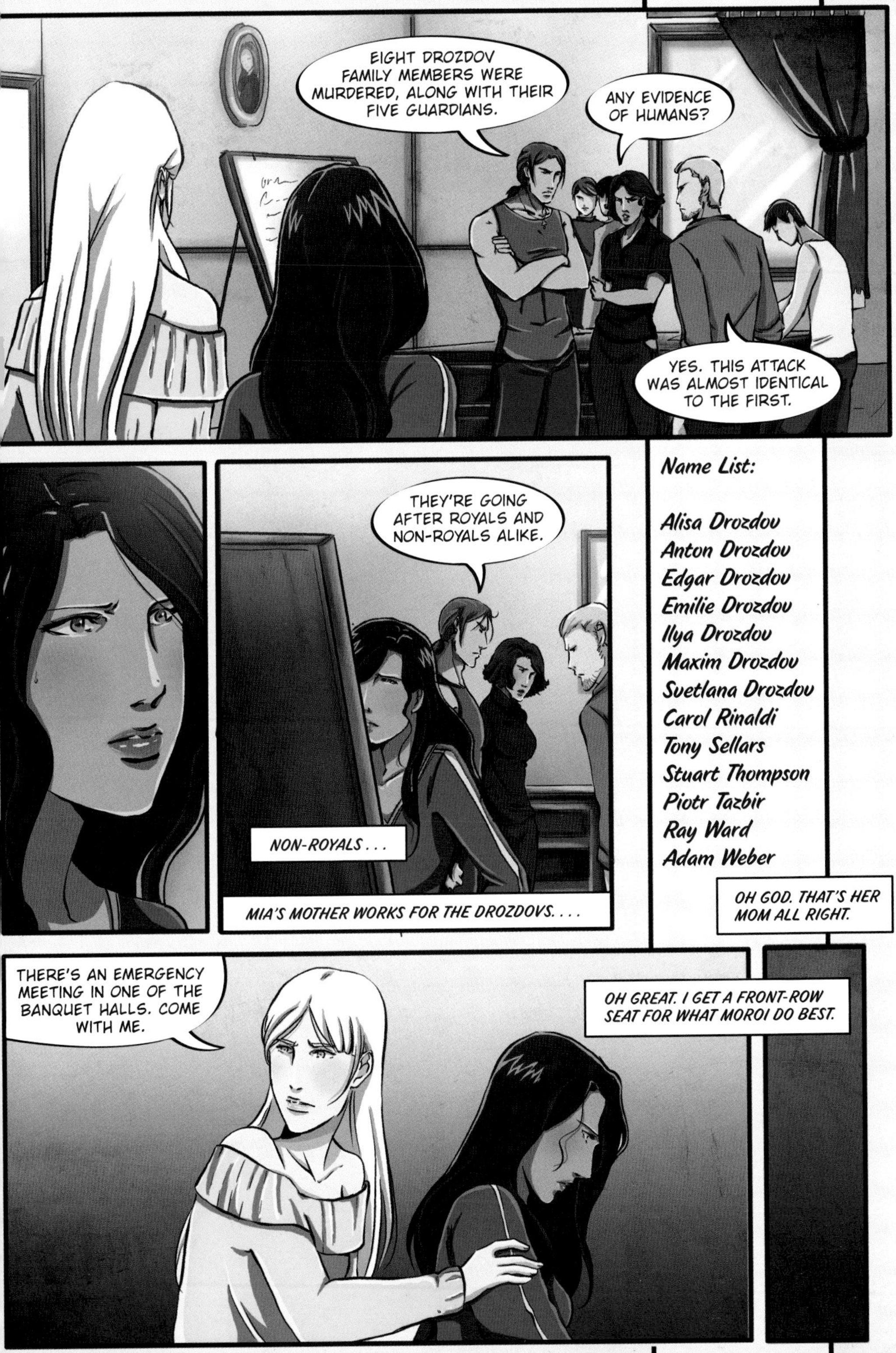
EIGHT DROZDOV FAMILY MEMBERS WERE MURDERED, ALONG WITH THEIR FIVE GUARDIANS.
ANY EVIDENCE OF HUMANS?
YES. THIS ATTACK WAS ALMOST IDENTICAL TO THE FIRST.
THEY'RE GOING AFTER ROYALS AND NON-ROYALS ALIKE.
NON-ROYALS . . .
MIA'S MOTHER WORKS FOR THE DROZDOVS. . . .
Name List:
Alisa Drozdov
Anton Drozdov
Edgar Drozdov
Emilie Drozdov
Ilya Drozdov
Maxim Drozdov
Svetlana Drozdov
Carol Rinaldi
Tony Sellars
Stuart Thompson
Piotr Tazbir
Ray Ward
Adam Weber
OH GOD. THAT'S HER MOM ALL RIGHT.
THERE'S AN EMERGENCY MEETING IN ONE OF THE BANQUET HALLS. COME WITH ME.
OH GREAT. I GET A FRONT-ROW SEAT FOR WHAT MOROI DO BEST.

TALK. AND TALK AND TALK AND TALK AND TALK AND TALK.

THE ANSWERS ARE ALL AROUND US, IN PLACES LIKE THIS LODGE AND ST. VLAD'S.

WE SHOULD ALL LIVE LIKE THIS! THERE'S SAFETY IN NUMBERS. WE COULD POOL OUR RESOURCES, OUR GUARDIANS, AND OUR MAGIC.

POOR MIA. I WOULDN'T WISH THIS ON ANYONE.

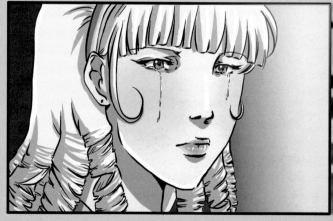

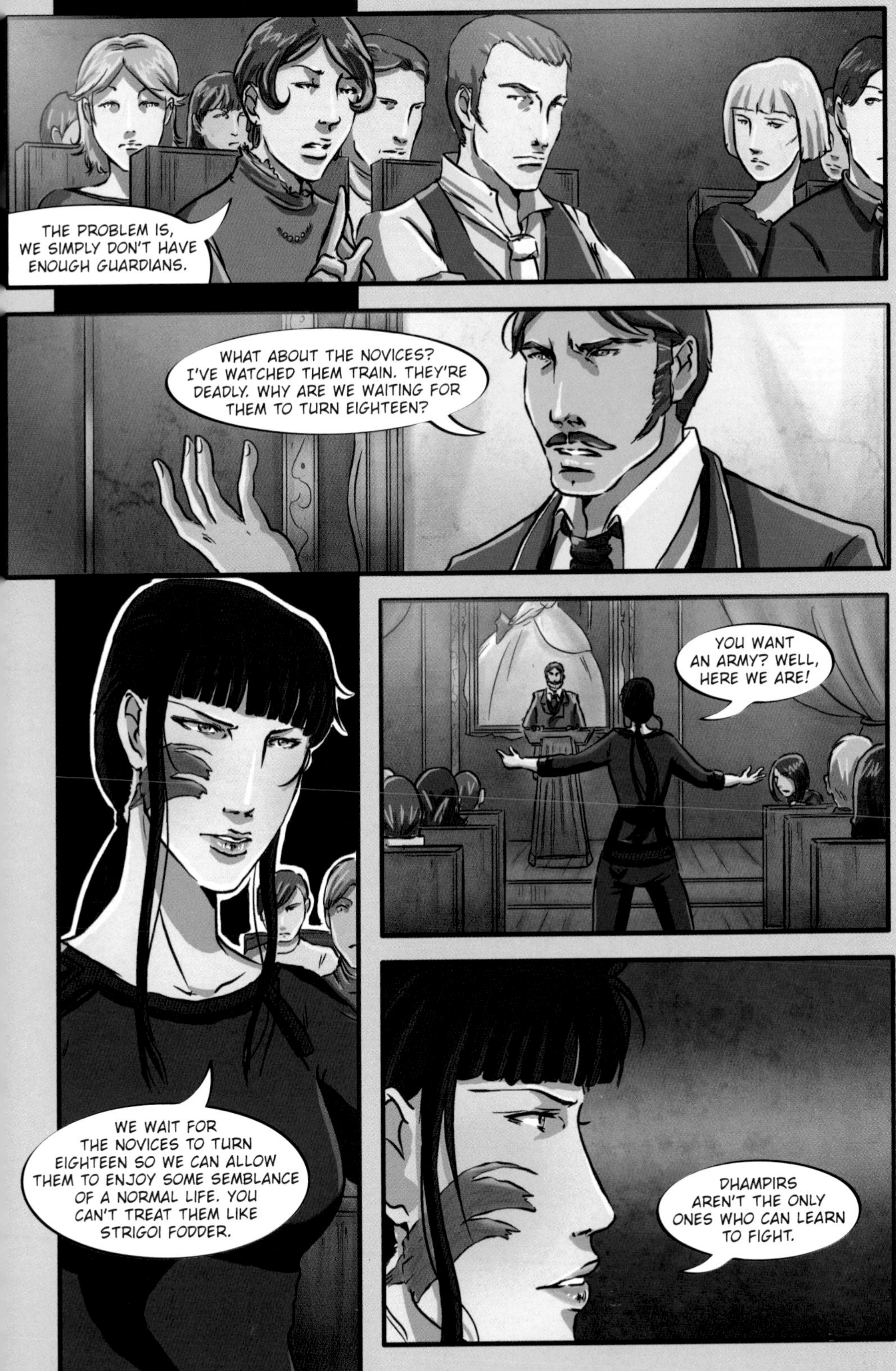
THE PROBLEM IS, WE SIMPLY DON'T HAVE ENOUGH GUARDIANS.
WHAT ABOUT THE NOVICES? I'VE WATCHED THEM TRAIN. THEY'RE DEADLY. WHY ARE WE WAITING FOR THEM TO TURN EIGHTEEN?
WE WAIT FOR THE NOVICES TO TURN EIGHTEEN SO WE CAN ALLOW THEM TO ENJOY SOME SEMBLANCE OF A NORMAL LIFE. YOU CAN'T TREAT THEM LIKE STRIGOI FODDER.
YOU WANT AN ARMY? WELL, HERE WE ARE!
DHAMPIRS AREN'T THE ONLY ONES WHO CAN LEARN TO FIGHT.

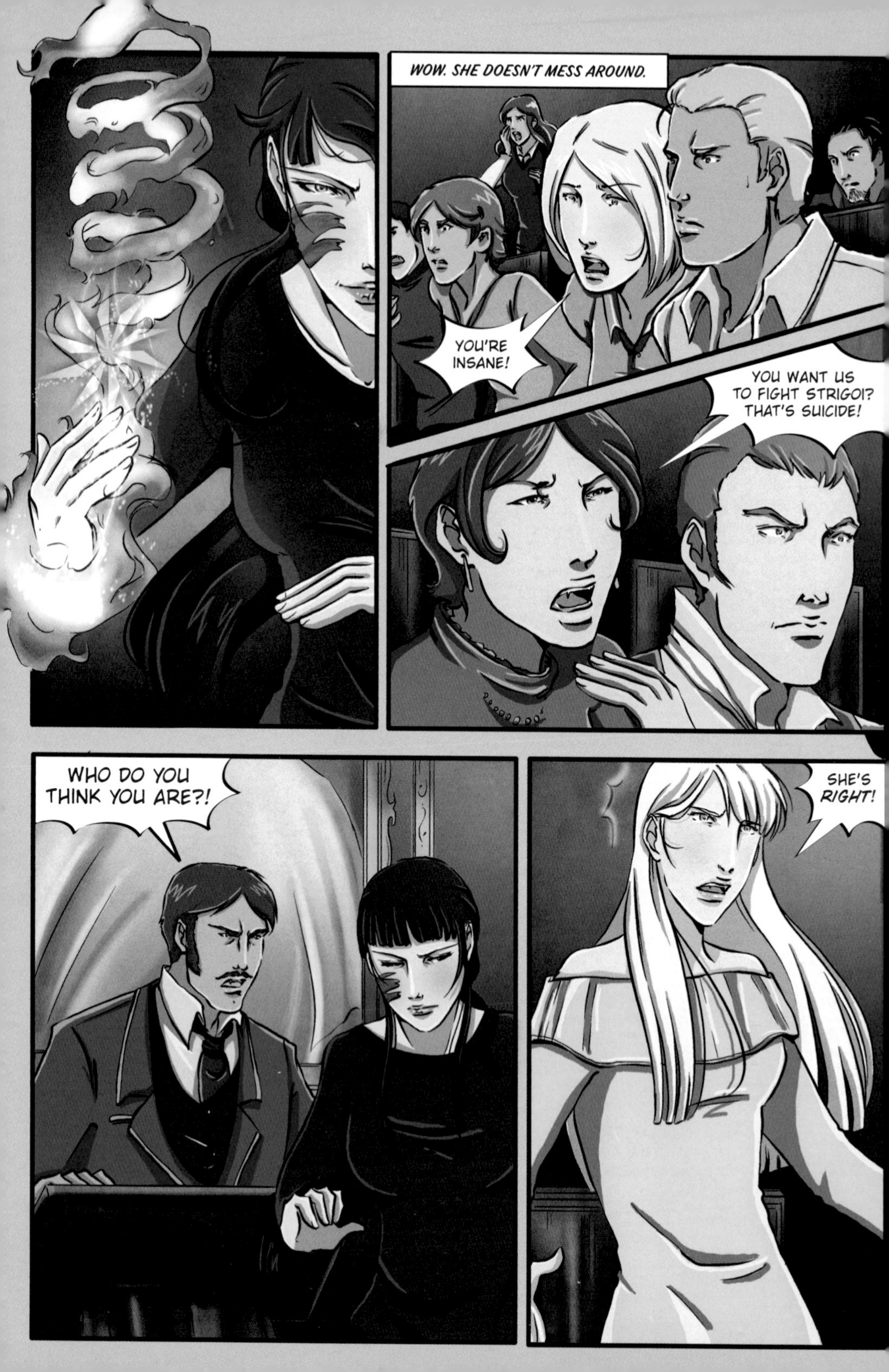
WOW. SHE DOESN'T MESS AROUND.
YOU'RE INSANE!
YOU WANT US TO FIGHT STRIGOI? THAT'S SUICIDE!
WHO DO YOU THINK YOU ARE?!
SHE'S RIGHT!

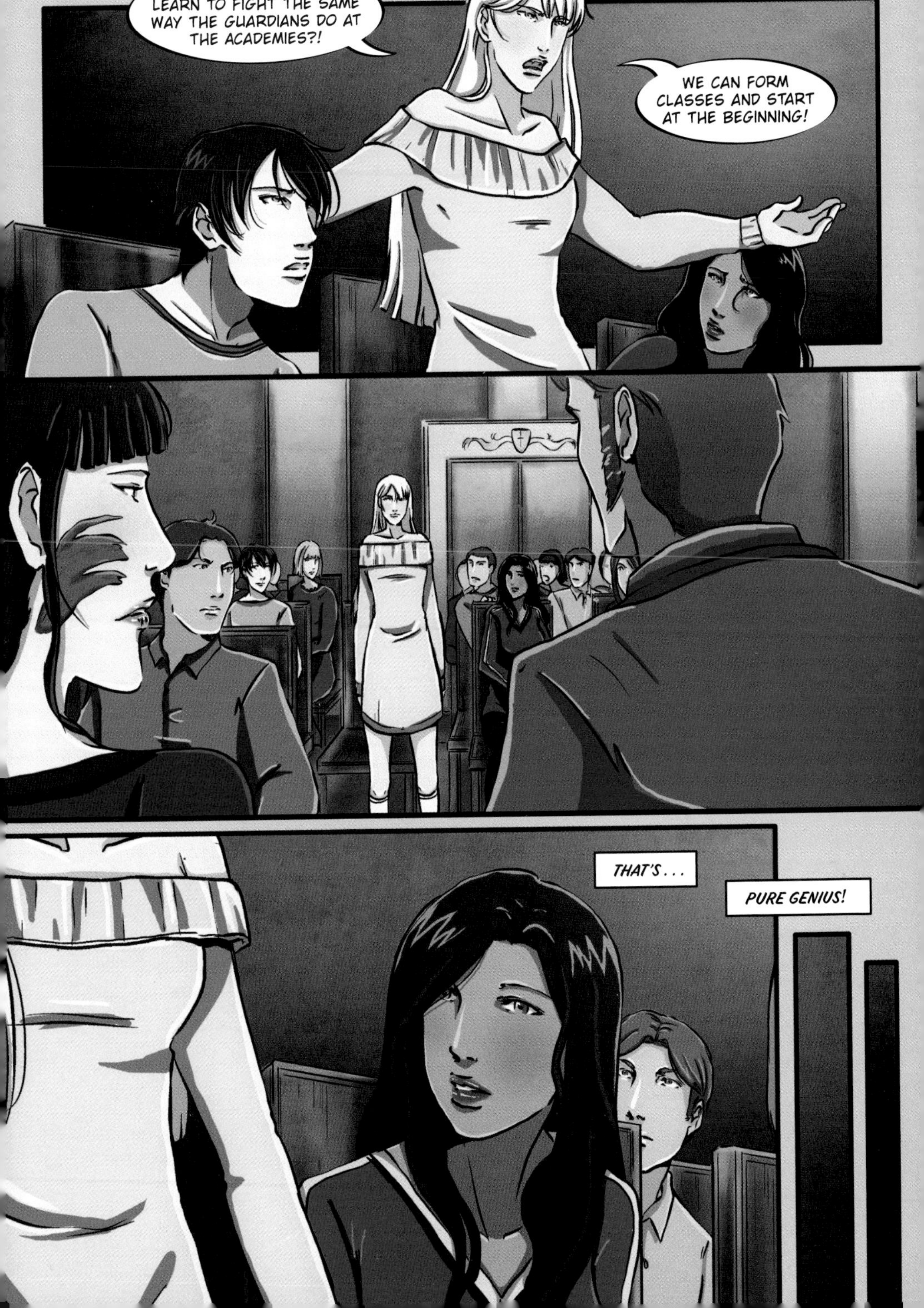
WHY CAN'T WE LEARN TO FIGHT THE SAME WAY THE GUARDIANS DO AT THE ACADEMIES?!
WE CAN FORM CLASSES AND START AT THE BEGINNING!
THAT'S . . .
PURE GENIUS!

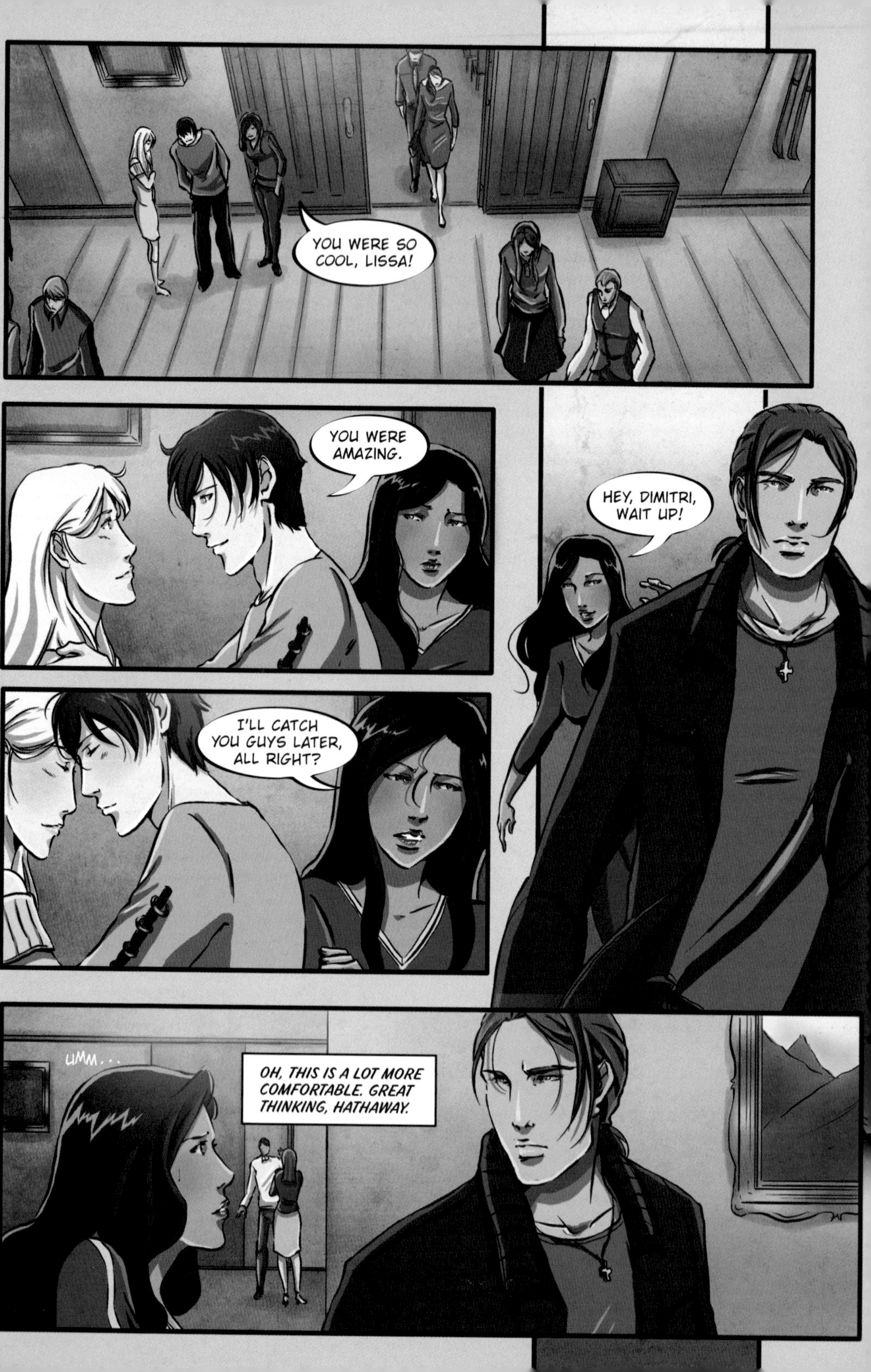
YOU WERE SO COOL, LISSA!
YOU WERE AMAZING.
I'LL CATCH YOU GUYS LATER, ALL RIGHT?
HEY, DIMITRI, WAIT UP!
UMM...
OH, THIS IS A LOT MORE COMFORTABLE. GREAT THINKING, HATHAWAY.

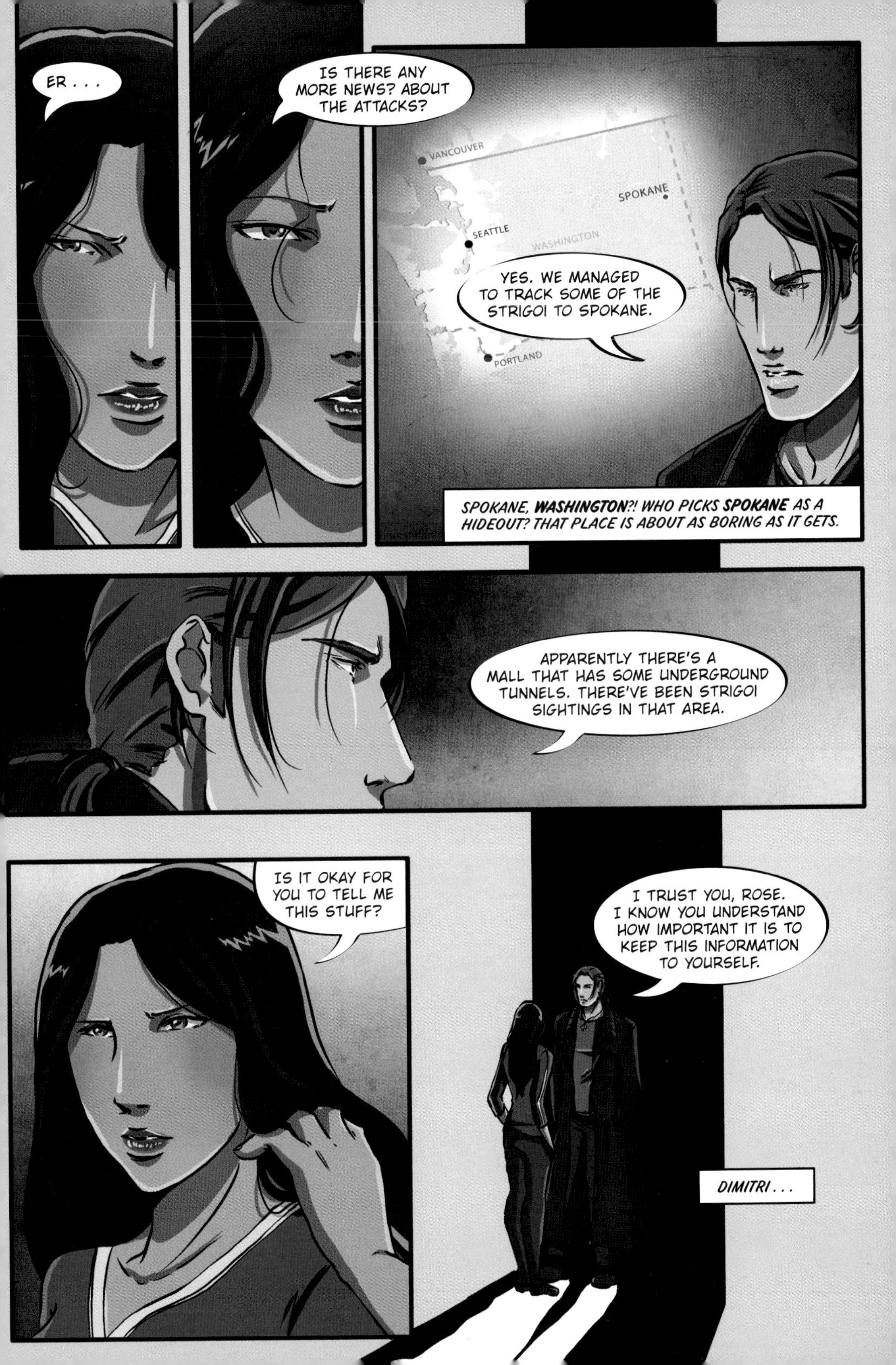
ER . . .
IS THERE ANY MORE NEWS? ABOUT THE ATTACKS?
VANCOUVER
SPOKANE
SEATTLE
WASHINGTON
PORTLAND
YES. WE MANAGED TO TRACK SOME OF THE STRIGOI TO SPOKANE.
SPOKANE, WASHINGTON?! WHO PICKS SPOKANE AS A HIDEOUT? THAT PLACE IS ABOUT AS BORING AS IT GETS.
APPARENTLY THERE'S A MALL THAT HAS SOME UNDERGROUND TUNNELS. THERE'VE BEEN STRIGOI SIGHTINGS IN THAT AREA.
IS IT OKAY FOR YOU TO TELL ME THIS STUFF?
I TRUST YOU, ROSE. I KNOW YOU UNDERSTAND HOW IMPORTANT IT IS TO KEEP THIS INFORMATION TO YOURSELF.
DIMITRI . . .

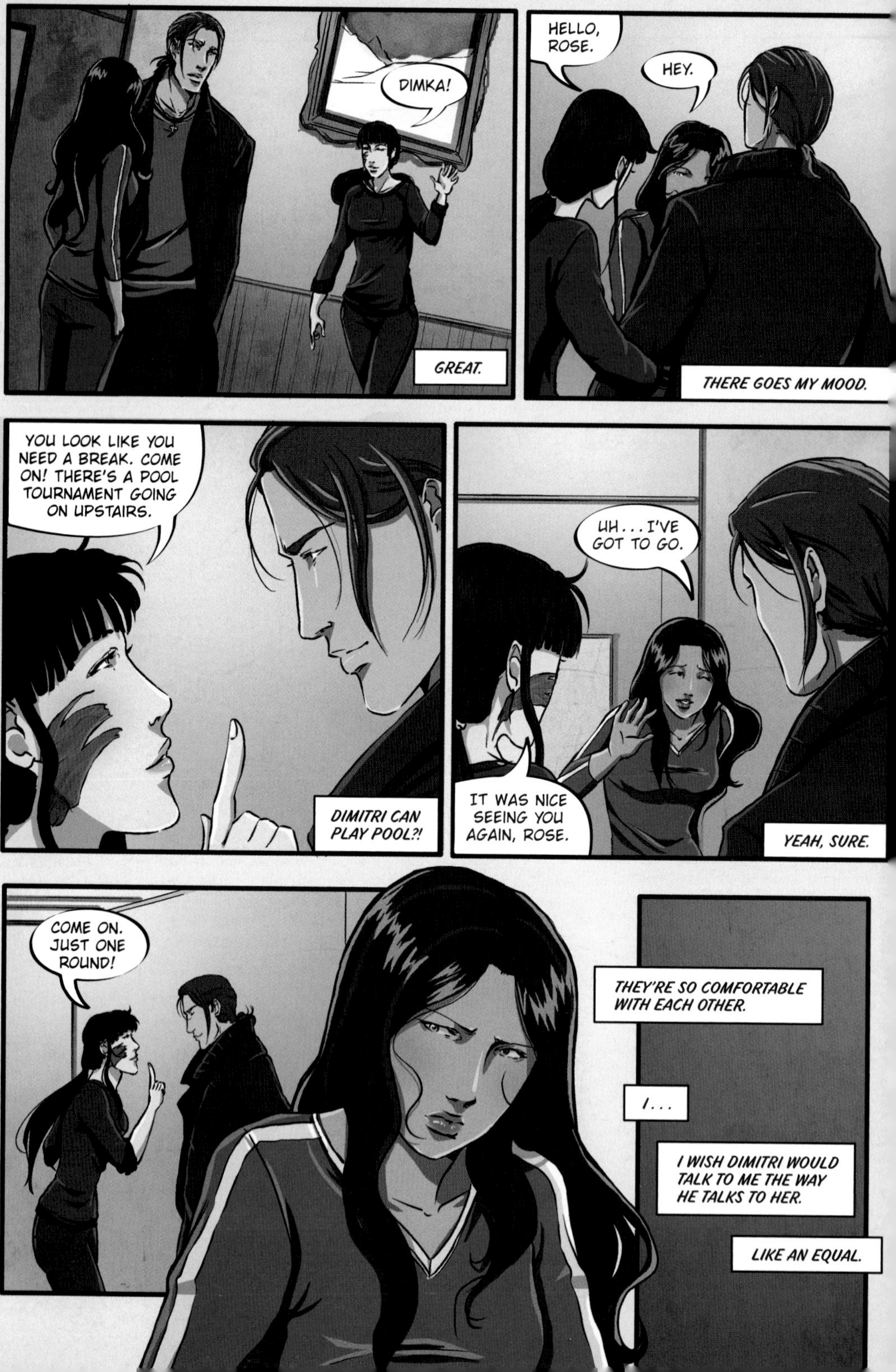
DIMKA!
GREAT.
HELLO, ROSE.
HEY.
THERE GOES MY MOOD.
YOU LOOK LIKE YOU NEED A BREAK. COME ON! THERE'S A POOL TOURNAMENT GOING ON UPSTAIRS.
DIMITRI CAN PLAY POOL?!
UH . . . I'VE GOT TO GO.
IT WAS NICE SEEING YOU AGAIN, ROSE.
YEAH, SURE.
COME ON. JUST ONE ROUND!
THEY'RE SO COMFORTABLE WITH EACH OTHER.
I . . .
I WISH DIMITRI WOULD TALK TO ME THE WAY HE TALKS TO HER.
LIKE AN EQUAL.

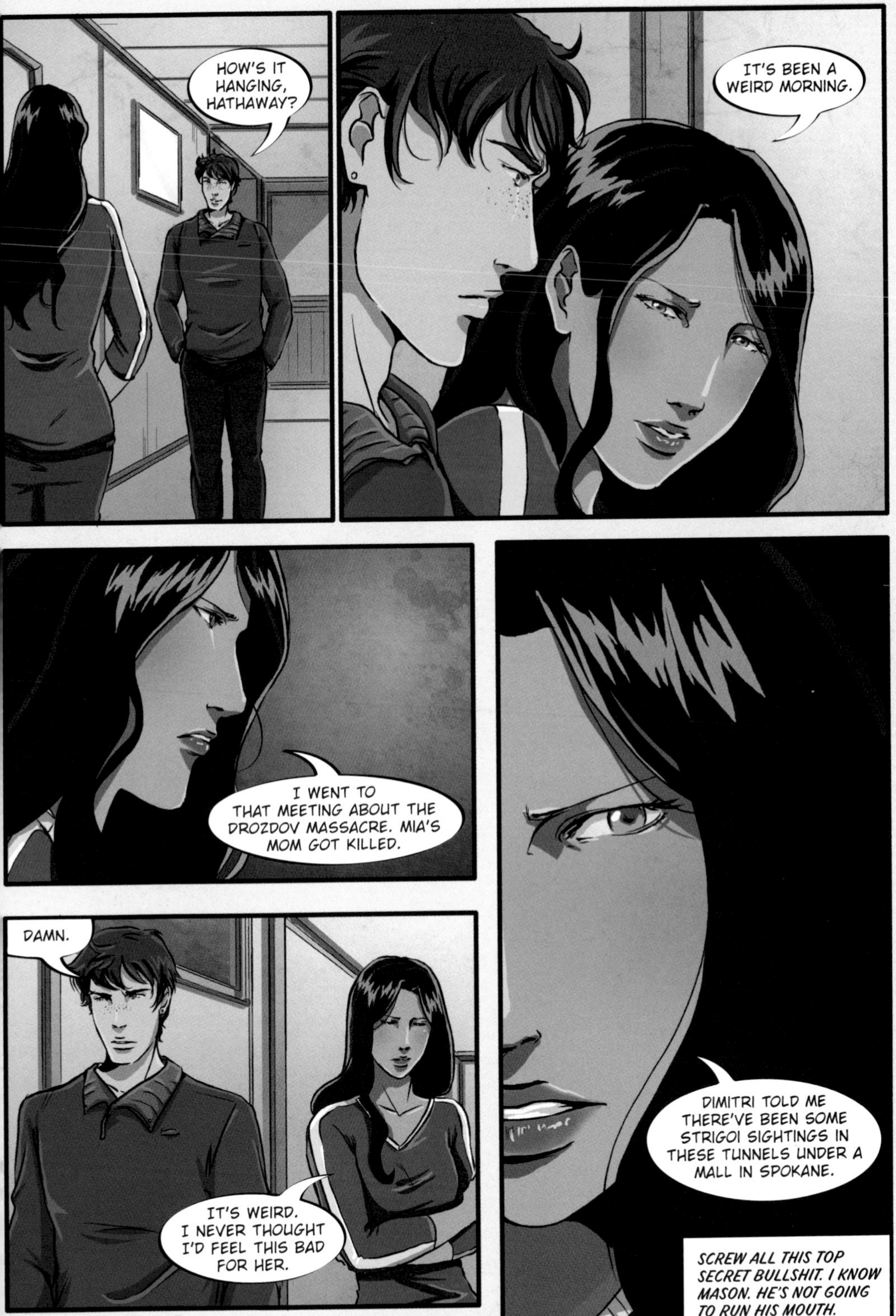
HOW'S IT HANGING, HATHAWAY?
IT'S BEEN A WEIRD MORNING.
I WENT TO THAT MEETING ABOUT THE DROZDOV MASSACRE. MIA'S MOM GOT KILLED.
DAMN.
IT'S WEIRD. I NEVER THOUGHT I'D FEEL THIS BAD FOR HER.
DIMITRI TOLD ME THERE'VE BEEN SOME STRIGOI SIGHTINGS IN THESE TUNNELS UNDER A MALL IN SPOKANE.
SCREW ALL THIS TOP SECRET BULLSHIT. I KNOW MASON. HE'S NOT GOING TO RUN HIS MOUTH.

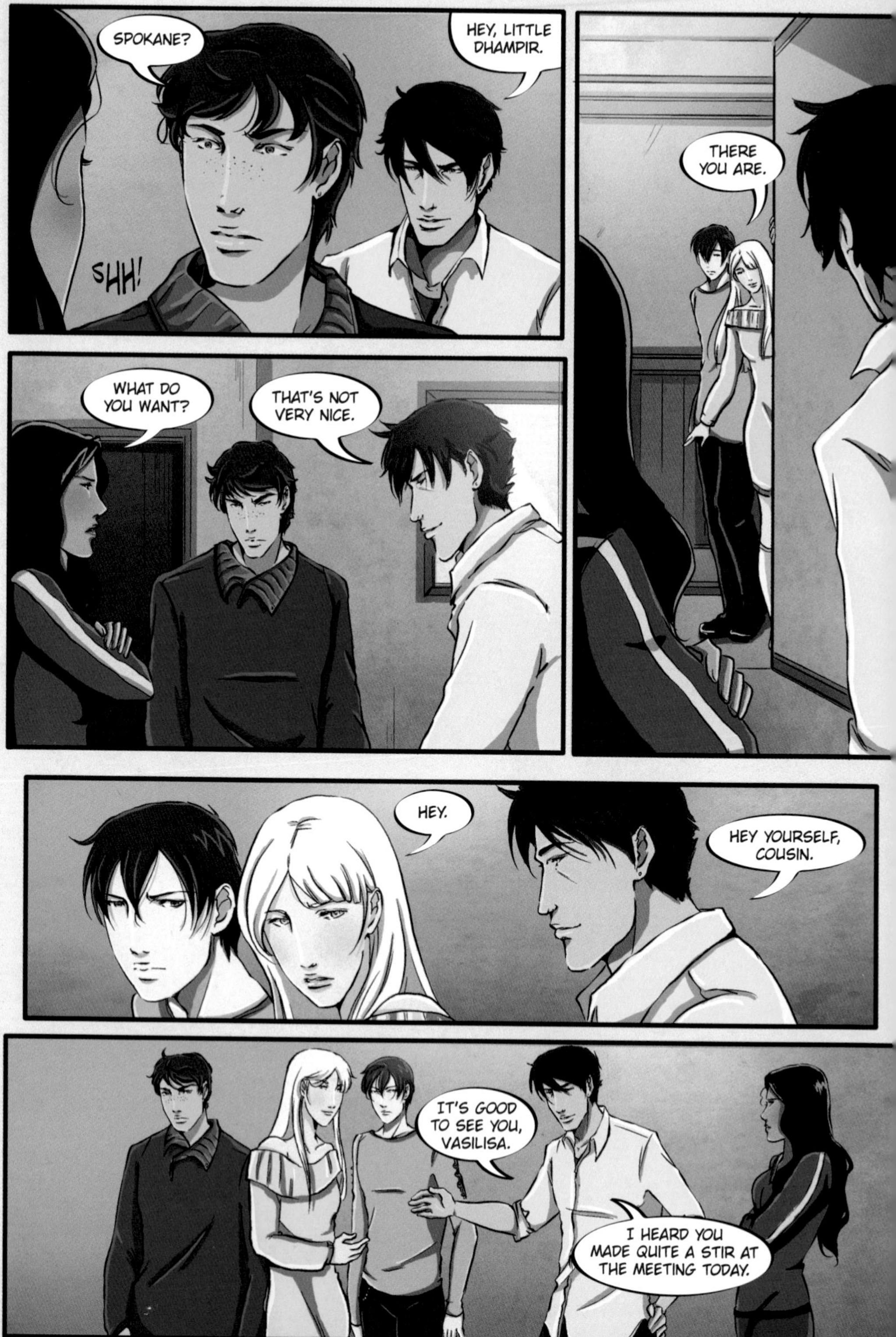
SPOKANE?
HEY, LITTLE DHAMPIR.
SHH!
WHAT DO YOU WANT?
THAT'S NOT VERY NICE.
THERE YOU ARE.
HEY.
HEY YOURSELF, COUSIN.
IT'S GOOD TO SEE YOU, VASILISA.
I HEARD YOU MADE QUITE A STIR AT THE MEETING TODAY.

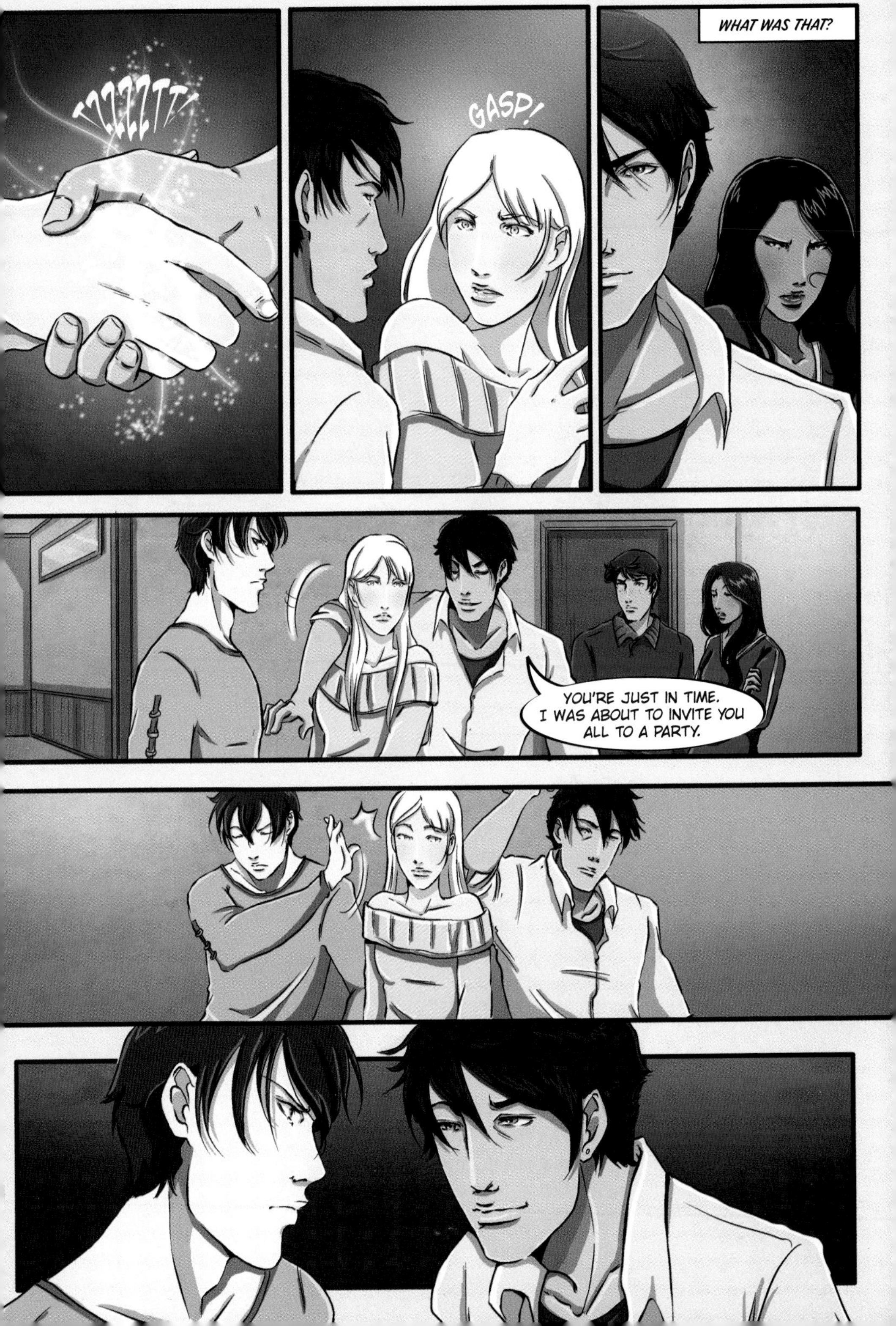
ZZZZZTT!
GASP!
WHAT WAS THAT?
YOU'RE JUST IN TIME. I WAS ABOUT TO INVITE YOU ALL TO A PARTY.

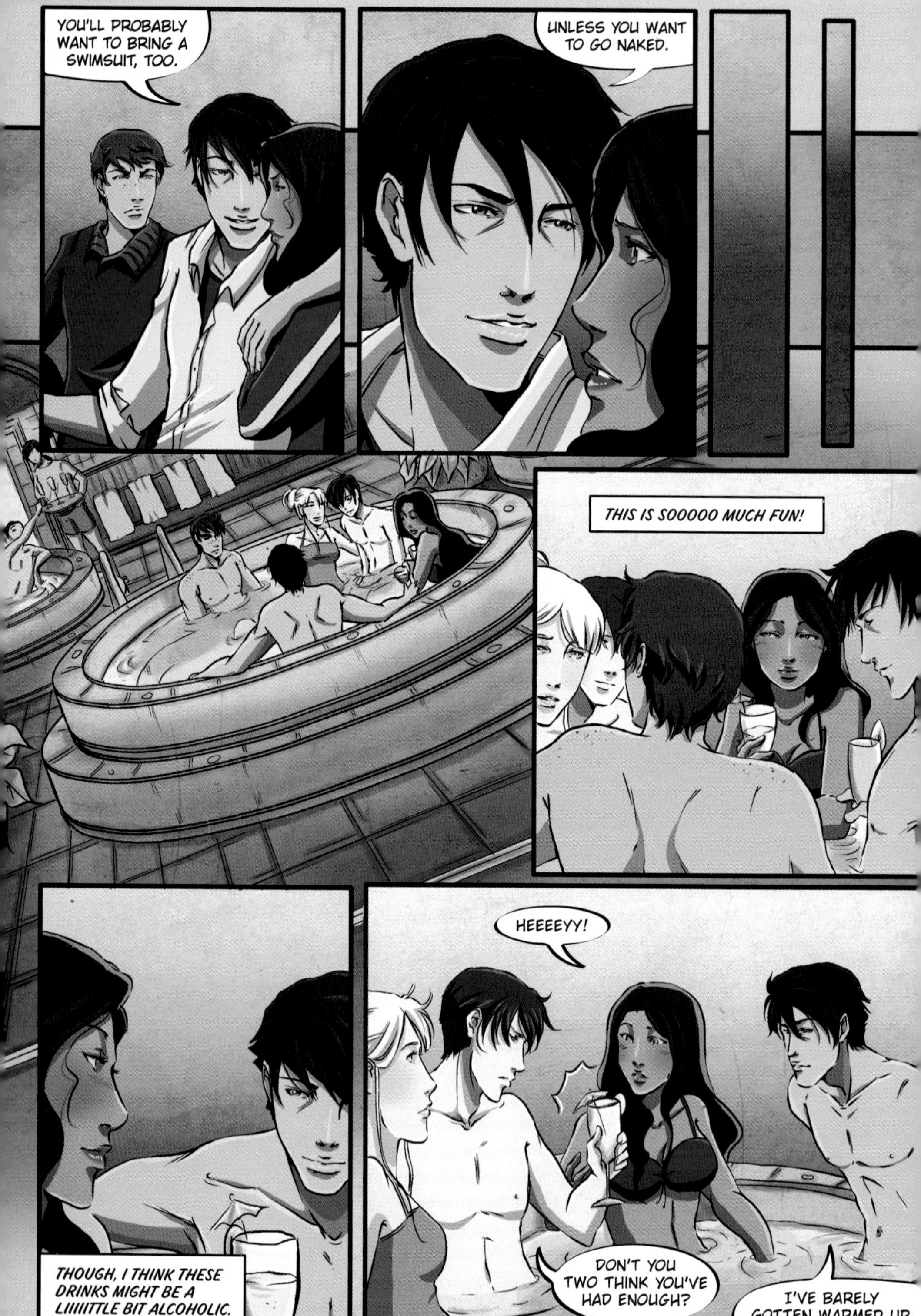
YOU'LL PROBABLY WANT TO BRING A SWIMSUIT, TOO.
UNLESS YOU WANT TO GO NAKED.
THIS IS SOOOOO MUCH FUN!
THOUGH, I THINK THESE DRINKS MIGHT BE A LIIIIITTLE BIT ALCOHOLIC.
HEEEEYY!
DON'T YOU TWO THINK YOU'VE HAD ENOUGH?
I'VE BARELY GOTTEN WARMED UP.

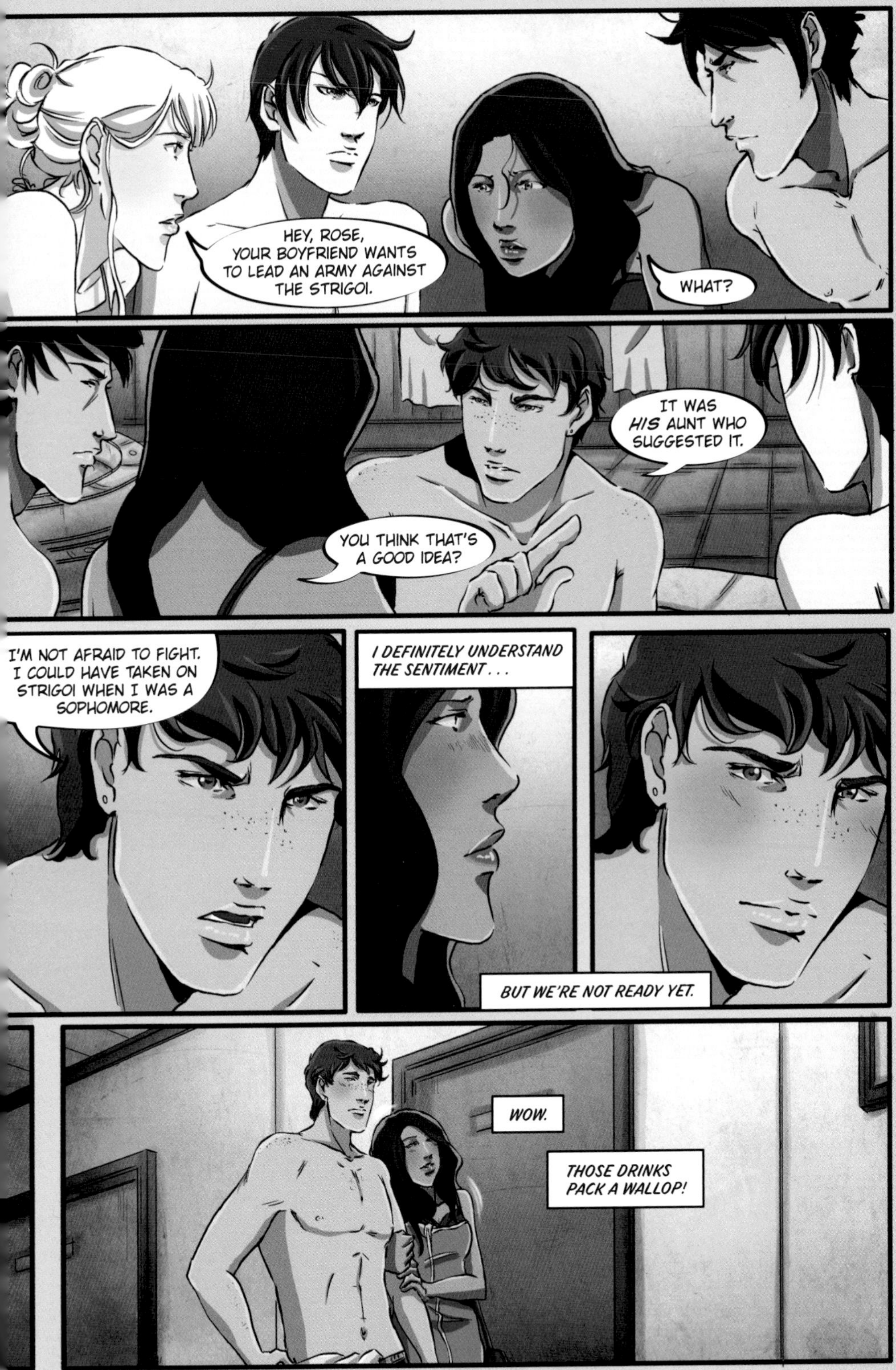
HEY, ROSE, YOUR BOYFRIEND WANTS TO LEAD AN ARMY AGAINST THE STRIGOI.
WHAT?
IT WAS HIS AUNT WHO SUGGESTED IT.
YOU THINK THAT'S A GOOD IDEA?
I'M NOT AFRAID TO FIGHT. I COULD HAVE TAKEN ON STRIGOI WHEN I WAS A SOPHOMORE.
I DEFINITELY UNDERSTAND THE SENTIMENT . . .
BUT WE'RE NOT READY YET.
WOW.
THOSE DRINKS PACK A WALLOP!

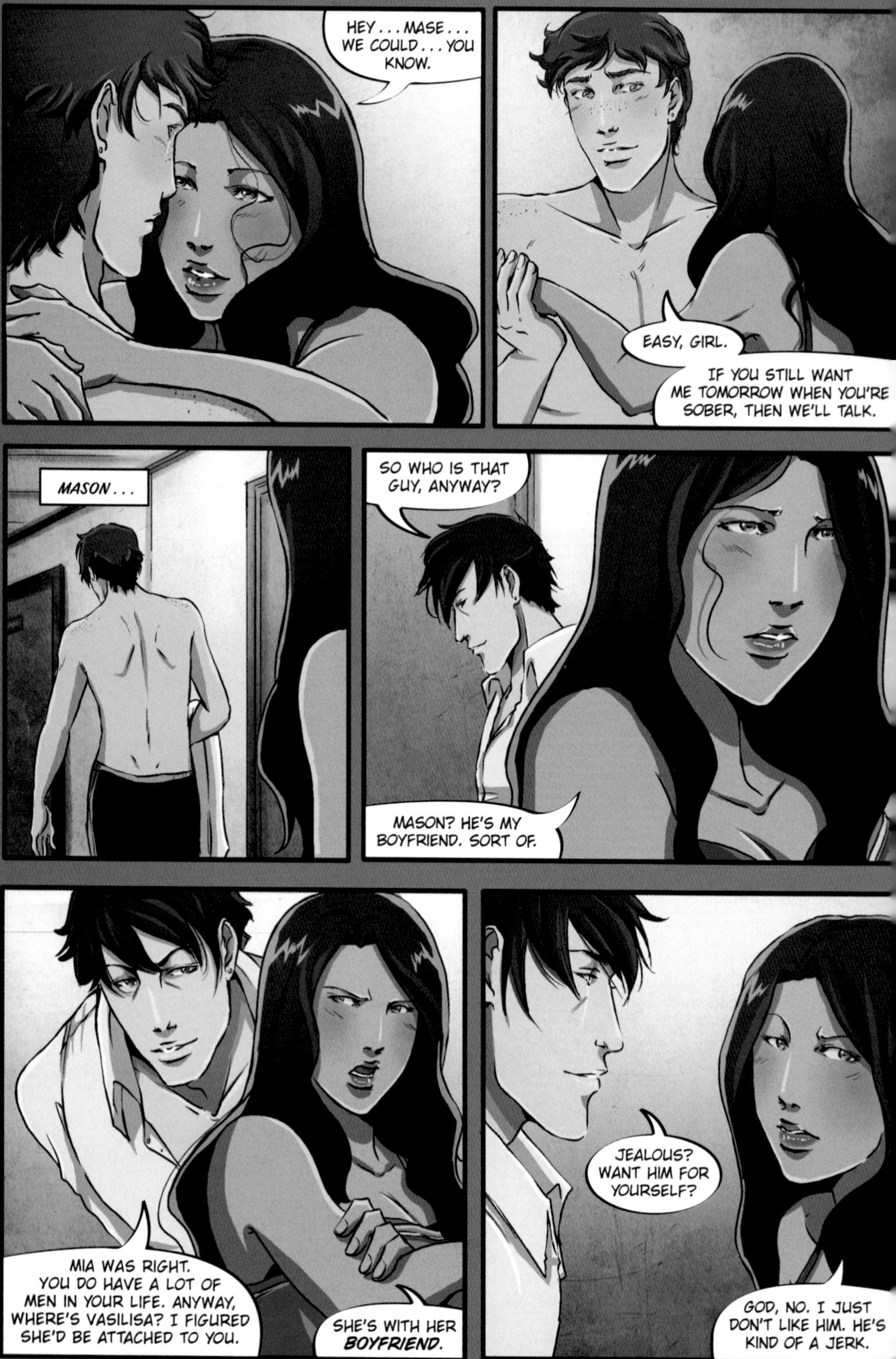
HEY . . . MASE . . . WE COULD . . . YOU KNOW.
EASY, GIRL.
IF YOU STILL WANT ME TOMORROW WHEN YOU'RE SOBER, THEN WE'LL TALK.
MASON . . .
SO WHO IS THAT GUY, ANYWAY?
MASON? HE'S MY BOYFRIEND. SORT OF.
MIA WAS RIGHT. YOU DO HAVE A LOT OF MEN IN YOUR LIFE. ANYWAY, WHERE'S VASILISA? I FIGURED SHE'D BE ATTACHED TO YOU.
SHE'S WITH HER *BOYFRIEND*.
JEALOUS? WANT HIM FOR YOURSELF?
GOD, NO. I JUST DON'T LIKE HIM. HE'S KIND OF A JERK.

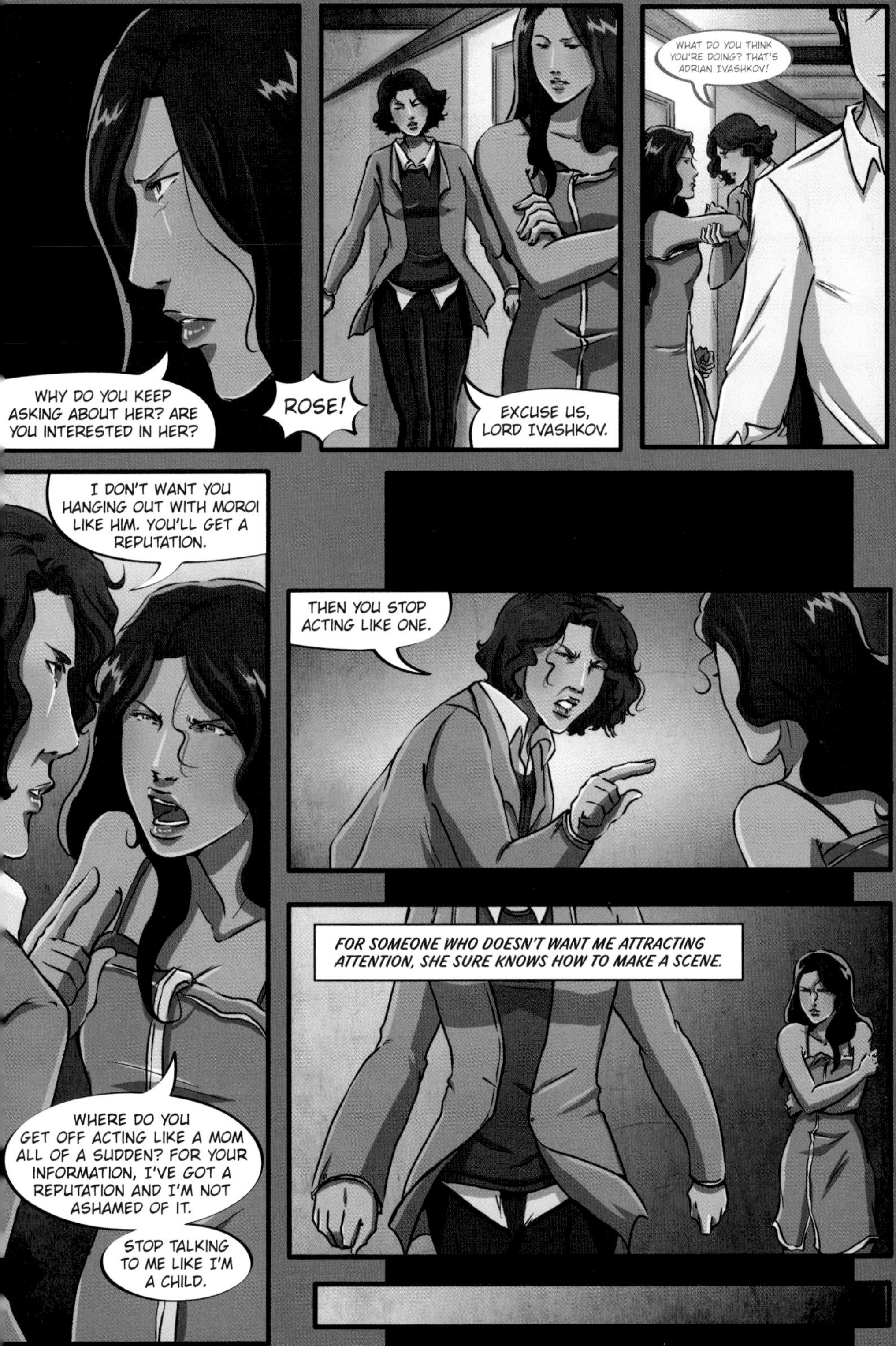
WHY DO YOU KEEP ASKING ABOUT HER? ARE YOU INTERESTED IN HER?
ROSE!
EXCUSE US, LORD IVASHKOV.
WHAT DO YOU THINK YOU'RE DOING? THAT'S ADRIAN IVASHKOV!
I DON'T WANT YOU HANGING OUT WITH MOROI LIKE HIM. YOU'LL GET A REPUTATION.
WHERE DO YOU GET OFF ACTING LIKE A MOM ALL OF A SUDDEN? FOR YOUR INFORMATION, I'VE GOT A REPUTATION AND I'M NOT ASHAMED OF IT.
STOP TALKING TO ME LIKE I'M A CHILD.
THEN YOU STOP ACTING LIKE ONE.
FOR SOMEONE WHO DOESN'T WANT ME ATTRACTING ATTENTION, SHE SURE KNOWS HOW TO MAKE A SCENE.

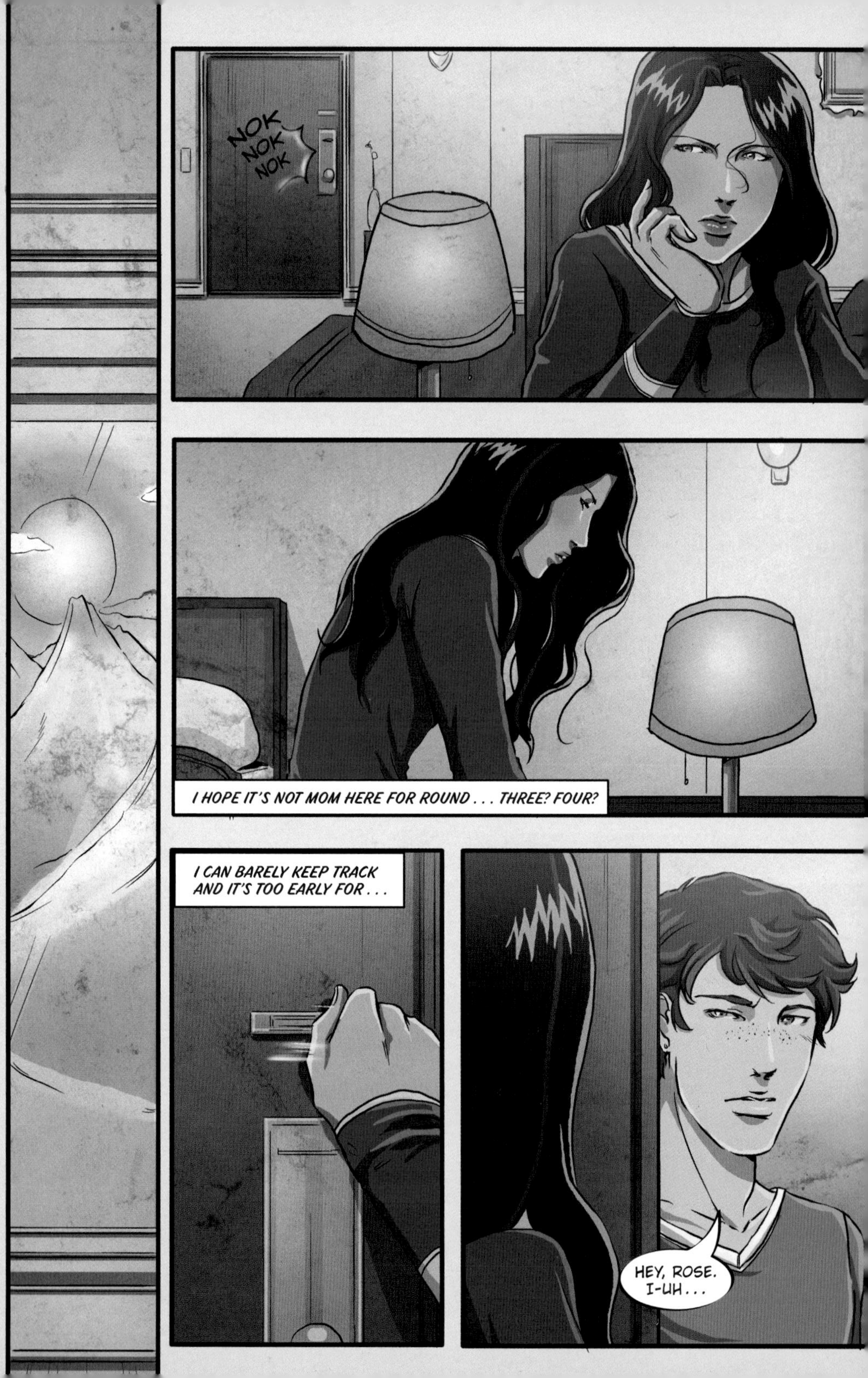

NOK NOK NOK
I HOPE IT'S NOT MOM HERE FOR ROUND . . . THREE? FOUR?
I CAN BARELY KEEP TRACK AND IT'S TOO EARLY FOR . . .
HEY, ROSE. I-UH . . .

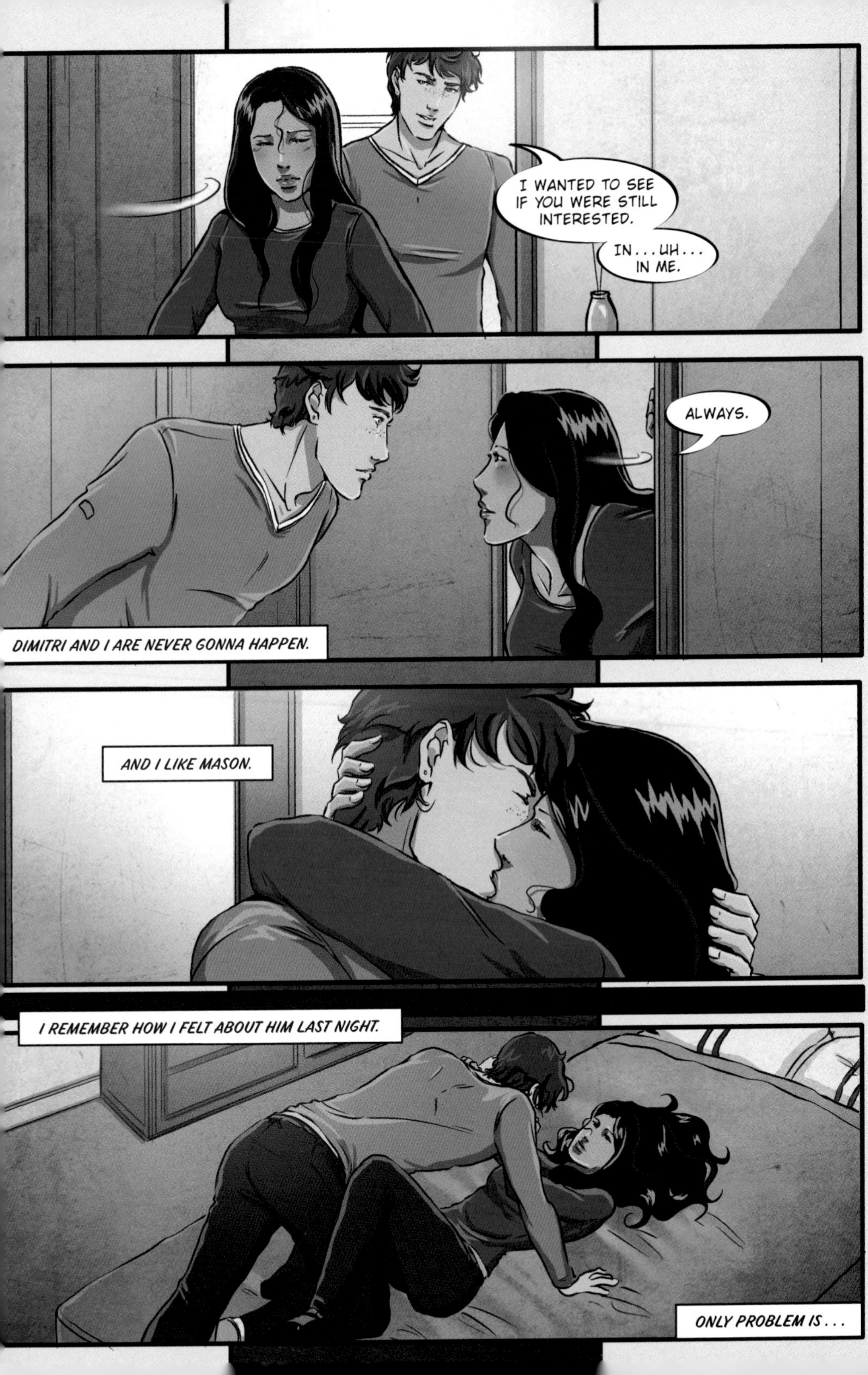
I WANTED TO SEE IF YOU WERE STILL INTERESTED.
IN . . . UH . . . IN ME.
ALWAYS.
DIMITRI AND I ARE NEVER GONNA HAPPEN.
AND I LIKE MASON.
I REMEMBER HOW I FELT ABOUT HIM LAST NIGHT.
ONLY PROBLEM IS . . .

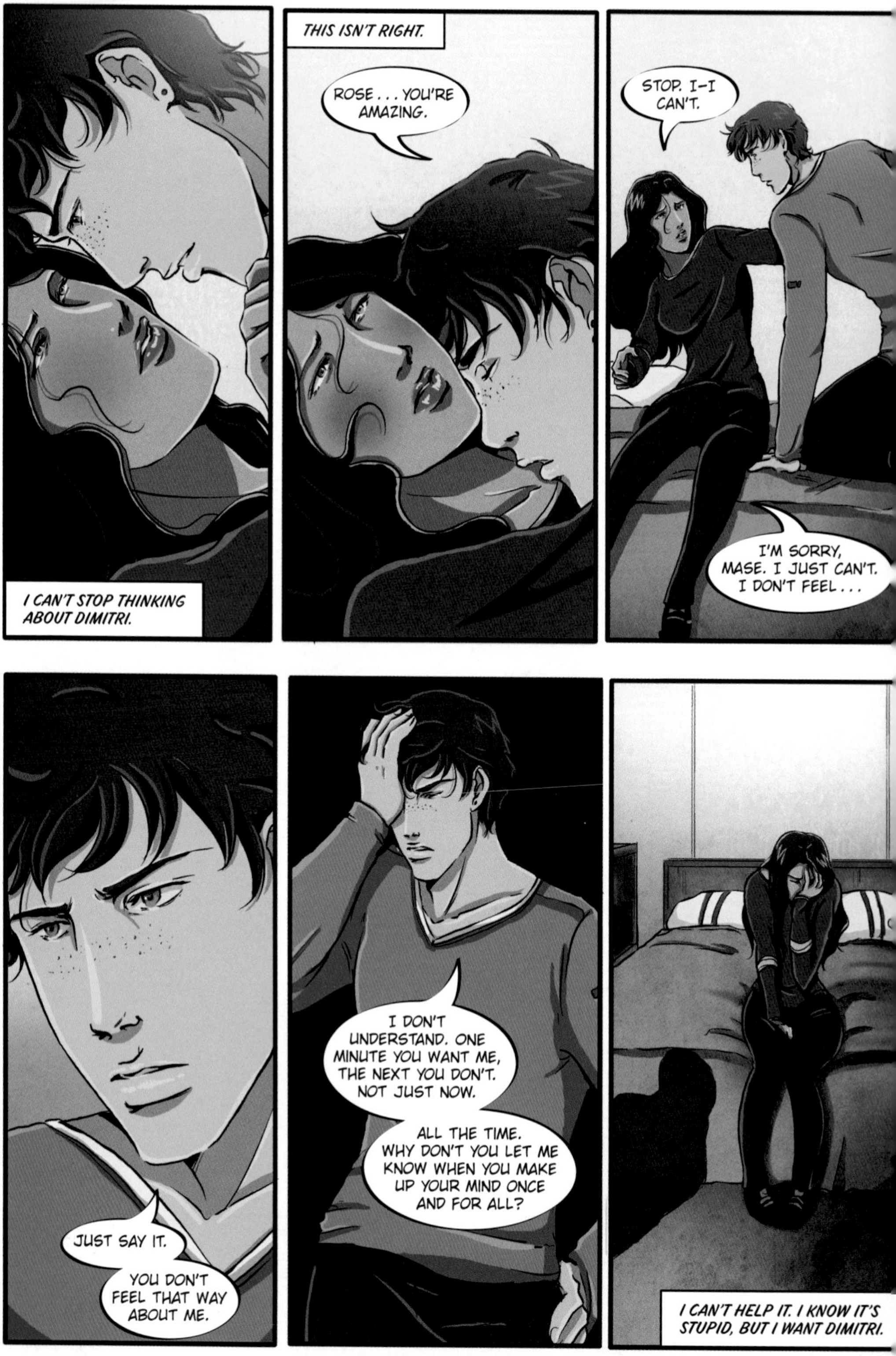
I CAN'T STOP THINKING ABOUT DIMITRI.
THIS ISN'T RIGHT.
ROSE . . . YOU'RE AMAZING.
STOP. I–I CAN'T.
I'M SORRY, MASE. I JUST CAN'T. I DON'T FEEL . . .
JUST SAY IT.
YOU DON'T FEEL THAT WAY ABOUT ME.
I DON'T UNDERSTAND. ONE MINUTE YOU WANT ME, THE NEXT YOU DON'T. NOT JUST NOW.
ALL THE TIME. WHY DON'T YOU LET ME KNOW WHEN YOU MAKE UP YOUR MIND ONCE AND FOR ALL?
I CAN'T HELP IT. I KNOW IT'S STUPID, BUT I WANT DIMITRI.

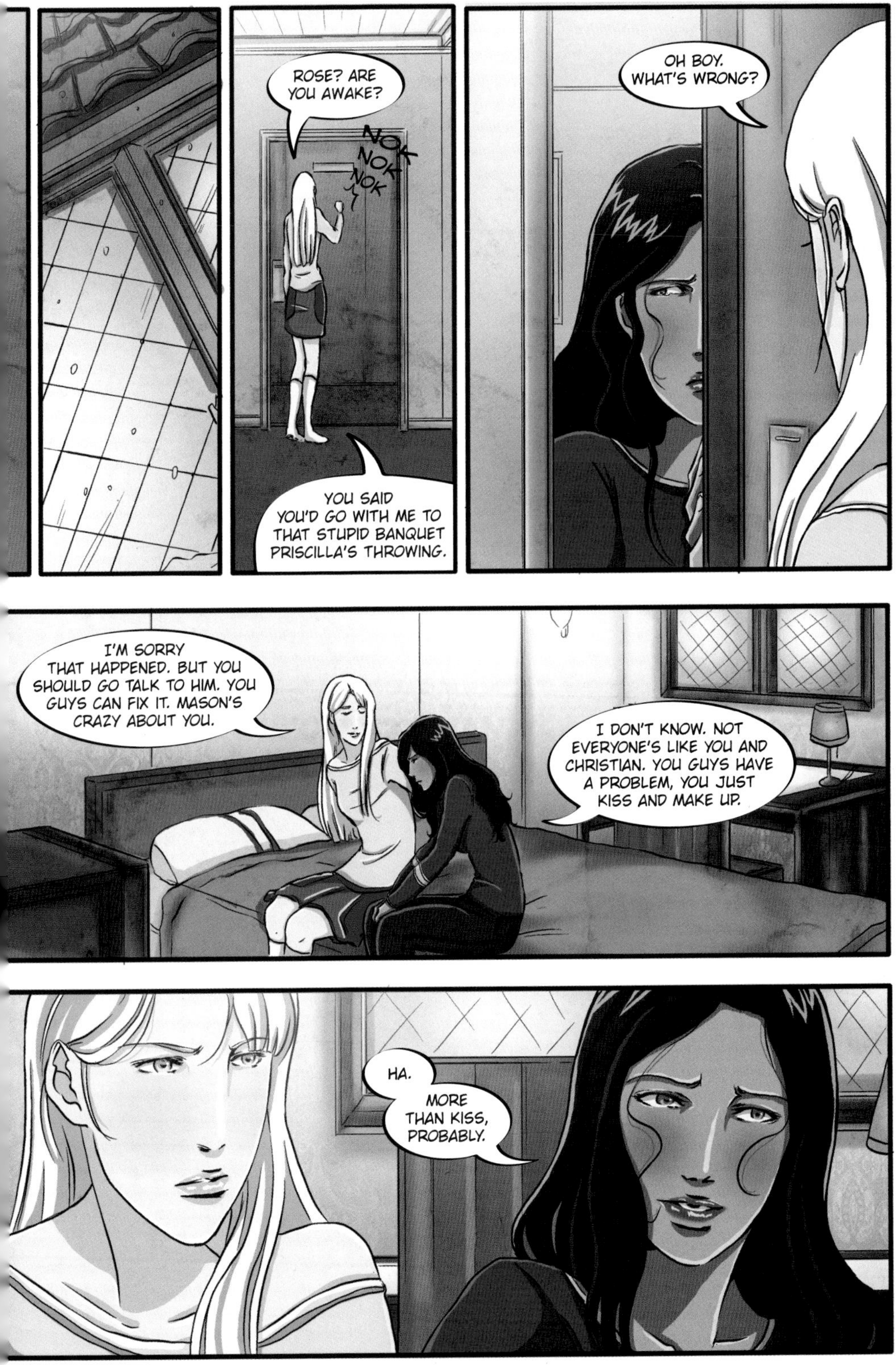
ROSE? ARE YOU AWAKE?
NOK NOK NOK
YOU SAID YOU'D GO WITH ME TO THAT STUPID BANQUET PRISCILLA'S THROWING.
OH BOY. WHAT'S WRONG?
I'M SORRY THAT HAPPENED. BUT YOU SHOULD GO TALK TO HIM. YOU GUYS CAN FIX IT. MASON'S CRAZY ABOUT YOU.
I DON'T KNOW. NOT EVERYONE'S LIKE YOU AND CHRISTIAN. YOU GUYS HAVE A PROBLEM, YOU JUST KISS AND MAKE UP.
HA.
MORE THAN KISS, PROBABLY.

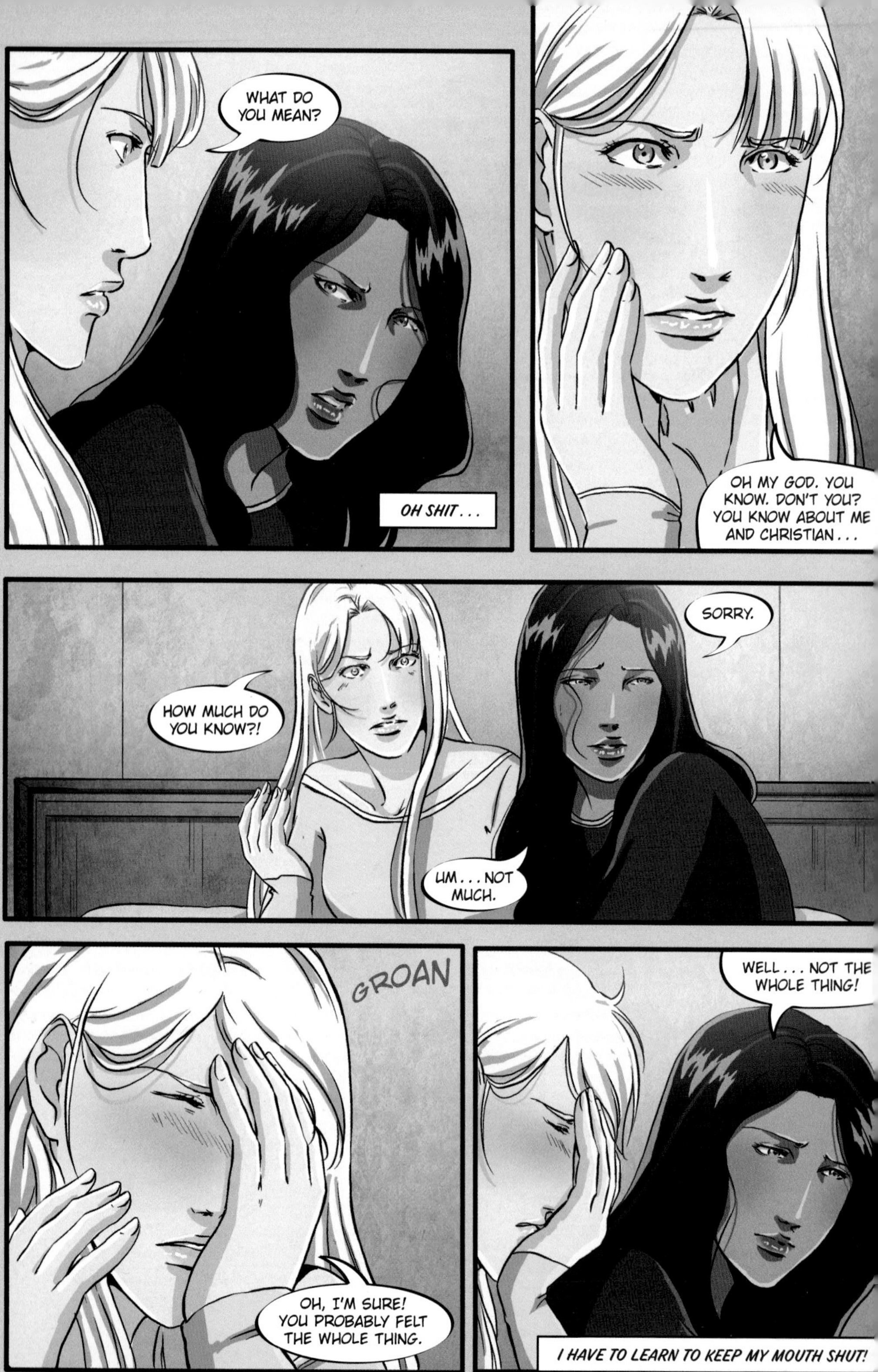
WHAT DO YOU MEAN?
OH SHIT . . .
OH MY GOD. YOU KNOW. DON'T YOU? YOU KNOW ABOUT ME AND CHRISTIAN . . .
SORRY.
HOW MUCH DO YOU KNOW?!
UM . . . NOT MUCH.
GROAN
OH, I'M SURE! YOU PROBABLY FELT THE WHOLE THING.
WELL . . . NOT THE WHOLE THING!
I HAVE TO LEARN TO KEEP MY MOUTH SHUT!

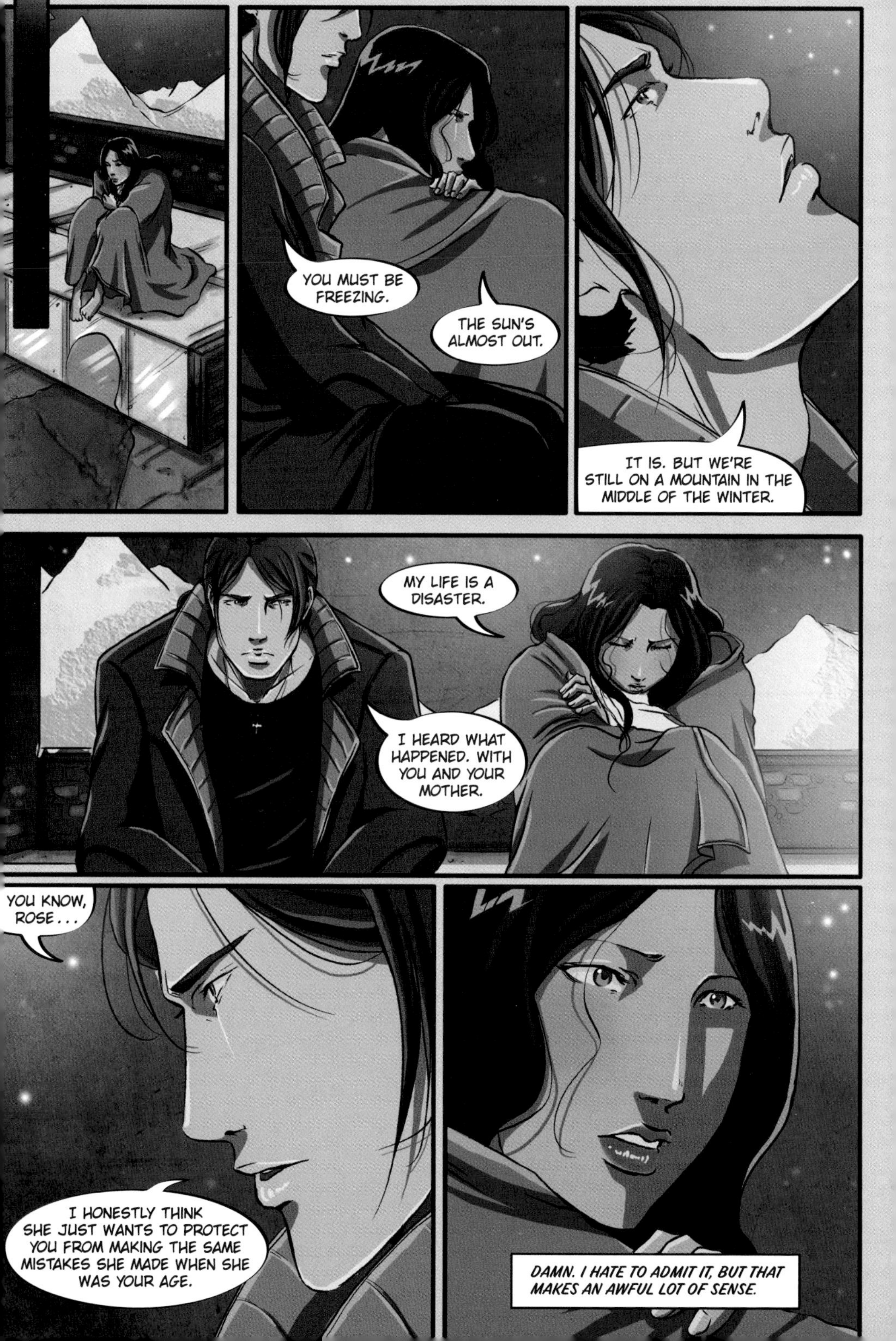
YOU MUST BE FREEZING.
THE SUN'S ALMOST OUT.
IT IS. BUT WE'RE STILL ON A MOUNTAIN IN THE MIDDLE OF THE WINTER.
MY LIFE IS A DISASTER.
I HEARD WHAT HAPPENED. WITH YOU AND YOUR MOTHER.
YOU KNOW, ROSE . . .
I HONESTLY THINK SHE JUST WANTS TO PROTECT YOU FROM MAKING THE SAME MISTAKES SHE MADE WHEN SHE WAS YOUR AGE.
DAMN. I HATE TO ADMIT IT, BUT THAT MAKES AN AWFUL LOT OF SENSE.

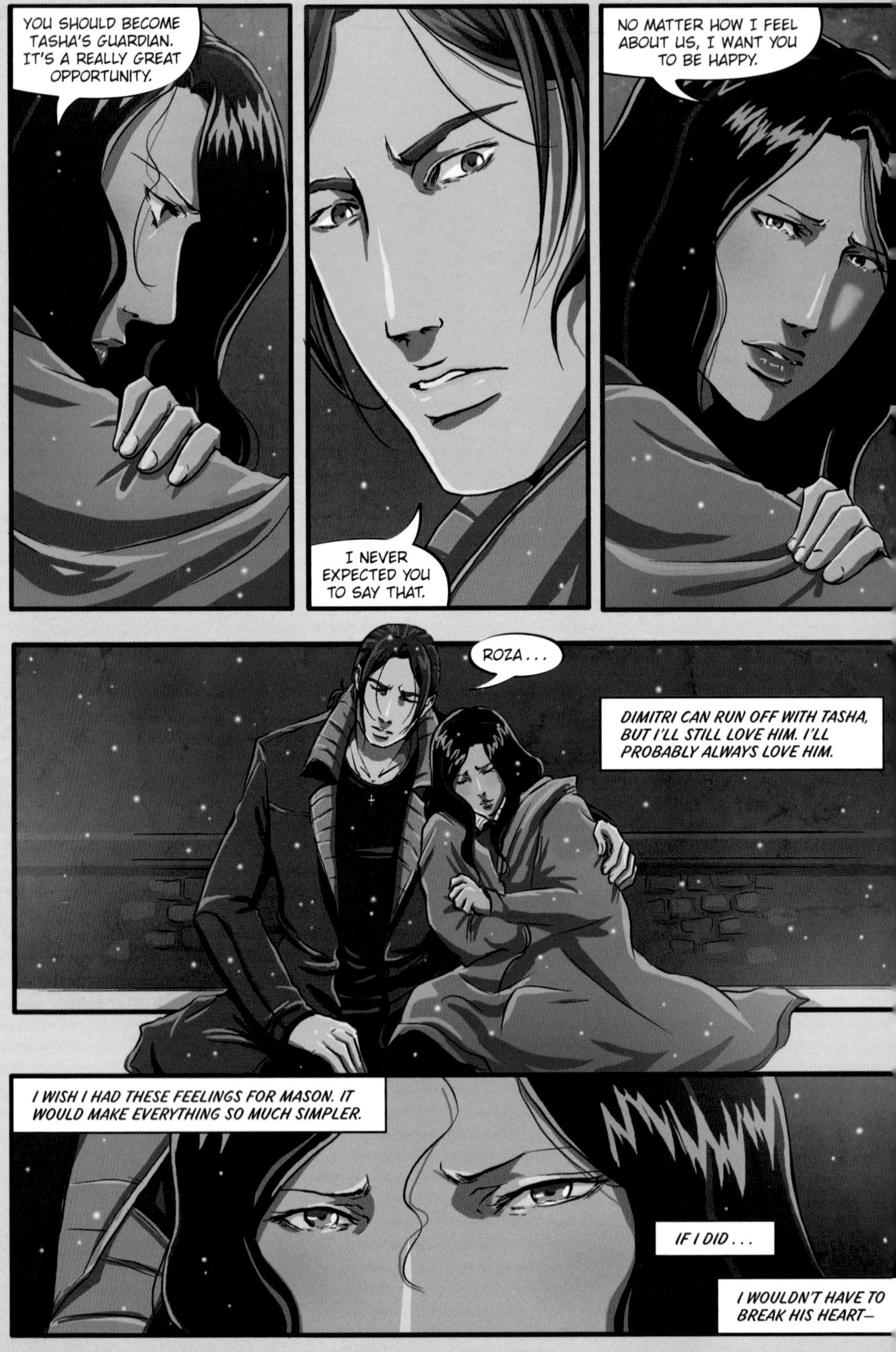
YOU SHOULD BECOME TASHA'S GUARDIAN. IT'S A REALLY GREAT OPPORTUNITY.
I NEVER EXPECTED YOU TO SAY THAT.
NO MATTER HOW I FEEL ABOUT US, I WANT YOU TO BE HAPPY.
ROZA . . .
DIMITRI CAN RUN OFF WITH TASHA, BUT I'LL STILL LOVE HIM. I'LL PROBABLY ALWAYS LOVE HIM.
I WISH I HAD THESE FEELINGS FOR MASON. IT WOULD MAKE EVERYTHING SO MUCH SIMPLER.
IF I DID . . .
I WOULDN'T HAVE TO BREAK HIS HEART—

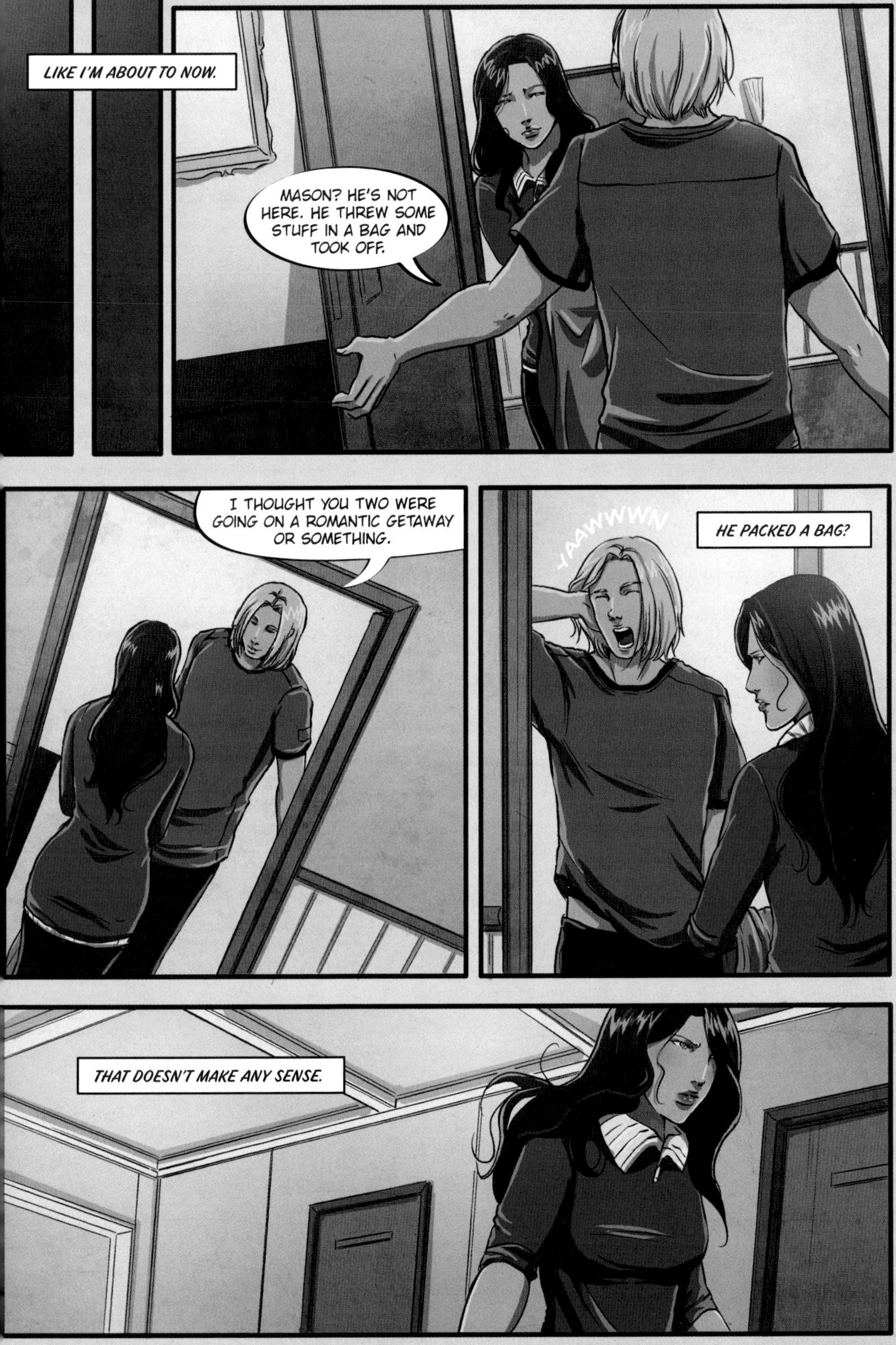
LIKE I'M ABOUT TO NOW.
MASON? HE'S NOT HERE. HE THREW SOME STUFF IN A BAG AND TOOK OFF.
I THOUGHT YOU TWO WERE GOING ON A ROMANTIC GETAWAY OR SOMETHING.
YAAWWWN
HE PACKED A BAG?
THAT DOESN'T MAKE ANY SENSE.

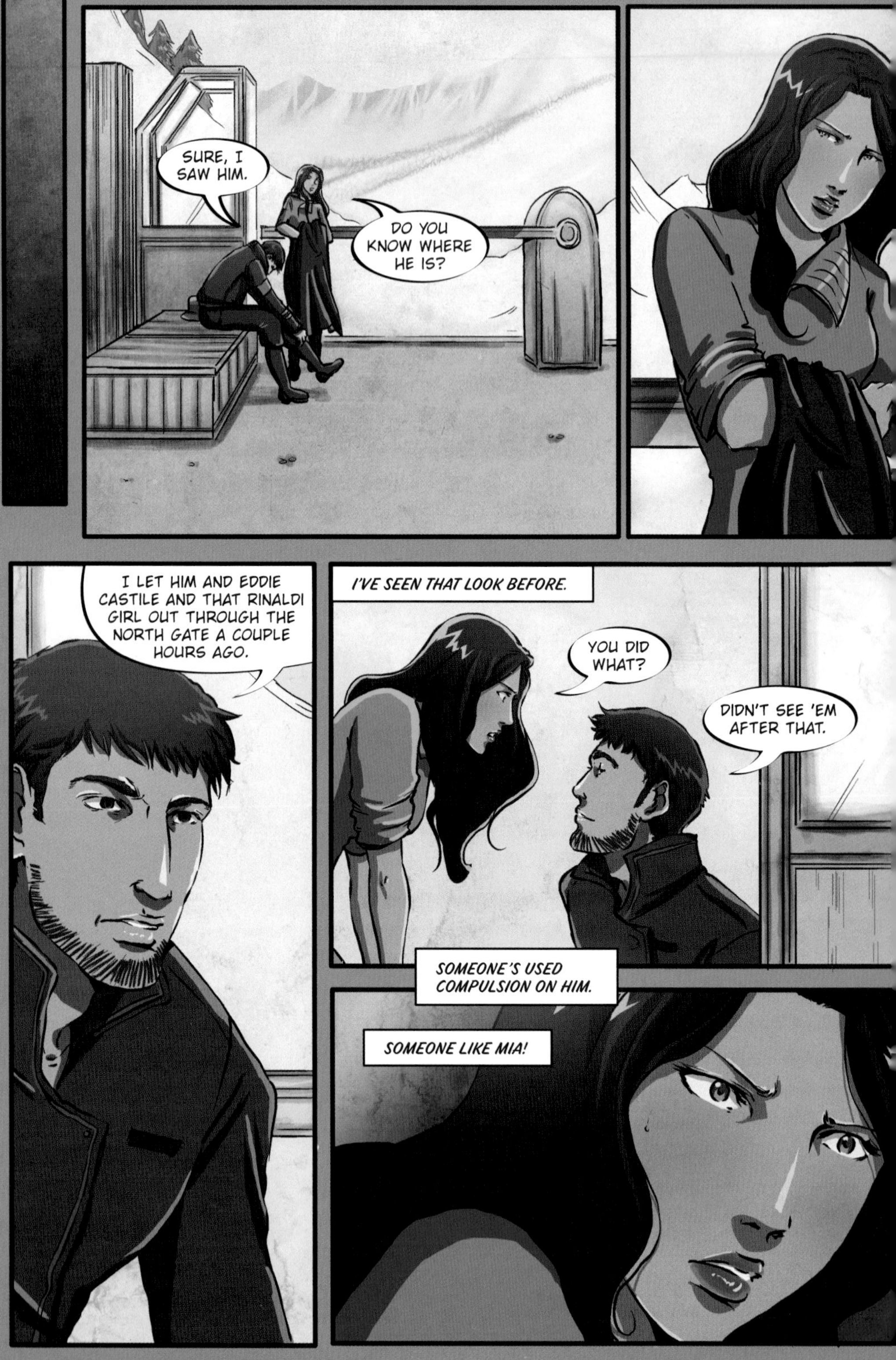
SURE, I SAW HIM.
DO YOU KNOW WHERE HE IS?
I LET HIM AND EDDIE CASTILE AND THAT RINALDI GIRL OUT THROUGH THE NORTH GATE A COUPLE HOURS AGO.
I'VE SEEN THAT LOOK BEFORE.
YOU DID WHAT?
DIDN'T SEE 'EM AFTER THAT.
SOMEONE'S USED COMPULSION ON HIM.
SOMEONE LIKE MIA!

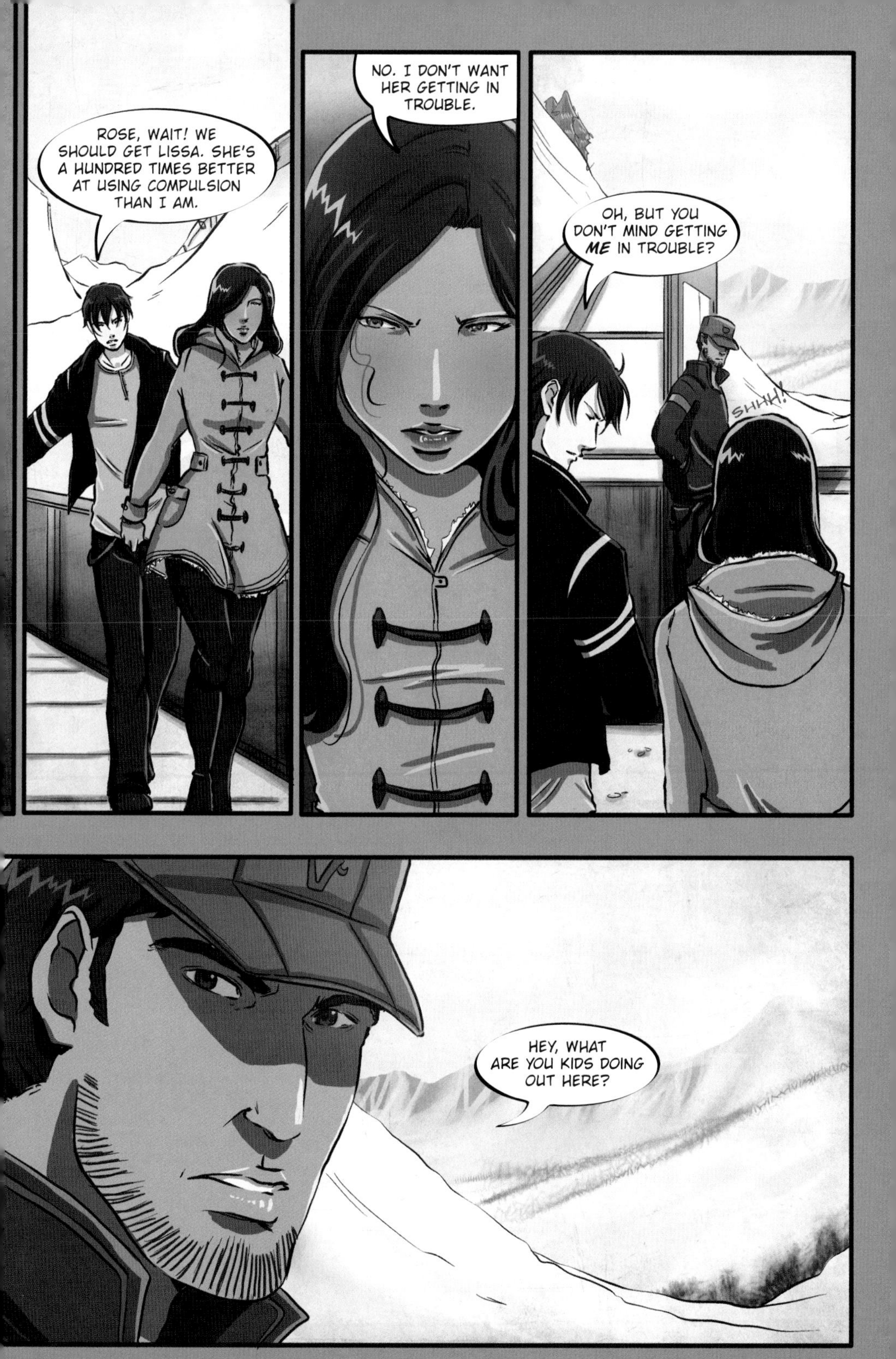
ROSE, WAIT! WE SHOULD GET LISSA. SHE'S A HUNDRED TIMES BETTER AT USING COMPULSION THAN I AM.
NO. I DON'T WANT HER GETTING IN TROUBLE.
OH, BUT YOU DON'T MIND GETTING *ME* IN TROUBLE?
SHHH!
HEY, WHAT ARE YOU KIDS DOING OUT HERE?

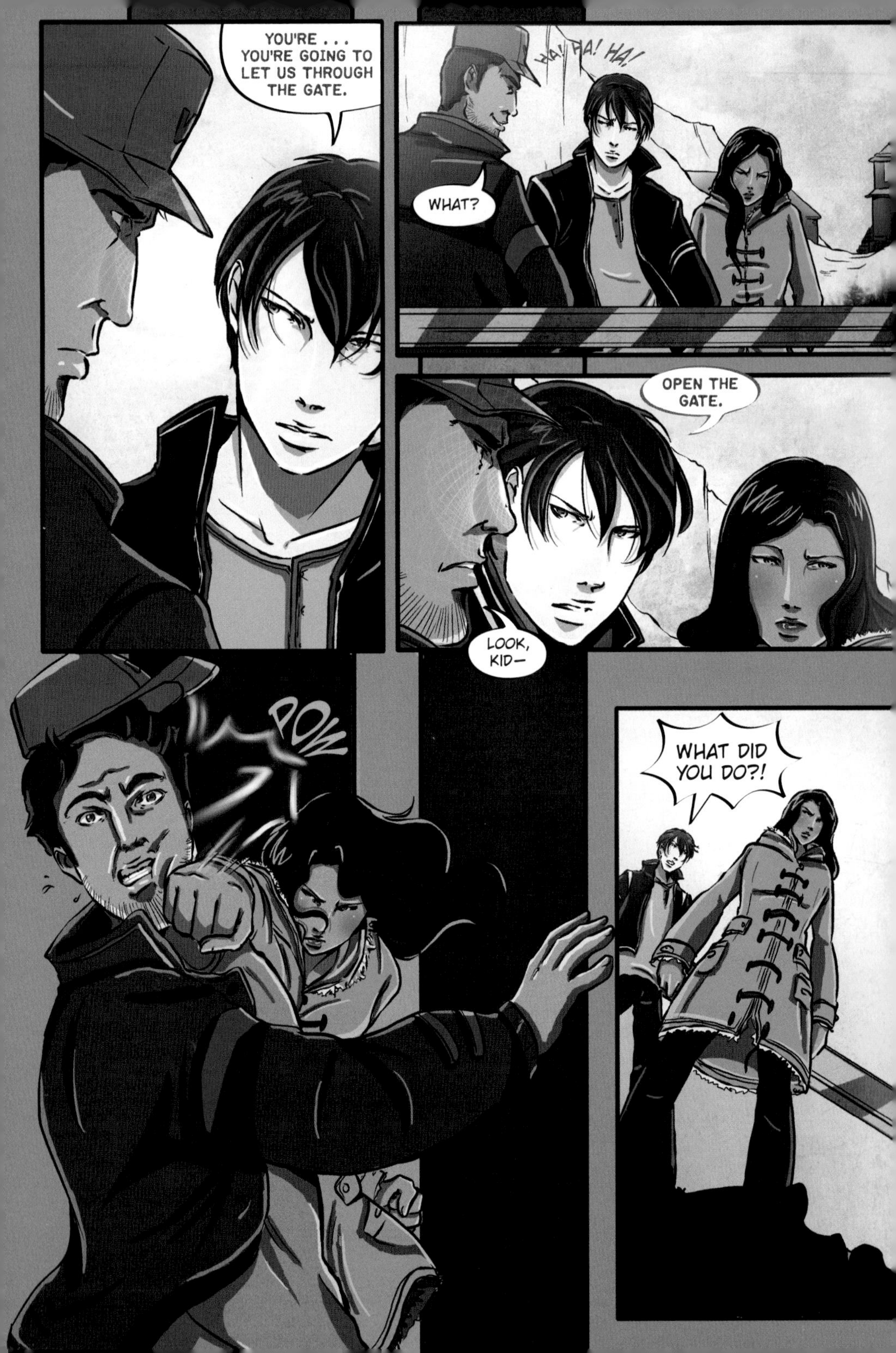
YOU'RE . . . YOU'RE GOING TO LET US THROUGH THE GATE.
HA! HA! HA!
WHAT?
OPEN THE GATE.
LOOK, KID—
POW
WHAT DID YOU DO?!

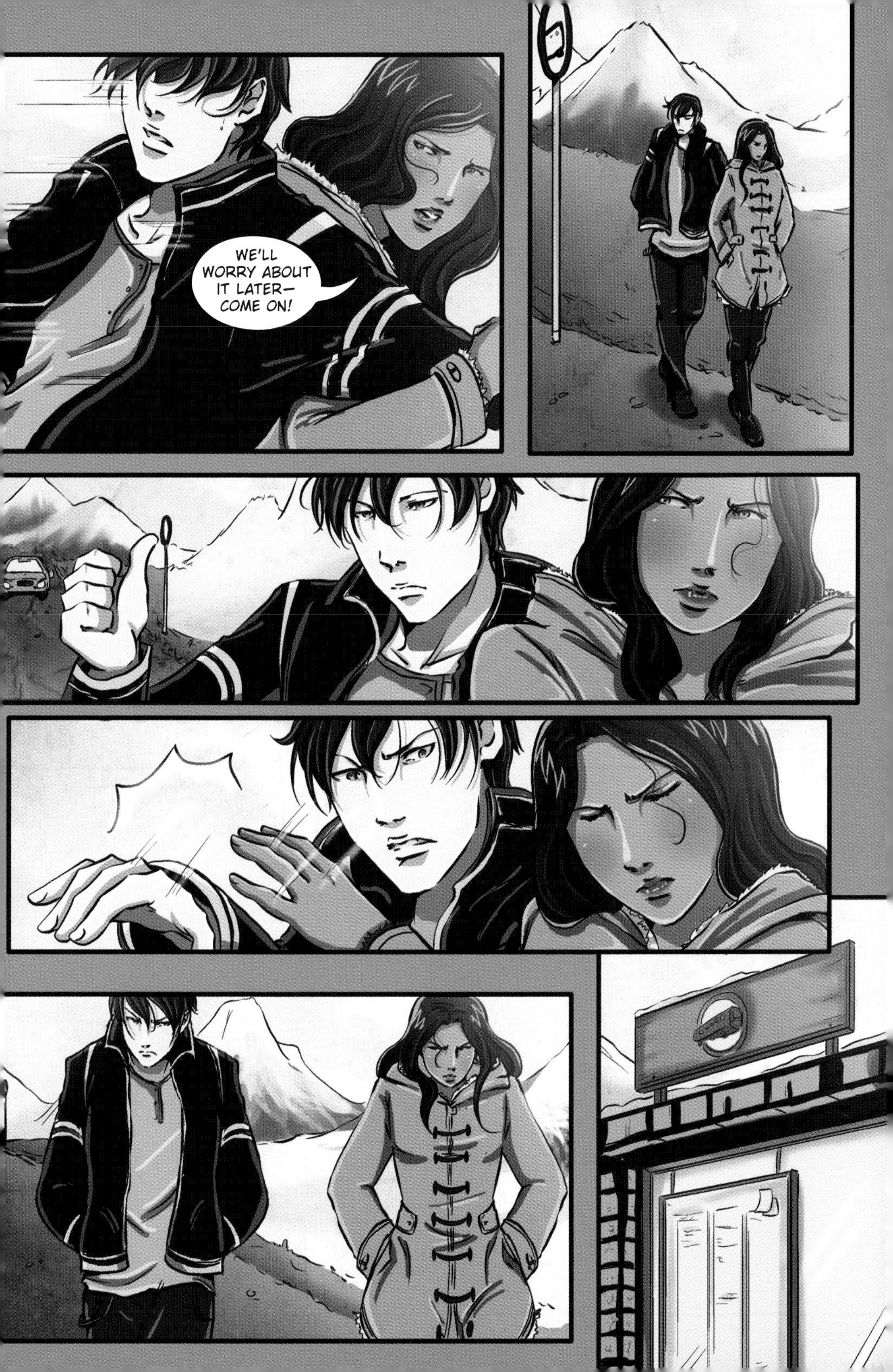
WE'LL WORRY ABOUT IT LATER— COME ON!

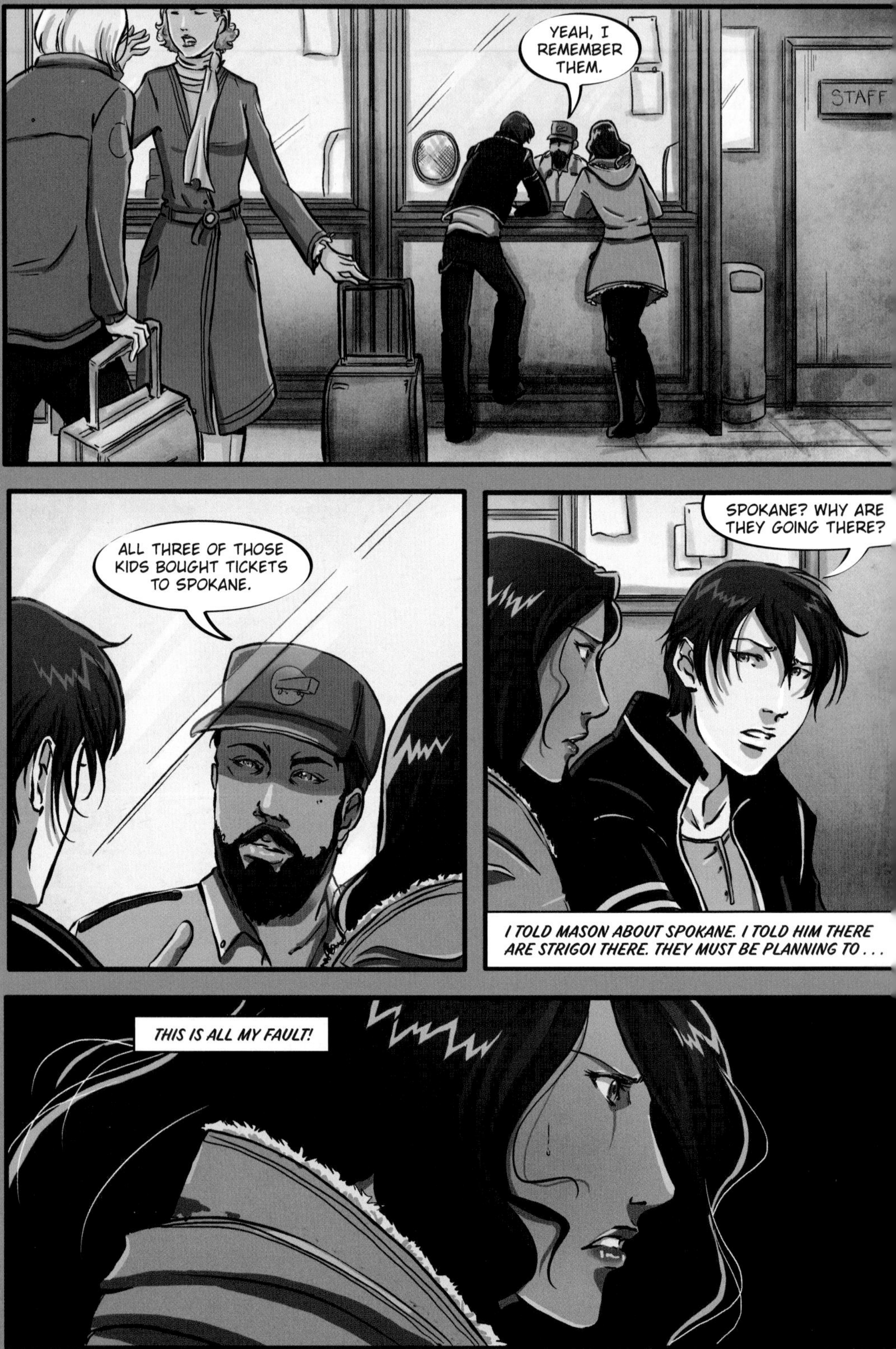
YEAH, I REMEMBER THEM.
ALL THREE OF THOSE KIDS BOUGHT TICKETS TO SPOKANE.
SPOKANE? WHY ARE THEY GOING THERE?
I TOLD MASON ABOUT SPOKANE. I TOLD HIM THERE ARE STRIGOI THERE. THEY MUST BE PLANNING TO . . .
THIS IS ALL MY FAULT!

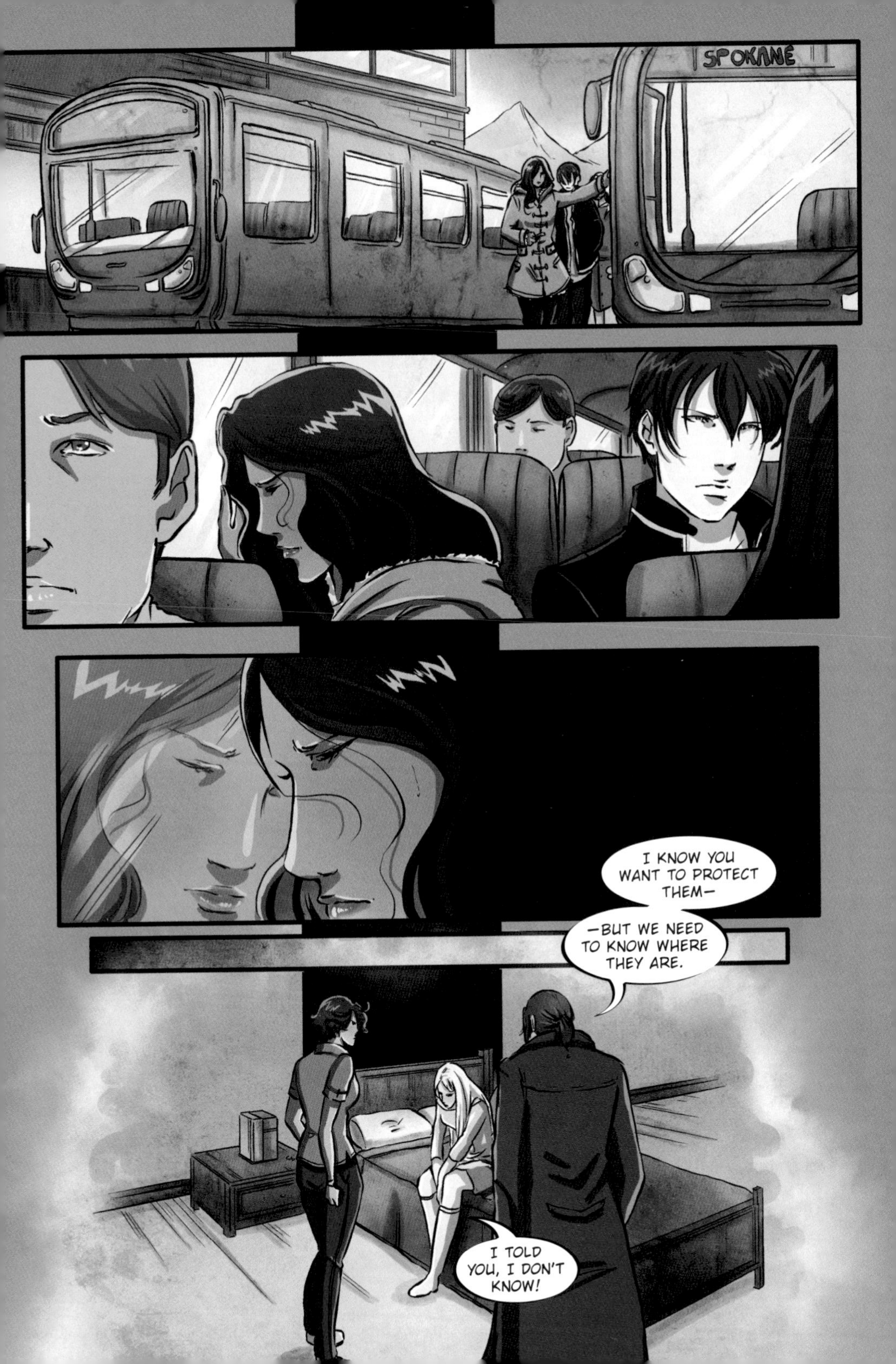
SPOKANE
I KNOW YOU WANT TO PROTECT THEM—
—BUT WE NEED TO KNOW WHERE THEY ARE.
I TOLD YOU, I DON'T KNOW!

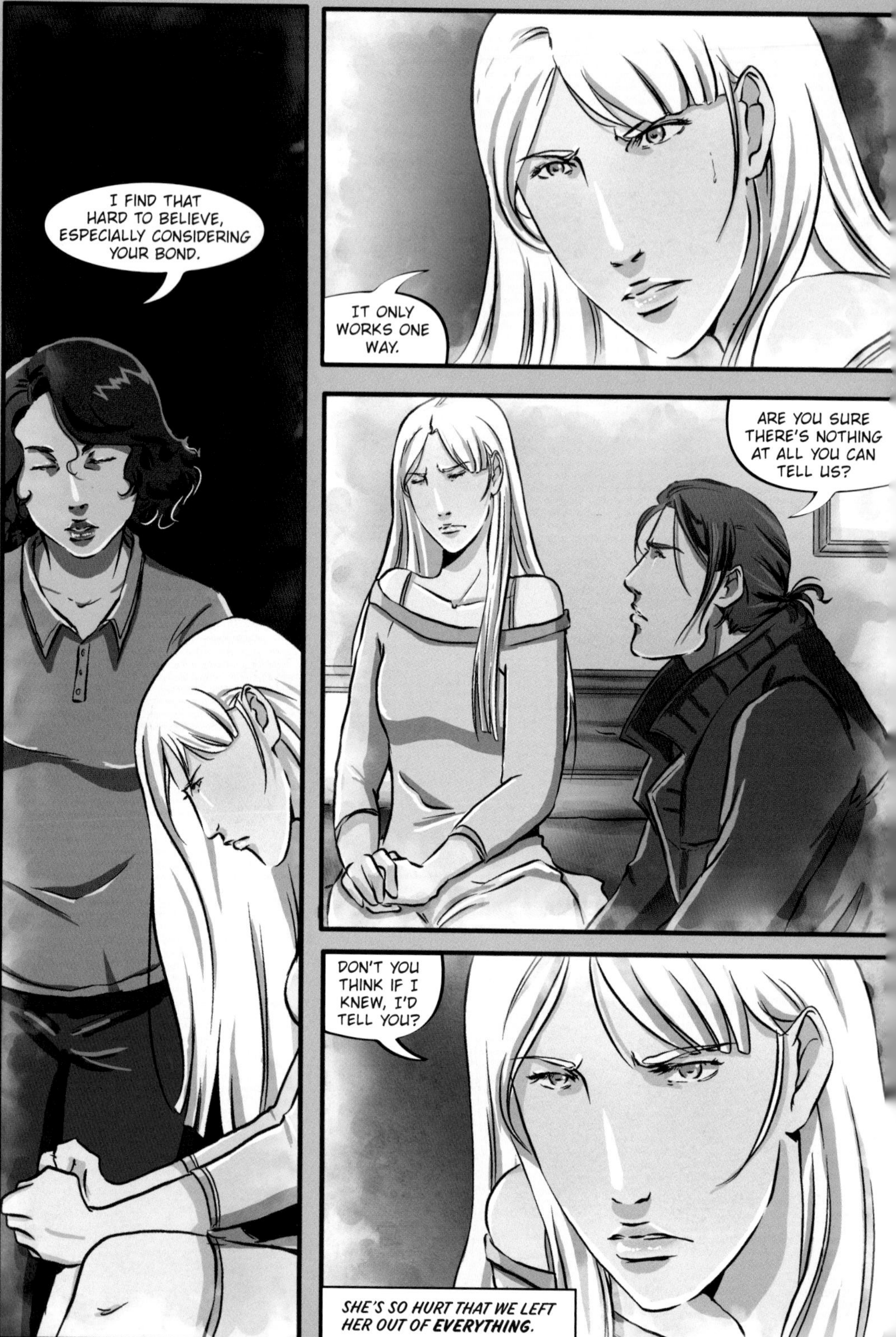

I FIND THAT HARD TO BELIEVE, ESPECIALLY CONSIDERING YOUR BOND.
IT ONLY WORKS ONE WAY.
ARE YOU SURE THERE'S NOTHING AT ALL YOU CAN TELL US?
DON'T YOU THINK IF I KNEW, I'D TELL YOU?
*SHE'S SO HURT THAT WE LEFT HER OUT OF **EVERYTHING**.*

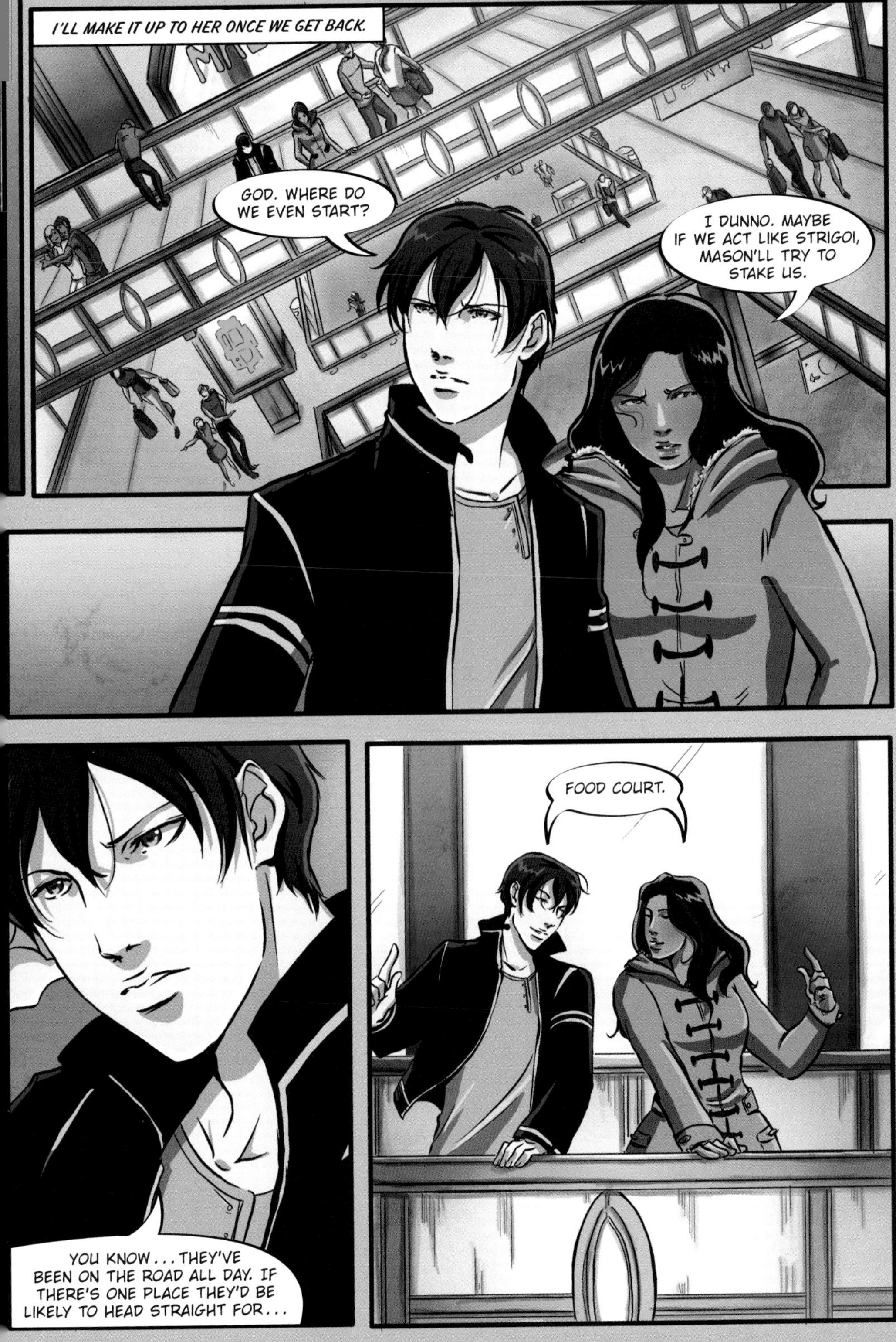
I'LL MAKE IT UP TO HER ONCE WE GET BACK.
GOD. WHERE DO WE EVEN START?
I DUNNO. MAYBE IF WE ACT LIKE STRIGOI, MASON'LL TRY TO STAKE US.
YOU KNOW . . . THEY'VE BEEN ON THE ROAD ALL DAY. IF THERE'S ONE PLACE THEY'D BE LIKELY TO HEAD STRAIGHT FOR . . .
FOOD COURT.

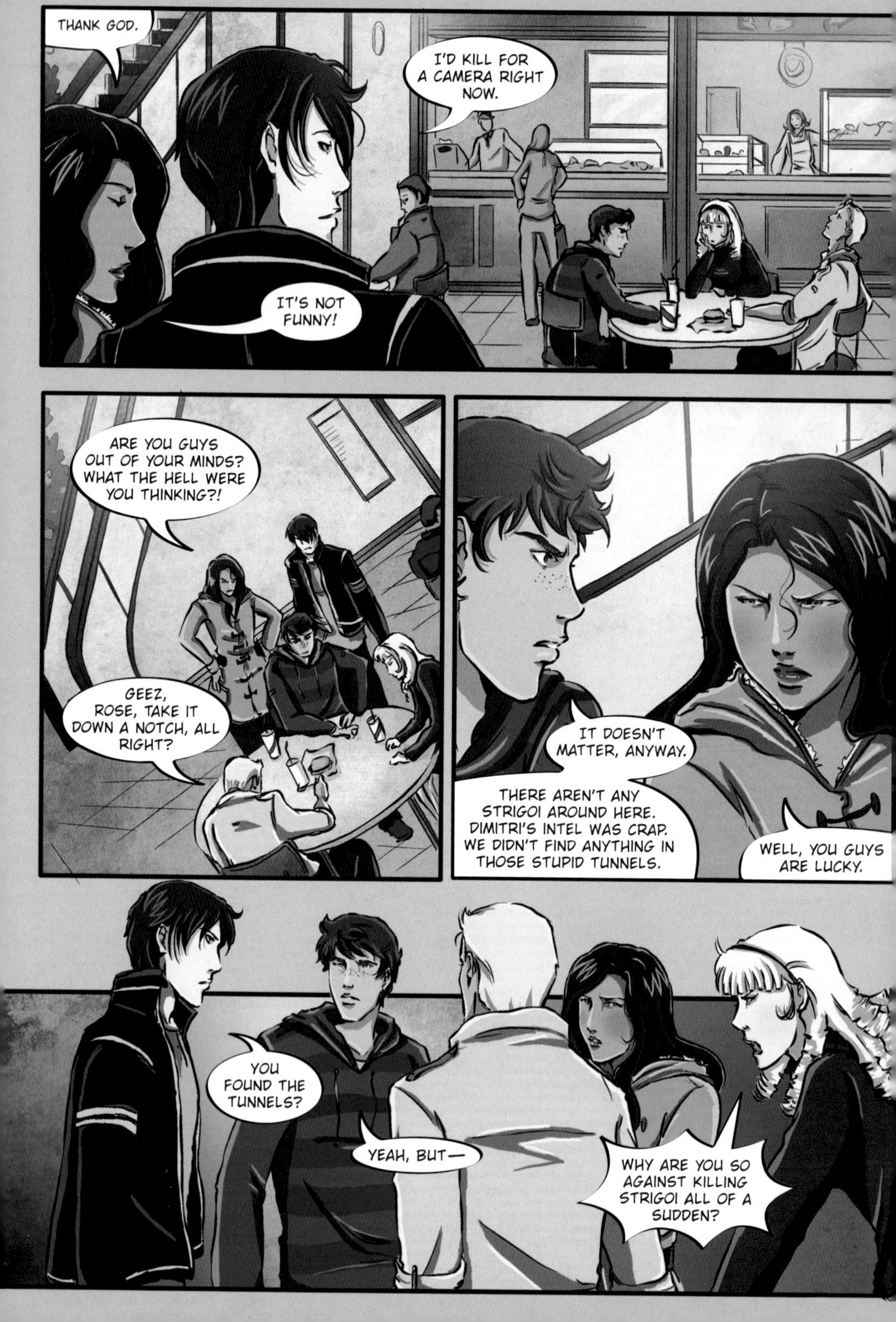
THANK GOD.
I'D KILL FOR A CAMERA RIGHT NOW.
IT'S NOT FUNNY!
ARE YOU GUYS OUT OF YOUR MINDS? WHAT THE HELL WERE YOU THINKING?!
GEEZ, ROSE, TAKE IT DOWN A NOTCH, ALL RIGHT?
IT DOESN'T MATTER, ANYWAY.
THERE AREN'T ANY STRIGOI AROUND HERE. DIMITRI'S INTEL WAS CRAP. WE DIDN'T FIND ANYTHING IN THOSE STUPID TUNNELS.
WELL, YOU GUYS ARE LUCKY.
YOU FOUND THE TUNNELS?
YEAH, BUT—
WHY ARE YOU SO AGAINST KILLING STRIGOI ALL OF A SUDDEN?

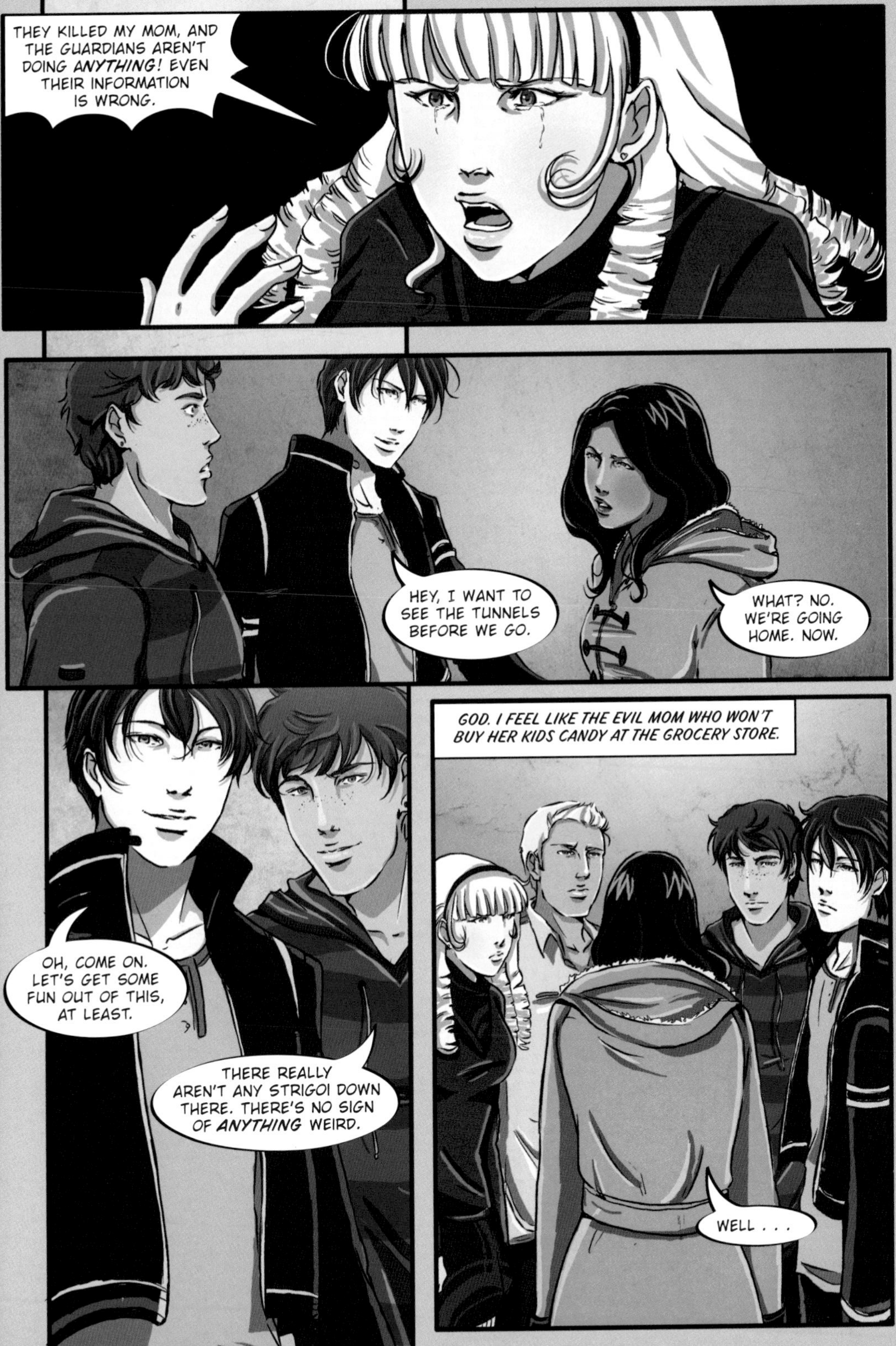
THEY KILLED MY MOM, AND THE GUARDIANS AREN'T DOING *ANYTHING*! EVEN THEIR INFORMATION IS WRONG.
HEY, I WANT TO SEE THE TUNNELS BEFORE WE GO.
WHAT? NO. WE'RE GOING HOME. NOW.
OH, COME ON. LET'S GET SOME FUN OUT OF THIS, AT LEAST.
THERE REALLY AREN'T ANY STRIGOI DOWN THERE. THERE'S NO SIGN OF *ANYTHING* WEIRD.
GOD. I FEEL LIKE THE EVIL MOM WHO WON'T BUY HER KIDS CANDY AT THE GROCERY STORE.
WELL . . .

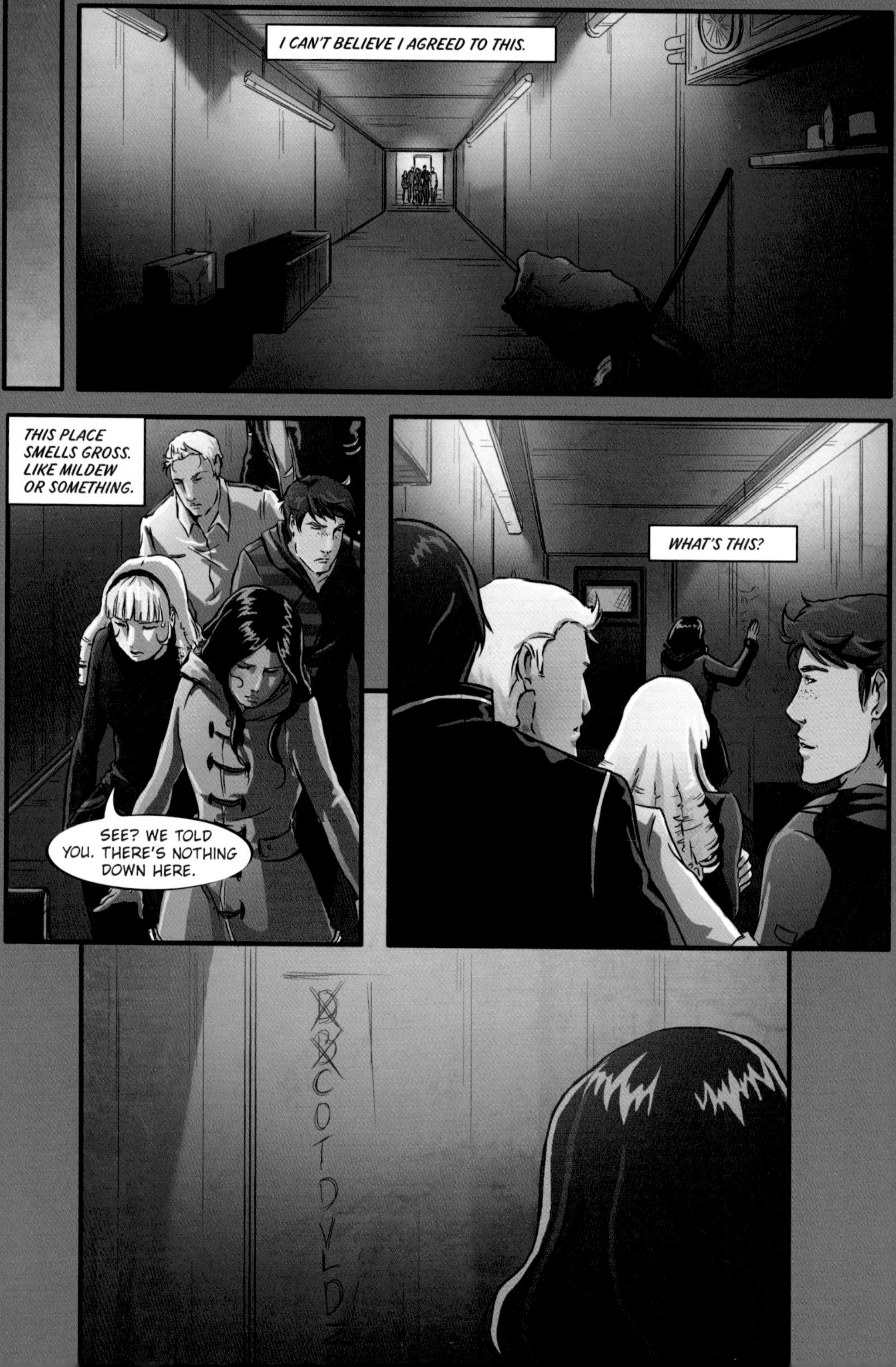
I CAN'T BELIEVE I AGREED TO THIS.
THIS PLACE SMELLS GROSS. LIKE MILDEW OR SOMETHING.
SEE? WE TOLD YOU. THERE'S NOTHING DOWN HERE.
WHAT'S THIS?

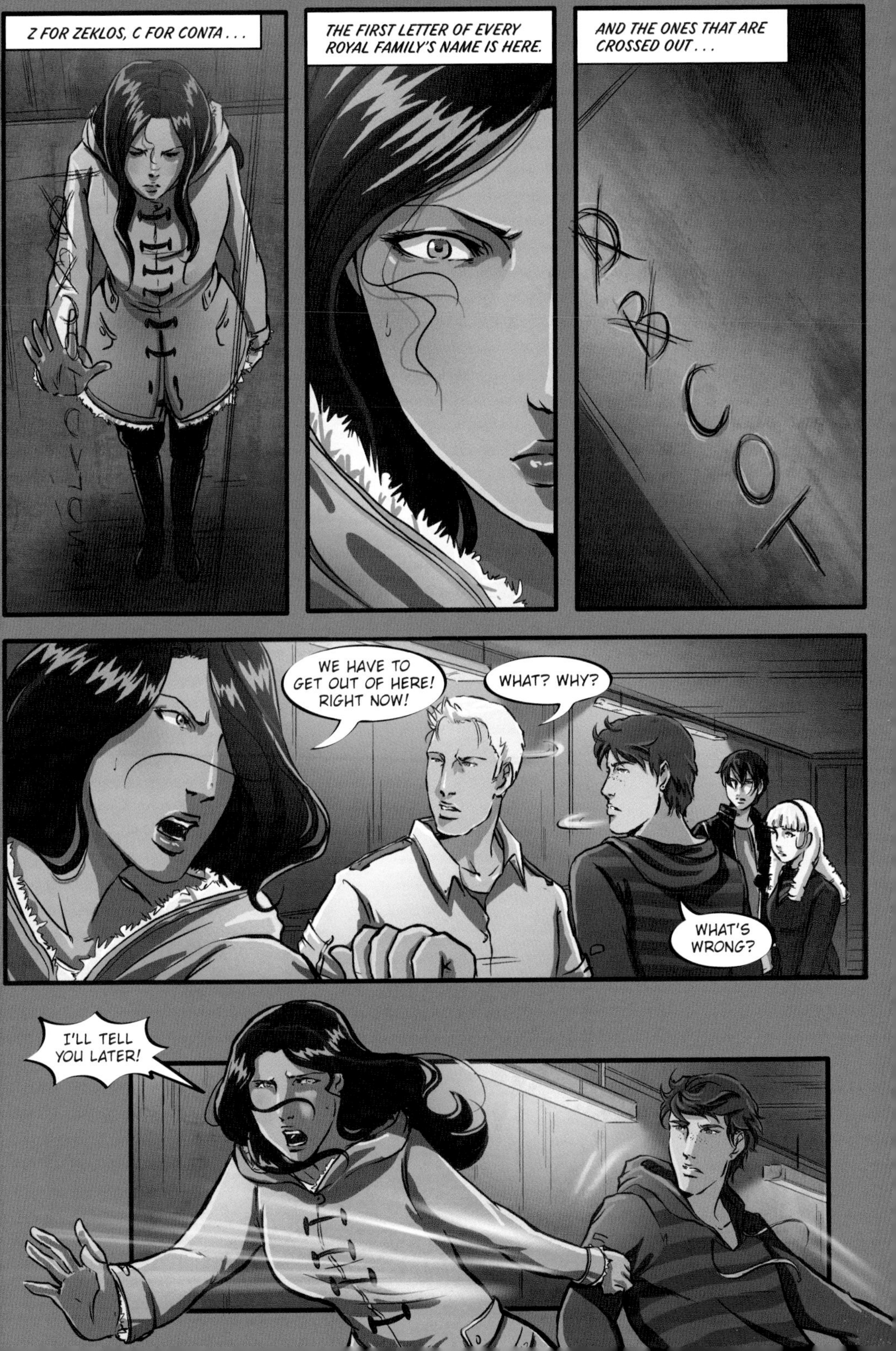
Z FOR ZEKLOS, C FOR CONTA . . .
THE FIRST LETTER OF EVERY ROYAL FAMILY'S NAME IS HERE.
AND THE ONES THAT ARE CROSSED OUT . . .
WE HAVE TO GET OUT OF HERE! RIGHT NOW!
WHAT? WHY?
WHAT'S WRONG?
I'LL TELL YOU LATER!

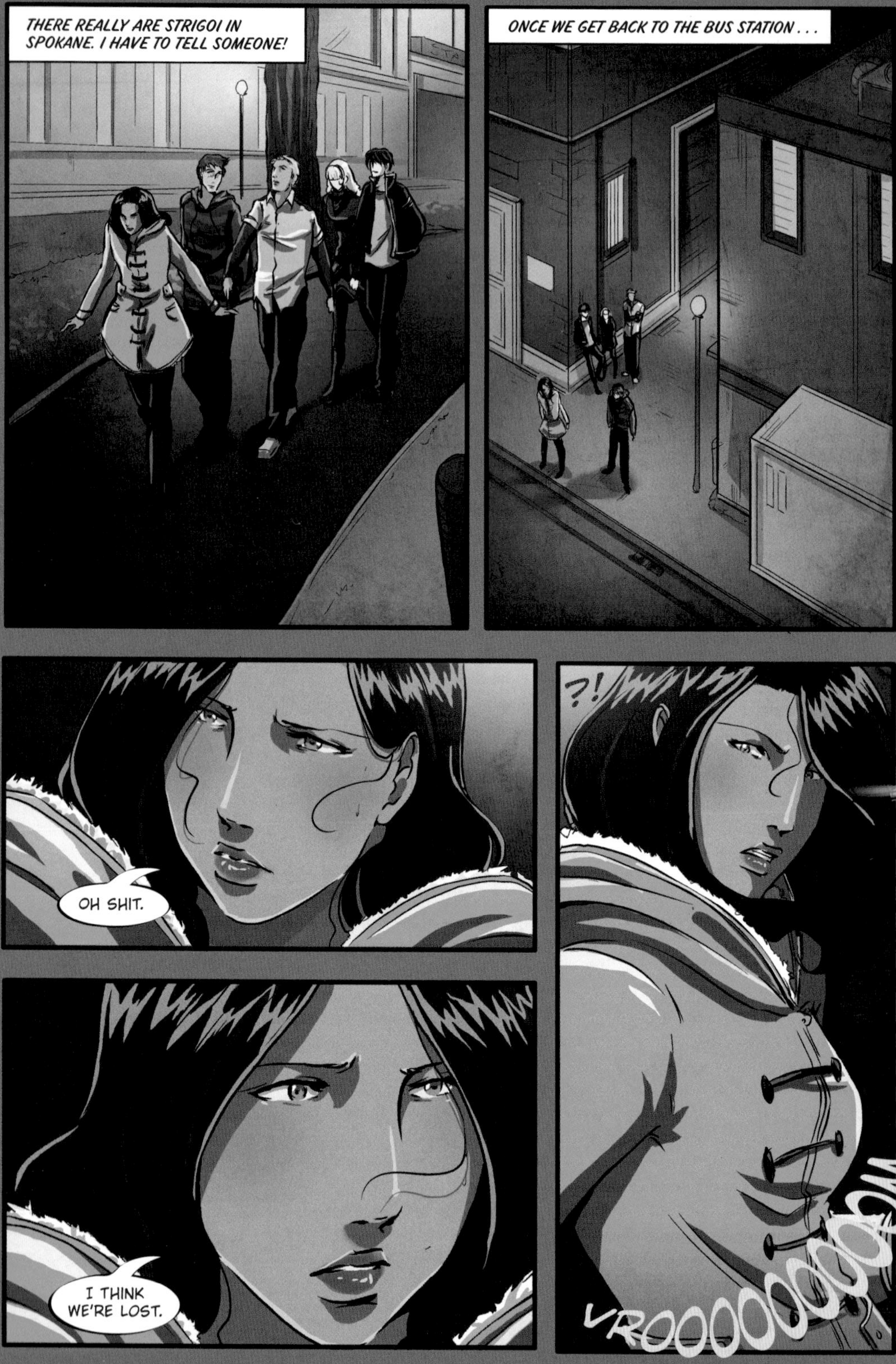
THERE REALLY ARE STRIGOI IN SPOKANE. I HAVE TO TELL SOMEONE!
ONCE WE GET BACK TO THE BUS STATION . . .
OH SHIT.
I THINK WE'RE LOST.
?!
VROOOOOOOOOOM

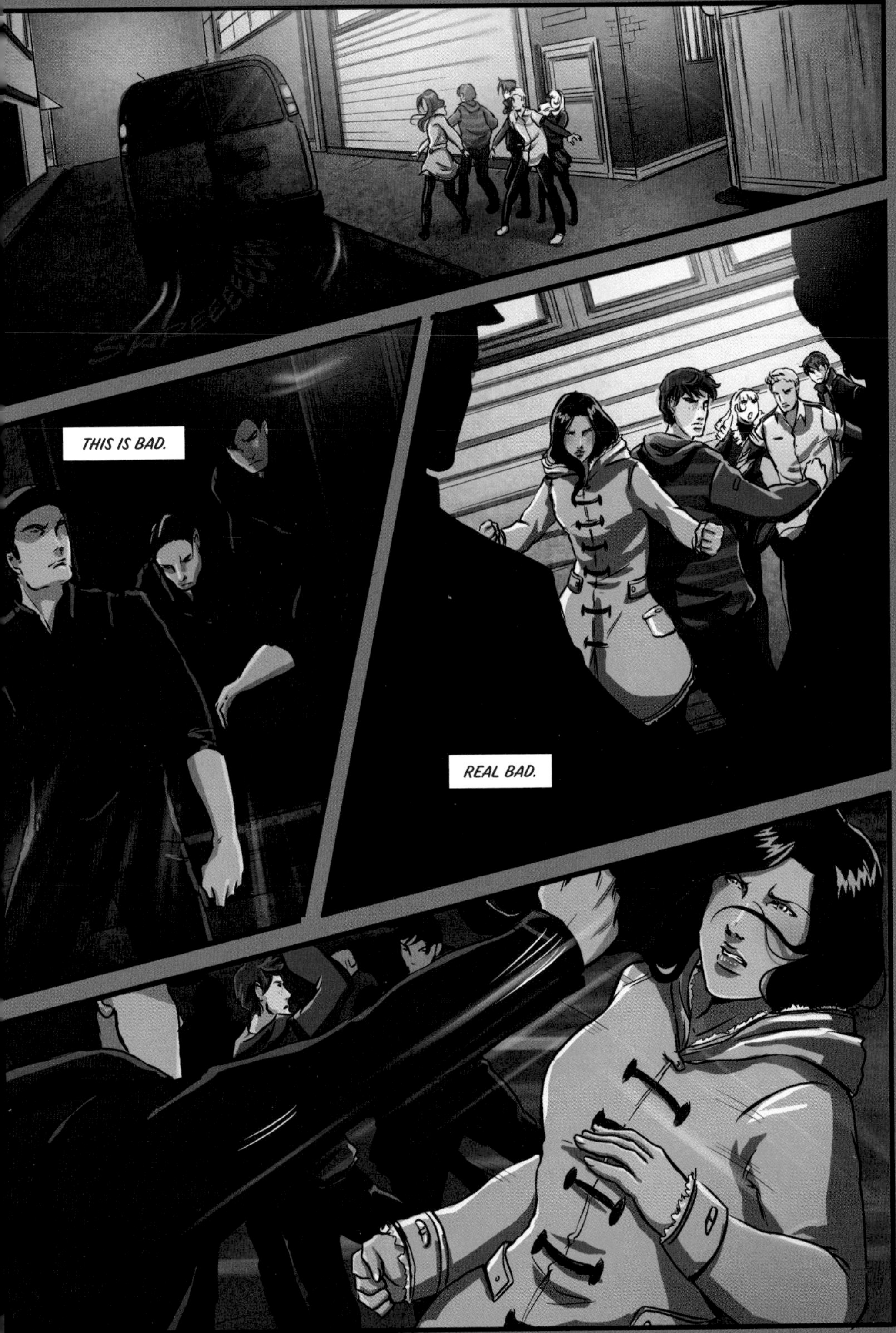
THIS IS BAD.
REAL BAD.

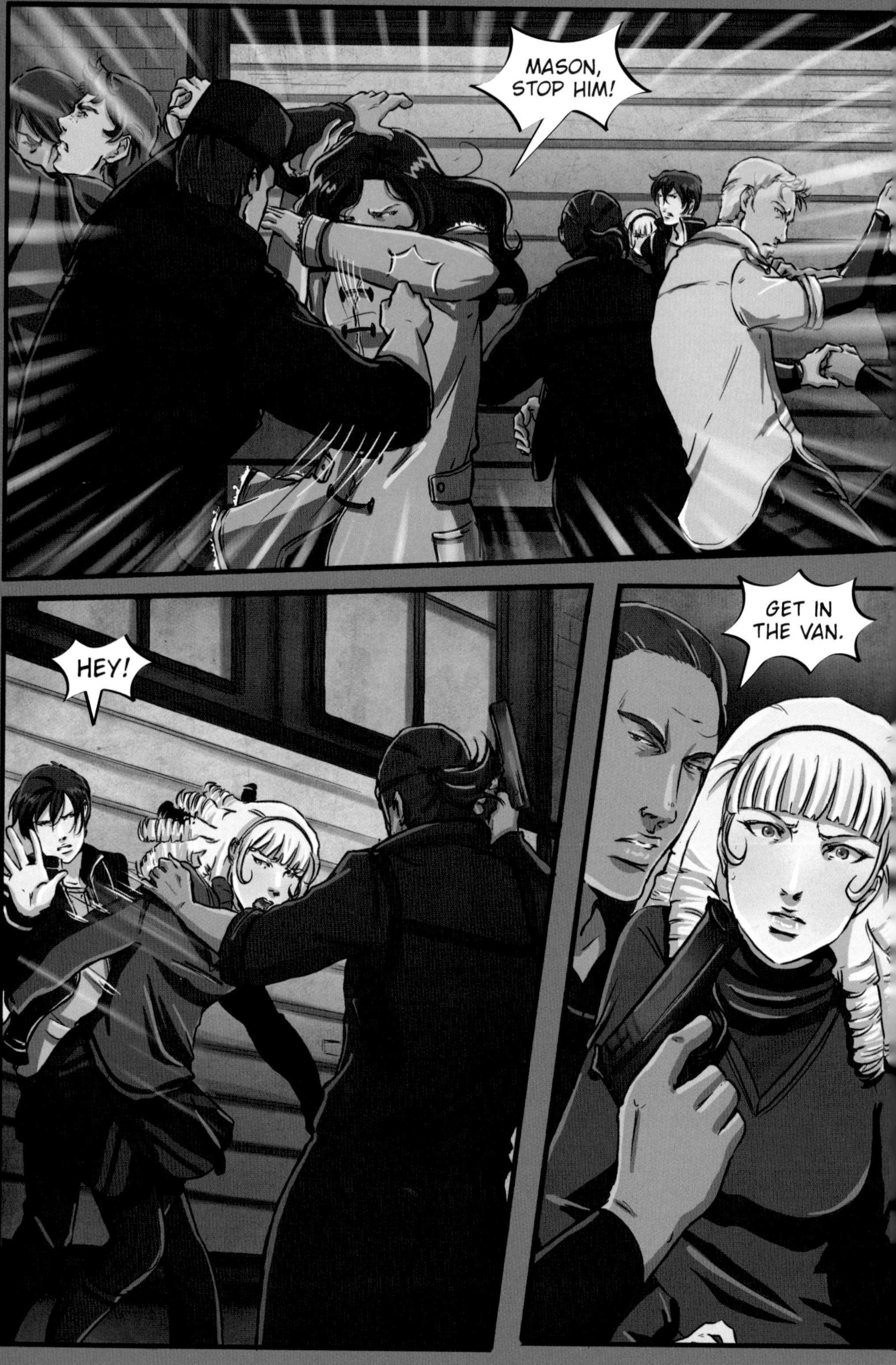
MASON, STOP HIM!
HEY!
GET IN THE VAN.

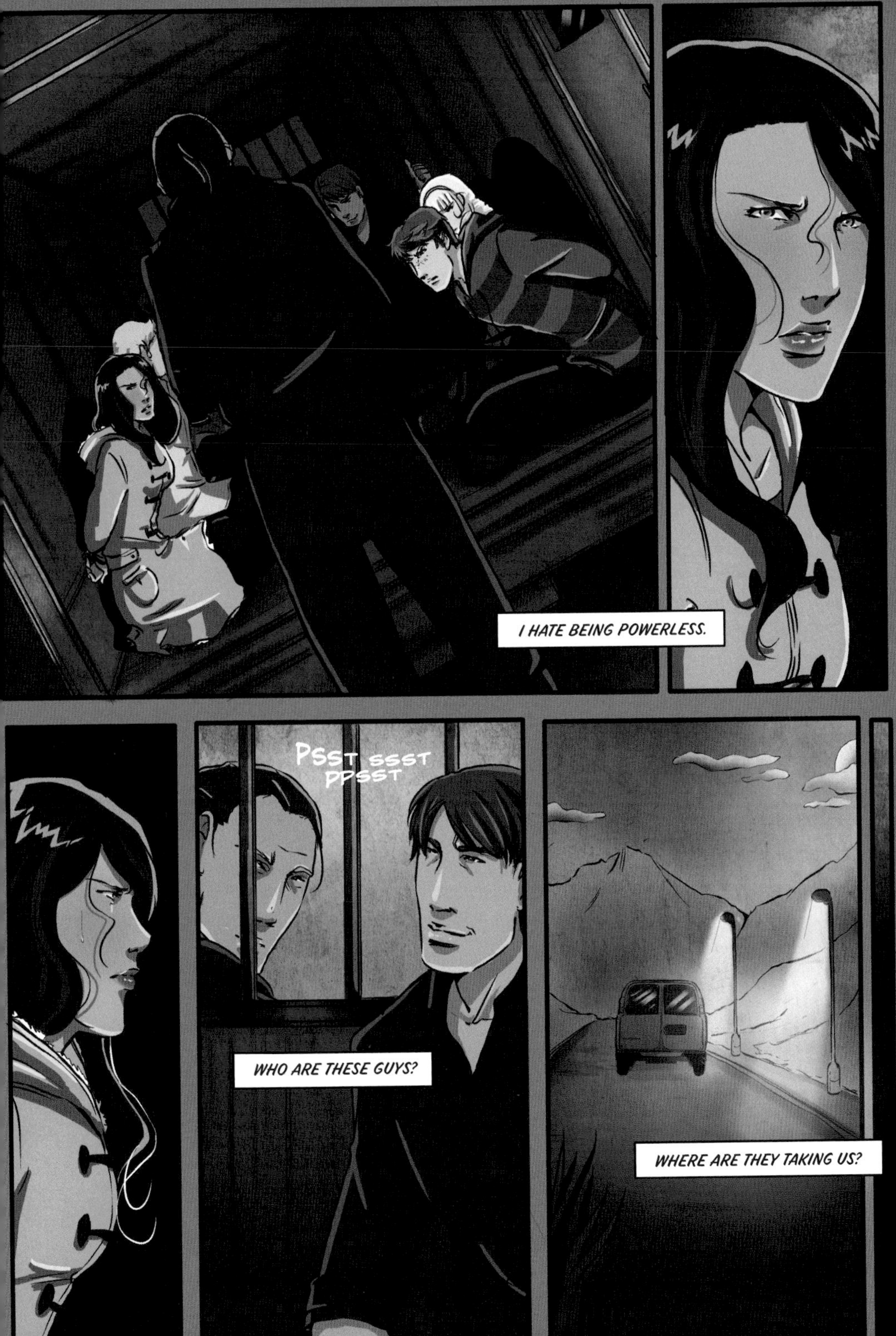
I HATE BEING POWERLESS.
PSST SSST PPSST
WHO ARE THESE GUYS?
WHERE ARE THEY TAKING US?

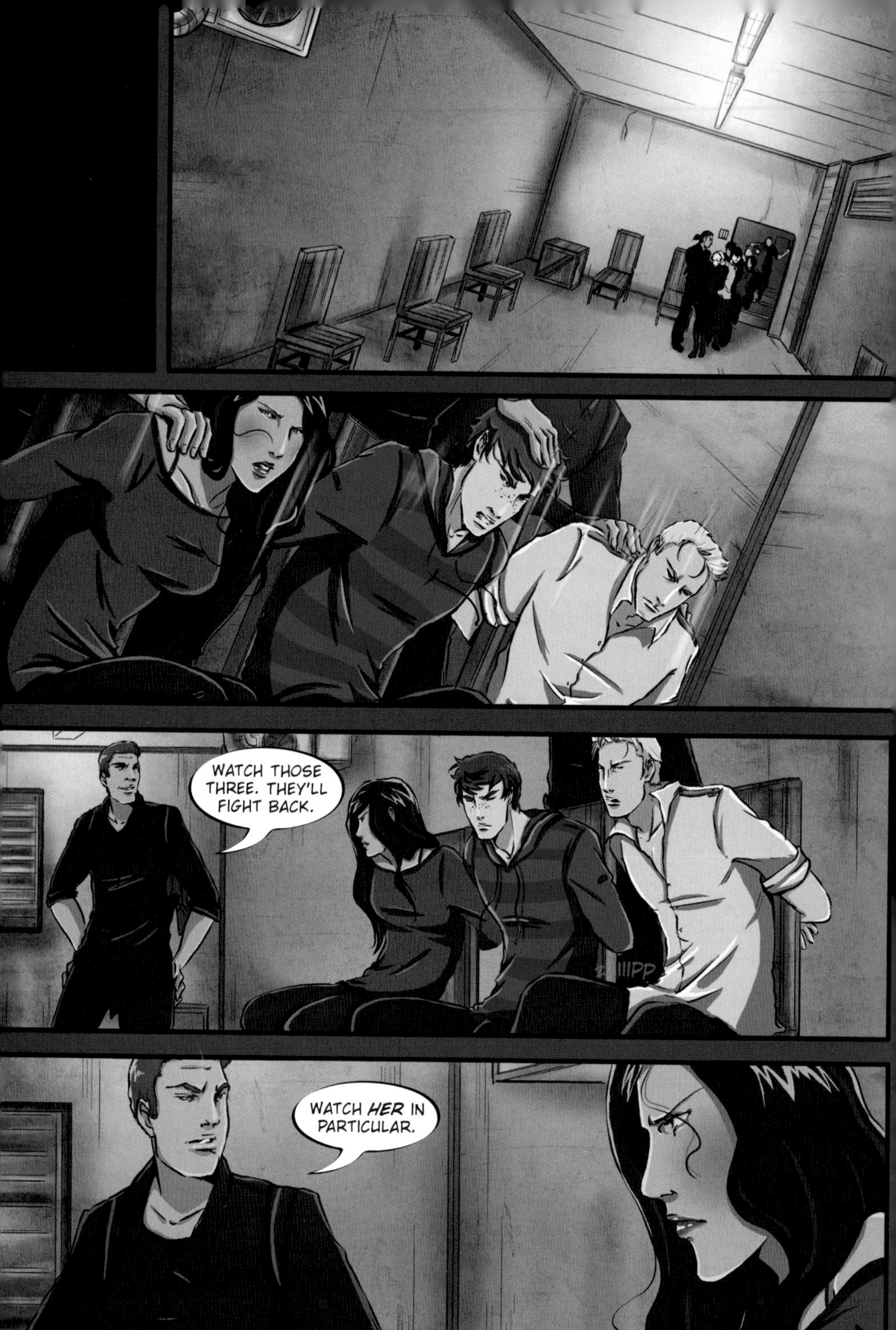
WATCH THOSE THREE. THEY'LL FIGHT BACK.
WATCH *HER* IN PARTICULAR.

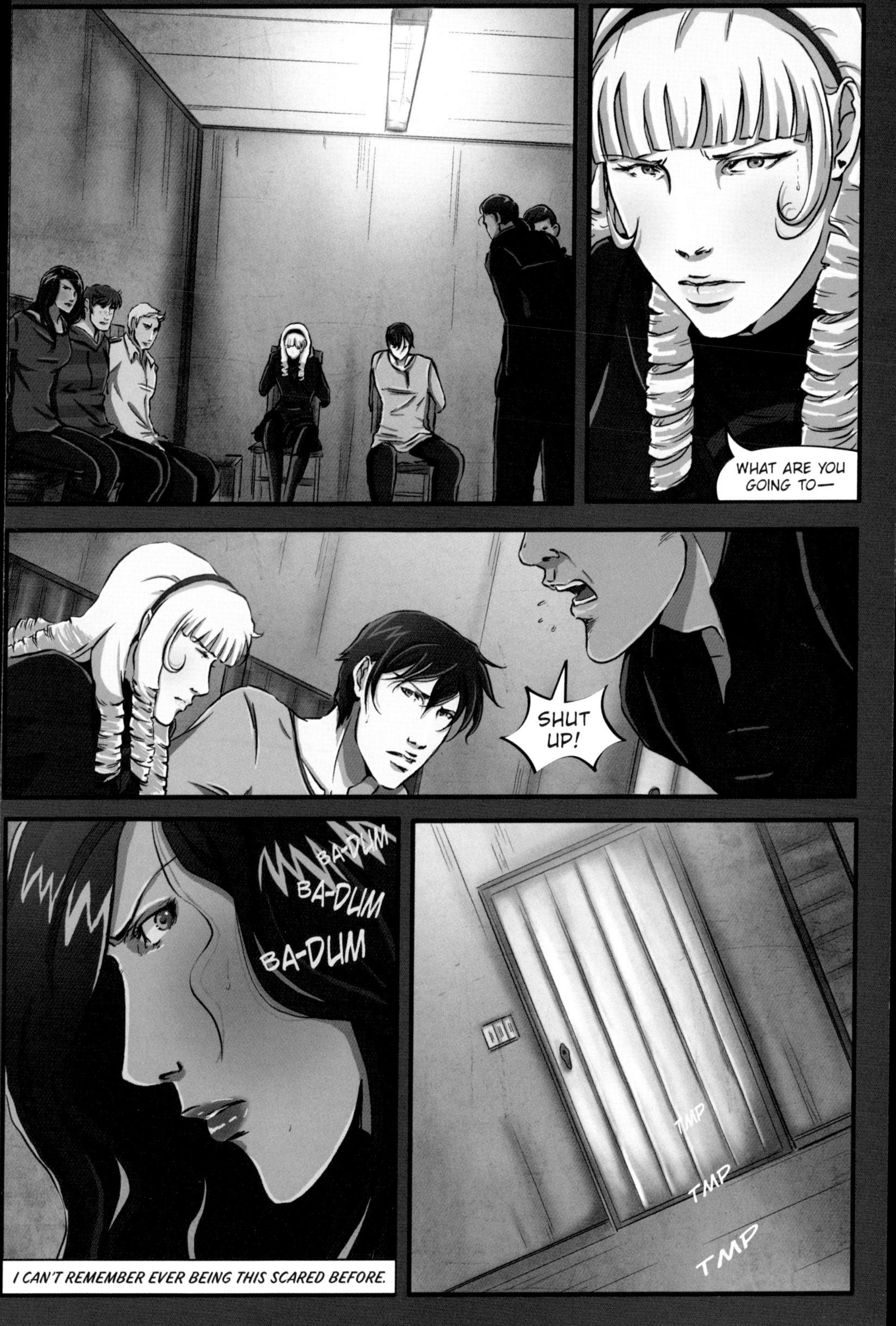
WHAT ARE YOU GOING TO—
SHUT UP!
BA-DUM
BA-DUM
BA-DUM
I CAN'T REMEMBER EVER BEING THIS SCARED BEFORE.
TMP
TMP
TMP

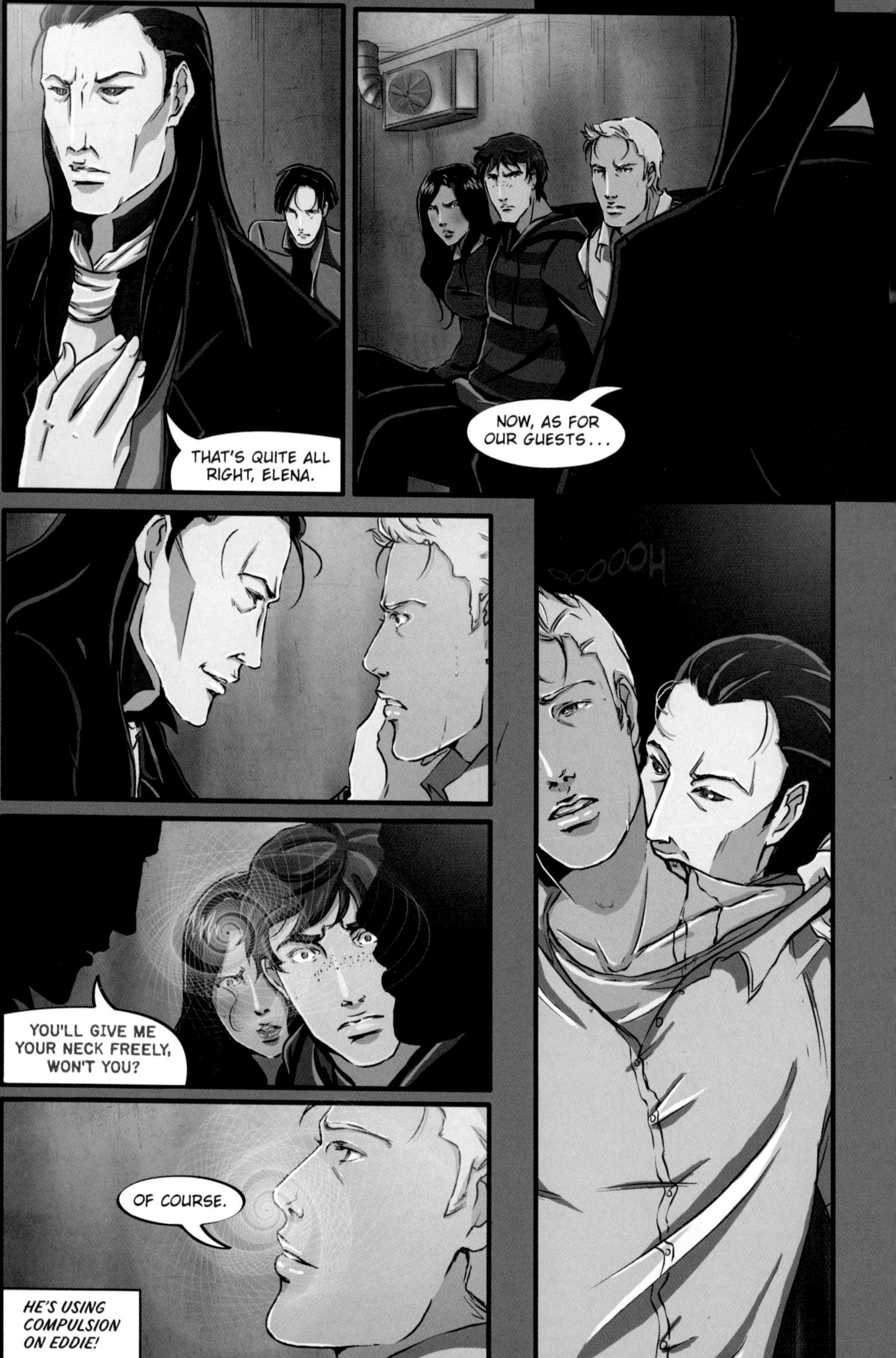
THAT'S QUITE ALL RIGHT, ELENA.
NOW, AS FOR OUR GUESTS . . .
YOU'LL GIVE ME YOUR NECK FREELY, WON'T YOU?
OF COURSE.
HE'S USING COMPULSION ON EDDIE!

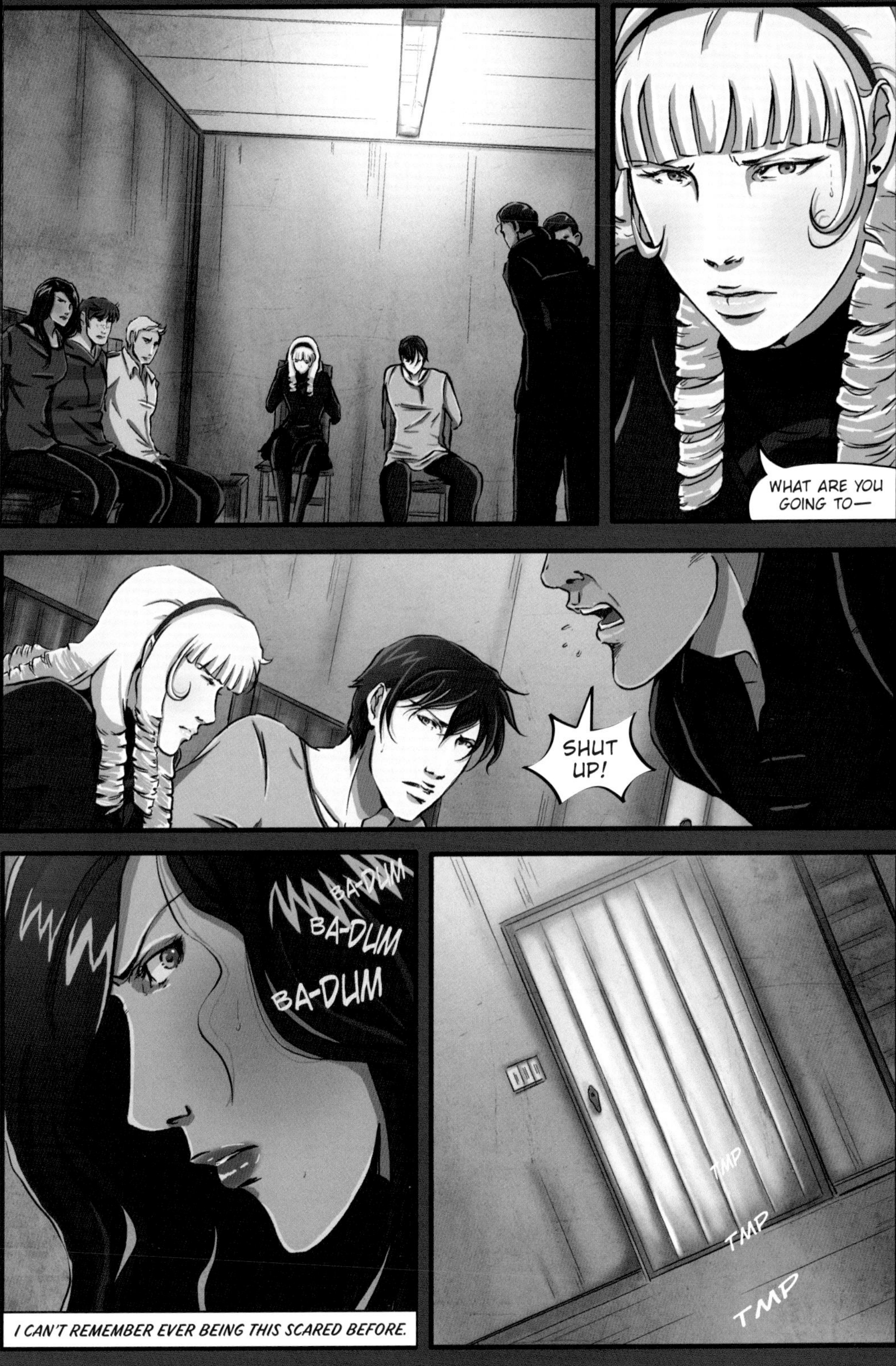
WHAT ARE YOU GOING TO—
SHUT UP!
BA-DUM
BA-DUM
BA-DUM
I CAN'T REMEMBER EVER BEING THIS SCARED BEFORE.
TMP
TMP
TMP

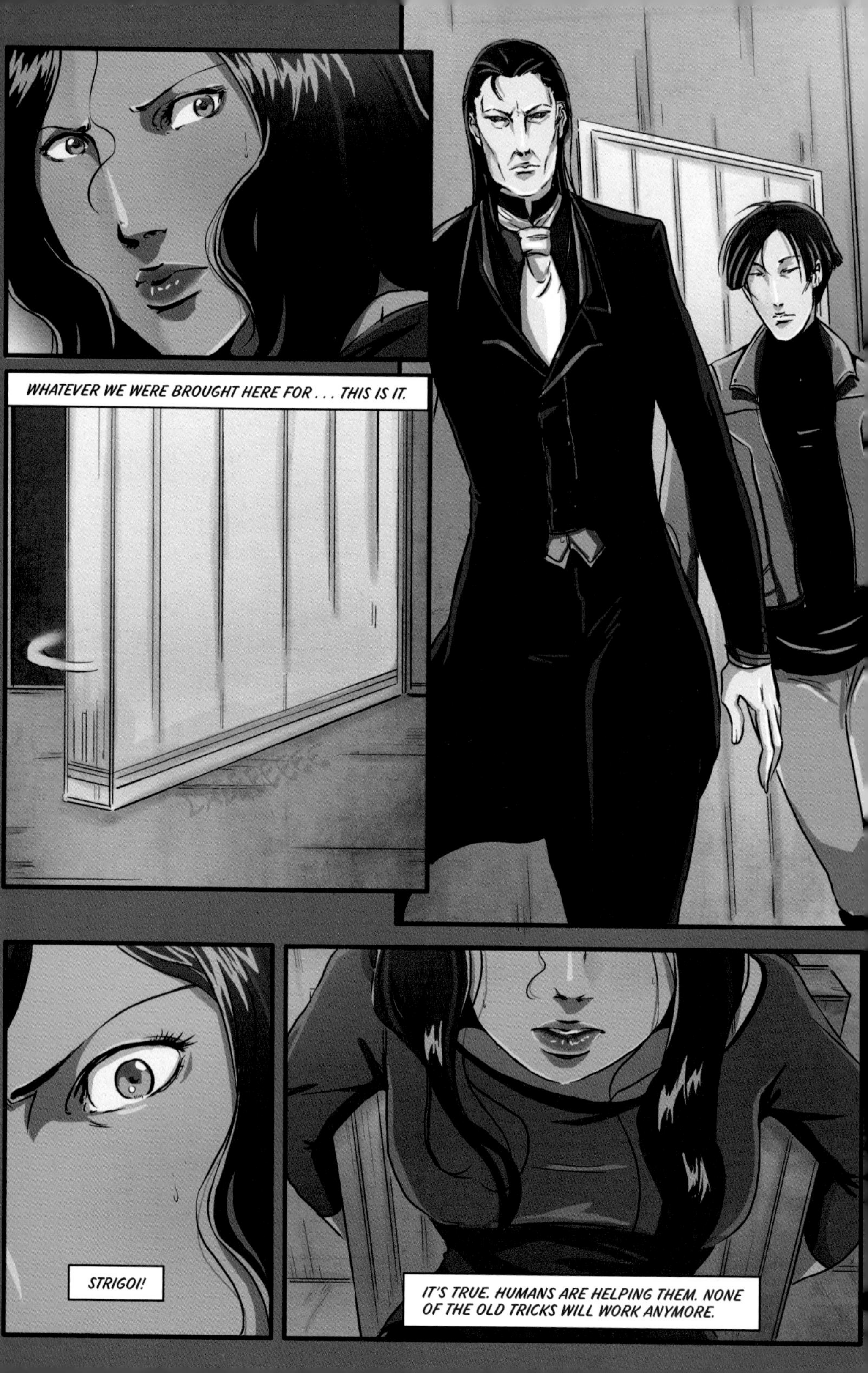
WHATEVER WE WERE BROUGHT HERE FOR . . . THIS IS IT.
STRIGOI!
IT'S TRUE. HUMANS ARE HELPING THEM. NONE OF THE OLD TRICKS WILL WORK ANYMORE.

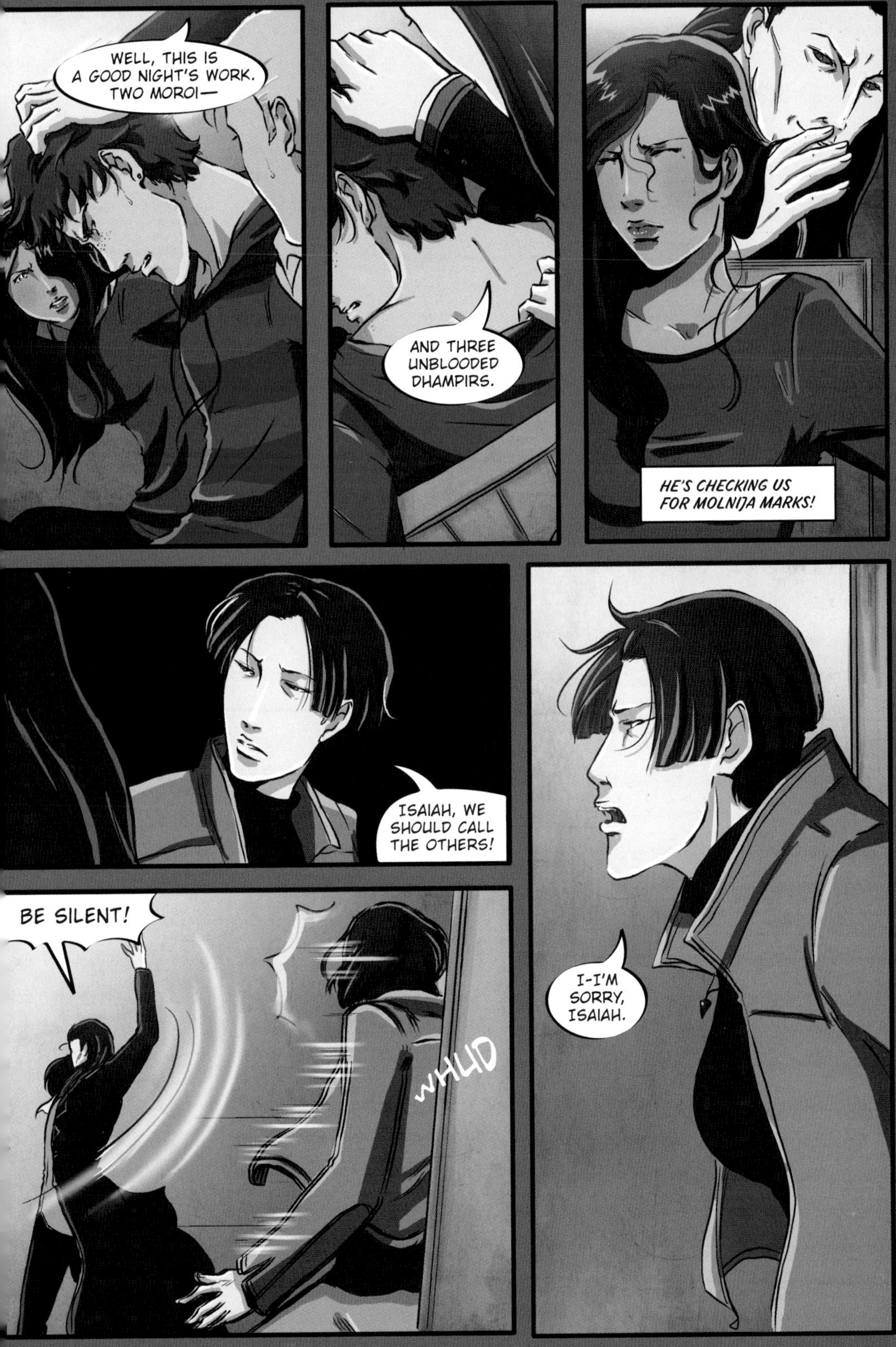
WELL, THIS IS A GOOD NIGHT'S WORK. TWO MOROI—
AND THREE UNBLOODED DHAMPIRS.
HE'S CHECKING US FOR MOLNIJA MARKS!
ISAIAH, WE SHOULD CALL THE OTHERS!
I-I'M SORRY, ISAIAH.
BE SILENT!
WHUD

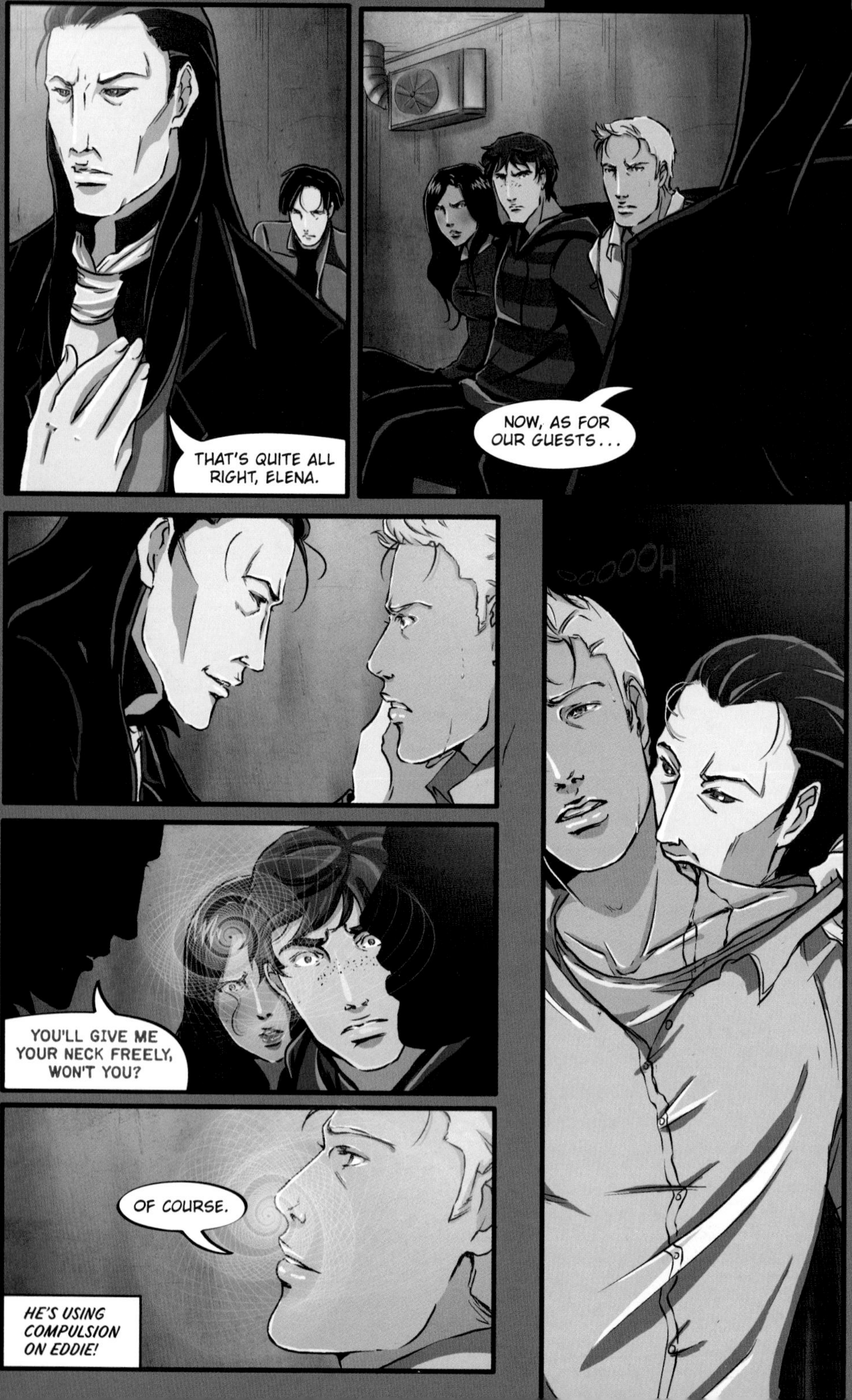
THAT'S QUITE ALL RIGHT, ELENA.
NOW, AS FOR OUR GUESTS . . .
YOU'LL GIVE ME YOUR NECK FREELY, WON'T YOU?
OF COURSE.
HE'S USING COMPULSION ON EDDIE!

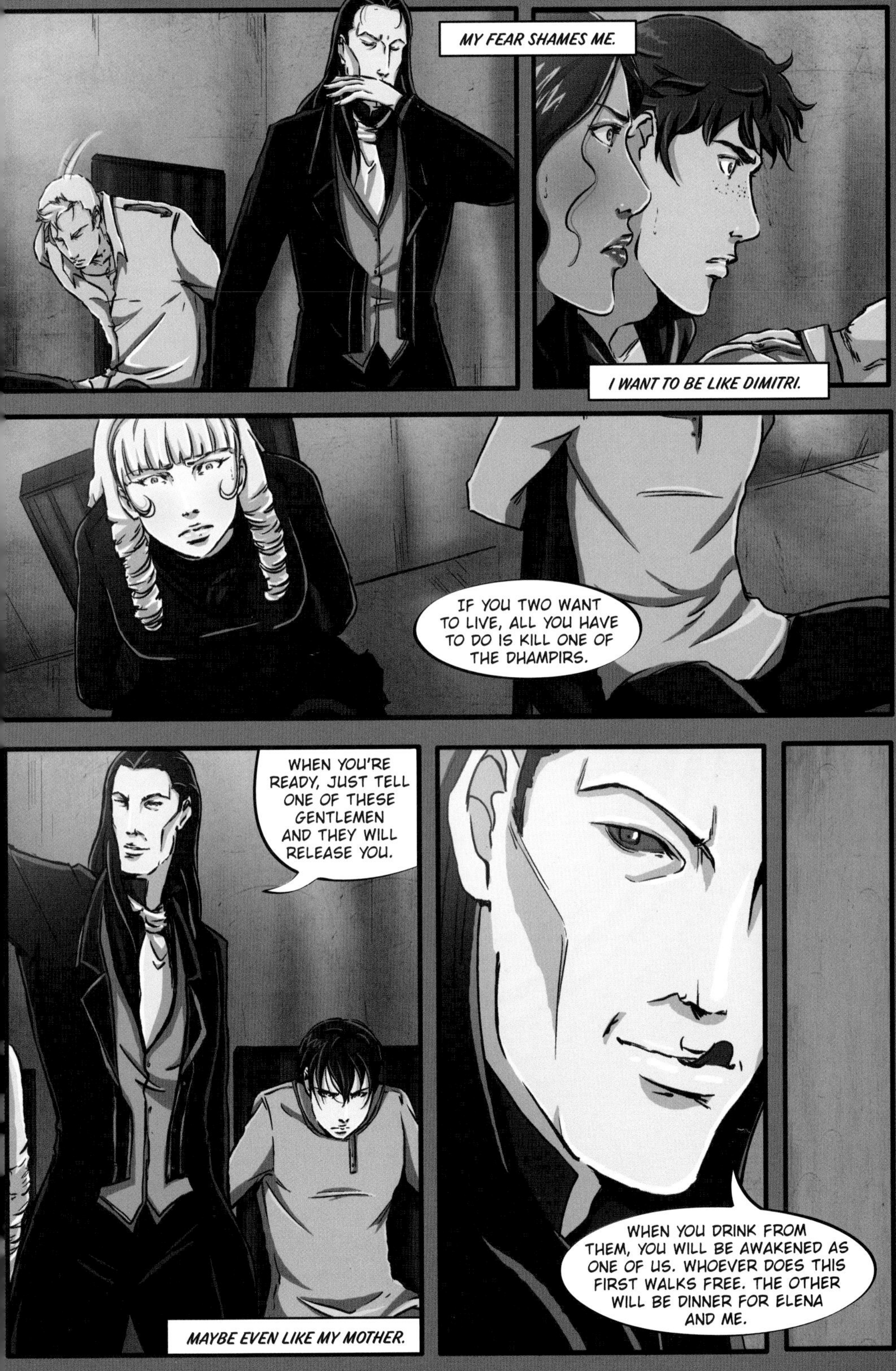
MY FEAR SHAMES ME.
I WANT TO BE LIKE DIMITRI.
IF YOU TWO WANT TO LIVE, ALL YOU HAVE TO DO IS KILL ONE OF THE DHAMPIRS.
WHEN YOU'RE READY, JUST TELL ONE OF THESE GENTLEMEN AND THEY WILL RELEASE YOU.
MAYBE EVEN LIKE MY MOTHER.
WHEN YOU DRINK FROM THEM, YOU WILL BE AWAKENED AS ONE OF US. WHOEVER DOES THIS FIRST WALKS FREE. THE OTHER WILL BE DINNER FOR ELENA AND ME.

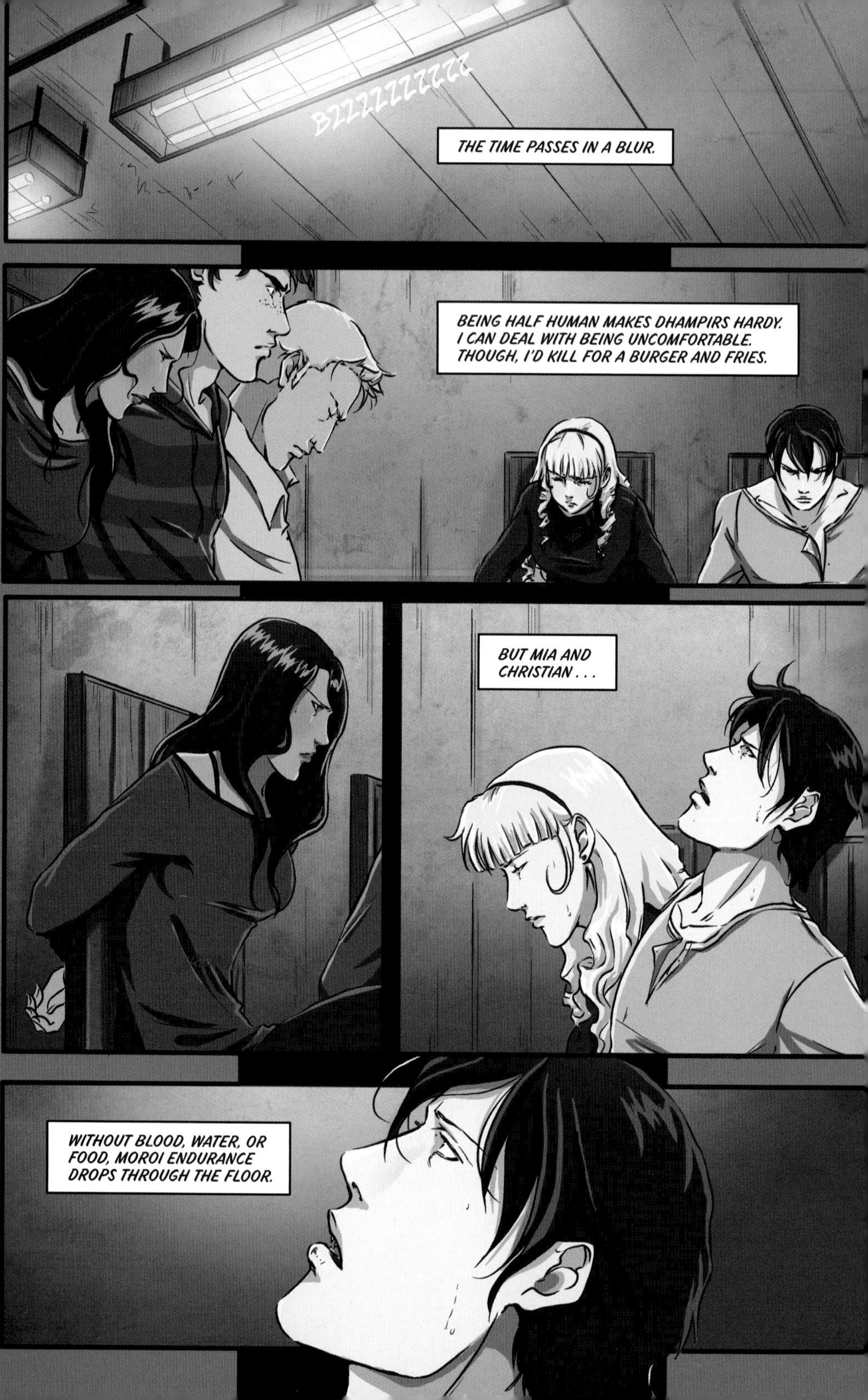
BZZZZZZZZZZZ
THE TIME PASSES IN A BLUR.
BEING HALF HUMAN MAKES DHAMPIRS HARDY. I CAN DEAL WITH BEING UNCOMFORTABLE. THOUGH, I'D KILL FOR A BURGER AND FRIES.
BUT MIA AND CHRISTIAN . . .
WITHOUT BLOOD, WATER, OR FOOD, MOROI ENDURANCE DROPS THROUGH THE FLOOR.

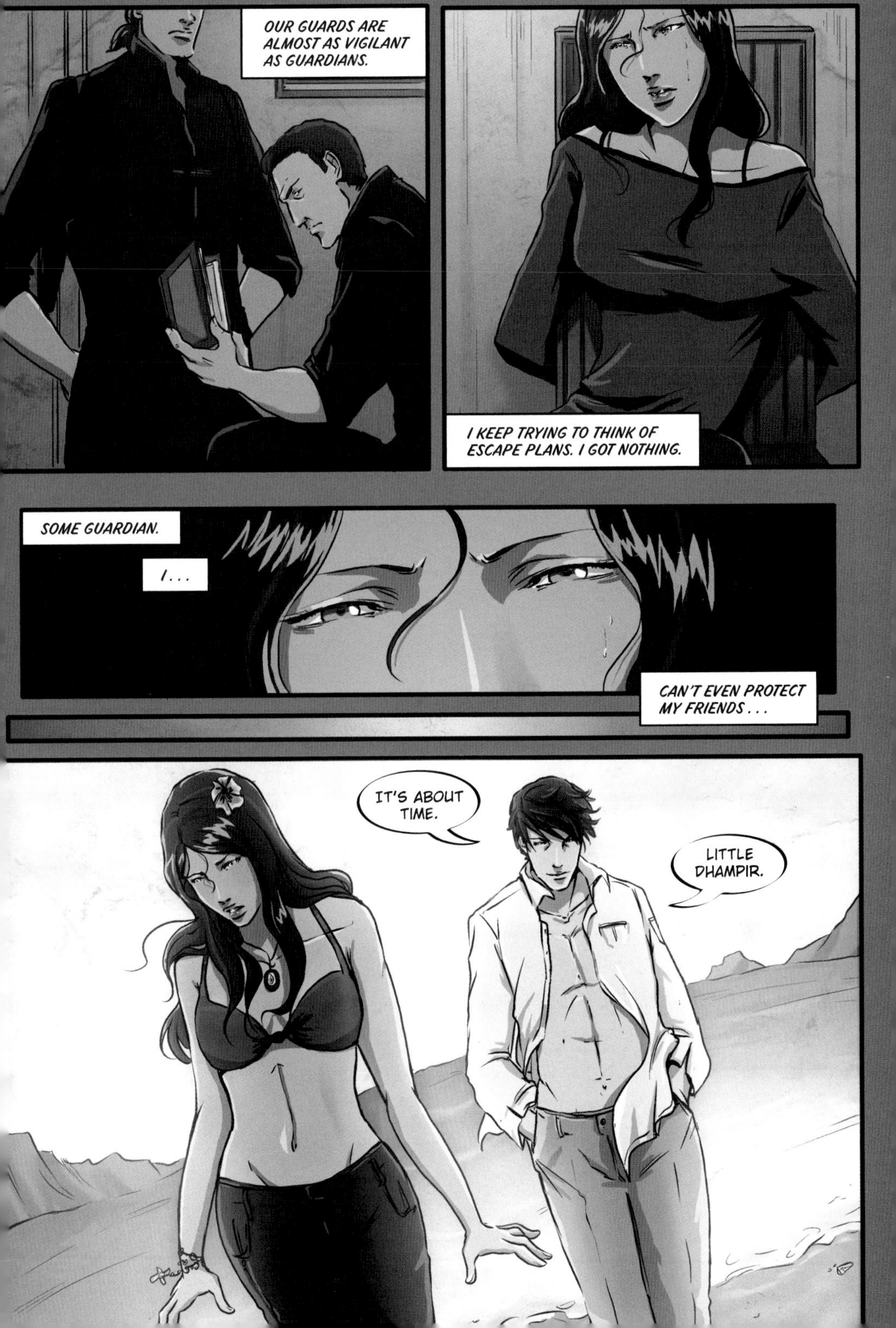
OUR GUARDS ARE ALMOST AS VIGILANT AS GUARDIANS.
I KEEP TRYING TO THINK OF ESCAPE PLANS. I GOT NOTHING.
SOME GUARDIAN.
I . . .
CAN'T EVEN PROTECT MY FRIENDS . . .
IT'S ABOUT TIME.
LITTLE DHAMPIR.

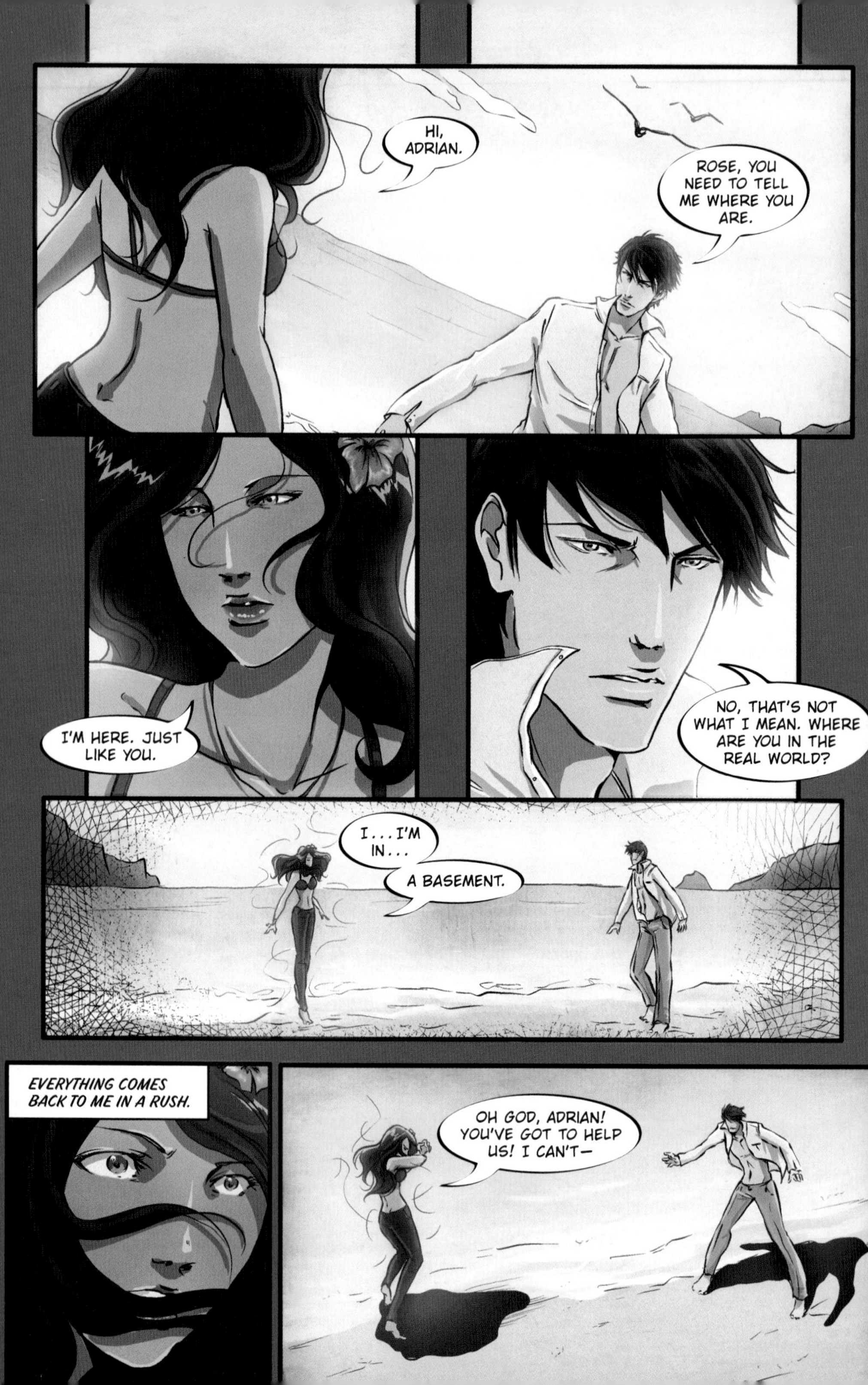
HI, ADRIAN.
ROSE, YOU NEED TO TELL ME WHERE YOU ARE.
I'M HERE. JUST LIKE YOU.
NO, THAT'S NOT WHAT I MEAN. WHERE ARE YOU IN THE REAL WORLD?
I . . . I'M IN . . .
A BASEMENT.
EVERYTHING COMES BACK TO ME IN A RUSH.
OH GOD, ADRIAN! YOU'VE GOT TO HELP US! I CAN'T—

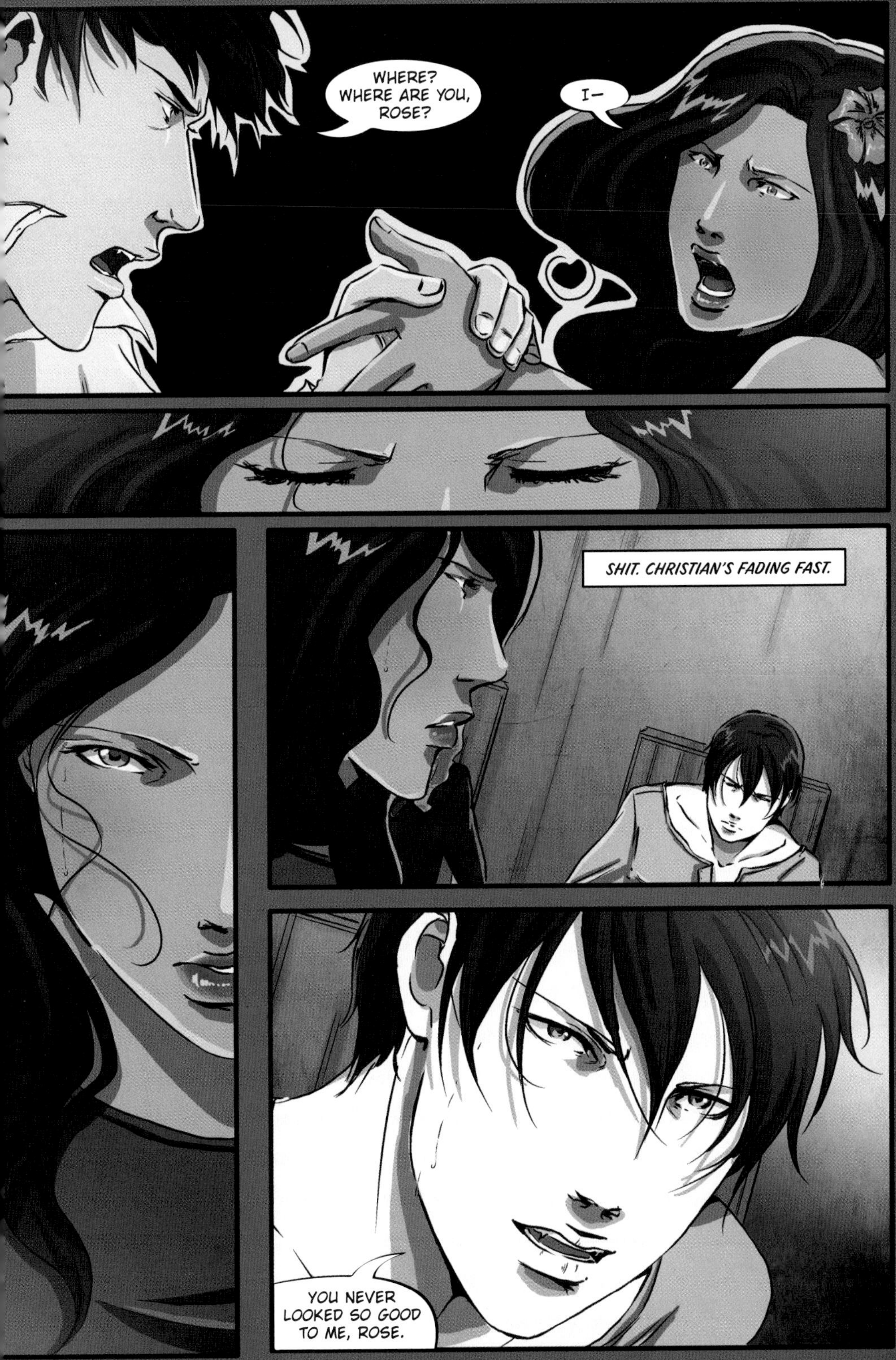
WHERE? WHERE ARE YOU, ROSE?
I—
SHIT. CHRISTIAN'S FADING FAST.
YOU NEVER LOOKED SO GOOD TO ME, ROSE.

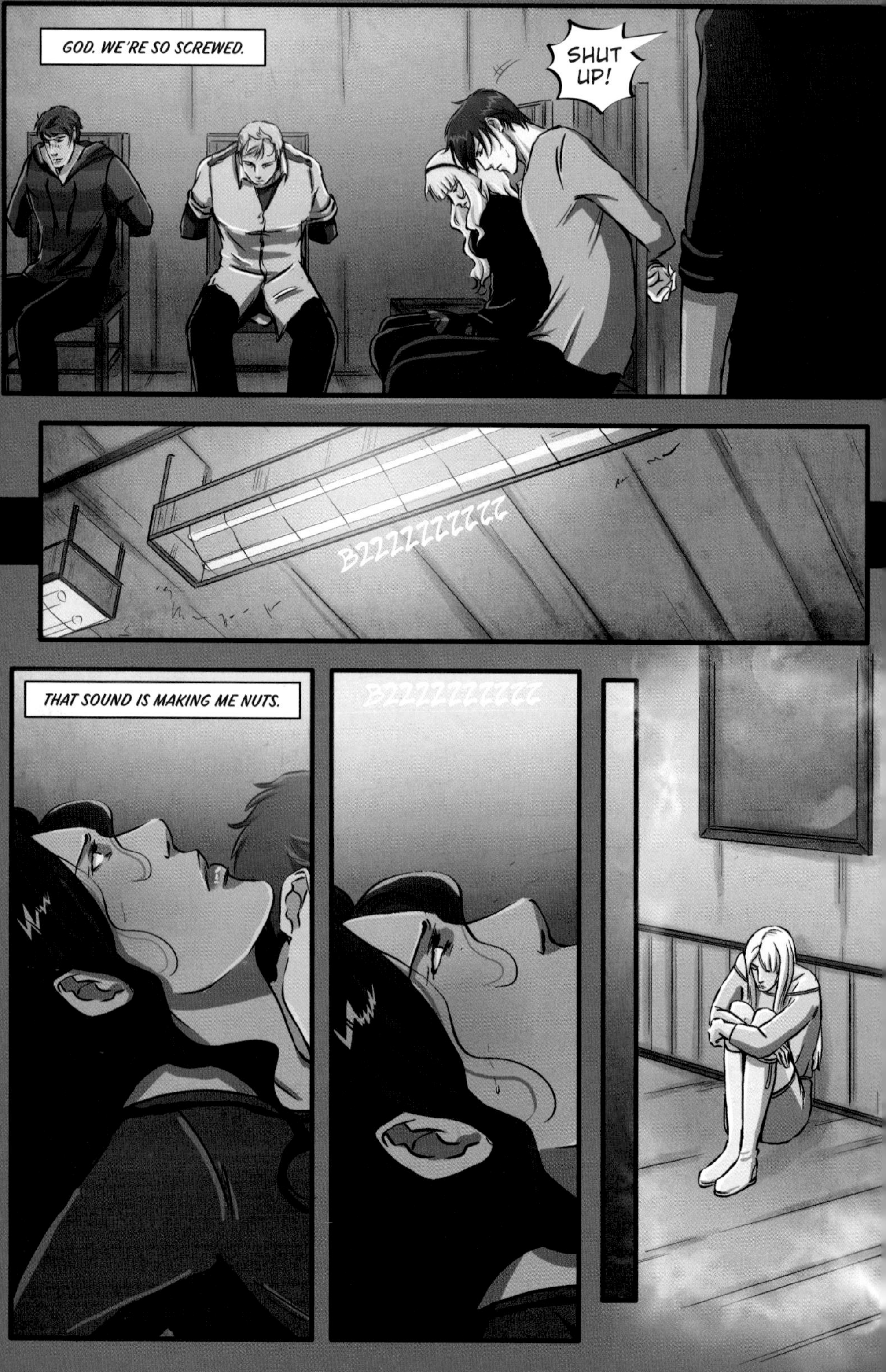
GOD. WE'RE SO SCREWED.
SHUT UP!
BZZZZZZZZZZZ
THAT SOUND IS MAKING ME NUTS.
BZZZZZZZZZZZ

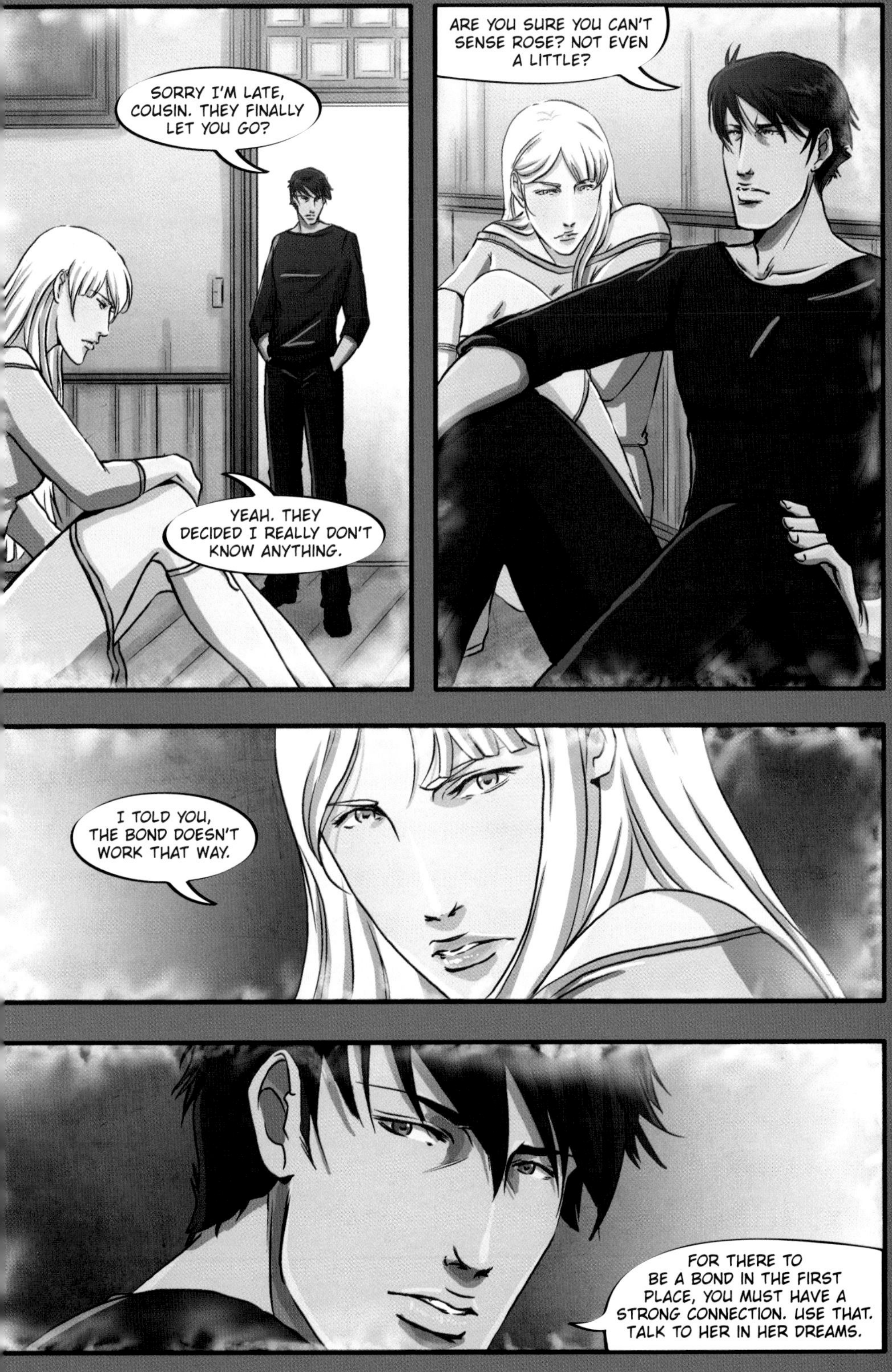
SORRY I'M LATE, COUSIN. THEY FINALLY LET YOU GO?
YEAH. THEY DECIDED I REALLY DON'T KNOW ANYTHING.
ARE YOU SURE YOU CAN'T SENSE ROSE? NOT EVEN A LITTLE?
I TOLD YOU, THE BOND DOESN'T WORK THAT WAY.
FOR THERE TO BE A BOND IN THE FIRST PLACE, YOU MUST HAVE A STRONG CONNECTION. USE THAT. TALK TO HER IN HER DREAMS.

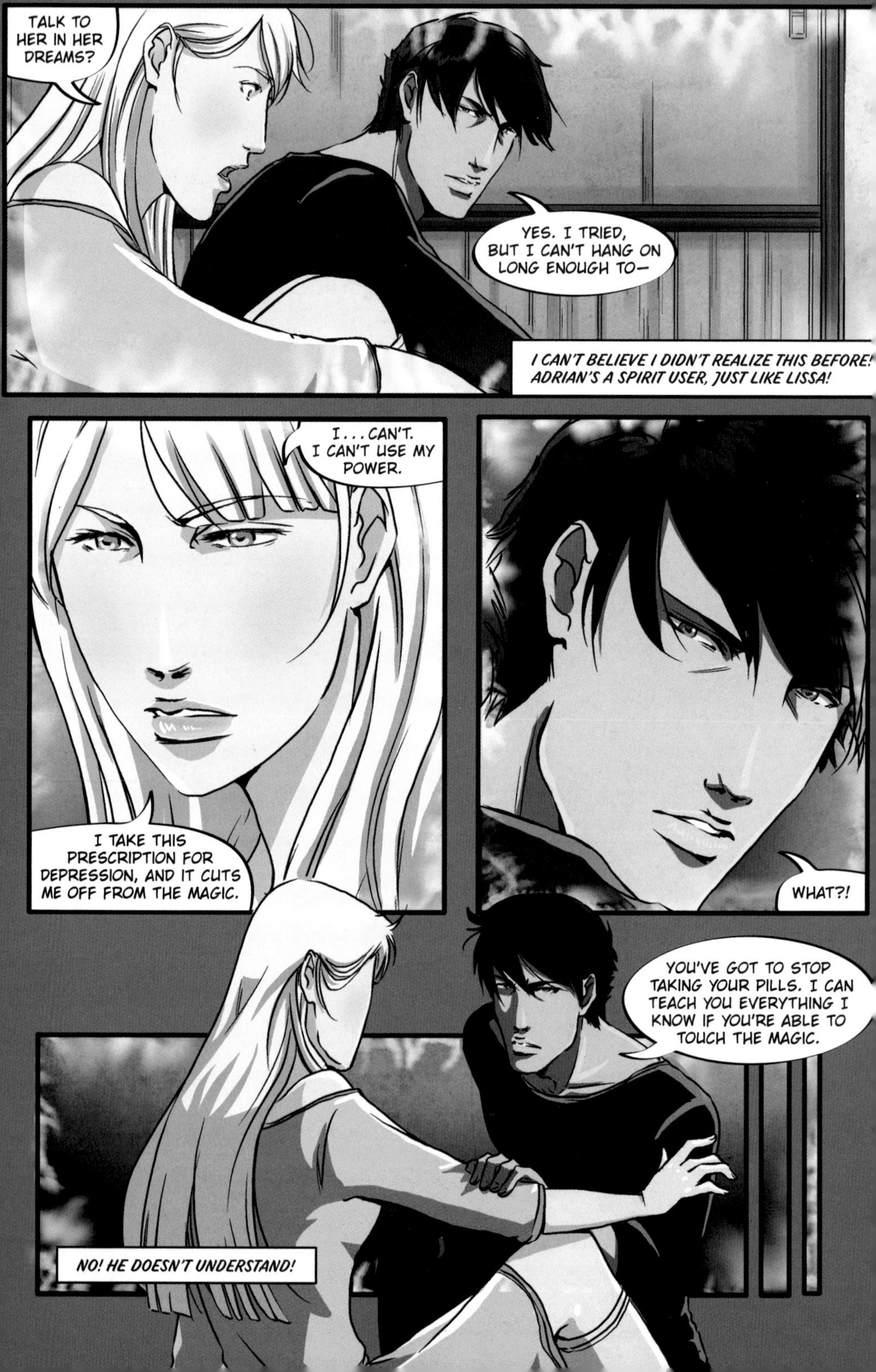
TALK TO HER IN HER DREAMS?
YES. I TRIED, BUT I CAN'T HANG ON LONG ENOUGH TO—
I CAN'T BELIEVE I DIDN'T REALIZE THIS BEFORE! ADRIAN'S A SPIRIT USER, JUST LIKE LISSA!
I . . . CAN'T. I CAN'T USE MY POWER.
I TAKE THIS PRESCRIPTION FOR DEPRESSION, AND IT CUTS ME OFF FROM THE MAGIC.
WHAT?!
YOU'VE GOT TO STOP TAKING YOUR PILLS. I CAN TEACH YOU EVERYTHING I KNOW IF YOU'RE ABLE TO TOUCH THE MAGIC.
NO! HE DOESN'T UNDERSTAND!

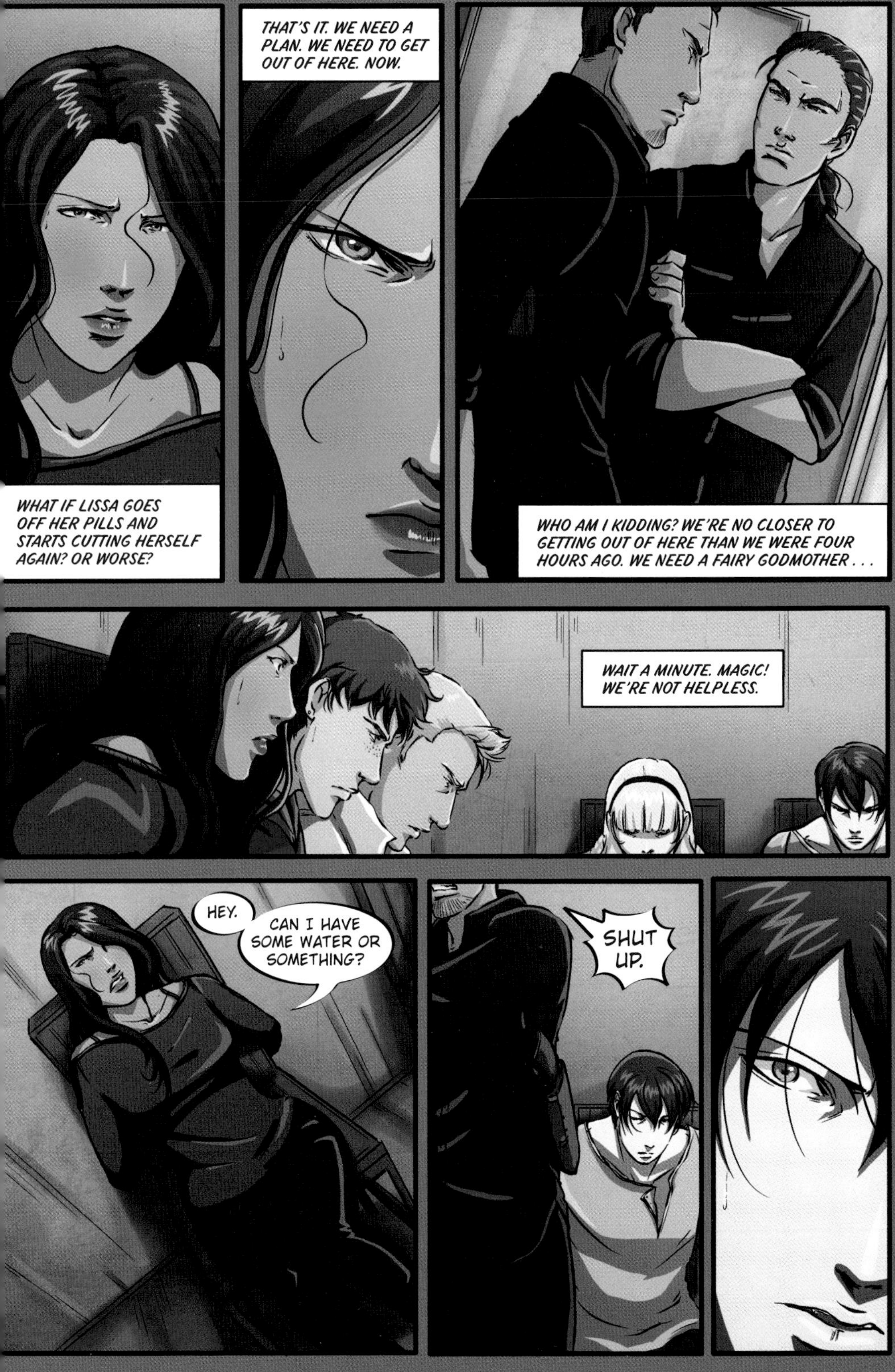
WHAT IF LISSA GOES OFF HER PILLS AND STARTS CUTTING HERSELF AGAIN? OR WORSE?
THAT'S IT. WE NEED A PLAN. WE NEED TO GET OUT OF HERE. NOW.
WHO AM I KIDDING? WE'RE NO CLOSER TO GETTING OUT OF HERE THAN WE WERE FOUR HOURS AGO. WE NEED A FAIRY GODMOTHER . . .
WAIT A MINUTE. MAGIC! WE'RE NOT HELPLESS.
HEY.
CAN I HAVE SOME WATER OR SOMETHING?
SHUT UP.

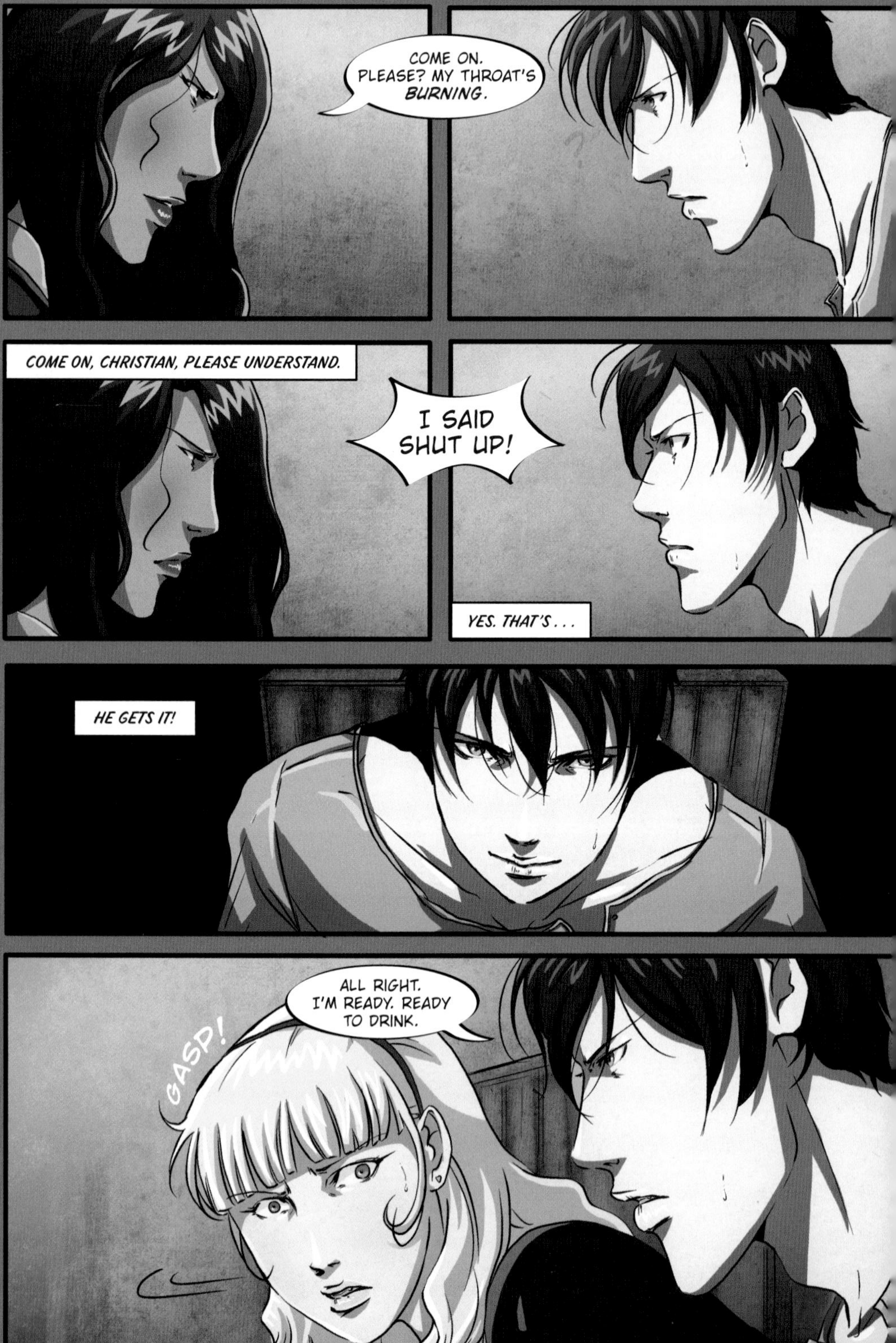
COME ON. PLEASE? MY THROAT'S *BURNING*.
COME ON, CHRISTIAN, PLEASE UNDERSTAND.
I SAID SHUT UP!
YES. THAT'S . . .
HE GETS IT!
ALL RIGHT. I'M READY. READY TO DRINK.
GASP!

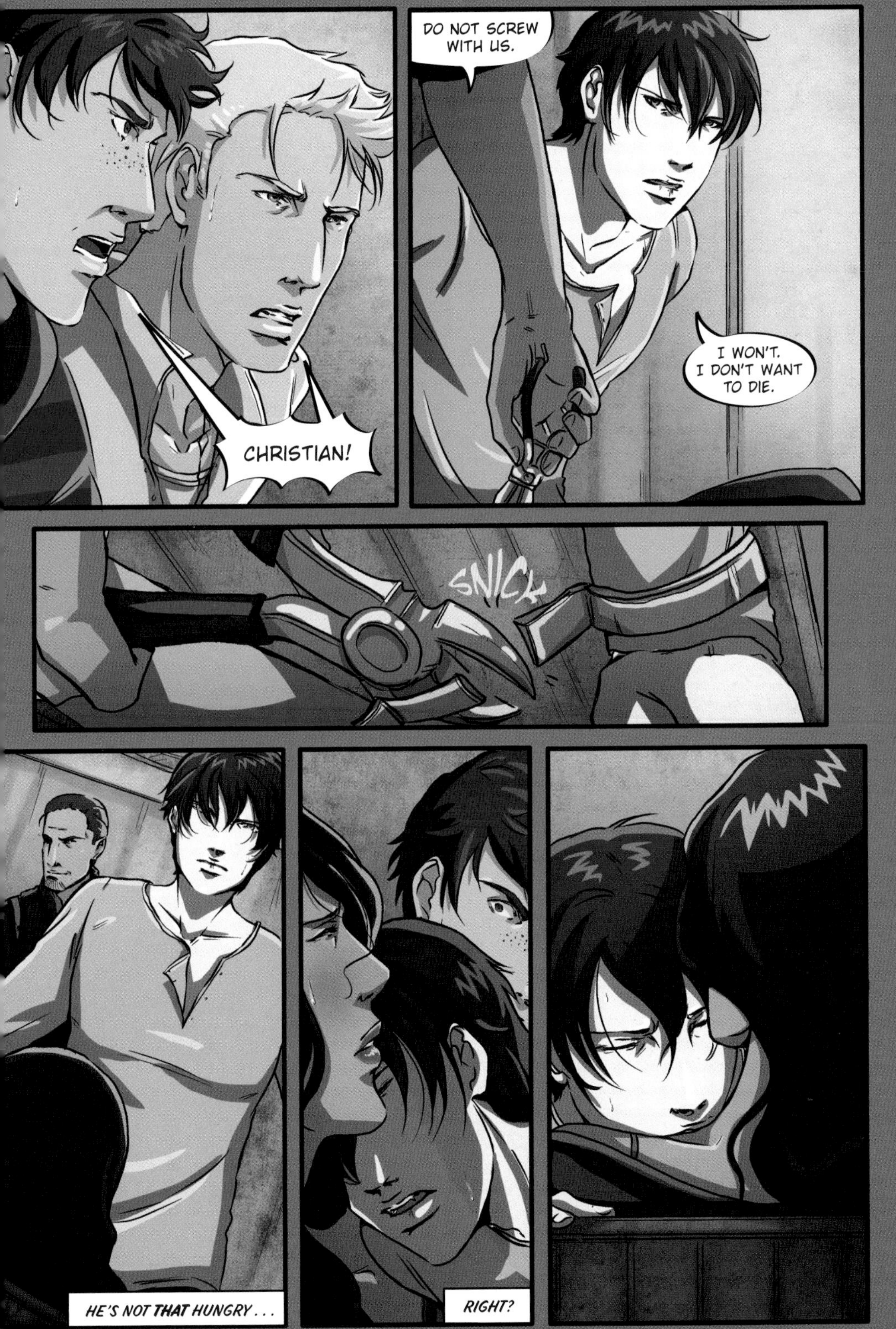
CHRISTIAN!
DO NOT SCREW WITH US.
I WON'T. I DON'T WANT TO DIE.
SNICK
HE'S NOT **THAT** HUNGRY . . .
RIGHT?

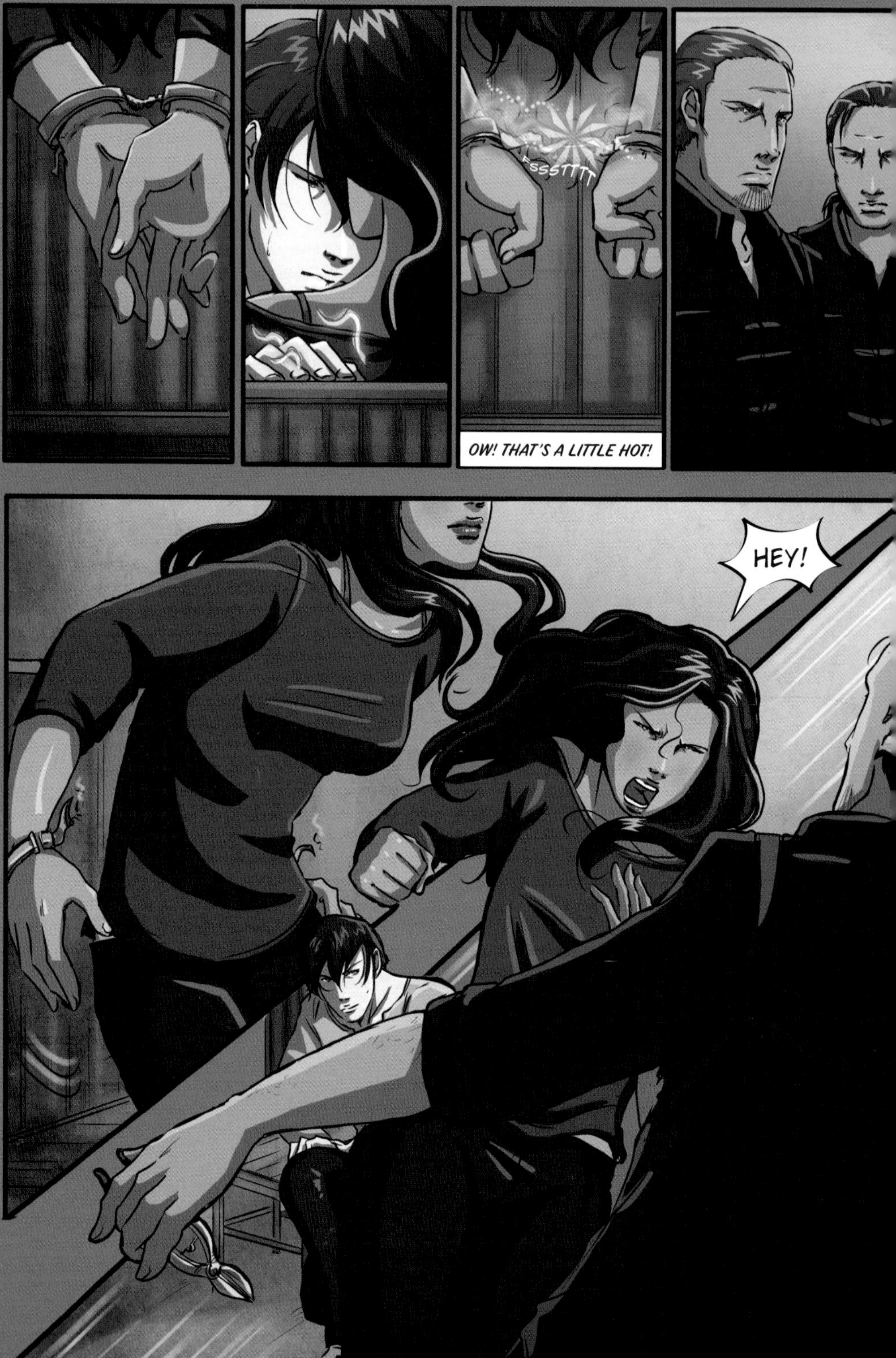
FSSSTTTT
OW! THAT'S A LITTLE HOT!
HEY!

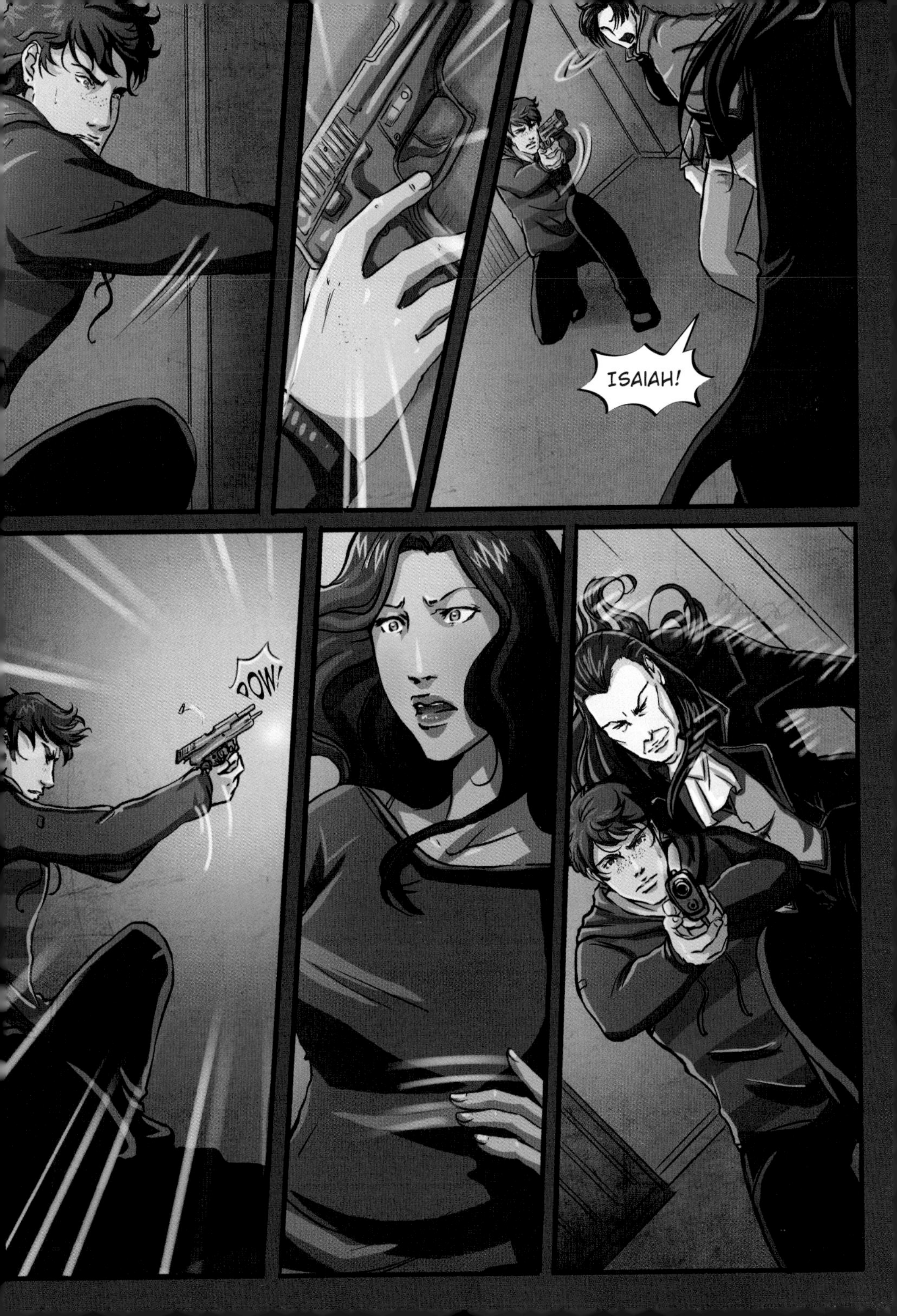
ISAIAH!
POW!

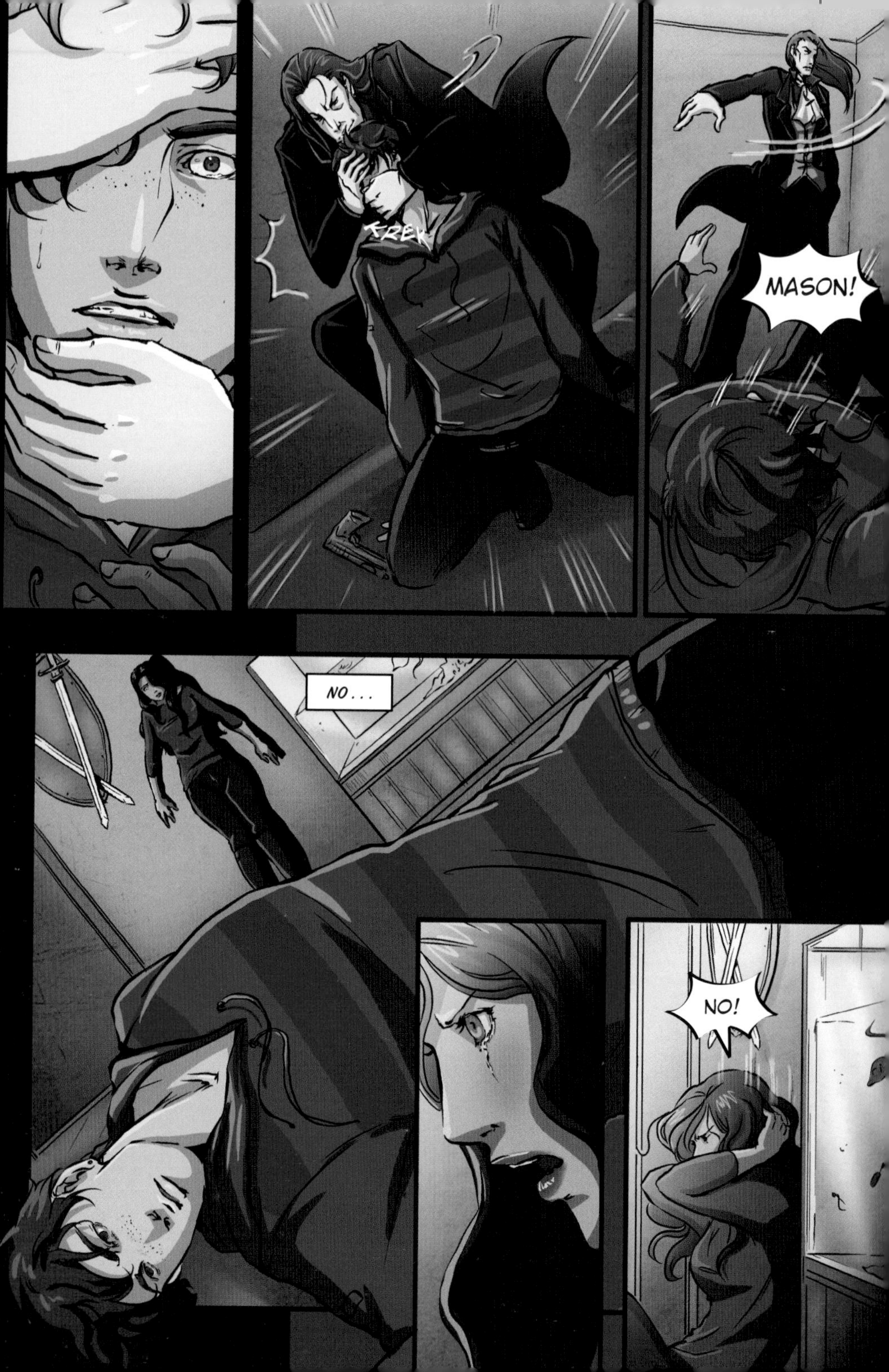
KREK
MASON!
NO...
NO!

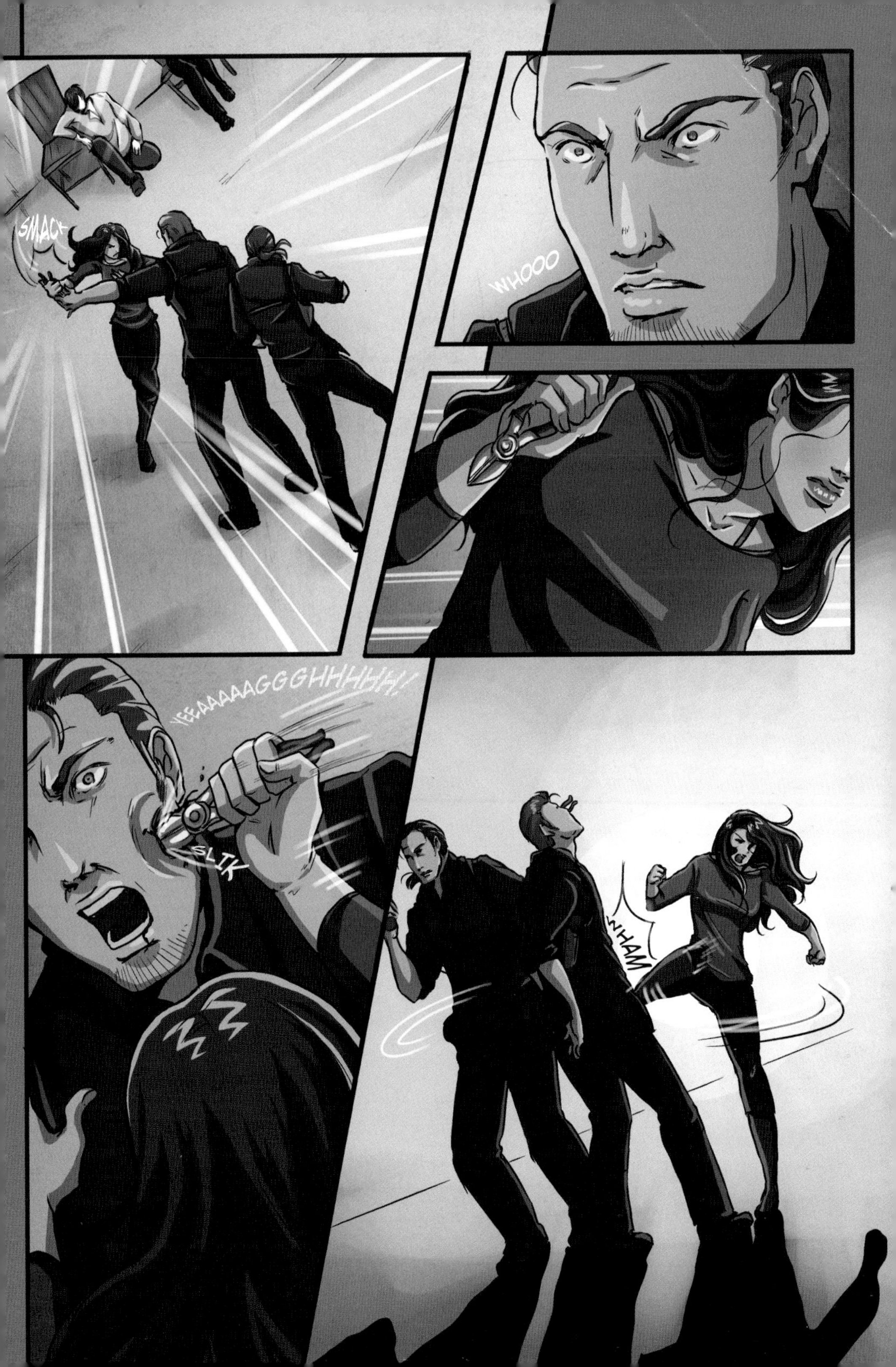
SMACK
WHOOO
YEEAAAAAGGGHHHHH!!
SLIK
WHAM

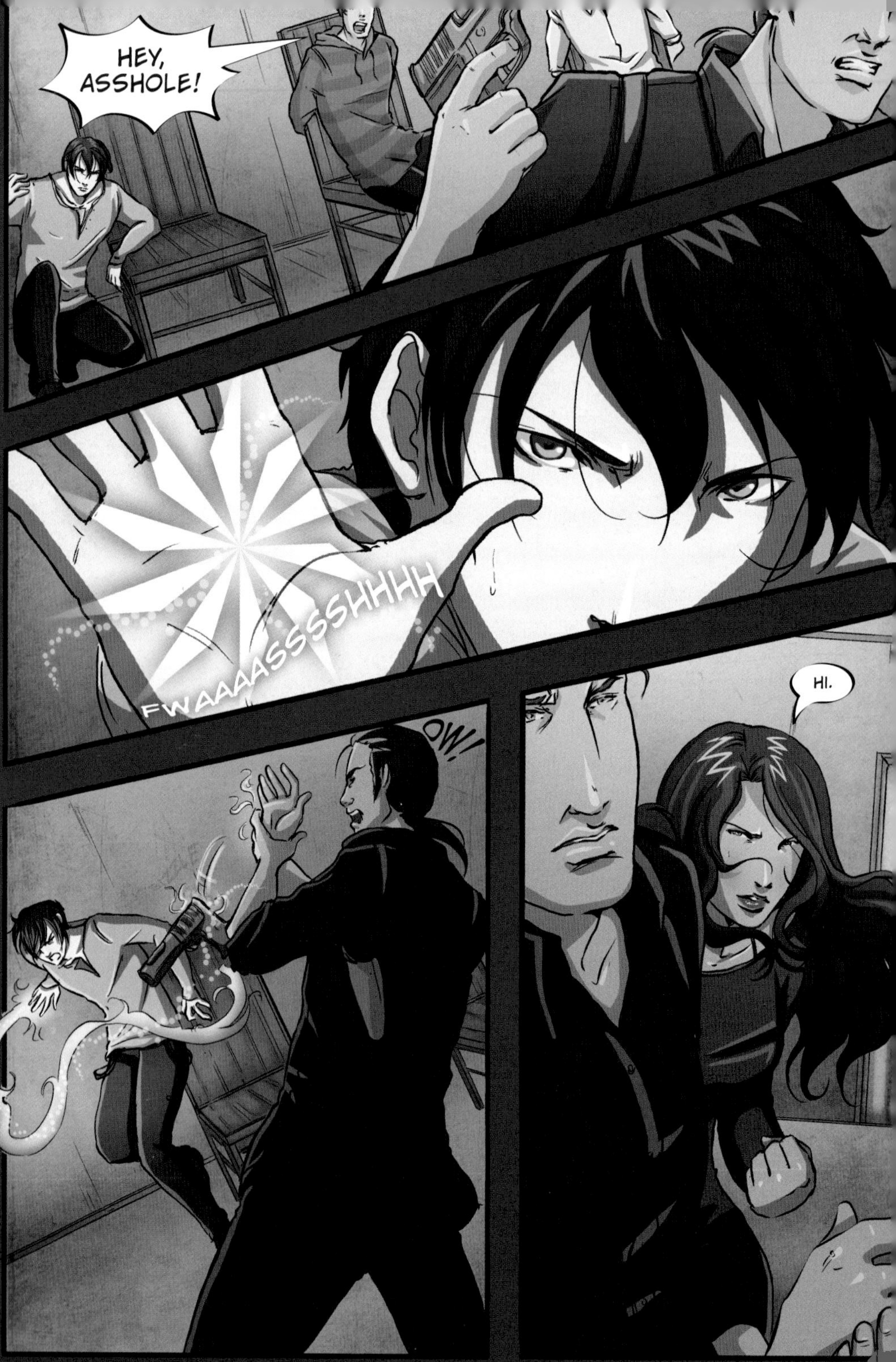
HEY, ASSHOLE!
FWAAAASSSSSHHHH
OW!
HI.

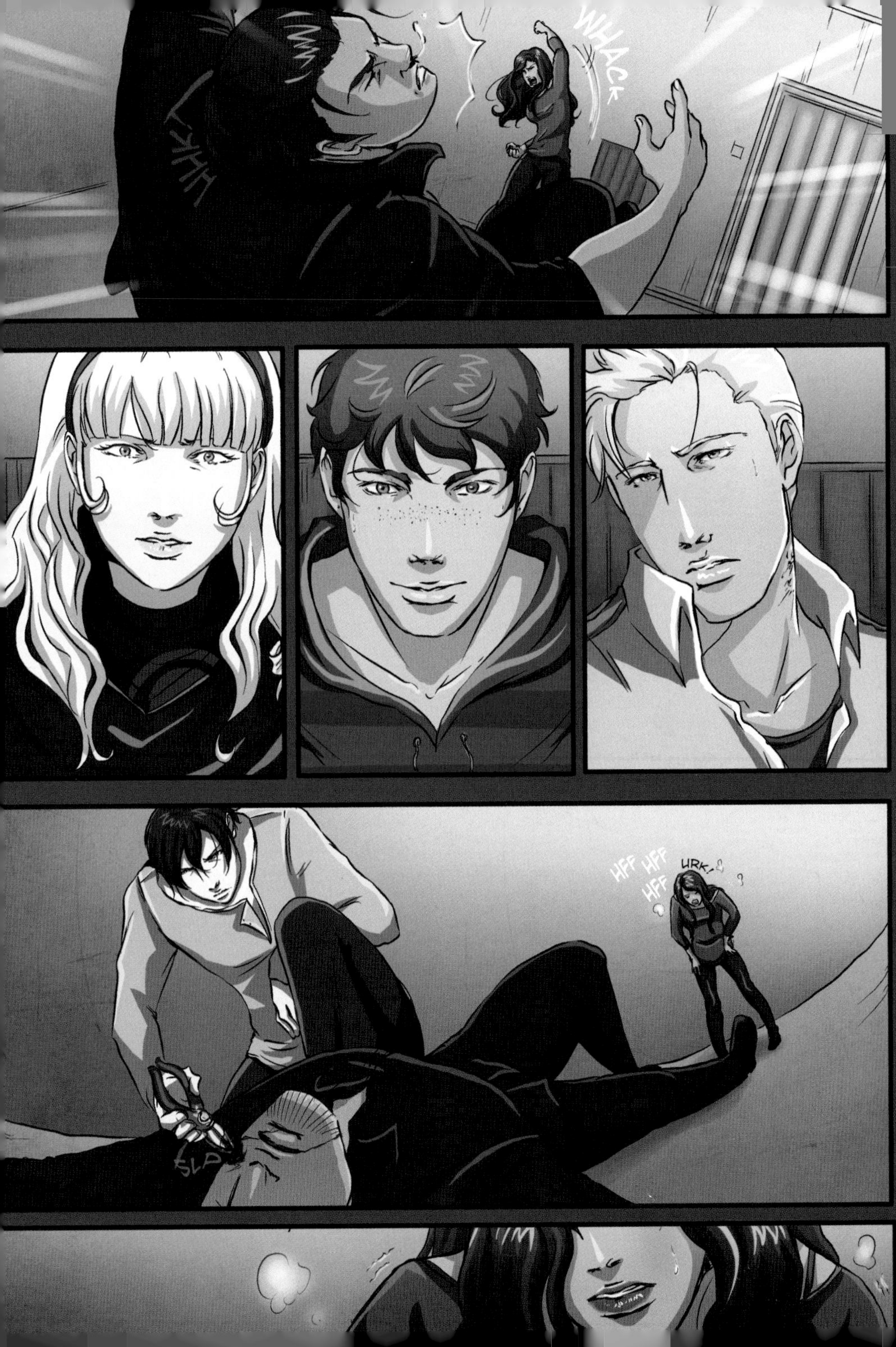

WHACK
HHRK!
HFF HFF HFF
URK!

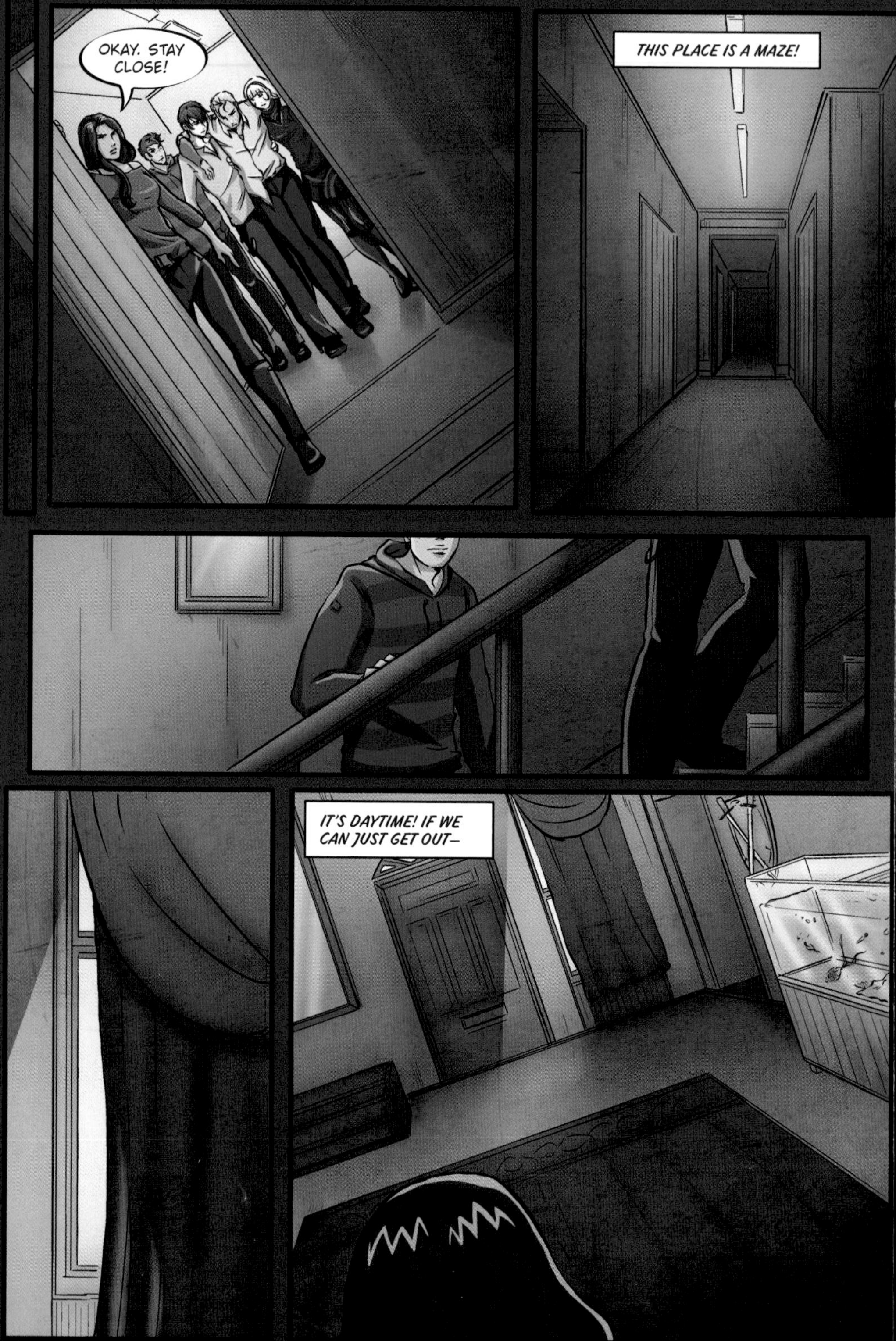
OKAY. STAY CLOSE!
THIS PLACE IS A MAZE!
IT'S DAYTIME! IF WE CAN JUST GET OUT—

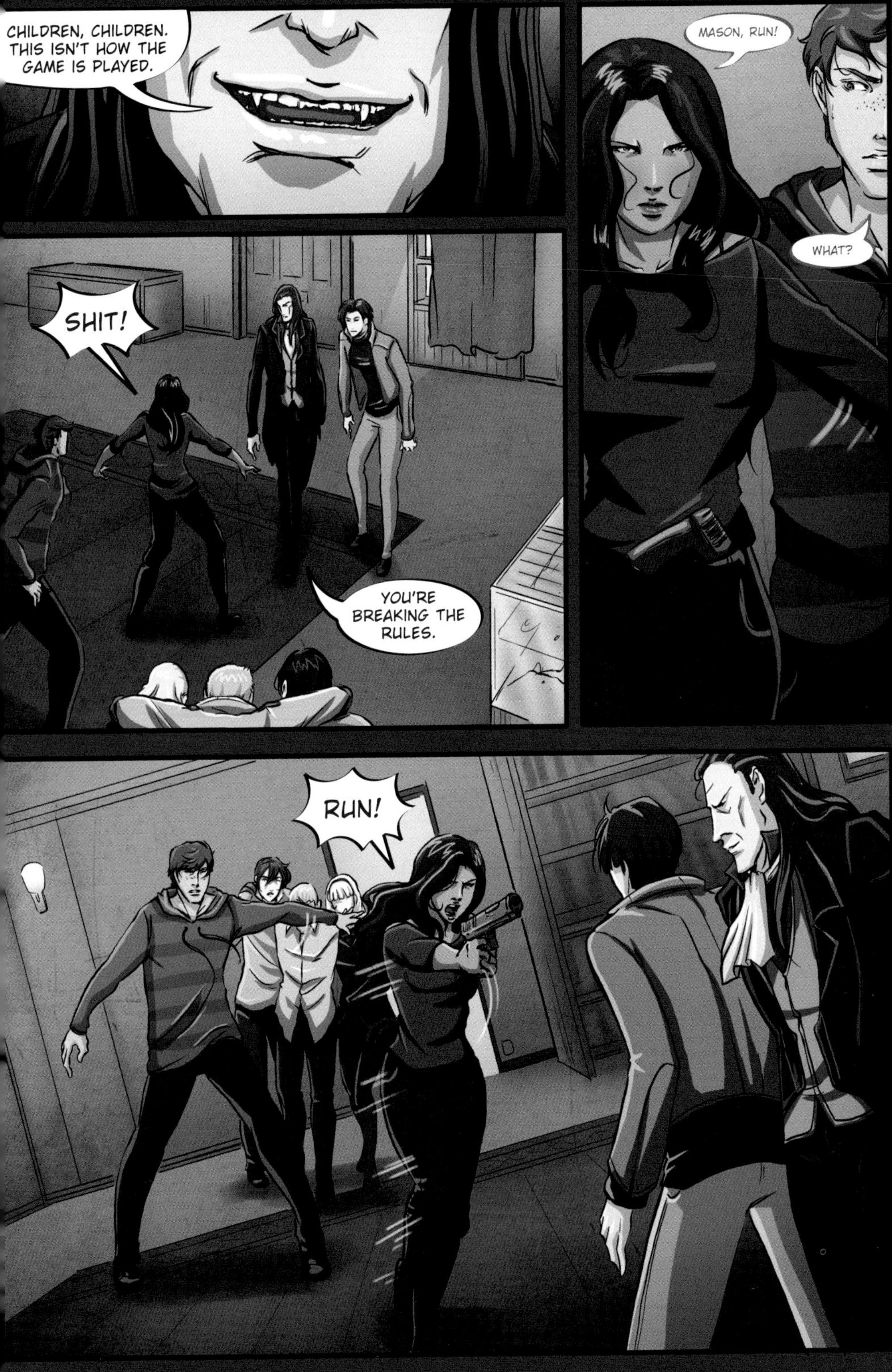
CHILDREN, CHILDREN. THIS ISN'T HOW THE GAME IS PLAYED.
MASON, RUN!
WHAT?
SHIT!
YOU'RE BREAKING THE RULES.
RUN!

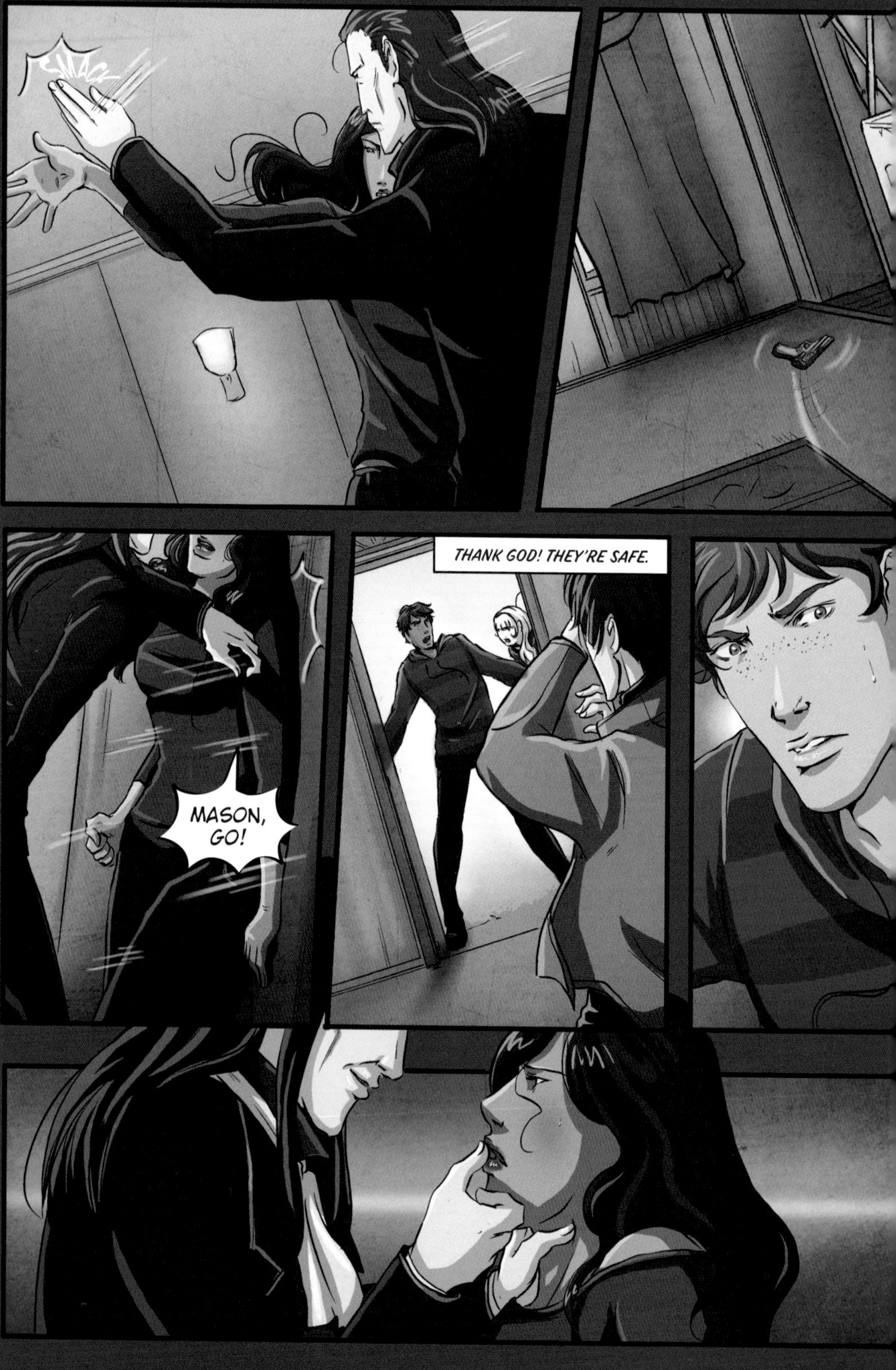
SMACK
MASON, GO!
THANK GOD! THEY'RE SAFE.

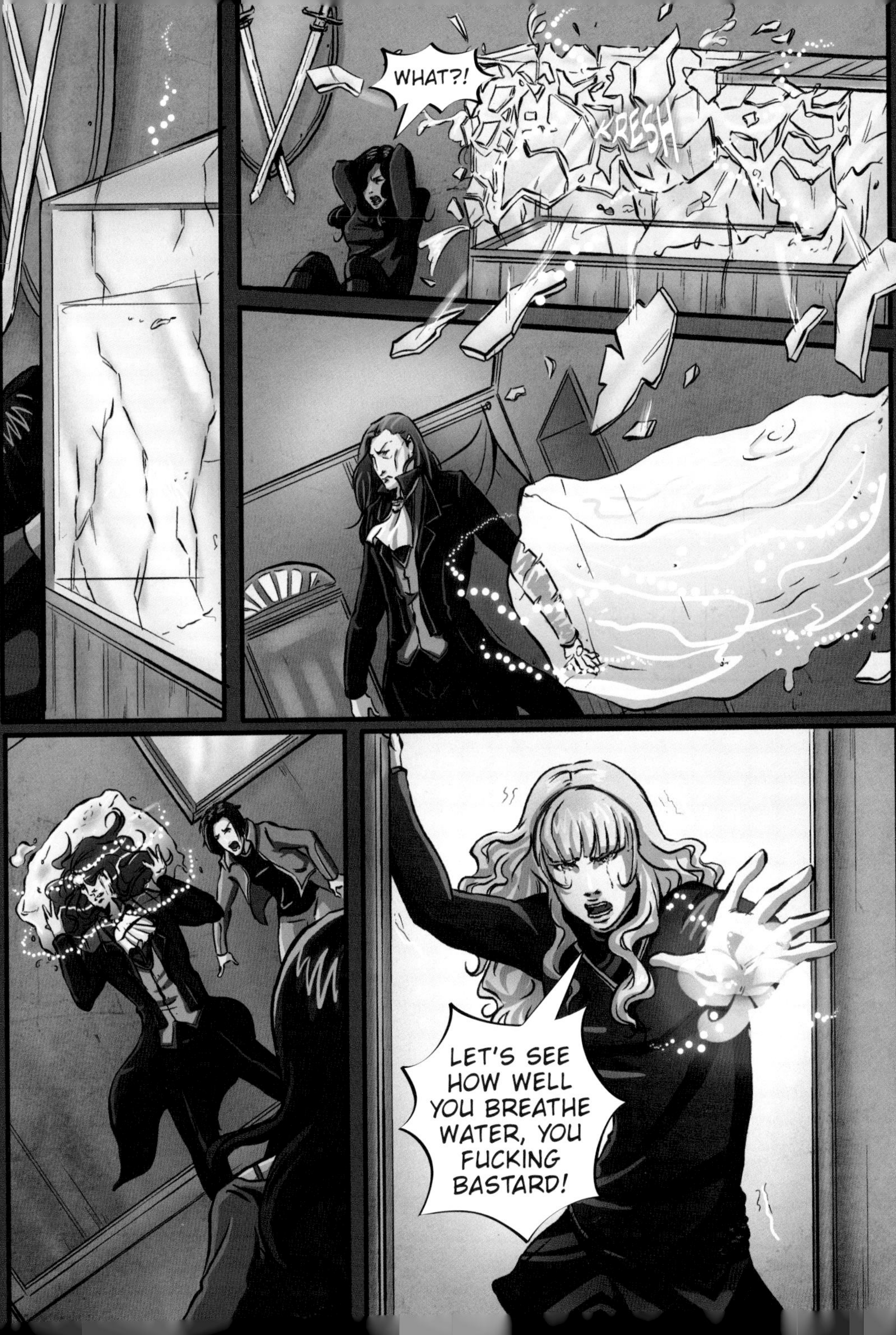
WHAT?!
KRESH
LET'S SEE HOW WELL YOU BREATHE WATER, YOU FUCKING BASTARD!

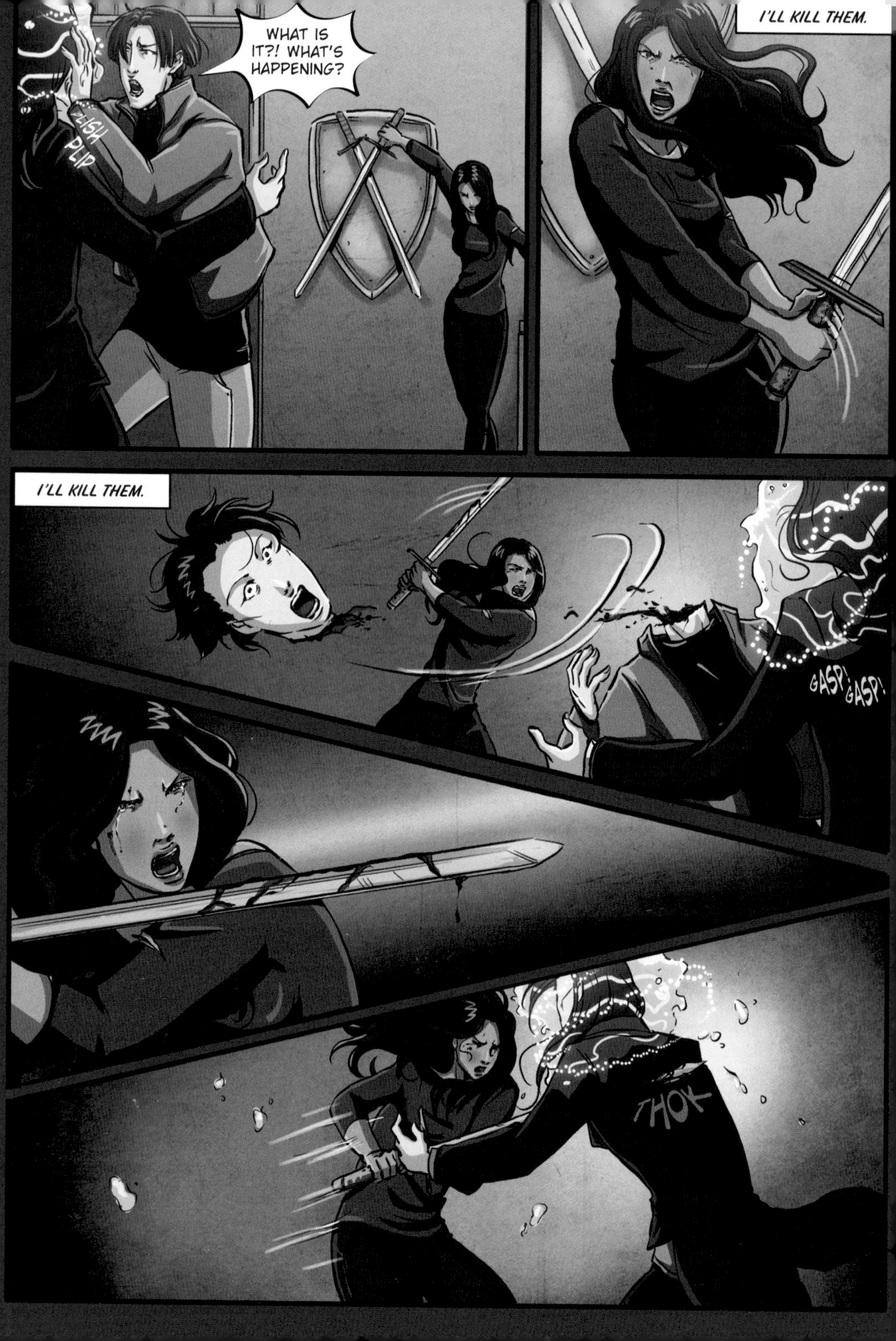
WHAT IS IT?! WHAT'S HAPPENING?
ZLISH
PLIP
I'LL KILL THEM.
I'LL KILL THEM.
GASP! GASP!
THOK

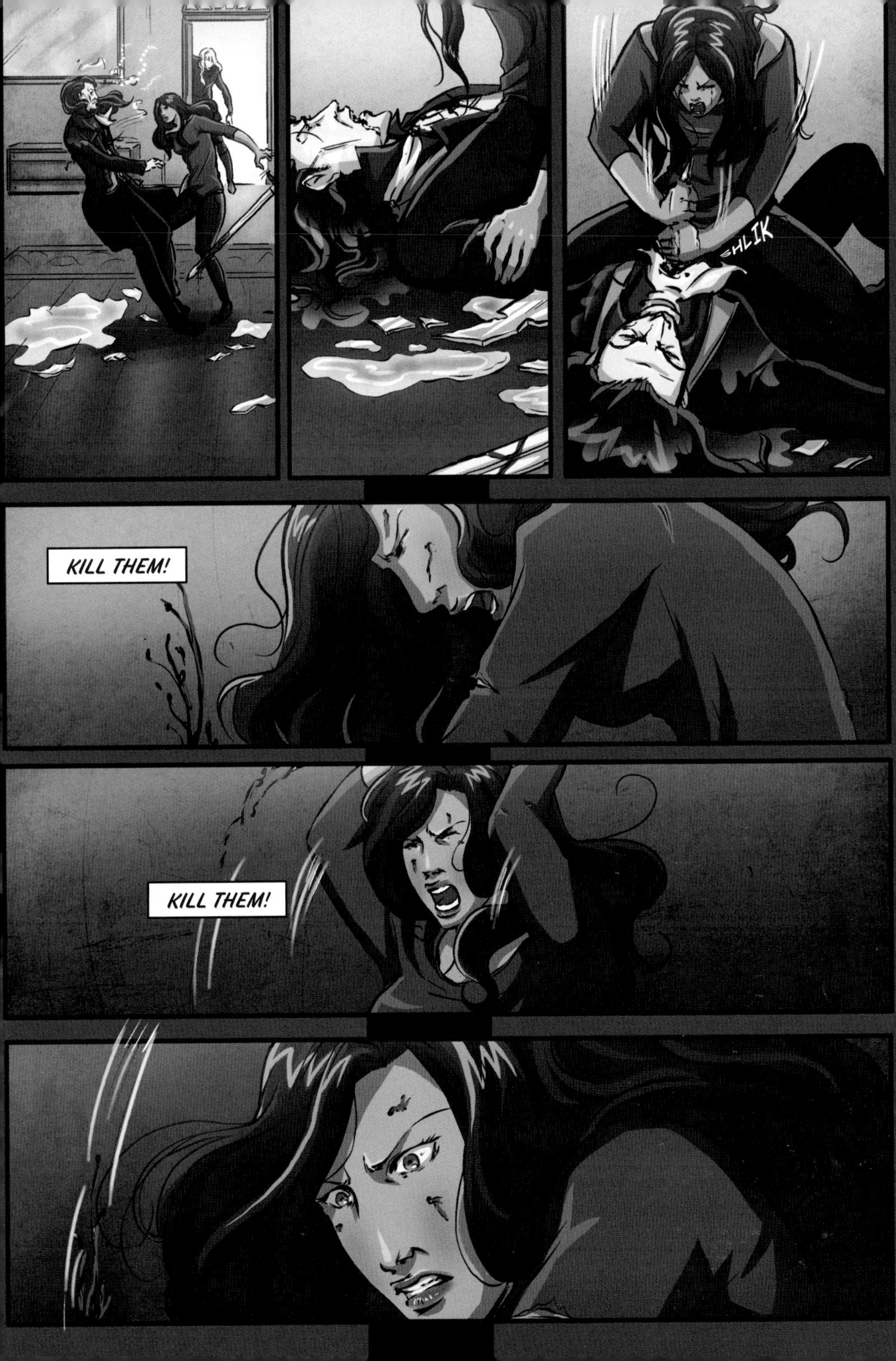
SHLIK
KILL THEM!
KILL THEM!

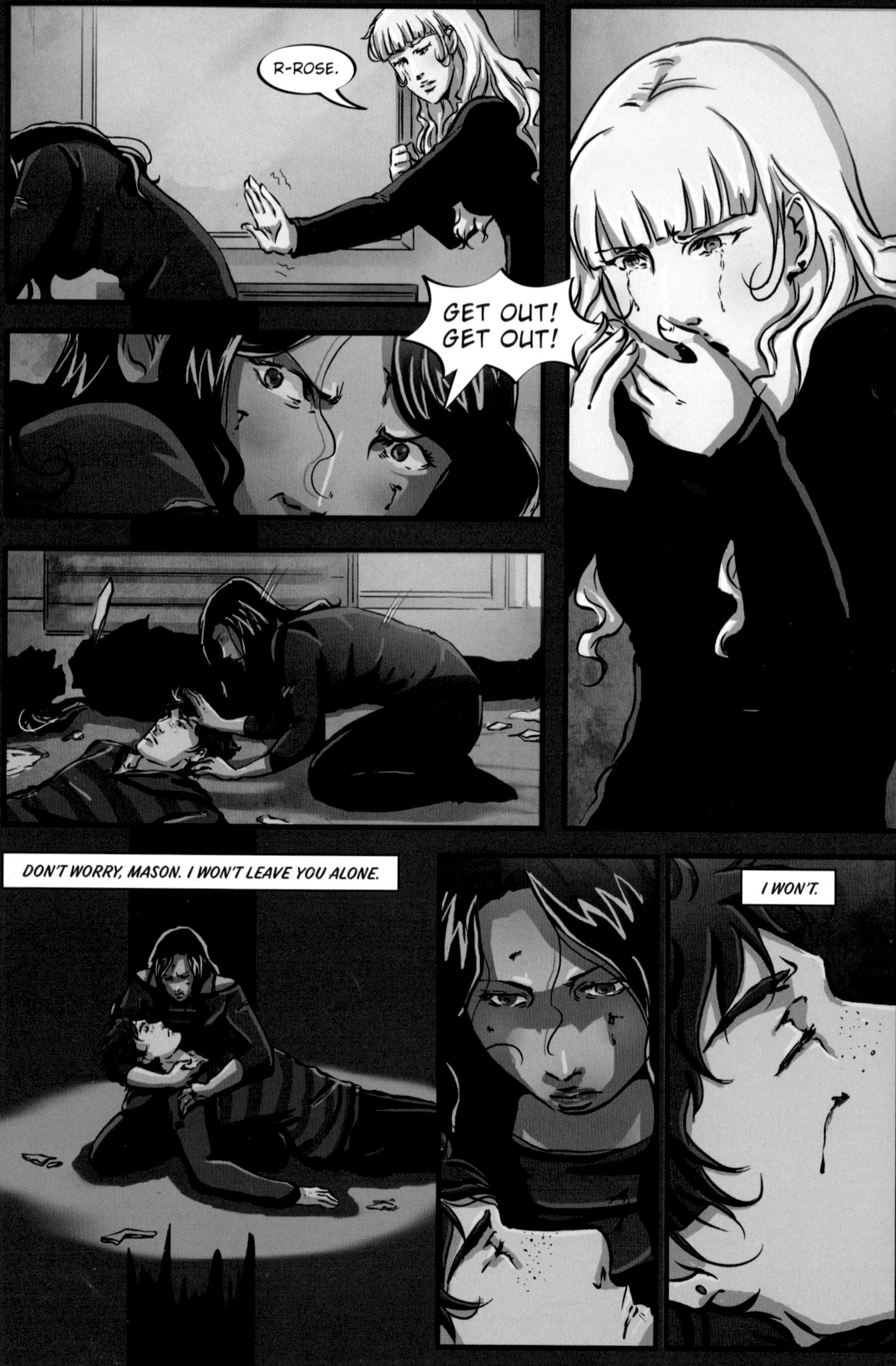
R-ROSE.
GET OUT! GET OUT!
DON'T WORRY, MASON. I WON'T LEAVE YOU ALONE.
I WON'T.

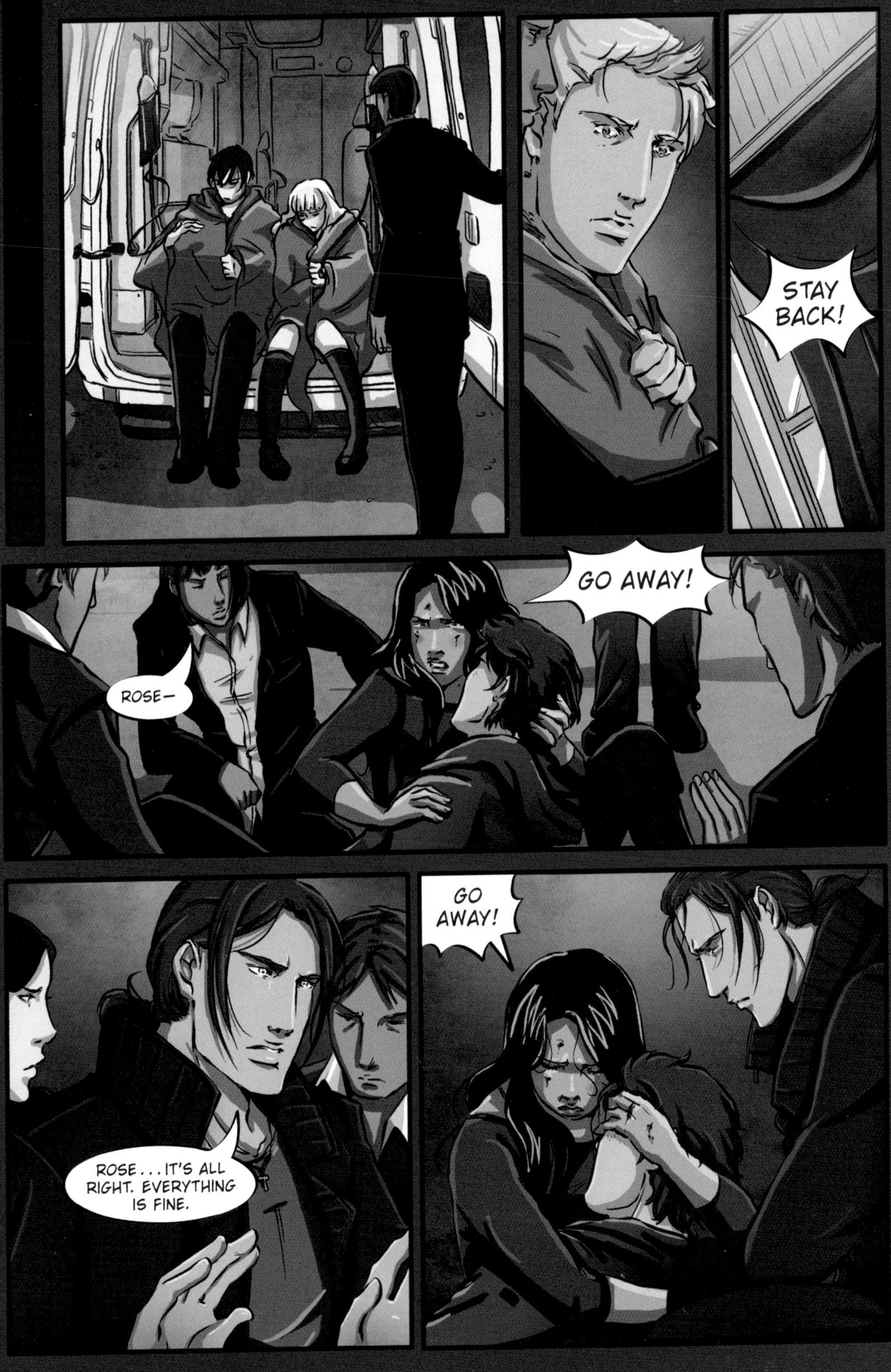
STAY BACK!
GO AWAY!
ROSE—
ROSE . . . IT'S ALL RIGHT. EVERYTHING IS FINE.
GO AWAY!

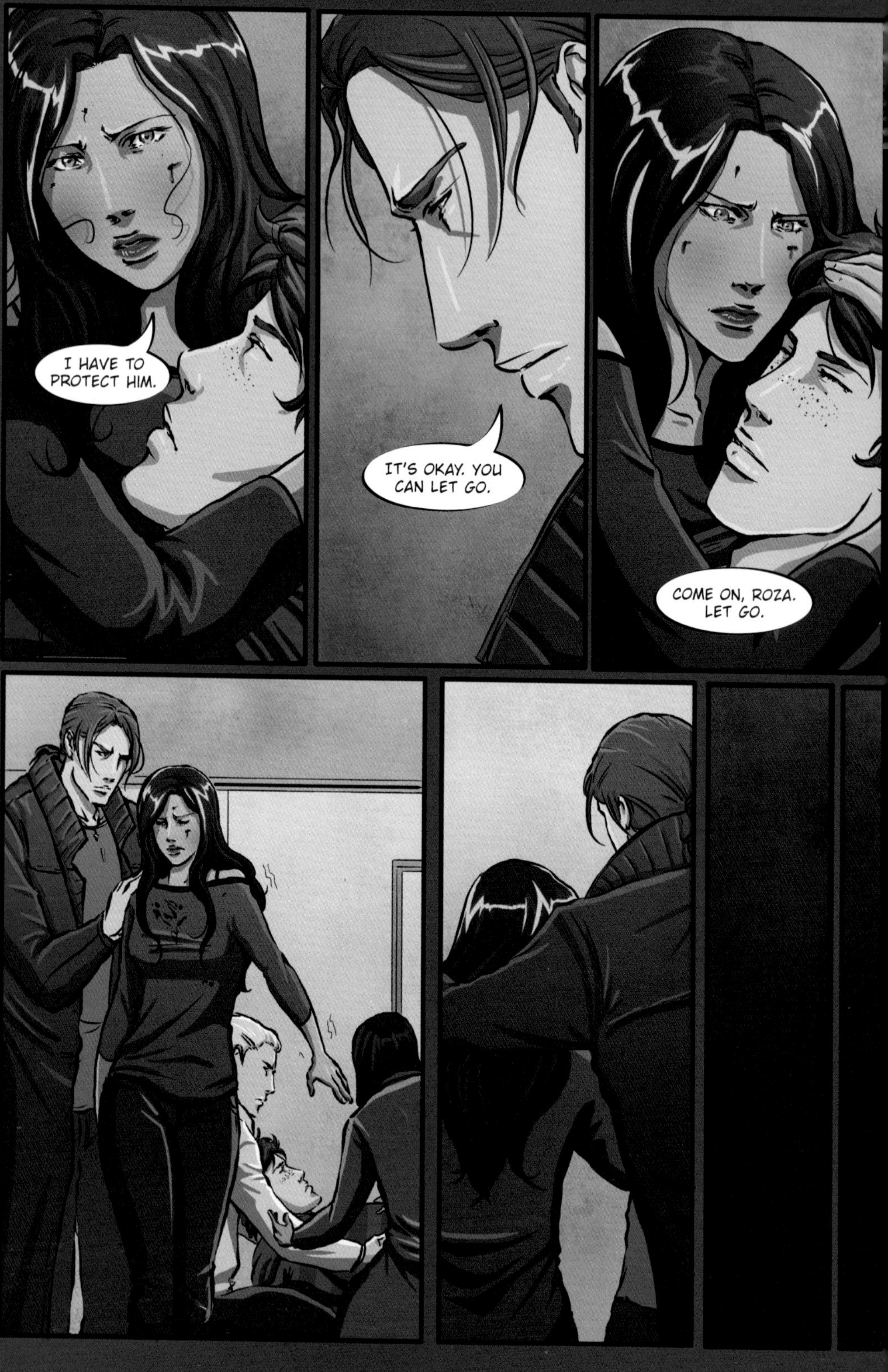
I HAVE TO PROTECT HIM.
IT'S OKAY. YOU CAN LET GO.
COME ON, ROZA. LET GO.

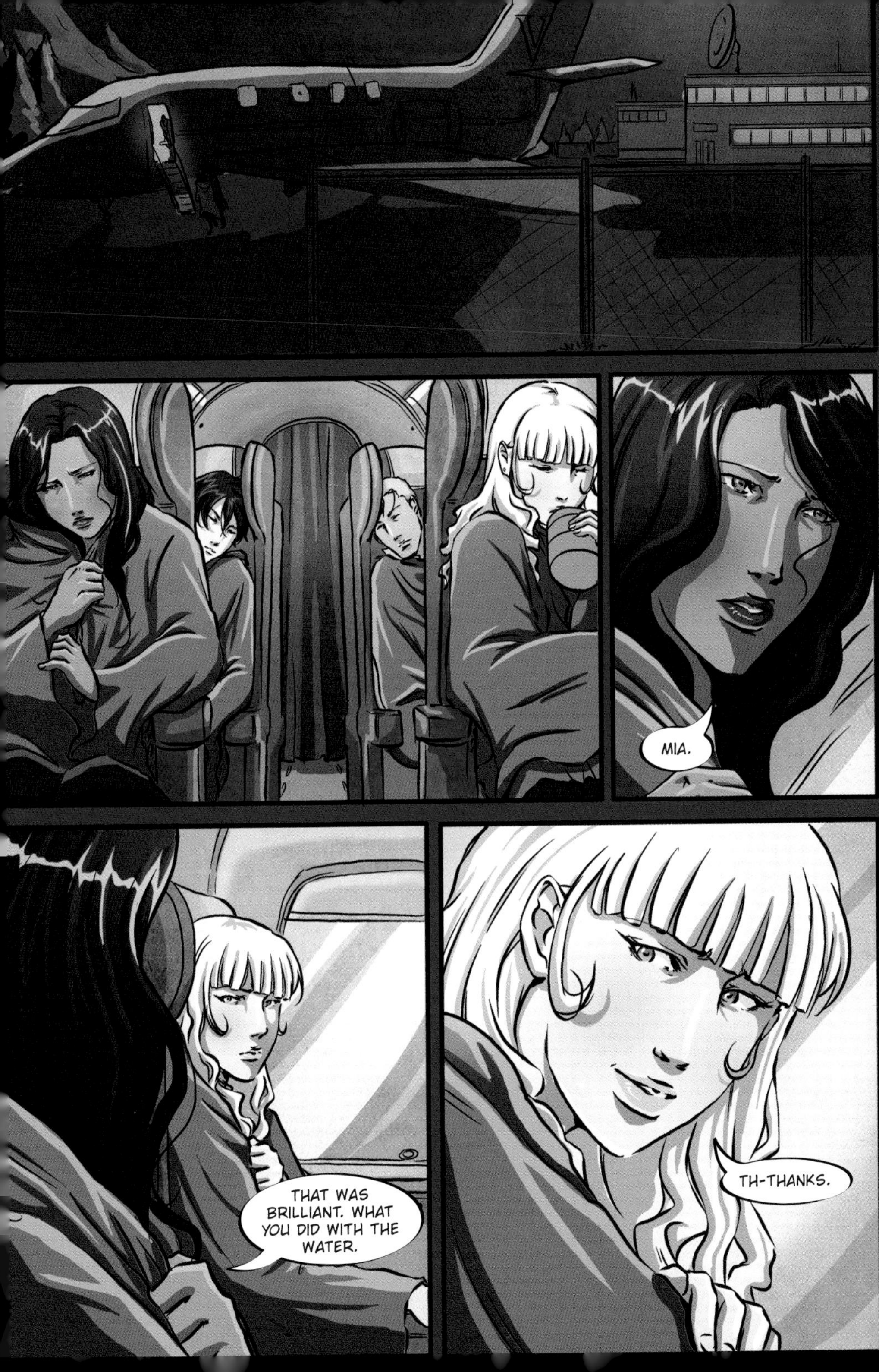
MIA.
THAT WAS BRILLIANT. WHAT YOU DID WITH THE WATER.
TH-THANKS.

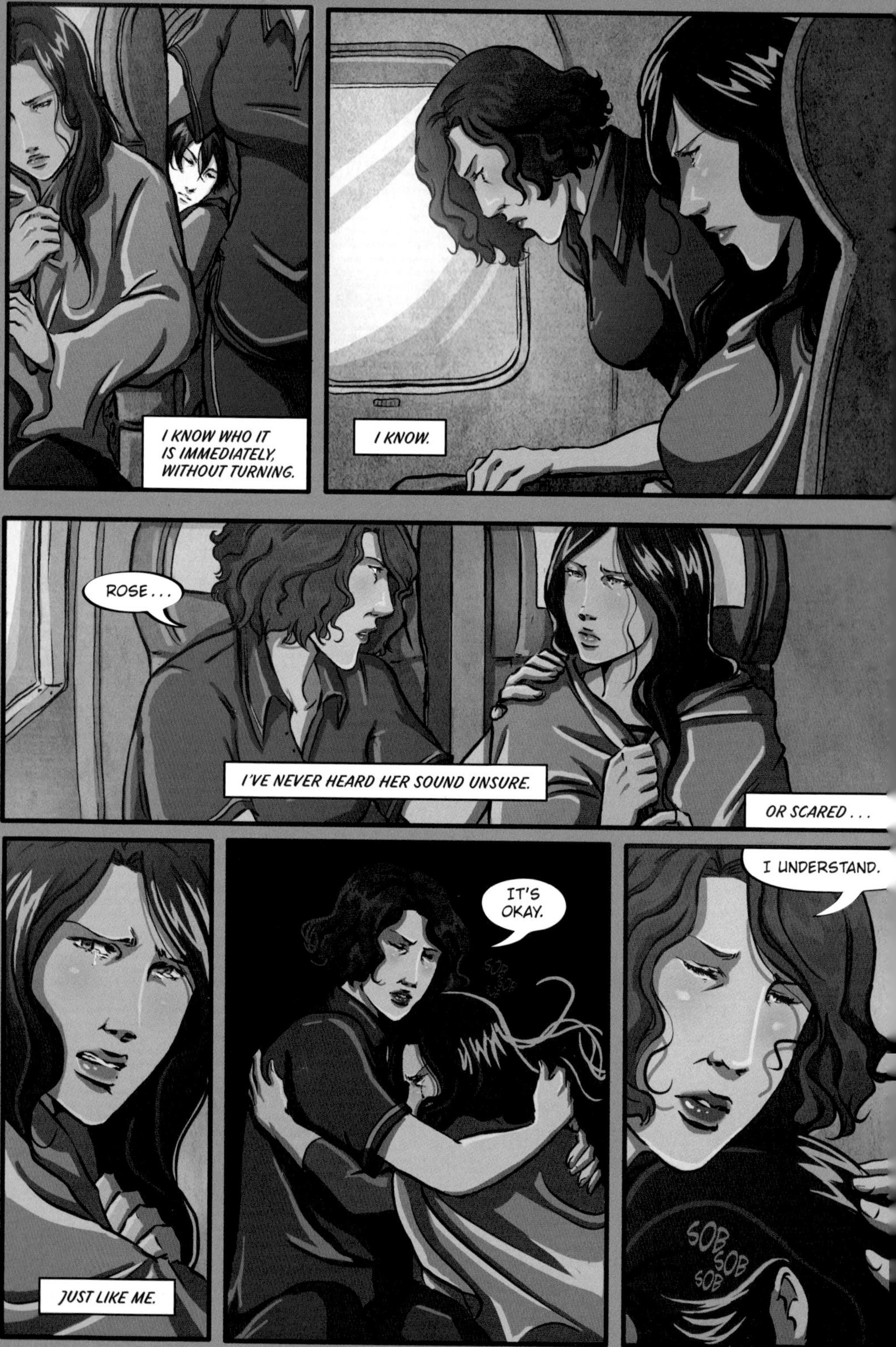
I KNOW WHO IT IS IMMEDIATELY, WITHOUT TURNING.
I KNOW.
ROSE . . .
I'VE NEVER HEARD HER SOUND UNSURE.
OR SCARED . . .
JUST LIKE ME.
IT'S OKAY.
I UNDERSTAND.
SOB SOB SOB

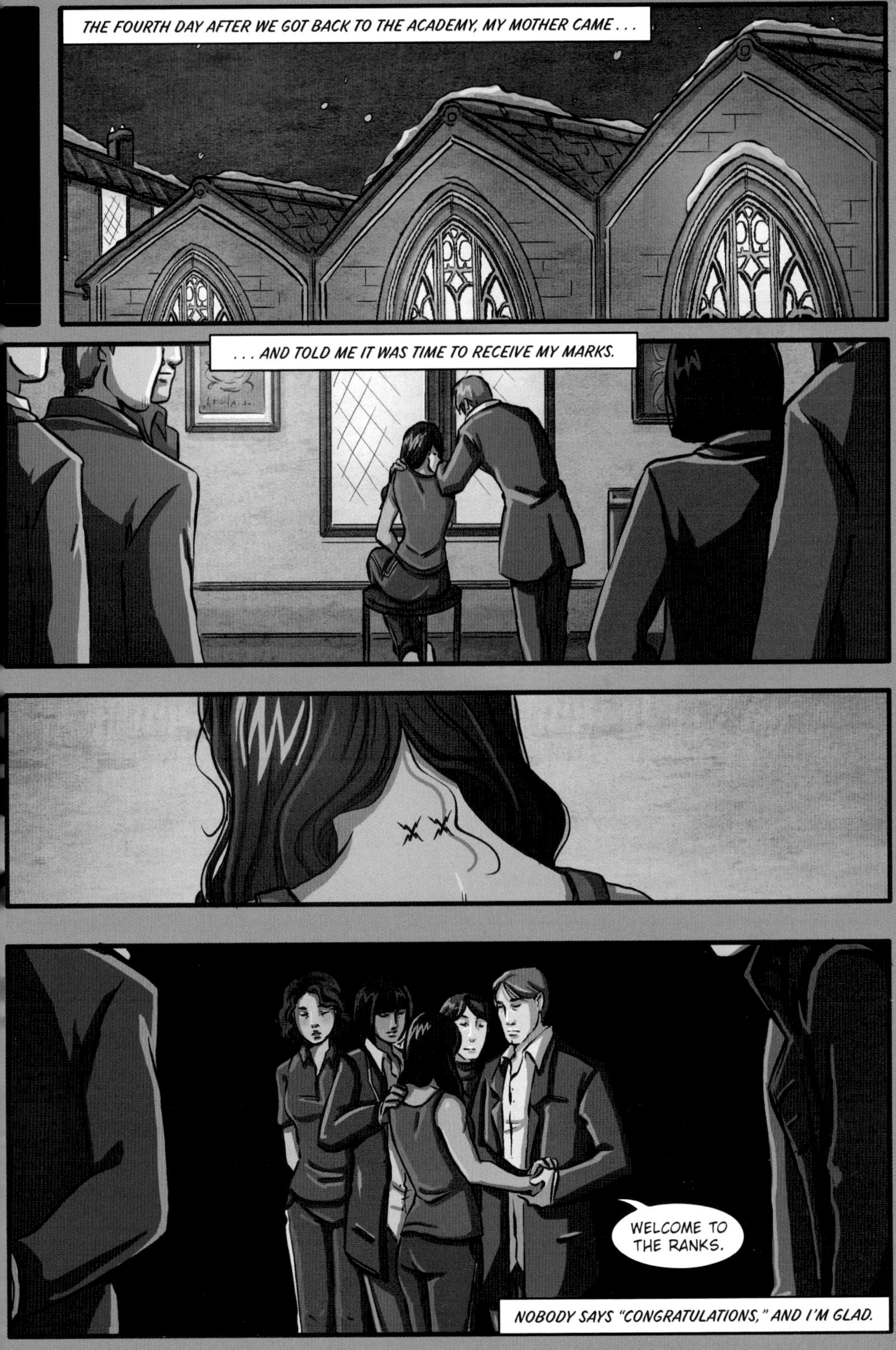
THE FOURTH DAY AFTER WE GOT BACK TO THE ACADEMY, MY MOTHER CAME . . .
. . . AND TOLD ME IT WAS TIME TO RECEIVE MY MARKS.
WELCOME TO THE RANKS.
NOBODY SAYS "CONGRATULATIONS," AND I'M GLAD.

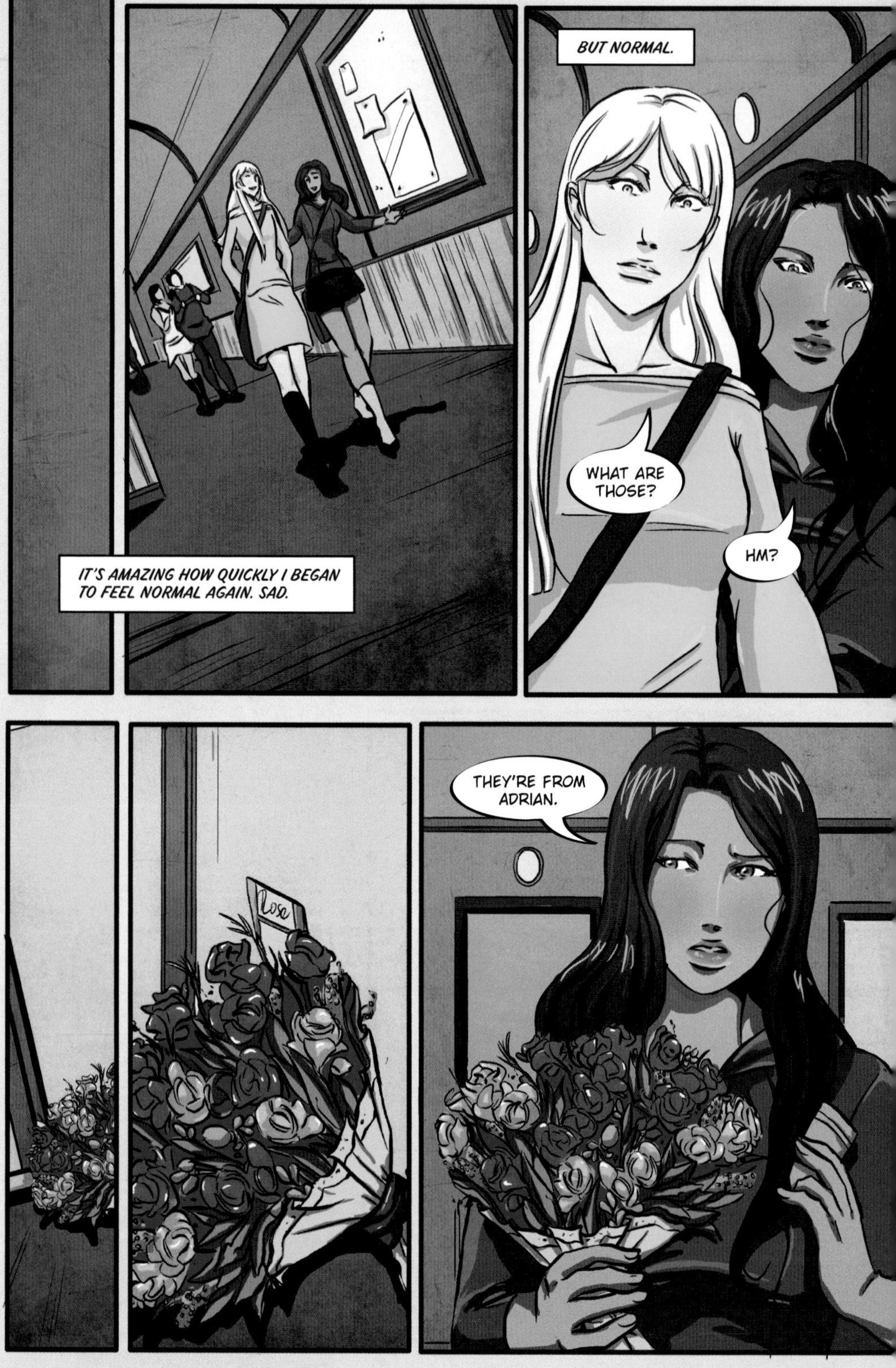
IT'S AMAZING HOW QUICKLY I BEGAN TO FEEL NORMAL AGAIN. SAD.
BUT NORMAL.
WHAT ARE THOSE?
HM?
Rose
THEY'RE FROM ADRIAN.

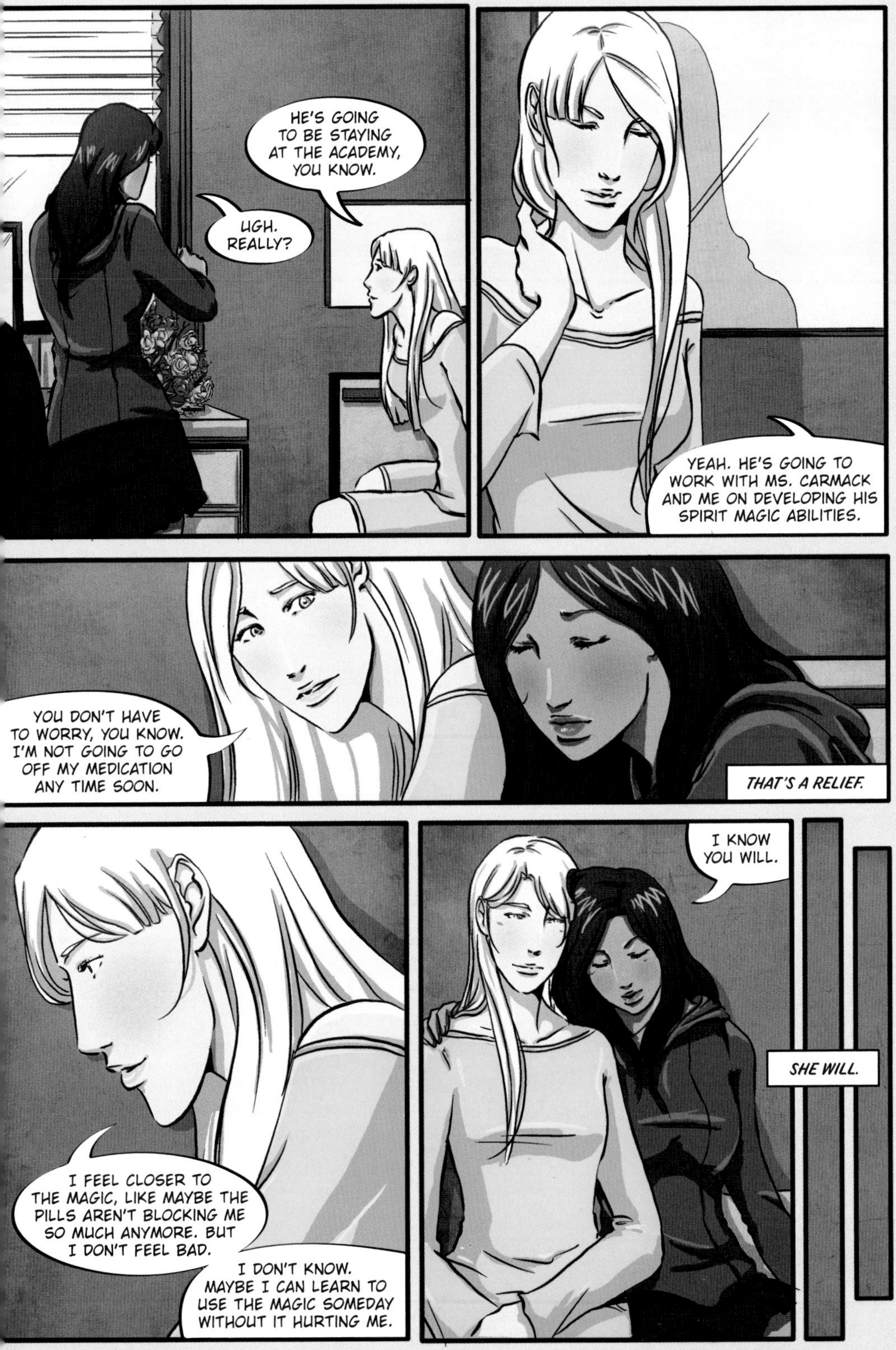
HE'S GOING TO BE STAYING AT THE ACADEMY, YOU KNOW.
UGH. REALLY?
YEAH. HE'S GOING TO WORK WITH MS. CARMACK AND ME ON DEVELOPING HIS SPIRIT MAGIC ABILITIES.
YOU DON'T HAVE TO WORRY, YOU KNOW. I'M NOT GOING TO GO OFF MY MEDICATION ANY TIME SOON.
THAT'S A RELIEF.
I FEEL CLOSER TO THE MAGIC, LIKE MAYBE THE PILLS AREN'T BLOCKING ME SO MUCH ANYMORE. BUT I DON'T FEEL BAD.
I DON'T KNOW. MAYBE I CAN LEARN TO USE THE MAGIC SOMEDAY WITHOUT IT HURTING ME.
I KNOW YOU WILL.
SHE WILL.

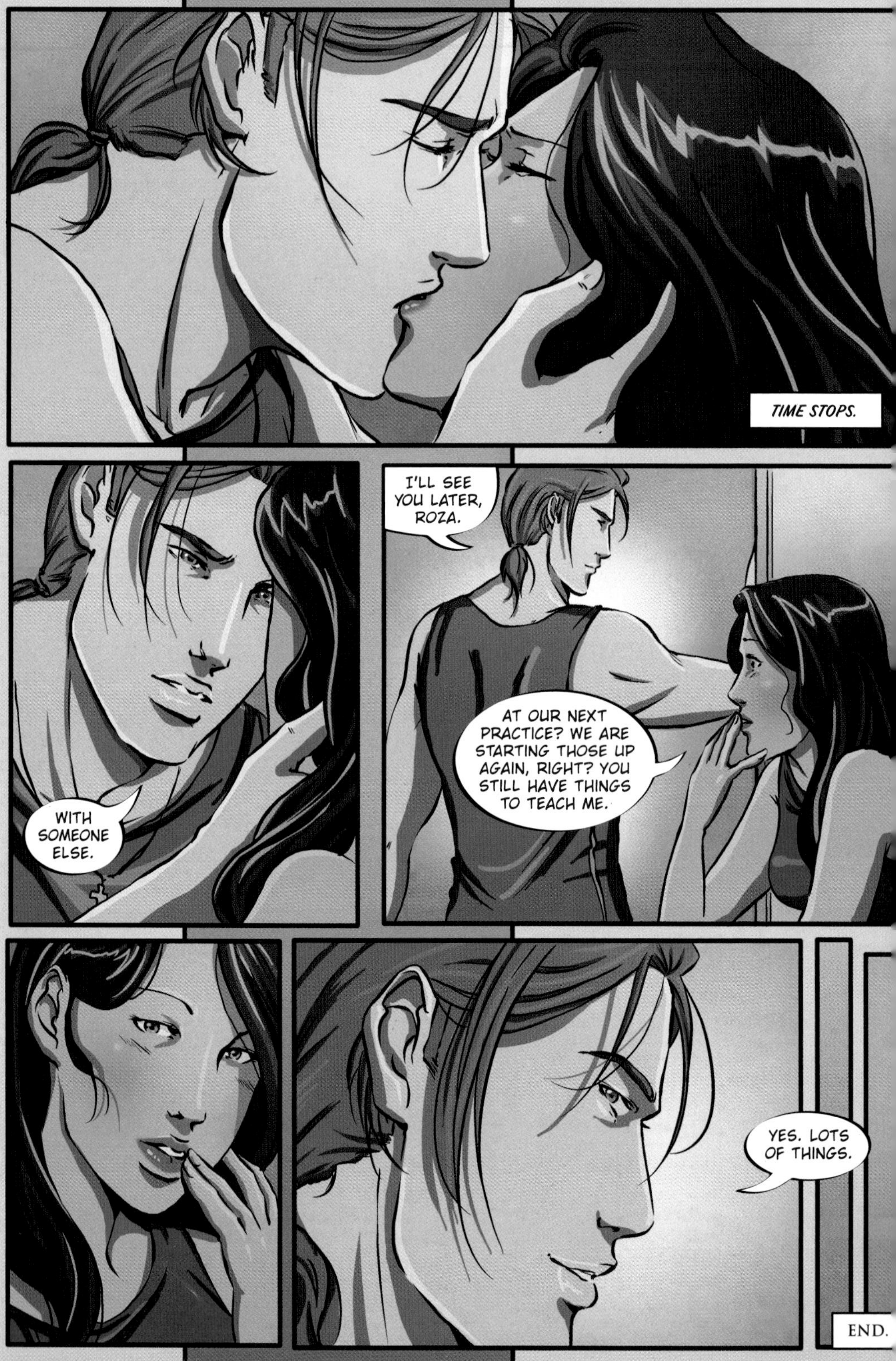
TIME STOPS.
WITH SOMEONE ELSE.
I'LL SEE YOU LATER, ROZA.
AT OUR NEXT PRACTICE? WE ARE STARTING THOSE UP AGAIN, RIGHT? YOU STILL HAVE THINGS TO TEACH ME.
YES. LOTS OF THINGS.
END.

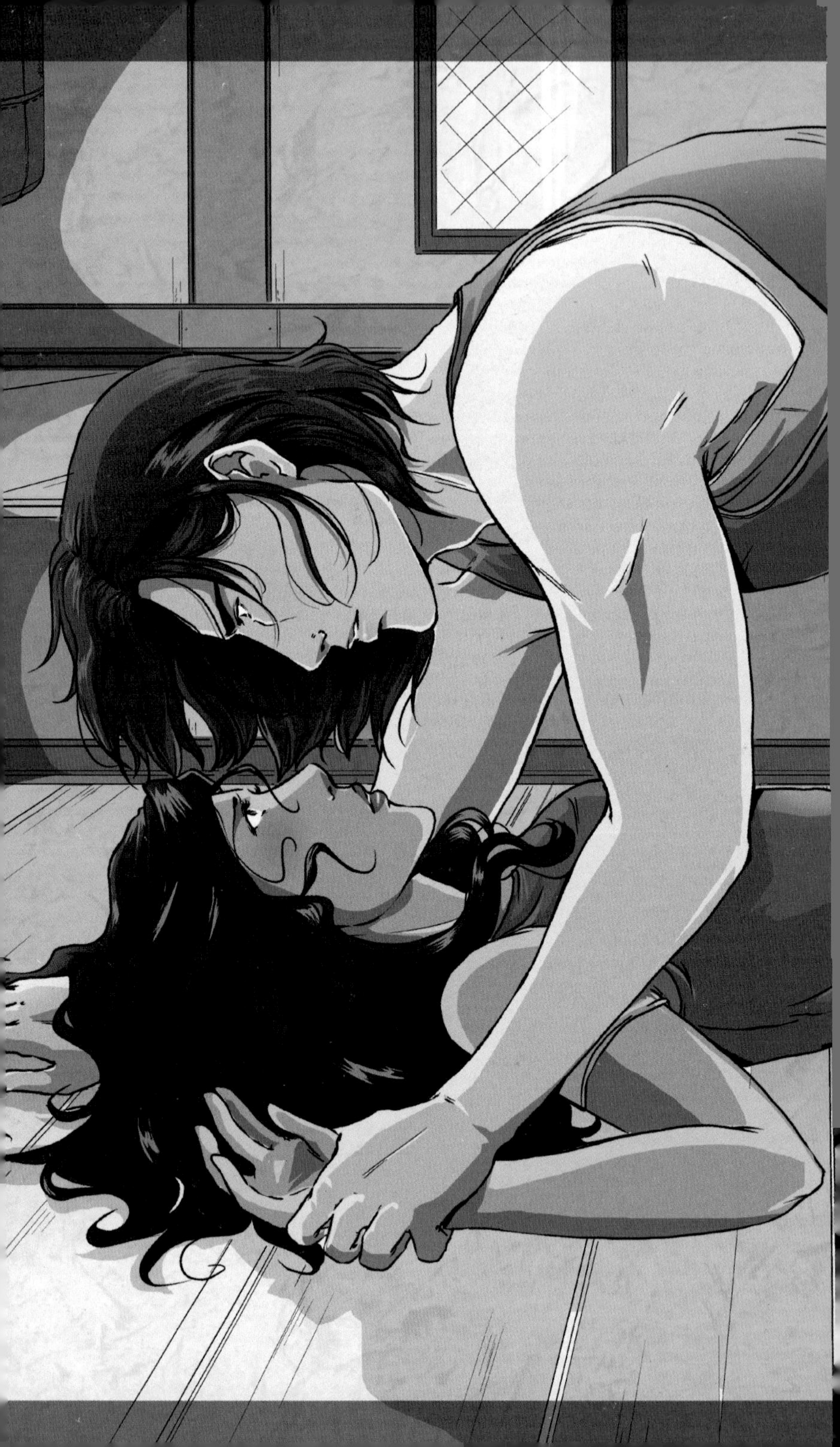

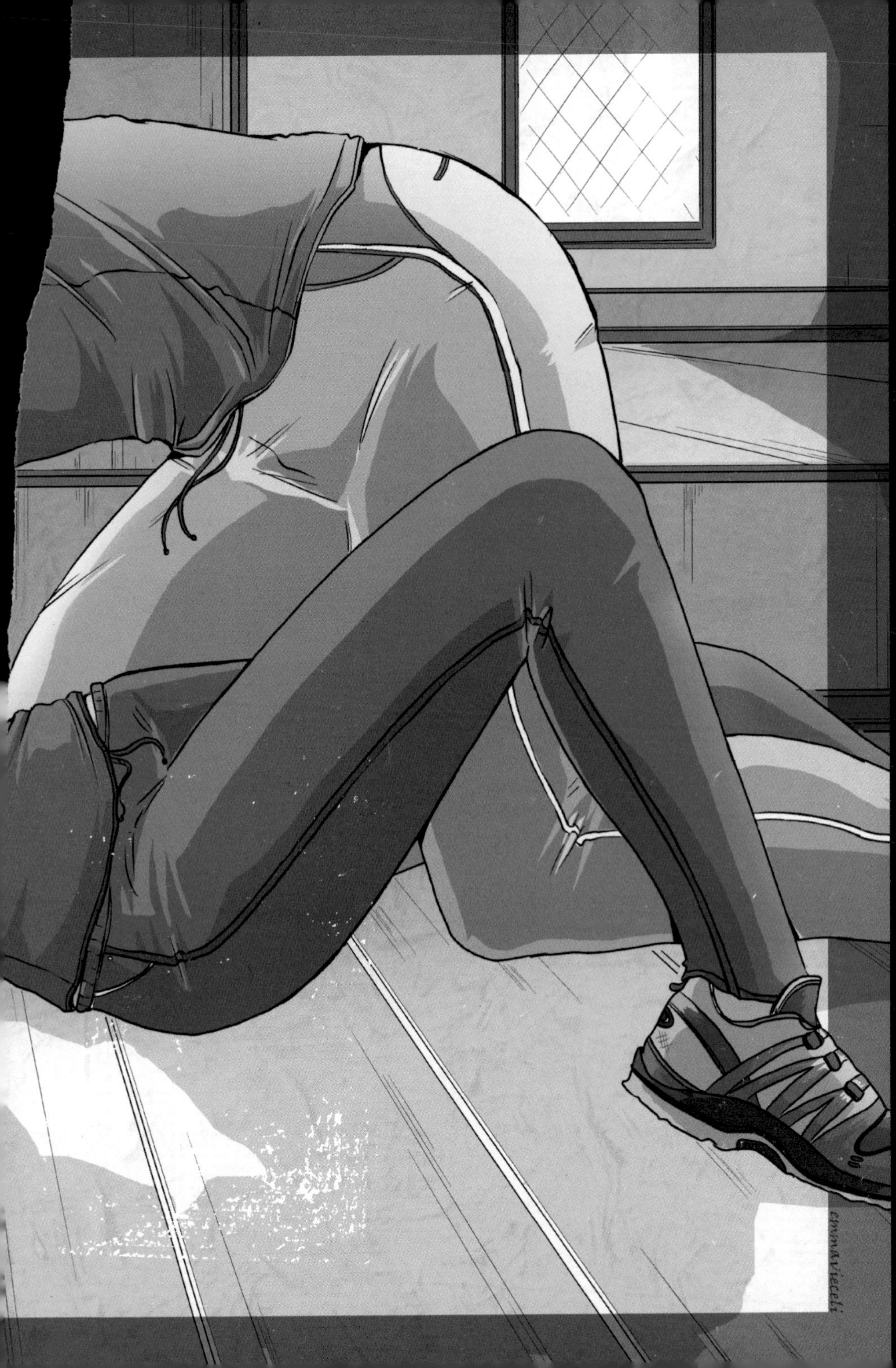
emmavieceli